Anthony Holt MBE was a pilot and Seaman Officer in the Royal Navy for over thirty years, leaving as a Commander in 1992 to run the Naval and Military Club in Piccadilly, and then the Army and Navy Club in Pall Mall.

He sailed and flew over all the oceans of the world, serving every type of ship, including two years ashore and afloat with the Australian Navy.

Married and living in Dorset, where he spends his time writing, sailing, working as a volunteer Coast Watcher and as a member of the Harbour Board, as well as entertaining his four grandchildren.

PRIVATEER

Also by the author

Spoofy
Vanguard Press (2012)
ISBN: 978 1 84386 886 6

At Least We Didn't Sink
Vanguard Press (2013)
ISBN: 978 1 84386 793 7

Anthony Holt

PRIVATEER

Anthony Holt

13 Jan 2016

Vanguard Press

VANGUARD PAPERBACK

A CIP catalogue record for this title is
available from the British Library.

ISBN 978 1 84386 774 6

*Vanguard Press is an imprint of
Pegasus Elliot MacKenzie Publishers Ltd.*
www.pegasuspublishers.com

First Published in 2013

**Vanguard Press
Sheraton House Castle Park
Cambridge England**

Printed & Bound in Great Britain

This book is dedicated to my wife, Irene, without whose never failing support it could not have been written.

Acknowledgements

I am indebted to my longstanding friend and naval colleague Mike, for his valuable help and photographic expertise, as well as to my son Richard for his continuing patience in resolving the little difficulties that all personal computers seem constantly to be able to generate.

Privateer is a work of fiction. The characters presented are not meant to represent any real person, alive or dead and any such resemblance is purely coincidental. None of the ships depicted represent any particular vessel but they are based on the generic types operating in and around what is known as the High Risk Area in the Gulf of Aden and the Indian Ocean.

None of the meetings, operations or actions described actually took place but they are set around the many incidents which have occurred over recent years when modern pirates have been active in the Indian Ocean.

The term 'Privateer' was originally used during the first Elizabethan era when privately owned vessels were commissioned under a 'Letter of Marque' to act as temporary warships, to attack, rob, plunder and destroy the ships of the Queen's enemies.

Loch Eriboll
Reay
Faslane
Glasgow
Edinburgh

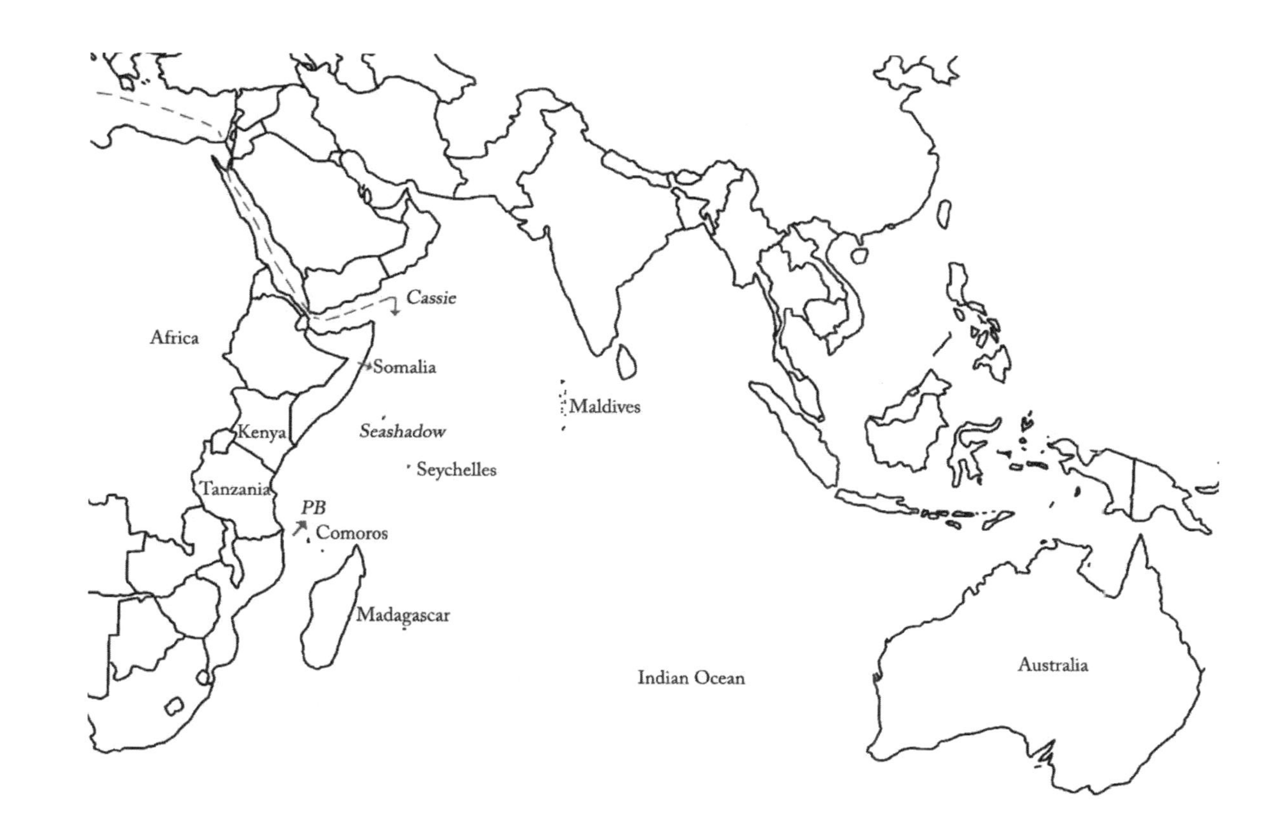
Cassie
Africa
Somalia
Maldives
Kenya
Seashadow
Seychelles
Tanzania
PB
Comoros
Madagascar
Australia
Indian Ocean

ONE

The boat moved slowly on the long ocean swell. The moonless, cloudless sky provided just sufficient light to enable the eight men crouched on the duckboards to pick out the horizon, which from their position a few feet above the surface of the water was only about three miles away. Most of the men were listening rather than looking for their prey. Some were asleep and one was murmuring over his beads. Hamid, wedged into the blunt stern section, sat bolt upright, one sinewy arm draped over the huge outboard motor, the other resting along the wooden gunwale, fingers trailing in the water.

As well as the eight men the boat was further laden with several automatic rifles and three steel grapnels wrapped with adhesive plastic tape, each attached to thirty feet or so of knotted rope. Belts and satchels containing ammunition and grenades completed the weaponry. The remaining space was taken up with leather water bags and plastic fuel cans. The boat carried no food or life jackets. Occasionally a man seated on the centre thwart would lean down to scoop up water with a leather bailer before emptying it lazily over the side.

Hours passed. Thin clouds began to obscure the glittering stars and the night became darker. By now most of the group were dozing. Only the bailer and Hamid remained awake, and only Hamid was alert.

Gradually Hamid's ears became attuned to a different, alien noise distantly competing with the gentle slap of wavelets against the side of the boat. He was not sure, at first, what it was or where it came from. It was not close and seemed to be intermittent. He drew himself even more erect, stretching his thin corded neck higher and turning his head from side to side, like a direction finding aerial. After several minutes he thought he knew which side the noise was coming from but he was still unable to identify the precise direction of the source. He moved his foot, stirring Ahmed, his climber, who was curled in a foetal crouch immediately to his front. Ahmed hardly moved but Hamid knew he was now awake and alert. At the same time Hamid pressed the electric starter on the outboard, grumbling the big engine into life. The boat began to move through the tiny surface wavelets of the otherwise still water, turning easily and slowly in a wide curve to starboard. As the boat climbed to the crest of each long oily swell the sound came a little clearer and louder. Hamid's face remained stony, unmoving, giving nothing away. But he was enjoying a stirring of grim satisfaction. He had identified the sound. It was music. Arabic music – now competing with the faintest background hint of a diesel engine.

But Hamid had guessed wrong on the direction of the sound. He reversed the turn and moved the boat in an even wider arc to port. Others in the crew had detected the new movement of the boat and were easing themselves into different positions, stretching cramped limbs and selecting weapons. A leather water bag was passed around and the Climber began to lay out and re-coil the knotted ropes. A tension gripped the whole boat as the sound became clearer.

The boat's position and its ability to remain unseen throughout the approach was crucial for success or failure of this night's work.

Everyone in the boat was now awake, alert and silent. The tinkling musical sound spilling intermittently out of the night remained frustratingly difficult to pin down. Hamid climbed stiffly to his feet, stretching to peer around the horizon. The sky was even darker as the night consumed its final hours. He thought he saw a glow – very briefly – away to the west, but so far as he could gather this did not match his estimate of the direction of the sound. He sank down again, squatting beside the burbling engine and turning his head this way and that. The boat continued to turn to port in an ever widening circle. He wondered, were his ears playing him tricks? Was he being taunted by some ocean borne djin? If this was the way of the Lord Allah, then so be it. Hamid continued to search.

Then he saw it. Not where he had expected but not far off. His ears were not playing him tricks. At first it was just a glow on the horizon but as he eased the boat's turn and settled on a course towards the glow, it began to increase in intensity until, as the boat was lifted on the long imperceptible ocean swell, it turned from glow to pinpoints of light.

Hamid could pick out with difficulty the high steaming light and the red port side navigation light of his quarry. He centred the tiller and allowed the boat to settle on a perfect interception course.

*

Feisal was enjoying himself. Away from his father's claustrophobic control he could take all that life might offer him. He remained devout, or so he believed, but he could also experience the good things in life. It was necessary, he sometimes reasoned to himself, otherwise how would a man know what is good and what is bad?

He rolled over and raised himself on one elbow, reaching out to take a sip of vintage champagne, while, beside him the girl stirred and pulled the dark blue satin sheet closer over her olive skinned nakedness. Feisal replaced the glass and lay back while he allowed his mind to rerun the last forty minutes of lovemaking. She had been skilled and exquisite, of that there was no doubt. However, when the yacht reached Oman it would be necessary to give her a present and send her on her way. She could not be found on board when they docked in Jeddah.

On the Bridge, Jose the Spanish First Mate was waiting while his eyes adjusted to the night before beginning the process of taking over from Manuel, the Philippino Second Mate. He peered through the forward Bridge window and as his eyes grew accustomed, the line of the horizon marking the boundary between black empty ocean and starlit sky slowly became clearer to him. He fished in his shirt pocket for his matches and cigarettes. Squinting to shut out the flare of the match he bent his head to light up. Manuel slid out of the tall padded Captain's chair and moved across, passing behind the helmsman, who was leaning back in his chair, watching the illuminated tape showing the ship's heading which was being maintained very precisely by the steering autopilot.

"Coffee?" said Manuel. He nodded to the helmsman who disappeared into the chartroom to boil the kettle.

"Thanks Mano. What's the picture?" replied Jose, expelling smoke.

"Quiet, very quiet. We've been on nor'-nor'-east all watch, the sea is quiet, there are no warnings and the boss has been entertaining himself screwing his new tart since dinner."

"I wouldn't mind a go at that." Jose's leer was hidden by the darkness.

"Don't even think about it."

"You're probably right," said Jose. "Where's the old man?"

"Came up on the Bridge at midnight, and then again about two hours ago."

"I dunno why he doesn't sleep. We're in mid-ocean five hundred miles from anywhere," growled Jose.

"Anyway, course is nor'-nor'-east, speed reduced to eight knots to keep the love birds happy, Duty Engineer is 'Third', there's nothing on the radar out to twenty miles, radio's fairly quiet but there is a warship somewhere around within VHF range. OK? You happy?"

"I have the watch," said Manuel, formally. He climbed into the chair and leaned forward to crush the remains of his cigarette in a small metal ashtray.

Jose moved wearily towards the exit door before turning and calling, "Oh yes, call the old man as usual and at six thirty."

"Got it," replied Jose as he turned to accept the steaming cup of coffee held out by the returned helmsman.

*

In the tiny Machinery Control Room, Third Engineer, 'Sharkey' Fisher leaned back in his chair and, running his eyes over the panel of dials and switches before him, reached out for his dog-eared vintage copy of *Penthouse* magazine. He flipped the pages glancing at the glossy pictures of semi-naked girls almost without seeing them. He had thumbed through the same magazine many times before and as he had frequently explained to his 'oppo', Ossie, it wasn't the same as the real thing.

A shadow darkened the frosted glass panel of the control room door. As the door opened, Sharkey was alerted by the sharp smell of fresh coffee.

"Coffee, Third?" said Carlos the Philippino Second Engineer as he eased his bulk through the door. The turn-over of duties here was less formal and took much less time than on the Bridge. Sharkey took the coffee, sipped at the once hot liquid and slid out of the swivel chair.

"Everything's ticking along nicely and the greaser's still out dipping the tanks. It's all yours."

Carlos put the second mug of coffee on the control panel shelf and wriggled himself to a position of comfort in the chair. "Sweet dreams," he said. "It's all mine."

"Night," said Sharkey as he closed the door and headed for the ladder.

"What's left of it!" came the rejoinder from behind the door. The engine room watch – or most of it – had been relieved.

*

Louis, Head Steward, and tonight, since his boss was entertaining, Head and only Barman, continued clearing away the remains of the evening. Waterford crystal glasses were hand washed, polished and carefully returned to their individual stowages. The two vintage champagne bottles were hand painted and so were stowed away carefully because they would fetch an attractive few dollars when next the *Sea Shadow* eventually docked in Bahrain. Louis wondered how long it would be before he could discreetly close up and slip away without risking the receiving end of yet another tantrum. For a true believer, he thought, he could certainly put the sauce away. And the steady boozing didn't seem to have any detrimental effect on the equally steady screwing of the scrubber who had flown in to embark before they left Jeddah. By the look of her and the style of her she must be bloody expensive. 'Well,' thought Louis as the remains of the oysters and lobster went into the gash bin. 'Why should I worry? The pay is exceptionally good and the job will continue so long as I keep my mouth shut.' There were also lots of little extra perks like the champagne bottles. Life was sweet but the hours were long – and the rich young man he served was an unpredictable evil-hearted bastard.

TWO

Hamid eased the outboard throttle open a little more as he settled on a course towards the lights. Ahmed moved forward quietly through the boat pushing and nudging the silent, reclining forms. Those who had been sleeping were now awake, carefully adjusting and checking their weapons. The silence was broken only by the clicks of oiled metal as weapons were cocked, and by the swish of the water past the hull of the now rapidly moving craft.

The distant navigation lights on the horizon had by now resolved themselves into the shape of a ship and had then almost disappeared behind the cluster of deck lights and glowing cabin windows. However, the pinpoint navigation lights still served sufficiently to indicate the direction of the ship.

A slight relaxation crossed the otherwise stony expression on Hamid's face. He was in a good position for the attack, broad on the port bow of his target so that if he maintained this course and his quarry remained unaware of his existence, then he would be able to sweep round behind the ship and come alongside on the starboard side near the stern. They had about two or three miles to run and all through the boat preparations were being made for the attack. Hamid kept the boat heading in at the same steady speed. He did not want to risk an increase in power on the outboard, which would create a luminescent wash, although he was fairly confident that any increase in sound would be unlikely to penetrate into the interior of the ship and the lateness of the hour and lack of movement on deck suggested that there was nobody in a position to listen to the noises of the night.

As they closed the last few hundred yards towards the starboard quarter Hamid tried to judge the height from waterline to the deck and reckoned it was within the reach of his ladders but he could see that Ahmed, agile as a monkey, was already prepared, feet braced on either side of the middle thwart, the grapnel rope coiled in his hands, ready to throw.

The distance between the boat and the gleaming white paint on the side of the ship grew steadily less and still the ship maintained her course, her people blissfully unaware of the disaster which was about to overtake them.

The boat leaned outward as it recoiled from the touch of the ship's side. Ahmed threw his grapnel, straight and true; it caught on the top guardrail, slid silently along the mahogany rail until it stopped and held against the steel stanchion. Ahmed was swarming up the rope even before the grapnel held, disappearing over the top and moving soundlessly away along the deck.

Hamid caught the loose rope and leaned his weight on it to hold the boat alongside the white hull now towering above him, while Khalid braced the ladder from the middle of the boat against the white steel side. The other five men raced up the ladder and over the rail, guns strapped to their backs and long knives hanging from their waists. Khalid dropped the ladder back into the boat before tossing a second grapnel over the rail, pulling it tight and tying it to the metal ring on the bows.

All of this took less than one minute, but Hamid took time to glance around before climbing easily up the ladder, once again held and braced by Khalid, before slipping over the rail, drawing his old but serviceable Browning Automatic and walking purposefully forward along the deck.

An easy external stairway, a 'ladder' in nautical terms, led up from the starboard side deck to a heavy screen door at the side of the Bridge. As he climbed the ladder, Hamid glanced around him with increasing satisfaction. 'Truly, this is a good choice,' he thought. 'At last, the Lord Allah has smiled upon me.' The door into the enclosed Bridge was swinging open, revealing a darkened scene inside, with three of the ship's crew standing with backs to the front windscreens hands raised to shoulder level as they stared with stunned, shocked expressions at the three Arabs facing them, gesticulating and prodding with a variety of weapons. Ahmed, small and wiry, was standing above the other companionway ladder, an Uzi machine pistol pointing down the ladder.

Two of the absent pirates were already making their way towards where they expected to find the entrance to the engine room. As the Bridge was captured they walked silently and carefully back down the ladder and along the deck, trying various doors into the superstructure as they went. The first few of these opened into dimly lit passageways of extreme opulence, obviously the part of the ship devoted to passengers. They ignored these, moving back out onto the deck and continuing their progress towards the stern of the vessel until they opened a door into a stark, white painted lobby illuminated by brilliant white strip lighting and decorated only by looms of coloured electric cables fastened to the bulkheads as well as several large metal pipes running through the compartment. A steeper ladder led through an open hatch to the next deck down, from which emerged the unmistakable hum of electric fans and the growling rattle of powerful diesel engines.

Although the progress of these two had been swift and silent it had not passed entirely without notice. Louis had heard the screen doors along the main accommodation passageway opening and shutting one after another and had stopped his clearing up to stand still in his pantry and listen. After a few moments he turned and unlocked the big door at the back of the pantry which led to his private empire. This was a cleverly combined wine cellar, food store, and butler's store with expensive table silverware, cutlery, crockery and linen. At the back of all this was a space which Louis had converted into his own comfortable hideaway, with a couple of easy chairs, table, radio, writing matter and his private library. It was his bolt hole and known, so far as he was aware, to no-one else, certainly not to his masters. Most important of all it was where he kept his prized possession, a satellite phone, stored in a small grip packed with his passport, some clothing, money and one or two other items he regarded as essential. It was his 'grab bag', for use in any of the emergencies to which ships at sea might be at risk.

Louis eased past the half open door into the pantry, peered out into the bar then stepped through the doorway and locked it behind him. He padded across the thick carpet and out into the dimly lit corridor, keeping away from the outside bulkhead and dodging into adjacent lounges from time to time. In this way he tracked the pair of Arabs moving down the deck until they passed beyond the accommodation. Louis pocketed the keys and moved silently along the thickly carpeted accommodation section. He had little doubt as to where they were heading and as he made his way back towards his pantry and his bolt hole he began to assemble the other facts of which he was aware. He knew the ship was cruising through the most dangerous part of the Somali pirates' operating area, he knew that the movements along the deck had no other explanation and he knew that the ship would be a valuable catch. But she was Arab owned – would the pirates attack one of their own? Within seconds he had decided. 'Yes they would,' he thought.

What should he do? The most obvious course would be to report what he had seen to the Bridge, but if there were men creeping about the deck, what was happening on the Bridge? Louis decided to lock himself into his store, hunker down and await developments.

*

In the alley running through the machinery spaces, the two Somalis inched towards the partially open door of the Machinery Control Room. Inside the control room, Carlos was lounging back in his swivel chair, his coffee mug now half empty and cold. He knew that it was time to do rounds of the machinery spaces but all of the needles on the dials were where they should be, no amber or red lights were showing and his chair was very comfortable. He decided to put off rounds for just five minutes. Within three of these his eyelids were drooping and within four his eyes were closed.

He woke with a terrible, convulsive start. The door to his small office had crashed open and he felt himself pinioned in the seat. His reaction was to launch his considerable bulk forward unthinkingly, taking Ali, the youngest and most nervous of the attackers completely by surprise. Before his supporter could get through the door, Ali found the positions reversed and he was being overwhelmed by the sheer weight of his opponent. His old revolver was knocked from his hand and fell clattering across the floor. As he was forced back he swung his free arm, holding a rusty bladed knife and slashed wildly with it. Luck stayed with him and deserted Carlos. Without any guiding aim the knife caught Carlos's throat, sliced across it and, covered with a jet of blood, both men fell to the floor. Melak, the second man was now through the doorway and into the compartment, jabbing viciously down on the exposed head of Carlos with the butt of his automatic. He need not have bothered. Carlos was already dead.

*

"Who is officer?" Hamid spoke in thickly accented English. His very deep rumbling timbre added further menace to his words. Manuel was sweating heavily. "I am," he said.

"What name is ship?" demanded Hamid.

"*Sea Shadow*, out from Bahrain, bound for Oman," replied Manuel, trying to avoid looking towards the communication console where a tiny flashing red light was giving away the fact that an automated emergency signal had already been transmitted on the Digital Selective Calling VHF set.

Hamid stared at the face glistening with sweat before him and his mind began to conjure questions and possible answers. His hand tightened around the butt of his automatic pistol as he advanced menacingly towards Manuel. Suddenly the radio speaker, set in the overhead panel, burst into life. "*Sea Shadow, Sea Shadow, Sea Shadow*, this is United States Ship *Andrew James*. What is the nature of your emergency, over?"

All eyes turned towards the bulkhead mounted speaker. Abdullah, standing closest to the panel raised his ancient Sten, pointing it towards the panel. "Stop!" commanded

Hamid. He waved his gun hand towards Abdullah, pointed towards the helmsman, and speaking rapidly in Arabic said, "Take him and find the Captain. Bring him here to me." Abdullah turned and pushed the helmsman towards the internal Bridge stair and prodded him in the lower back with the muzzle of his gun. As an afterthought, Hamid shouted in English, "Find Captain!"

The radio burst into life again. "Ship transmitting on international distress, this is British Warship *Carlisle*. I have received your distress message and I believe I have you on radar thirty-eight miles to the west of me. I am closing your position at best speed and I am assuming you are under attack by pirates as shown in your auto-transmission. Please acknowledge if you are able to, over."

Hamid spoke slowly and quietly as though he wished to hide his words from the radio. "You." He pointed his gun towards Manuel. "Take radio, tell him mistake, tell him go away. Now!" Manuel remained rooted to the spot. "Do it now!" roared Hamid, spittle flying from his beard.

Manuel lowered his arms, sidled tentatively across the Bridge until he was standing pressed against the communication console. He looked down at the handset and hesitated.

"Now! Do it now! Tell British! Tell American!" roared Hamid shaking his gun at the terrified Manuel. Manuel picked up the hand microphone and held it to his lips. "British Ship, British Ship," he stammered, hesitated and then said, "This is *Sea Shadow*, my emergency transmitted in error, very sorry, no problem here, all well here. Out."

THREE

"Captain, sir, Officer of the Watch."

"Yes, what is it?" The drowsy voice of Commander Craig Wilson emerged from the intercom speaker on the Bridge of Her Majesty's Ship *Carlisle.*

"We have an automated distress signal from a Saudi registered, privately owned vessel which suggests a pirate incident, sir."

"OK, I'm coming up, wake Number One, the Navigator and Ops Officer."

"Aye aye sir. I'm coming up to full power." There was no answer to this. The Skipper was already on his way up. Thirty seconds later a tall figure clad in a dark blue reefer jacket with three salt stained gold stripes on each sleeve, and a pair of striped pyjama trousers sprang up the last three steps of the bridge ladder and, crossing the Bridge in three strides, eased himself up into the Captain's tall leather padded swivel chair.

"OK, brief me." Craig Wilson was known as a man of few words who took every opportunity to demonstrate that listening was more useful than talking.

"Well sir," began the Officer of the Watch. John Temple had joined the *Carlisle* as Anti-Submarine Warfare Officer in Bahrain only four weeks beforehand and he was still finding his feet in the ship, as well as judging where he stood with his new Commanding Officer. "There was a brief automated transmission on DSC VHF about ten minutes ago. First response was from the *Andrew James* in clear voice and there was no answer to that. They said to us, that the emergency transmission was a mistake. Our own ECM has identified the transmission as coming from a position about thirty-five miles now to the west of us which matches an S band surveillance radar contact. I've brought all engines on line, turned towards and we are now running down the bearing at twenty-six knots with revs set for thirty knots. I made a response call which did get an answer after a few minutes but it was very brief, said the call was transmitted in error and signed off. The operator sounded nervous in the extreme."

A steaming mug of Kai – the Navy's special thick cocoa – had magically appeared on the shelf alongside the Captain's chair. Craig Wilson reached for it and sipped the scalding liquid while he thought. Temple waited expectantly while other figures began to appear on the Bridge. The Watch Signalman, pad in hand, stood dutifully to one side of the Captain and a young Boatswain's Mate had joined the Quartermaster at the wheel, ready to act as a messenger if required. Wilson turned to the Officer of the Watch, peered over the rim of his mug and asked, "When's sunrise, Officer of the Watch?"

Before the Lieutenant could answer, a different voice chipped in from the top of the bridge ladder, "Just coming up to first light now sir, sunrise proper in half an hour, about oh six hundred. Morning sir, First Lieutenant on the Bridge." Lieutenant Commander George Lee concluded his entrance with a familiarly casual salute before placing his battered off-white cap on the chart table at the back of the Bridge.

"Morning George, could be a busy one by all accounts," said the Captain without looking round. "I think we'll need to call the hands half an hour early and go to Action Stations immediately after they have had breakfast. If the initial position is accurate we should be at the datum in an hour." He slid off the chair and strode to the chart table at the back of the Bridge calling over his shoulder, "Hold her at twenty-five knots will you, John."

"Aye aye, sir." Turning to the Quartermaster, John Temple called, "Set revolutions two four zero."

"Two four zero set sir, ship steering in auto," came the almost instant reply.

After a short quiet conversation the two senior officers turned towards the Bridge ladder, the Captain calling over his shoulder, "I'm going to the Ops Room with Number One, send Pilot and Ops down there if they turn up here and you had better roust out the aviators."

"Aye aye sir."

The Bridge was just filling with the cool grey light of the pre-dawn as the traditional first 'pipe' of the day boomed out over the ship's main broadcast. "Call the hands, call the hands, call the hands," followed the penetrating shrill of the boatswain's call, made even more startling by the electronic amplification of the main broadcast system.

Before the first grumble had been uttered from a warm bunk, the broadcast started again. "D'ye hear there! First Lieutenant speaking. We have been alerted to a possible piracy incident and we are closing the probable datum position now, which is why you have all been invited to greet the day half an hour early. Breakfast for those off watch will be at zero six three zero. The ship will go to Flying Stations at zero six four five and modified Action Stations at zero seven hundred, stand fast morning watchmen. That is all." Throughout the ship, two hundred men and twenty-eight women tumbled out of bunks and headed for ‘heads’ and shower rooms.

In the Operations Room surrounded by banks of radar, sonar, and computer screens, a brief conference had just been concluded. Commander Wilson called the Signals Yeoman from his desk on the other side of the room – “Signal, Yeo. Make to the *Andrew James:* ‘Am proceeding WSW at twenty-five knots to estimated position of unknown vessel having declared emergency. Single suspicious VHF response received, then no further contact. Request you pass any information this contact A.S.A.P. Also request you move to the west of your box in readiness to provide support if required. Launching helo imminent. Will pass sitrep when helo makes contact’.”

The Chief Petty Officer Yeoman disappeared back to his desk to type out the message for auto transmission to the *Andrew James*.

On the flight deck the ship’s Lynx Mark Eight helicopter was already held in place on the centre spot with four light nylon lashings in addition to the ‘Harpoon’ system, a metal probe extending from underneath the aircraft into a hole in a circular grid set into the deck. The Observer was settling into his seat and the pilot was walking round the aircraft carrying out final pre take-off checks, pulling at fastenings, kicking the tyres and peering at the rotor blades. The side nettings and guardrails were lowered to the horizontal and the ‘lashing numbers’ stood on either side of the Flight Deck officer, ready to crouch low, dash in to the aircraft and remove the final four deck lashings at the last minute prior to take off.

*

On board the USS *Andrew James*, some forty miles further to the east of HMS *Carlisle,* things were not quite so hectic. *Andrew James* was an Air Defence Aegis missile armed cruiser, slightly bigger than *Carlisle* but designed with much the same task in mind. Both Captain and XO were on the Bridge examining the report from the Combat Communications Centre and the signal from *Carlisle* which had just arrived.

"Bring the Seahawk to readiness," ordered the Captain, "and increase to twenty knots." Turning to the XO and the other officers gathering around him he said, "Coffee gentlemen, my cabin, I think."

*

The Lynx helicopter climbed away from the deck of *Carlisle* in a wide climbing turn. Joe Hardisty, the Flight Commander and Observer switched on his radar set and pressed the 'preset' button for the operational UHF frequency. "Four zero three airborne, on ops, descending cherubs three." He spoke into the boom microphone attached to his helmet. A single blip on the frequency was his only answer. Both ship and aircraft were maintaining minimum communications. The pilot settled on a westerly heading and as he reached his cruising speed of a hundred knots he eased the aircraft down to three hundred feet above the sea before stabbing at the radio altimeter button, holding for a second to confirm that the speed heading and height of the aircraft were set rock solid, and then allowing himself to relax into his seat, all the while scanning the flight and engine instruments in front of him.

As they sped west over the sea, the sun climbed, red and fiery behind them and at the same time a little orange light began to flash below the radar screen. Near the top of the screen a single contact appeared and Joe pressed another button to put an auto-track on the contact. Joe spoke on the intercom to Lieutenant Keith Walker, the pilot, who responded by slowing down the aircraft to sixty knots as they altered course slightly towards the south, maintaining a distance of about thirty miles from their target while Joe twiddled with his controls, using his sophisticated electronic sensors to learn all about the ship still only represented by a blip on his radar screen. As he worked he scribbled notes on his kneepad, occasionally flicking the radar into sector scan. After about five minutes he thumbed the transmit button in front of him and spoke into the boom microphone, "Zulu Lima, this is zero three. Returning." With that they turned back towards *Carlisle's* position, increased speed and dived down to sixty feet above the sea surface. Within fifteen minutes they could see the destroyer racing towards them through the slight sea, with a foaming bow wave and a dead straight line of wake behind. Within twenty minutes Joe was reporting his findings to the Captain in the Operations Room.

FOUR

Onboard *Sea Shadow* the pirates were consolidating their position. Thirty-nine officers and crewmen had been rounded up and locked in four adjacent cabins with Ali on guard outside the doors. Khalid was now the sole occupant of the Bridge and he had altered course to head southwest for the Somali coast. The blood soaked body of the murdered Second Engineer had been manhandled up from the Machinery Control Room to the upper deck with considerable difficulty, leaving a trail of gore, torn clothing and the small contents of his pockets. He had then been tipped unceremoniously over the side to land with a noisy splash in the sea. Even as the body drifted astern, a single triangular dorsal fin could be seen homing in on it looking for a gratuitous meal.

Hamid had taken over the Captain's comfortable and spacious cabin below the Bridge deck, the former occupant having been bundled away to join his officers and crew, after first, with some encouragement having opened the large safe welded to the steel bulkhead of his cabin.

Hamid finished rooting through the ship's papers. He went back to the wide open safe and carefully removed all the bundles of banknotes in various currencies. Ignoring the rest of the money he methodically stuffed a selection of United States dollars, euros and Saudi rials in various pockets about his person. He found a small zipped overnight bag in the sleeping cabin and filled it with the remainder of the hard currency. With the ship seemingly firmly under his control he left the cabin, closing the door behind him. He climbed the ladder to the Bridge, checked with Khalid that he had switched off the navigation lights and the upper deck lights and told him in Arabic that he was going to look around to examine the prize they had won.

Hamid trotted back down the ladder from the Bridge, walked a short distance towards the stern, dropped through a hatch and down a second ladder to enter the passenger accommodation area. He passed two more of his men, armed, alert and looking trigger happy.

As he made his way along the opulent passageway he marvelled that anyone would want to decorate a ship in such a way. Hamid was no expert in art of any kind but even his untutored eye could see that the paintings, sculptures and glass encased artefacts were expensive and unusual. He planned to take them out of the ship once they returned to base, musing that they would make a very nice bonus over and above the ransoms that the ship and her crew would generate.

Much as Louis had done less than an hour previously, Hamid cautiously opened each door he came across, looking into sumptuous dining rooms, lounges and bars, then a small gymnasium, then a series of guest cabins. These cabins became increasingly more grand, bigger and more ornate as he continued to make his way aft. When he found each room empty his caution ebbed away and he began to throw successive doors wide without ceremony. At the fourth cabin door he recoiled with shock as he stepped into the cabin. It was occupied. How could it be that this had been overlooked?

The cabin stretched across the width of the ship. The room was decorated in a kind of early Hollywood style with crimson satin curtains, gold embroidered armchairs and low tables. Two doors led from the cabin, one of which was open. Through this he could see the marble walls and gold fittings of a sumptuous bathroom. On the other side of the cabin set against the bulkhead and fitted into an ornate panelled surround was a giant bed. The bed, covered in dark blue heavy satin sheets was occupied by a man and a woman. Hamid hefted the gun in his hand and cocked it noisily. There was no movement from the bed. Hamid moved closer and took in the details before him. Clothing lay scattered on the floor, and a shelf at the same level as the bed on the far side was occupied by two empty glasses and an equally empty but ornate, hand painted champagne bottle. Scattered across the surface and around the glasses was a covering of white powder. This, thought Hamid, could explain why neither of the cabin's occupants had been woken by his intrusion. The man, furthest away, was naked, with a jumble of the shining dark blue satin sheets thrown haphazardly back from his body. The woman, olive skinned and strikingly beautiful, was loosely covered by the tousled sheets. Hamid carefully lifted a corner. She was also naked. Thick raven hair covered the pillows, contrasting strikingly with the white cotton. Olive skinned with Latin features she was slightly taller and significantly younger than her slumbering companion, who was now emitting an occasional gentle snore. The sleeping man, of Arabic appearance, had once been muscled and fit but was now running to fat.

Hamid crossed the room, still holding the gun in his right hand, and paused before sitting carefully on the bed beside the woman. She moved slightly and a heavy breast tumbled from beneath the satin. Hamid, glancing briefly across at her companion, gently pulled the covering sheet away from her waist.

As Hamid leaned forward the cabin door burst open and Ali shouted, "Hamid, come quick – to the Command Bridge, come quick!" With that, he was gone, the door swinging lazily back and forth behind him.

Hamid cursed as he sprang away from the bed, crossed the luxuriant purple carpet and peered through the door. The corridor was empty. Ali had already gone and Hamid stood alone for a moment. Ali, he thought, should be in the engine room but his message seemed to come from the Bridge, where Khalid the Navigator was in charge. Had something gone wrong?

Hamid stuck his gun in the waistband of his jeans and hurried up the ladder and forward towards the Bridge. As he moved he glanced towards one of the big picture windows lining the corridor and was briefly shocked to see the unmistakable shape of a large warship heading towards the *Sea Shadow* at high speed.

As he reached the Bridge he saw Khalid staring through a set of powerful binoculars towards the approaching warship. "British destroyer," Khalid said without turning from the binoculars. "What do we do, leader?"

"Nothing," growled Hamid. He stared intently towards the destroyer, now closing to parallel the yacht's course about two hundred yards distant and slowing down to maintain station alongside. "Keep to your course."

"I see no people," said Khalid still staring intently through the binoculars. "Only maybe two or three inside the Command Bridge."

"They are prepared for action. Watch to see if they launch boats." Khalid turned towards Ahmed, now the only other occupant of the Bridge.

Suddenly a loudspeaker boomed out from the destroyer, first in English, then repeated in Arabic. "*Sea Shadow*, heave to. Stop your engines."

Hamid looked around him, noting that Ali had arrived on the Bridge. The boy looked nervous and was waving his Kalashnikov about. "Do nothing. No guns. Keep down," he ordered, glaring pointedly towards Ali. The young man reluctantly lowered his gun. Khalid placed the binoculars carefully on the shelf running under the Bridge windows and reached into his trouser pocket, pulling out a small Garmin 72 GPS Navigator. He pressed a couple of buttons, examined the screen, and announced to no-one in particular, "We have six hundred miles to run to the Bay. At this speed it will be nearly two days."

As he spoke, Khalid pocketed the GPS and moved towards the multi-coloured radar screen in the centre of the navigation consol. "We have another contact," he said. "Maybe forty miles away. Coming towards us."

"Do nothing," repeated Hamid. "Change nothing. Do not shoot. Do not slow down."

"The warship is getting closer," Khalid responded, deadpan.

Hamid moved to the tall chair fixed at the front of the Bridge and climbed into it. He beckoned Ali towards him. "Ali," he said carefully and slowly, "leave your weapon here and go to each of our men. Tell them they are not to show themselves and there is to be no shooting. Do you understand?"

"Yes leader," said Ali.

"Go now. But first send a brother to the big cabin where they will find two people asleep. Lock them in."

"Yes leader," said Ali again, as he turned and clattered away down the Bridge ladder.

*

HMS *Carlisle* was at a high state of alert. Her entire ship's company was now closed up at 'Modified Action Stations' with all systems manned but no crew members exposed on the upper deck. Guns crews who would otherwise be stationed out on deck were held at instant readiness inside the nearest section of the ship's superstructure. This system had been adopted following lessons hard learned by other ships of the protection force, who had lost crew members to haphazard gunfire from the marauding pirate gangs as they had closed with their quarries to attempt communication by loud-hailer.

Craig Wilson slouched in his chair as his First Lieutenant tried once again to get some response out of the captured superyacht, still heading stoically towards the distant coast of Somalia. The Bridge exuded a hushed state of expectancy. "No response sir," called George Lee as he scanned the adjacent ship through binoculars.

"Officer of the Watch, get 'Ops' on the phone will you," said the Captain, without taking his eyes off the other ship.

"Aye aye sir."

"George, give them another try, will you?"

"Aye sir," the First Lieutenant responded as he picked up the external broadcast microphone and thumbed the transmit button.

"Ops officer on the phone sir," said the new Officer of the Watch, Sub Lieutenant Carole Clarke, as she held out the handset on the end of its long curly lead.

Craig Wilson nodded a perfunctory thanks as he took the telephone.

"Ops?"

"Sir?"

"Quote the current Rules of Engagement to me, please."

"Yes sir," said the Operations Officer. "We remain under Policy Two. The Dominant rule is three four oh. We may interrogate but may not attack unless we are fired on first. We may not attempt to board unless there is clear evidence from two sources that hostages are being killed. We may display weapons and attempt by non-lethal means to halt or deter enemy progress."

Craig snorted. "I'm surprised we aren't told to invite the evil bastards to dinner. Fucking useless rules," he ended lamely. Carol Clarke stared out over the bows and ignored the outburst. She had heard it all before.

"Yeo," called the Captain.

"Here sir." Chief Petty Officer Signals Yeoman Tom McBride stepped forward, signal pad in hand.

"Thanks Yeo. Make to Commander Task Group 2.01 and to C-in-C Fleet, copy to MoD London, FCO etc."

"Flash priority sir?"

"Yes make it Flash, Secret. From *Carlisle* to CTG 2.01 and C-in-C Fleet Ops. Have responded to auto-alarm received 0540 local this morning from Motor Vessel *Sea Shadow*. No subsequent response from *Sea Shadow* to repeated VHF and HF interrogation. Have closed contact at max speed and am now in close company. No response to English or Arabic loud-hailer comms. No indication of crew or other personnel on deck. Two, possibly three persons sighted within enclosed Bridge. Vessel has twenty-eight foot outboard powered open boat on long-stay tow. *Sea Shadow* is making way at fifteen knots heading two nine five true with no reaction to repeated demands to stop engines. *USS Andrew James* has also responded to initial signal and is expected to reach my position within two hours. *Sea Shadow* Lloyds listed as Saudi owned. Request approval to raise

Rules of Engagement and additional approval to attempt opposed boarding by helicopter."

The Chief Yeoman finished scribbling on his pad.

"Read that back will you Yeo." Tom did so.

"OK, get it away as soon as you can," said Wilson.

"Aye aye sir."

"Captain sir, warship in sight red one four zero. I think it's the '*James*', sir," intoned the Officer of the Watch.

"Thank you Sub," said Craig as he twisted around in the chair in a vain attempt to spot the approaching American warship. Turning towards the Bridge Duty Signalman, he called, "See if you can raise the '*James*' by light. Use the disengaged side and send 'Suspect pirate attack. Awaiting approval to respond'." He climbed out of his chair and wearily eased down the ladder to his cabin, calling from the bottom of the stairs, "Keep me informed Number One."

"Aye sir," responded the First Lieutenant.

*

Onboard *Sea Shadow* Hamid and his crew were settling into a routine. The somnolent passenger had been awakened and dragged into the sumptuous main saloon, together with his companion. Both had been subjected to rudimentary interrogation by Hamid and were now sitting quietly, clad in matching terrycloth bathrobes. As the combined effect of alcohol and drugs wore off the man had become more truculent and less co-operative. Now he barely spoke at all. Hamid had extracted the information that he was a Saudi Prince and that his name was Feisal. This both pleased and worried Hamid. On the one hand a member, even a minor member of the Saudi Royal dynasty was an exceptional catch capable generating huge amounts of dollars in a hostage exchange. On the other hand, he was an Arab, a brother, but more to the point Hamid was acutely aware that the Saudis with their enormous wealth had already demonstrated that they could reach far and wide to deal savagely with those who had created offence. The woman who spoke no Arabic and little English was a different matter. Although tired and dishevelled she still emanated a distracting sultry beauty and interrogating her had been frustrating, disturbing and unproductive. Hamid had found that her name was Nina and her nationality was either South or Central American, possibly Panamanian. She seemed typical of a certain class of expensive and exclusive prostitutes who travelled the world providing discreet but expensive diversion for the very rich and very famous.

In order to preserve his options Hamid decided to treat these captives leniently. He had their bedroom suite thoroughly searched and then locked them both inside, posting one of his men outside.

Behind the locked door of the wine and dry goods store, Louis heard much of what was going on. It confirmed his fears that he was in the middle of a piracy situation and he decided immediately that he would do all he could to avoid, so far as he was concerned, allowing it to turn into a hostage situation. The door into his hideaway was strong and it was locked from the inside. He had access to food and water as well as unlimited supplies of the finest wines, beers and spirits. He could urinate in the large sluice system and had worked out how to deal with other bodily functions. He had his radio, but could not raise a signal and he had his satellite phone but he had not yet dared to use it. One further advantage of which he was not aware was that Hamid had already determined that he would not allow any of his men to go near or attempt to enter the wine store because he feared the consequences.

FIVE

It was eighteen minutes past four when the signal from *Carlisle* was carried in to the Duty Commander in the Navy Operations and Trade Cell deep in the bowels of the Ministry of Defence Main Building on the west side of Whitehall. Within two minutes the same signal came rattling off a teleprinter on the long grey metal desk of the Surface Operations Officer in the Fleet Operations Centre of the Combined Operations and Fleet Headquarters at Northwood. This network of cellular rooms was if anything buried even deeper than its equivalent in the Ministry of Defence in London. It was from here that the first response would be made to *Carlisle's* signal.

A standard procedure had been established within the Fleet Headquarters which was to reply immediately to urgent signals such as the one just received but to do no more than acknowledge the signal and remind the sender to maintain the status quo and do nothing to inflame the situation. Certainly, no decision could be made to relax the Rules of Engagement without political approval. Captain Oliver Harding, whose day job was Assistant to the Fleet Supply and Logistics Officer was a methodical man who would never ever contemplate even a little dent in the rules. He picked up the red scrambler telephone on the desk and pressed the third key which connected him directly to the Chief of Staff. After four or five rings the phone was picked up and following a longish pause a sleepy voice said, "Yes – this had better be good."

"We have a piracy alert sir. *Carlisle* is investigating a Saudi vessel called *Sea Shadow*. They are in company now and are asking for the Rules of Engagement to be lifted to allow a boarding attempt."

"Have they copied MoD?"

"Yes sir."

"Well it's a political one, so wait and see what response MoD gets from FCO. Keep me informed, only if there are developments. Got that?"

"Yes sir," said Oliver Harding unhappily.

*

In his horribly cramped and hot set of rooms beneath the Ministry of Defence, Frank Macauley was faring a little better but not much. His immediate reaction had been to pass the contents of the signal, with emphasis on the Rules of Engagement request by telephone to an office in the upper part of the Foreign and Commonwealth Offices. In contrast to his own surroundings Frank knew that the location of the FCO 'Duty Clerk' was more akin to a comfortable bachelor flat than a sweaty grey underground office. He disliked having to contact the Duty Clerk largely because it brought to mind the unfairness of their relative situations and because most of the Duty Clerks, none of whom had any other duty to occupy them, tended to effect a rather grand and supercilious manner when dealing with lowly naval officers from the Ministry of Defence. Frank also suspected that in decision making they tended to take too much on themselves. This turned out to be the case. The Duty Clerk thought for a moment and then said, without preamble, "No. Tell them to wait in position and take no further action until instructed."

Frank thought that this was the wrong answer but he had learned that argument with these people was futile. He simply said, "Please confirm that by internal signal," and put the phone down. Then he sat at his desk to compose a reply to the *Carlisle*.

*

An hour later, after a substantial breakfast, Craig Wilson climbed the ladder back to his Bridge followed a few moments later by his leading steward bearing an aromatic steaming mug of strong coffee.

"No change sir." Carole Clark turned away from the central compass stand, smiling a greeting. "We've moved out a bit and the *Andrew James* is just coming up on the other side of the target."

"It's not quite a target yet, Carole," replied the Captain.

At that moment a clatter of feet on the ladder heralded the arrival of the Chief Yeoman. "Reply, sir," he said, slightly out of breath as he reached the Bridge deck.

"About time, too." Wilson read the flimsy signal form, frowned, read it again and then scowled out of the starboard window towards the *Sea Shadow*. "Shit!" he intoned quietly, but with considerable feeling injected into the single syllable. Addressing no-one in particular he said, "It seems we are to remain here and do bugger-all while the relevant people in the Foreign Office and the MoD prize their fat arses out of their comfortable chairs and reach for their instructions on procrastination." He sipped his coffee while the remainder of the Bridge team looked diplomatically out of the windows or studied the instruments before them. The Chief Petty Officer

Yeoman waited silently to one side of the tall swivel chair. Craig passed a hand over his eyes, stared down at his coffee and said quietly, "Yeo, make to the *James*, by light if you can, 'I am stuck without approval to proceed. What about you?' Let me know if anything else relevant turns up."

"We'll need to move ahead if we are to use a discreet light to the *James*, sir," said McBride.

"Make it so." This, to the Officer of the Watch.

"Aye aye sir. Quartermaster, increase to eight zero revolutions, go to hand steering. Steer two four zero."

"Revolutions eight zero ma'am. Ship in hand steering. Ship's head two four zero." The destroyer began to draw steadily ahead of the *Sea Shadow*. Wilson changed his mind. "Take her all the way round to starboard of the *James*, Officer of the Watch."

"Aye aye sir," responded Carole and began quietly but firmly to issue a series of orders to drive the ship further ahead and around in a wide turn to starboard, eventually matching the course and speed of the *Andrew James* about a quarter of a mile on her beam. The big signal lamp began to clatter from the flag deck above the Bridge. Everyone waited, no one noticing the white overalled figure of the Ship's Mechanical Engineer Officer, who now stood just inside the port wing door.

The Chief Yeoman reappeared holding a slip of paper. Craig took it and read it. He frowned. "Seems they haven't done any better than us," he said.

The figure in white overalls took a tentative step forward and cleared his throat. Ben Crossley was old for his rank. A 'Special Duties List' officer he was proud of the fact that despite his ability, as he put it, to call a spade a fucking shovel, and his record of never being cowed from speaking the technical truth, no matter how important the recipient, he had successfully made the transition from the lower deck to the wardroom. He was widely respected by the whole ship's company, not only for his technical expertise but also for his pragmatic wisdom which many of the younger ratings had learned to value.

"Hello Chief," said Wilson. "What can I do for you?"

"You can go and get us some fuel sir," replied Crossley, adding, "unless you've got a secret stock of sails, that is."

"Oh. What's the state?"

"We're already down to fifty per cent sir, which means we should report that to Fleet."

"I know that," replied Wilson, sharper than he had intended. "We'll tell Fleet when they wake up and find out what they want us to do. We'll be alright for a couple of days and I don't want to drag the tanker down into the middle of the pirate's nest." At this point the Bridge signalman turned from his telephone and interrupted.

"Flash signal coming up from Fleet sir," he called.

"Bring it up."

Within thirty seconds or so, Wilson had the signal in his hand. At best, he believed, it was unhelpful. Turning to the Officer of the Watch he said, "Heads of Department Conference in my cabin in fifteen minutes. Then take us round to the other side of *Sea Shadow*. Keep the upper deck clear and let me know immediately of any change in the situation." Still clutching the signal he strode off the Bridge and down the ladder.

*

There were seven officers in all, seated on a variety of chairs placed haphazardly around the Captain's Cabin. A chart of the Northern Indian Ocean was spread across the table, with various positions and tracks marked on it in pencil.

As the First Lieutenant, last to arrive, settled into a lonely dining chair, Wilson started to speak. "Well," he said, "It is much as we thought. For the present at least we stay with the same Rules of Engagement. Obviously nobody has raised the energy to reach a decision and we are instructed to stay in contact with *Sea Shadow*, reporting any change in status to C-in-C Fleet."

"What about fuel, sir?" This from Ben Crossley.

"We are authorised to move away in order to refuel providing we are back within 24 hours and the *Andrew James* remains in contact while we are away."

"That means bringing the tanker south," interjected the young Navigating Officer.

"Can't be helped, Pilot," said Wilson. "Ops, brief the Flight Commander that we will launch the Lynx to sanitise the approach corridor for the tanker. Chief, how long will you need to be alongside drawing fuel?"

Crossley replied, "If all goes well, we should be able to top up within an hour, say possibly an hour and a half max."

Lieutenant Commander Mike Sheppard, Logistics Officer, chipped in, "Any chance of a brief stores transfer? We need bread making and WEO [Weapons Engineering Officer] needs some essential 'Greeny' bits and pieces."

"That may be possible, Mike, but it has to take second priority. We will try a coincidental Jackstay transfer and may be able to do a vertrep with the helicopter. No guarantees though."

"Thank you, sir." Mike made a note on his pad. Beside him the Weapons Officer looked glum. At that point the meeting broke up, most of the officers going about their business, leaving Wilson with Paul Bycroft, the Operations Officer, drafting the necessary instructions and signals.

SIX

In London the working day had started, the various overnight duty officers had handed over to the experts and things were beginning to happen, although inevitably there was much more talking than doing and little overall progress was being achieved.

The ad hoc Naval Operations Committee led by the Assistant Chief of Naval Staff was reviewing all possible choices open to the ships 'In Theatre' and listing possible actions attributable to the pirates. There was near uproar at one point when a diminutive representative of the Navy Board Legal Staff raised the question of the need to ensure the Health and Safety of the pirates, and when this subsided the Assistant Chief of Staff summarised progress to date. It amounted to agreement as to the only course open to *Carlisle* and her international consorts which was to watch and wait but to allow some minimum latitude of action, since it remained almost impossible and certainly unwise to attempt to predict what the pirates might do. The meeting lasted nearly two hours and actually decided little of consequence.

So far as they were able to determine there were no British citizens involved in the incident and it appeared that no lives had been lost. The captured ship was registered in Saudi Arabia and was owned by a Saudi company. No request for assistance had been received from the owners or the Government of Saudi Arabia and although recognised as an international problem it was not specifically a British problem. The committee concluded that the international force of warships in the Indian Ocean had already failed in their principal duty in that they had not been able to prevent the seizure of the *Sea Shadow*. The meeting had decided not to approve the required political request to change the Rules of Engagement, but then to instruct *Carlisle* to break off from close surveillance forthwith in order to withdraw to the north to refuel, and to carry out this task as quickly as possible before returning to close surveillance, reporting any occurrences on return to the scene of activity. It could be, and was, described as 'do nothing but watch and wait'.

In a different building across on the other side of Whitehall another committee was in session. This was a sub-committee of the standing Cobra Committee and it was meeting informally – that is without notes or minutes being taken by anyone present – to review the latest development in what had become an ongoing and intractable international sore. The Committee was rather smaller than the Naval Operations Committee but it carried more clout and was able to range far and wide in its consideration of various 'what if' scenarios.

The Prime Minister had opened the meeting, listened to the various reports and then handed over the chairmanship to the Foreign Secretary. By this stage there were only two other men and one woman in the room. The tall, spare sallow skinned man opposite the Foreign Secretary represented MI6. The woman, matronly and fiftyish, spoke for the Eastern Committee, a covert government organization charged with maintaining surveillance on all events taking place in the regions of North Africa and the Middle East which might be considered to affect British interests at some stage. In effect, but known only to a few, she *was* the Eastern Committee.

The fourth member of the committee did a lot of listening but said little. Colonel Jack Lang ran the Special Operations Group. These were the people who were sometimes called in, usually following recommendation from the Eastern Committee, to resolve problems on behalf of the British Government and to take actions which could be subsequently utterly deniable.

"We are, of course, only monitoring the possible outcome of the *Sea Shadow* incident," said the Foreign Secretary.

"Yes," said MI6. "But we all know that this is one that is likely to develop, leaving us with egg, or more probably oil, all over our faces. Neither the owner," he continued, "nor their government can actually do much about it and when the ship's occupants are identified and the degree of private and national insult registers, let me tell you, the shit will fly far and wide."

"The Eastern Committee has repeatedly stated that some wide ranging and serious response is necessary in general terms to send a signal to these people that their activities are not acceptable," said the woman from the other end of the table.

The Foreign Secretary sighed. "There you go again, Maggie. Gunboat diplomacy is a thing of the past," he said.

"That's why they do what they do," came the rejoinder.

The Foreign Secretary glanced towards the end of the table, looked away then whirled his head round again. "Maggie!" he demanded. "Are you knitting?"

"Helps me think," Maggie replied, as her needles continued to click.

Jack Lang, who had so far contributed little to the discussion, said, "The real point is that there is nothing we can do within our present constraints to relieve or resolve today's situation. However it is possible, likely even, that given the target the dunderheads have chosen this time, we might soon receive sufficient support within the region to set up a more permanent solution."

"That will take time – a lot of time." Maggie's needles continued to click. "Damn," she said, drawing the attention of her companions as she stared intently at the woolly mess in her hands. "Dropped a stitch."

Jack looked pained. He had been through this charade before but was prepared to indulge Maggie because behind the grandmotherly exterior lurked a brain of lightning speed and brilliant ability. All the signs were that it was now working furiously at maximum capacity. He turned towards the Foreign Secretary. "I think we need to continue to monitor and record the present incident and at the same time the Eastern Committee and the S.O.G. might do a preliminary study to work towards a permanent but unattributable solution to the whole problem."

"The Americans tried that a few years ago and came away with a bloody nose," muttered the Foreign Secretary unenthusiastically.

MI6 sniffed disdainfully. "Americans," he said, moving his head to one side as if suddenly assaulted by an offensive smell. "Foreign Secretary, I am surprised that you should ever consider American actions an appropriate model for us."

"No, of course not," said the Foreign Secretary, chastened.

MI6 continued. "I like the idea of pursuing a more lasting solution but there are two questions. In principle how long would it take and how long have we got?"

Jack leaned back in his chair while Maggie knitted on. "We haven't even worked out what we may be able to do yet. How can I tell you how long it will take?"

"OK, question two then. How long have we got?" said MI6, turning pointedly to face the Foreign Secretary.

The Foreign Secretary looked down at the notepad he had been doodling on and pondered. The silence stretched on, broken only by the click click of Maggie's needles and the occasional scrape of a chair. At length he said, slowly and carefully, "It depends of course on what the renegades get up to next but when this one is talked up and over, protests, threats and promises made and broken, I would say… I would say, a month, two at the outside, to plan, mount and recover an operation – if it's a permanent solution. In the short term of course, the time we have depends on how long it takes the pirates to get the ship to port." He looked enquiringly around the table. MI6 nodded but said nothing.

Maggie paused in her knitting, leaned down as if to examine her work and said quietly, "Then we will have to delay them a bit, won't we?"

Jack said, "I wonder how long we can delay them?" They all looked towards Maggie. The needles clicked on while the air of expectancy grew. "OK," she said at length. "We need to stop their captive from moving without letting them know what we have done. We should also be able to put a *cordon sanitaire* around them to prevent their friends getting involved. Of course this means keeping expensive assets tied to this incident."

Jack was already pondering an alternative solution.

*

The meeting broke up. The Foreign Secretary strode off along a wide corridor in the direction of his office while the other three made their way down a shabby set of service stairs towards the back entrance of the building where three unexceptional black cars collected each of them in turn.

As soon as the Foreign Secretary entered his enormous, palatial office he was surrounded by aides and minions competing for his attention. The Permanent Under Secretary appeared in the doorway of his connecting office and announced, "Good morning Minister." Magically the crowd of hopefuls dispersed leaving only the Private Secretary and the PUS in the room. The Private Secretary edged in front of the very senior 'mandarin' to grab her boss's attention.

"There are some urgent and pressing telephone calls, Minister," she said in her precise clipped tones.

"Yes?" The Foreign Secretary looked enquiringly towards the prim young lady standing on the other side of his desk now holding her spectacles and a pencil in one hand while she read from a shorthand notebook held in the other. He wondered, not for the first time if the heavy rimmed glasses were just for effect, concluding that they probably were. He also noted that Sir Gerald had eased his way around the desk to stand behind and slightly to one side of his master. 'To appear as one', he had been known to say.

Alice Hepplewhite had served several Foreign Secretaries and knew how to play the part assigned to her. Carefully paraphrasing the enraged and emotional phone calls she had reluctantly listened to, she said, "There were several calls sir, and they were all by or on behalf of Prince Khalid bin Saliz al Zubari. There were others of course which do not require your personal attention and they have been dealt with..."

“What about the Prince?” interrupted the Foreign Secretary.

Alice effected not to notice the rude interruption and continued her report. “The Prince wishes you to be aware of an incident which has occurred involving his private yacht. It seems that the vessel may have been attacked by pirates. A son of the Prince is on board and the Prince wishes the British Navy to recover his yacht, rescue his son and kill the pirates involved – sir.”

Sir Gerald slid a sheet of paper smoothly and noiselessly on to the desk. “I have taken the liberty of preparing an appropriate holding reply, Minister,” he said.

The Foreign Secretary glanced down at the paper. The response was as smooth and bland as the man who had prepared it. ‘That should infuriate the evil old bastard even more,’ he thought. He said nothing but stared into space over steepled hands, elbows resting on his desk.

“Yes,” he said at length, “send it.” Sir Gerald glided noiselessly from the room. Alice remained, holding her notepad, pencil poised above it. “Sit down,” said the Foreign Secretary, “I need to think.”

*

Almost as soon as the three cars left the Foreign Office and turned into Birdcage Walk they split up and headed in different directions. The MI6 car drove in the general direction of the massive headquarters building overlooking the Thames, but then switched into a network of ‘rat runs’ known to few, other than taxi drivers, emerging eventually in Burnt Ash Lane heading for the M3.

In his large heavy car, MI6 eased back, stretched across the comfortably upholstered fine leather seat and allowed his mind to wander.

Each of the other two cars were moving north on different roads and at some speed. Jack Lang was heading for a modest 'Gentleman's Residence' to the north of High Wycombe in the wooded Oxfordshire countryside. Maggie was bound further to the west where her car would eventually disappear into a tunnel at the end of a narrow lane leading into a small private estate on the eastern border of Wiltshire.

Before the day was out they would speak again and they would be discussing a plan within thirty-six hours.

*

Maggie McGuigan had been brought up in the school of hard knocks. Born some sixty years ago in the tiny village of Strangford on the southern edge of the sea loch of the same name, she had entered the world in a moderately protestant household unfortunately situated on the wrong side of the street, with staunch republican catholic families on either side. By the time she left school at the age of sixteen the 'troubles' in Northern Ireland had already begun. The McGuigan family had been forced out of their tiny but comfortable cottage and then out of the village, moving at first across the loch to the village of Portaferry. This home proved no more secure than the previous ones for a family who had been branded as the enemy by their neighbours for nothing more than the simple fact that their faith did not fit into the tribal warfare which had engulfed their homeland. They moved further north to the greater security afforded by the coastal town of Bangor. It was here that the family enjoyed the support and protection of their own kind and it was here that Maggie resolved to do what she could to contribute to the defeat of the evil gangs that held sway in so much of Northern Ireland. She joined the police reserves, then a year later she left and joined the British Army.

Within six months of completing her basic training Maggie had been drafted into the Intelligence Corps with the temporary rank of acting corporal. This led, inevitably, to undercover work at which she proved remarkably successful. By the application of cunning, quick wit and the ability to sense danger she skated out of situations that sadly claimed the lives of many other undercover operatives. Eventually her success meant that she became more identifiable to her enemies, even in disguise, and for her own safety she was pulled back from this particular undercover front.

For the next fifteen years she served in the hottest parts of every hot spot frequented by the British Army until, at the age of forty and with the rank of Lieutenant Colonel she left the army and moved neatly sideways into the Security Services. For the last five years she had led the Eastern Committee, planning and organizing remarkable security coups, most of which would never be known to the ordinary man in the street.

Her headquarters was also her home. Having been a widow now for over twenty years following the death of her army officer husband from an unaimed round fired by a republican 'volunteer', she lived a solitary life in somewhat modest circumstances but within the splendid setting of Carrick House and its small estate deep in the 'army country' to the east of Salisbury. She believed she thrived and survived by shunning publicity but she was still glad for the protection of a small and unorthodox team called the 'guard force', nominally part of the Royalty and Diplomatic Protection Squad of the Metropolitan Police. Among the three men and one woman who comprised this team there was not one current or former police officer nor any who had ever been near a royal palace or a foreign embassy. A secretary, operations clerk, researcher and a husband and wife butler and housekeeper completed the permanent staff of the Eastern Committee. When the Committee was in session, doing its thinking, as Maggie described it, other experts were called in as and when required.

Maggie kept in touch with the outside world with the use of several computers linked to an encrypted private internet channel as well as the World Wide Web. She also had an array of telephones in various rooms; some for general use but others providing tamper proof secure communication with various Government offices, including the Foreign Secretary, and with other Security elements such as GCHQ. One of these lines provided a direct connection to Buckland House – the lair of Jack Lang and his Special Operations Group.

A casual visitor passing through the deciduous trees to arrive at the gravelled courtyard in front of Buckland House might assume that they were approaching the offices of an expensive practice of management consultants with a small amount of overnight accommodation for the boss and his family as well a few overnight guests. Further progress around the house with its modern garage block and into the grounds beyond might give a different impression – of a conference centre or perhaps a small resort hotel. In fact the buildings formed the base for an elite and unsung action group who could be deployed at very short notice to almost anywhere in the world. Although the group numbered upwards of a hundred men and women there were seldom more than twenty on the premises. This number was just sufficient to keep the Command, Control and

Communications Centre operating, to run the domestic and transport services and to provide discreet protection for the house and grounds, and occasionally for individuals. The remainder of Jack's group would either be away on operations or 'case building', otherwise called surveillance, or they would be relaxing at home either on call or on leave. Jack's policy of 'If there's nothing to do, don't try to invent it' was popular with his people and ensured that when they were required they came speedily, with loyalty and enthusiasm.

More than a third of Jack's group came, like himself, from a background in the Special Boat Service. Others had spent time in different branches of the Special Forces or as overseas operatives in the Security Services. A few of the older hands had been senior police detectives and one or two were electronics technicians. The group also encompassed the ability to operate almost every form of land, sea and air transport, from horses to jet fighters, but as Jack often observed, success came from good planning and surveillance, followed by moving in quietly, doing the work unobserved, then vanishing.

*

It was nearly midnight before the green phone on the occasional table, waiting beside the crystal tumbler of Benromach Speyside malt whisky trilled to announce its presence and irritate Jack out of his reading.

Jack placed his opened book face down on the table and picked up the phone with one hand and the glass with the other. He took a sip of whisky and said, "Hello Maggie, you took your time."

There was the slightest delay due to the phone's encryption system before Maggie replied.

"It needed a lot of thought," she said. "We need to meet."

"Not tonight, I hope," said Jack.

There was a pause. Jack imagined a surprised Maggie realising what time it was. "Yes I see," she said. "I've been thrashing the problem around and I am beginning to see daylight."

"That's clever," responded Jack. "It's midnight!"

"You know what I mean. I'm not going to trail it all through for you on the phone, so you go and get your beauty sleep and we can meet for breakfast."

"Maggie, it'll take me over an hour to get there. How about lunch?"

"You've got a nice comfortable car, haven't you? And the Foreign Secretary wants answers PDQ," said Maggie. "Lunch won't do. Tell you what – we'll agree on a late working breakfast, say nine thirty, then we can plough on through lunch as well if we need to. OK. Bye."

Jack looked at the phone in his hand, quietly buzzing with a dialling tone. He sighed, closed his book, turned out the reading lamp, gave a last baleful glance towards the telephone and stumped up the stairs to bed.

SEVEN

The big maroon Jaguar hummed down the A403 from High Wycombe, using the dual carriageway sections to glide past the scurrying morning rush hour traffic. It was an exceptionally heavy car due to the armour along the sides and underneath but the supercharged four litre engine didn't even notice.

They had encountered only one jam on the crossing over the M4 just outside High Wycombe but the driver had flicked on the two tone horn and the blue lights set into the front wings of the otherwise unmarked car. The jumble of stationary cars had melted quickly away and Jack eased back into the sumptuous red leather upholstery, using the time to contemplate his forthcoming meeting with Maggie. It seemed the Eastern Committee was about to re-form and he was to be half of it.

By a quarter past nine the car was crunching slowly along the gravel drive leading up to the big house. Jack was out of the car and moving almost before it had stopped. He sprang up the five steps to the double oak doors and stepped through the open one. He stopped and breathed in the unmistakable aroma of a traditional English breakfast.

"In here, Jack." Maggie's voice came from a half open doorway leading off the hall to the left. Jack followed his nose and the sound of her voice.

The dining room was an extraordinary sight. One end of the long mahogany table was set for breakfast for two. The rest of the table was covered with papers, books and charts, from the middle of which peered an open Toshiba laptop computer. Maggie was already seated at the head of the table. She smiled engagingly towards Jack and gestured towards a high backed oak and leather chair immediately to her left. Jack nodded hello and took the seat offered. Chilled orange juice was set before him accompanied by an individual pot of Earl Grey tea. Jack noticed that its companion, set in front of Maggie, sported several tags for Yorkshire Breakfast Teabags.

'Maggie's Butler', Tom Page moved silently towards the table carrying two plates laden with scrambled eggs on thin toast, mushrooms grilled in butter, several rashers of smoked back bacon, a sausage and a grilled tomato. Although hungry having departed with only one cup of coffee, Jack wasn't sure he could do justice to this impressive feast. He took a sip of his orange juice then picked up his knife and fork.

"Eat," said Maggie and then followed her own command by attacking the contents of her plate. They both concentrated on the task before them, eating steadily in silence until both plates were empty. By this time a rack of hot wholemeal toast had arrived but Jack politely declined and sipped his tea while Maggie buttered a slice of toast, bit off a chunk and looked over at Jack. "Do you know what the real problem is?" she said through a mouthful of toast.

"Well, it seems we can chase pirates but we can't take any effective action when we catch them," said Jack. "Add to that a huge amount of ocean, a limited hunter force, a force comprised of units that can't or won't talk to each other, small boats that are difficult to detect, fear of ending up with a load of the brutes as asylum seekers and no government worth the name in their home country. Need I go on…?" he tailed off lamely.

"You've got the picture," came from the other side of the table. "So what do we do about it?" Jack remained silent and waited for the revelation that he was sure would come.

"Look at it this way," said Maggie. "Think of them as wasps. Nasty little creatures who don't seem to have any constructive role in life but who just turn up when you don't want them, bugger up your Sunday afternoon and then sting anyone they feel like. Are you with me so far?"

"I think so," said Jack, "but I'm not sure where you are headed yet."

"Just listen and I'll explain. Think about it. If when every time you go out into the garden you are harassed by wasps, what do you do about it?"

"Probably set traps," responded Jack.

"What else? What if your traps don't solve the problem?"

"Well, I suppose I'd call in a pest controller." Jack picked up his tea cup only to see that it was empty.

"Yes! Got it!" returned Maggie triumphantly.

"In our case, where do we get the pest controller? I thought *we* were the pest controller." Jack looked unimpressed. "Some pest controller!" he continued. "All we can do is wait till the bastards strike, rush after them and then watch them as they trundle home."

"Yes, but why is it like that?" interrupted Maggie.

"Rules, International law, treaties, agreements…" Jack lapsed into silence.

"So how is it we can deal with wasps?" pressed Maggie.

"I don't know. I suppose we eradicate them and make sure there are none left around to sting us afterwards."

"Good boy. You're getting close. So are you saying that we should go after the nest?"

"Yes but go prepared and don't get caught by the wasps who are left."

"Right," said Maggie, "so we go after the nest, but we make sure that we don't get caught out by ensuring that nobody knows we are there and afterwards nobody knows we've been."

"Well," said Jack, "if you are going to create mayhem somebody will know you've been."

"No, no, no!" cried Maggie. "Somebody will know that somebody has been but the trick is to ensure that nobody actually knows *who* has been."

"You mean a covert operation," said Jack. "We've done dozens of those, some more successful than others," he finished lamely.

"You still don't quite get it," said Maggie with a little exasperation. "We do a full scale black operation."

"In this environment, we'd never get clearance," responded Jack.

"So we don't ask for specific clearance. We just say we can do the job but don't divulge the details."

"Look Maggie, you know as well as I do that the sort of op you are suggesting is going to cost money. A great deal of money in fact." Jack's cup had been refilled but had gone cold. Tom deftly removed it and started to replace it with a fresh cup of tea but Jack waved him away.

Maggie leaned across the table corner and beamed at Jack. "We could, if we are clever, use the current situation entirely to our advantage. The last we heard, a fancy boat belonging to a desperately rich Arab has just been grabbed by pirates – presumably Somali pirates, right?

"We know that the owner is already leaning on the British Foreign Office to get his toy back and the way these things work I would bet a pound to a pinch of horse manure that our hero would be prepared to pay handsomely to recover his boat, his crew and whatever rich playboy may have been making use of it."

"How do you know any rich playboy has been using this ship?" interrupted Jack.

Maggie touched the side of her nose and gave a wry smile. "I just do, so trust me," she said.

"So your idea is that we go back to the Foreign Secretary and tell him we can do the job but that we won't tell him how, then somehow we contact this Sheik or Prince or…"

"Prince actually, and an important one."

"…Whatever he is, and invite him to dole out a few million dollars without even so much as a guarantee? You must be losing it."

"I'm not losing anything," retorted Maggie, raising her voice somewhat. "But there will still be problems such as the ability to locate the kit we will need within the timescale, and the people. We will need a lot of people and they will all have to remain shtum, before, during and after the event."

She was clearly on a roll so Jack stayed silent for a moment and then said, "OK, in general terms, outline the plan and tell me what you, we that is, will need."

"Right," said Maggie. "We need an old but serviceable ship, a warship, that is. If we can't get that we need an equally old but serviceable merchant ship that we can kit up ourselves to look and act a bit like a warship. We need a small tanker, and a couple of assault craft, or in extremis I suppose we could get away with one. We will need a crew who won't be missed for a few months, some personal weapons, a bit of heavy artillery and something nasty that will put our friends out of business for the foreseeable future. Add to that the usual passports and personnel admin paraphernalia and – hey presto – we're in business."

"Are you sure you wouldn't like a spacecraft or two?" asked Jack. He shook his head and stared at the table.

Maggie was not to be shifted. Stubbornly she held to the concept she had outlined and the debate continued in much the same way through the morning until by mutual agreement they stopped what had by then become an argument. Tom Page produced a tray of sandwiches and a bottle of Australian Chardonnay.

They sipped the wine in silence, both now standing. Jack turned and walked towards the window. As he stared out at the lowered clouds that were gathering he tried to marshal the thoughts that were jumbled in his head. Every time that a way ahead seemed about to present itself the pattern was immediately destroyed by some factor that didn't fit or could not be achieved.

Maggie broke in on his thoughts. "Let's try to analyse the situation," she said.

"At the Staff College, they called it 'Appreciating the Situation'," retorted Jack.

"Well, try this," said Maggie. "Forget about whether or not we can find the ships, or aircraft, and the men. Assume funds are unlimited, and consider what it is that we might – I only say might – set out to do." Jack nodded assent and waited for her to continue.

"We want to find a ship that no one will miss, man it and take it down through the Atlantic, around the Cape and up into the Indian Ocean. We want it to remain unseen throughout. We want to find the main base of the pirates, cut adrift as many of the hostage ships we can find and then deal a blow to the pirates' base that will prevent them from operating from that place within the foreseeable future. We then need to recover our ship and either return home or destroy the ship and recover the crew. Our ship will need to travel about twelve thousand miles so we will need some form of covert refuelling. That is where my idea for a small tanker comes in. How does that sound?"

"Peachy, just peachy." Jack turned and wilted under the glare that was focused upon him and decided for the moment to co-operate as best he could. "Well," he said, "the appropriate response to your statement of requirements is to list the problems, I think. First, does a suitable ship exist? Second, if such a ship does exist, it presumably has an owner and it either floats or sits in a dry dock. If it is moved someone will notice. Third, we don't know how many men we would need nor what skills they would have to have. But I can hazard a guess and the problem of putting a crew and a supporting team together would, I think, be considerable, if not insurmountable. Fourth, we need to locate a comprehensive range of armament and fit it to the ship. There are rules about acquiring weapons and they are not easy to circumvent and getting it wrong could become very embarrassing indeed for all concerned including our political masters. We would be unlikely to win any friends under those circumstances. Fifth, you said the ship would need to remain unseen. The only way I can think of to achieve that would be to hire a submarine – and I don't think the world has too many spare submarines hanging about, save perhaps the dozen or so redundant Soviet subs left rotting in the Kola Inlet while their dodgy nuclear reactors cook themselves into oblivion. Sixth, what in God's name are we going to do when we arrive on station, and lastly, and most difficult, how do we recover the hundred or so men we would need – and get them home? We can't rustle up a trooping flight. There is more, much more of course but it isn't even worth wasting brain energy on unless we can have some hope of resolving all of these."

Maggie said nothing for a while but as the pile of sandwiches diminished she said, brightly, "Every problem gets easier when you break it down into its constituent parts. Take the ship..."

"If we can find one."

Maggie ignored the interruption. "With the cuts imposed on the Navy there must be ships available here and others probably abroad..."

"Forget abroad," said Jack. Foreign ships if available are likely to be laid up in foreign countries and easing them out from under the noses of the locals will be darn nigh impossible. Also, foreign ships tend to have instructions, notices, tallies and so forth written in their own language. We can't possibly expect to find a bunch of unemployed sailors who also happen to be skilled linguists. Finally, ships tend to be built to meet the operating systems in use in the country of ownership and they often differ widely to what we have here."

Before he could continue, Maggie interrupted, "OK, that refines the task. We need to locate a former British warship."

"Look," said Jack, showing his exasperation, "ships surplus to requirements are not stowed away in convenient boxes in a store. True, some of the more modern ones are cocooned and parked at the top end of Portsmouth Harbour or in Plymouth or some such but the vast majority are sold to other countries if they are any good – or more likely, they are scrapped. Let me tell you, ships, especially warships, are simply not found hanging on trees, waiting for Christmas."

"You are very negative," declared Maggie. "The very least we could do is have a look and these days it shouldn't be too difficult to use the net, and our own network to find out if there is anything at all."

Jack could feel the ground of his argument crumbling, and he was beginning to wilt under the argumentative onslaught as well as the 'thousand yard stare' that seemed to follow him round the room. He sighed. "OK," he said, fiddling in the inside pocket of his jacket which was now hanging over the back of his chair. He took out a small, silver backed mobile phone, tapped a five digit code into the keyboard and lifted it to his ear. It was answered almost immediately by Annette, his Anglo French Secretary and Personal Assistant. "Annie," he said, "I have a simple task for the ops control team. I need an unused or disused British warship, preferably one that nobody knows we've got. It needs to be capable of being made operational. A frigate or destroyer, or corvette or even a bloody minesweeper will do. Get the boys onto it please and get back to me as soon as you have a preliminary result – even if it's negative. Got that? Any questions?"

Annie announced that she had indeed 'got that' and she had no questions.

EIGHT

In Wiltshire it was twenty to two in the wintery afternoon when Jack made his phone call. In the Indian Ocean it was twenty to five.

Craig Wilson glanced again at the flimsy signal print-out in his hand. Swivelling his chair to face across the Bridge, he addressed the Officer of the Watch. "What time is sunset Officer of the Watch?" he called.

The answer came back instantly "eighteen twenty eight, sir."

He swivelled the chair back to face the First Lieutenant who was waiting expectantly. "OK Number One. We are instructed to break off close surveillance and refuel as soon as convenient, but our masters would like the Yanks to keep watch while we are away." Hardly pausing he called over his shoulder, "Make to *Andrew James* Yeo: 'I must withdraw temporarily to refuel. Can you remain in contact, max 24 hours until I return.' Quick as you can please Yeo."

"Aye aye sir." The Yeoman was already on his way to the Bridge wing and the ten inch signal lamp. Within two or three minutes he appeared back through the screen door and read from a scribbled piece of paper. "From *Andrew James* sir. No problem. Take your time. Intend to stay in close company until Somali national limit or until authorised for further action. Bon voyage."

"Acknowledge," said Wilson. "Officer of the Watch, come up to twenty-five knots and close the bearing towards the *Fort Brockhurst*." Picking up a microphone from the panel in front of him he continued, "Ops, Captain, inform the tanker on tactical that we are closing him for refuel and give him an estimated time for first gun-line. Ask the Chief for the tonnage required and an estimate of time alongside. Make the replenishment course up sea and contact 'Loggo' to get his list of bread and spares. Tell him the jackstay time will be governed by the refuel time. No longer – OK?"

The console speaker responded, "Very good sir." As he replaced the microphone, *Carlisle* was already healing hard to starboard as the ship surged around in a two hundred and seventy degree turn away to port of the *Sea Shadow* and across her stern to the north. As soon as the destroyer cleared the immediate area of the pirated ship, men began spilling out on to the upper deck. Despite the spray created by the 30-knot apparent wind, huge black hose sections and bronze deck connecters began to appear on the forecastle deck in front of the Bridge. Men and one woman in white overalls scurried about checking seals and pressures as the refuelling position was set up. Just abaft of that group, seamen began setting up ropes and heavy pulley blocks. The Gunner's Yeoman already dressed in his red surcoat arrived and carefully set in place his gun-lines and line throwing rifle. Wilson slipped out of his chair and moved out onto the Bridge wing. He was pleased with what he saw. By now, *Carlisle* had worked up to her required speed.

The console speaker burst into life again. "Captain, Ops sir. *Brockhurst* is actually at the southern end of her 'racetrack' and she is extending south at eighteen knots. We have ninety miles to run so we should be alongside the tanker by twenty ten, first gun-line say at twenty fifteen sir?"

“Yes, make it so,” said the Captain, “and tell Number One to get the RAS [Replenishment at Sea] team and Special Sea Dutymen to supper as soon as possible. Can you make a pipe from the Ops Room to the Ship’s Company to make sure that everybody knows what is going on? Also note it will be fully dark when we start. Pass the RAS course to *Brockhurst* as three two zero.”

“Aye aye sir.”

As HMS *Carlisle* settled at twenty-five knots heading north with the long ocean swell on her port bow, she began to smash through the waves so that every fourth or fifth swell broke over the bow, boiling white around the gun mounting and missile launcher, splattering and soaking the Bridge windows and the men working below.

NINE

In Wiltshire, as the afternoon wore away the debate between the two senior 'spooks' rumbled on. They addressed, considered and rejected thought after thought. Jack was privately convinced that Maggie's plan would never get off the ground because he could not accept that they would be able to locate any type of ship capable of travelling twelve thousand miles whilst remaining undetected by passing vessels or aircraft. "And we're not even thinking about satellites," he scoffed at Maggie. Money was also likely to remain a huge difficulty, despite the fact that Maggie's firm conviction that the 'Sheik', whom she had never met, nor been aware of until today, could be tapped for untold millions by people he didn't know for a plan he couldn't be told about. Finally, neither protagonist could work out how many men and women would be needed, nor what skills they must have, in order to fix up an old ship and take it halfway round the world, before tackling the pirates in their base.

*

In London, the Foreign Secretary was also having a difficult time. He was receiving telephone calls at least every hour either from the Prince or from a variety of individuals who claimed to speak on behalf of the Prince, or with his authority. Threats were uttered concerning international business deals, oil supplies, control of terrorists, overflying rights and various other even more bizarre activities, and all the while, the Foreign Secretary was trying to grasp why the loss of *Sea Shadow* should have anything at all to do with the British Government. While this was taking place, the British Legation in Riyadh was swamped with demands for assistance, all emanating, by various obscure routes, from the same source. Finally, within the Whitehall offices translators and secretaries were labouring under a storm of emails.

"But Gerald," said the Foreign Secretary, addressing Sir Gerald, the Permanent Under Secretary. "It isn't our fucking problem! We didn't steal his bloody boat!"

"Quite so, Foreign Secretary," replied Sir Gerald in his most formal tone.

"I wish I'd never heard of the fucking thing."

"Well sir, until today you hadn't," replied Sir Gerald, hiding a discreet cough behind an immaculately manicured hand.

The Foreign Secretary glared up at him from behind his desk. "Are you trying to be funny?" he snarled.

Sir Gerald dropped instantly into damage recovery mode. "Oh no, Minister. Certainly not. No, no, no." He began to wring his hands and lean further towards his master on the other side of the desk.

The red phone in the centre of the Foreign Secretary's desk clanged into life.

*

In Wiltshire another telephone rang. This was a white one.

Maggie picked up the phone, listened for a moment, and handed it to Jack without speaking.

"I 'ave found you a sheep," said Annette, her increasing French accent giving away her rising excitement.

"What?" exploded Jack. "I don't believe it – where?" he finished lamely.

"I weel send the details in an email," said Annette. "Au 'voir." And she was gone.

Jack sat in silence. Maggie leaned across from the armchair she was sitting in and said triumphantly, "We've got a ship! I can tell by the deflated look on your face." She beamed at Jack and could not resist clapping her hands, dropping her knitting into a tangle on the floor in the process. She had started knitting about an hour previously when the debate had lurched into an opposed stalemate.

"Annie's sending an email," said Jack blankly.

"I'll get some tea," said Maggie. Jack sat and waited.

An antique mahogany desk on the far side of the dining room contained an open laptop computer emerging like a mountain summit from a jumble of paper and booklets. After six or seven minutes an orange light began to flash in the bar at the base of the screen. Thinking that computer etiquette dictated that the computer owner should be the first to see incoming emails, Jack continued waiting patiently until Maggie emerged from the kitchen carrying two mugs of her Yorkshire Tea on a tray. Inconsequentially, Jack thought 'no more Earl Grey for me today then'.

Yet again, Maggie read his thoughts. "Sorry," she said. "Tom has put it away and I don't know where, so you will just have to join me in some genuine 'sergeant major's special'."

"Signal's come through on your machine," said Jack, ignoring the barb and nodding towards the desk.

Maggie put down the tea and moved across to the desk. She sat in the black leather swivel chair in front of the laptop and swept aside a pile of paper, allowing her to see the keyboard. After a couple of key strokes she peered intently at the screen, scrolled down using the mouse, peered again, then ran it back to the top. "Couldn't be better!" she exclaimed. Maggie fiddled with the mouse and swept more paper out of her way, revealing a small compact printer. As she did so, the printer began to buzz and grumble, eventually ejecting a dozen sheets of paper.

"Two copies, one each," said Maggie as she gathered up the paper and strode across the room. Jack sipped at his tea and waited for Maggie to arrange the sheaf of paper into two sets. They each took a set and, sinking back into their armchairs, studied the papers in silence.

Jack looked up first. "Well, I have to hand it to you," he said. "It's all here. The answer to a maiden's prayer."

"I'm not exactly a maiden," said Maggie. "But I'll settle for what we have got here. I think we should get up to Scotland as fast as we can and have a look at it."

The report was precise and comprehensive. There were three possible ships that might have met the requirement but initial investigation had determined that two of them should be discarded. One was an old World War Two Algerine class ocean going minesweeper which had ended its service days as the venue for various Damage Control experiments, most of which resulted in structural damage to the vessel. Also, even if it could be patched up it would be too slow and too small. The second prospect was a Type 14, 'Blackwood' Class frigate which was languishing in the Reserve Fleet Moorings up at the northern end of Portsmouth Harbour. This was proving the most likely prospect until it was noted that her extensive service during the 1960's Iceland Cod War had resulted in major structural damage to the hull. In fact the ship had all but broken her back. The fatal damage was evidenced by a jagged crack running from side to side across the ship just in front of the main galley. It was unlikely, the report went on to concede, that the ship would ever be capable of moving from her current resting place without breaking up.

The third ship was an old Leander Class frigate. These ships had once been the backbone of the Fleet – ubiquitous, universal workhorses seeing service in every part of the globe. Twenty-six ships had been built for the Royal Navy, two for the Royal New Zealand Navy and a further six for the Indian Navy. The subject of the report had been built initially as number seven for the Indian Navy but that contract had been cancelled when the Indian government had been seduced into re-arming their Fleet with ex-Soviet ships all offered at knock down prices by the Russians, who were anxious to use their inroad into the Sub-Continent to extend the reach of their political influence and achieve a lead in the arms races of the Cold War. This victim of international political intrigue had never entered proper service but had completed a series of sea trials, sailing under the red ensign, before being leased to various elements of the Ministry of Defence as a platform for maritime weapons and equipment trials. The trials had culminated in her steam engines and boilers being ripped out and replaced with an experimental layout of gas turbines and diesel engines. This became an arrangement subsequently used to power later destroyers and frigates and had been successfully employed in several future classes of ships, known by the acronym CODOG, standing for 'Combined Diesel or Gas'.

Leander Class frigates had been built in three different batches at a variety of commercial and government shipyards around the country. Most of them had undergone refits and modernisation programmes of one sort or another and so no two were exactly the same. The first two batches had been built to be anti-submarine frigates and the third batch, often called 'Gun Leanders', had been built with more emphasis towards surface warfare and gunnery, until several were further converted to enter the missile age. These ships were wider in the beam, occasioning the alternative epithet 'Wide Beam Leanders'. It was one of these that had apparently been rejected by the Indian Navy and which for the last fifteen years or so had been anchored fore and aft at the top end of one of the most remote sea lochs in Scotland. The ship apparently had not been given a name, at least not one that lasted long enough to be recorded. The Gun Leanders had been originally designed around a main armament consisting of two four point five inch guns in a single mounting in front of the Bridge. Capable of speeds just short of thirty knots with exceptional sea keeping qualities the Leanders had a range of over four thousand miles but this was based on a steam powered system. There was no indication of the state of the engines in this particular ship; indeed it was possible that, given the engine trials programme she had undergone, she might not now have any engines at all.

There were two photographs of, presumably, this particular ship and a diagram of the ship showing its principle sensors and weapon systems – or rather where they should have been if they had actually been fitted. One of the photographs had been taken from the air and had obviously been taken in weather typical of the north coast of Scotland. It showed a rather smudgy, long grey shape nestling under overhanging trees at the top of a long and narrowing sea inlet. The other photograph had been taken at sea level and had a tiny portion of the gunwale of an open boat superimposed across one corner. It was much clearer but not very encouraging. The ship seemed to be camouflaged with a mixture of rust, weed, algae, rotting leaves and green mould. There was no sign of a gun, nor of any other weapon, and the few aerials left looked as if they were rejects from a scrap yard.

"It's a ship," said Jack as he dropped his copy of the report on the coffee table beside his chair, "but I'm not sure I'd like to go to sea in it.

"Well," said Maggie, "We've made a start. It *is* a ship. Doesn't look much but we only have two old photographs to go on and it is still afloat."

"You don't know that. It could be sitting on the bottom."

"The report says it's in a Scottish sea loch – created by glaciers. I don't think so."

"If it was a viable, serviceable ship when the Indians said they didn't want it, why wasn't it sold to some other navy or used by the Royal Navy?" mused Jack, then turning back to riffle through the papers of the report he answered his own question. "Here it is," he said. "It suggests that there was a protracted dispute over ownership and payment. It drove the builders' yard out of business. The Royal Navy didn't take it because they already had their full whack of ships and didn't have the money to operate an extra one, nor probably the men to run it. It doesn't actually say so but it looks as though the government stepped in, too late as usual, smoothed things over with the Indians and paid off the receivers as well as trying to find a use for the ship. I think the ship was then just forgotten."

Maggie looked on with interest. "Interesting theory," she said.

"We need to go and look at it…" Jack was interrupted by the telephone beside Maggie's chair. Maggie picked it up and listened. After a few seconds she said, somewhat formally, "Yes, Foreign Secretary." Then, "I have been in conference with Jack all day and I think we may be getting close to the outline of a plan." As she spoke she pressed a button on the telephone base unit and the familiar North Country tones of the Foreign Secretary boomed out into the room. Jack sat still and listened.

The Foreign Secretary was saying, "…It's becoming more urgent to be seen to be doing something. I don't mind telling you that I'm getting a bucketful of pressure from Saudi Arabia. Prince Khalid Bin Saliz al Zubari is a Saudi Government Minister who seems to have the ear of the King, the Prime Minister and just about everybody else. He has lost his boat and wants it back. For some obscure reason that I can't bloody well understand he seems to think that I am responsible – I mean, that we are responsible. We, the British Government, he means. We are now approaching the blackmail phase: all about how the missing bloody boat is going to deflect resources away from making sure we – Britain – get our oil supplies. We are in a spot, Maggie, and we need to use everything we can to get out of it. We need to get this damn ship back and, I suppose the people on it, and we need to do it without anyone else noticing."

"A covert operation," interrupted Maggie.

"Got it in one," came from the telephone speaker.

"What about money?" Maggie seized her chance to get a word in.

"Well that's the only good thing – or should I say helpful thing to emerge from this mess so far," said the Foreign Secretary. "If we get his boat back, whatever the cost, it will be covered."

Maggie quickly interrupted again. "That's not good enough," she said. "If we set up an operation to resolve the situation we need to be sure that it is going to be funded, whether we succeed or fail. Foreign Secretary, I think we will be able to at least make a realistic attempt, but it will take time, money and people. We can only do our best but we are human. We could fail. You need to get money – cash that is – up front."

There was silence from the telephone speaker for thirty seconds, then noises of paper moving then more silence. At length the distinctive voice of the Foreign Secretary emerged from the speaker. "All right," he said. "This is what I will do to hold the status quo for say the next 24 hours…"

"We need at least 48 hours," interrupted Maggie once again.

The phone lapsed into silence once again. Then, "OK I think we can stall for 48 hours, but the money…"

"You definitely need money up front," said Maggie. "Put it this way. Say that preparations need to be made and we can't be seen to be removing money openly from any government budget…"

"But you've got an operating budget…" responded the Foreign Secretary.

"Not big enough," announced Maggie starkly. "Not nearly big enough."

The tiredness was evident in the Foreign Secretary's voice as he came back on the line. "Right, I'll try. How much am I bidding for?"

Maggie thought for a moment as she looked across at Jack, who held up a figure scrawled on a sheet of paper. "Twenty million, for starters," she said.

"What?" shrieked the Foreign Secretary from the phone speaker. Jack actually thought the base unit jumped a little on the coffee table. "Twenty million fucking dollars?"

"No," said Maggie, icily calm. "Twenty million fucking pounds, up front, in cash, and counted. Thirty-five million if we are counting in dollars. Oh, and by the way we want to borrow a ship."

Strangulated noises came from the speaker. "Did you get that?" cooed Maggie sweetly towards the telephone handset. There was no immediate answer so she continued in the same sweet tone, "If you ask nicely, Foreign Secretary, and considering the billions that the Sheik, sorry, Prince has got locked up in his piggy bank, I'm sure you can convince him that it will be money well spent. Tell him we will give him any change there is."

"I'll get back to you. Wait there." They heard the clatter of a replaced receiver, ending the conversation.

"Well done," said Jack. "That was pretty cool."

"Necessary though."

"Yes."

"OK. Assume we've got a ship," continued Maggie.

"A big assumption."

"Yes well, beggars and choosers and all that. We've got to start somewhere, so we assume we have a ship. How many men will we need? How far can it go on a load of fuel? What will we need to make it workable?"

Jack leaned back. "At this point," he said, "I think we need a sailor. However it says in the notes here that they had a crew of two hundred and sixty-three, so say we can economise a bit, maybe we can get it down to a hundred."

"We'll need to do much better than that," said Maggie.

"As I said, we need a sailor."

TEN

The lines came hurtling back across the gap between the two ships as the tall derrick at the midships station on the tanker hauled the great loops of heavy fuelling hose steadily back to hang above the replenishment tanker's well deck, ready for the next customer.

"Starboard ten," said the Officer of the Watch quietly to the helmsman.

"Ten of starboard wheel on, sir."

The destroyer peeled away from the tanker, opening the gap between the two ships and beginning to move ahead as speed was increased. Further aft along the port side of the upper deck, cardboard boxes and packages were being manhandled into the ship through a screen door, supervised by Mike Sheppard.

Craig Wilson studied the chart laid out on the chart table at the back of the Bridge, the Navigating Officer at his side. "How long to re-join the *Andrew James*, Pilot?"

"Assuming *Andrew James* and *Sea Shadow* are maintaining the same course and speed, sir, and allowing that the RAS course has been taking us northwest, we should have about one hundred and fifty miles to run to re-join, say six hours at this speed."

The replenishment operation had been relatively uneventful. The tanker had been where she said she would be, already settled on the Replenishment Course of 320 degrees at fifteen knots. The first gun-line from the tanker had been fired a fraction too early and had fallen uselessly into the sea as *Carlisle* made a final speed reduction to slot neatly into position alongside the tanker, but the second line, fired by *Carlisle's* Gunner's Yeoman had sailed perfectly over the tanker and had been quickly gathered up and attached to the messenger outhaul to begin the refuelling operation. Two hours later the whole thing, including the transfer of various packages of stores was complete.

"As soon as the gear is stowed, let's see if we can inch her up to twenty-eight knots for a while," said the Captain. "When he gets up to the Bridge ask the First Lieutenant to make a pipe to the ship's company to bring them up to date and tell them that we will be re-joining the Datum position by, say, zero four three zero with the upper deck out of bounds from that time."

The Navigating Officer's reply was drowned by the shrill clanging of alarm bells. The Captain spun round towards the Officer of the Watch who called over his shoulder, "Man overboard, sir." He was hanging on to the central compass repeater stand as the ship heeled violently into the first part of a 'Williamson Turn', designed to manoeuvre the ship into a position to track back exactly along its previous course.

"Get the speed off her, Sub," called the Captain as he clambered into his chair.

"Aye aye, sir."

"Away Seaboat's Crew, Watch on Deck stand by port side!" boomed the main broadcast.

"Fuck!" said the Captain.

"One of Mike's lads slipped and went over the side before the guardrails were fully made up, sir," added the Navigating Officer, helpfully.

"Fuck!" repeated the Captain, then, to the Officer of the Watch, "Bring her down to five knots once you're settled on the reverse track. Have you posted extra lookouts?"

"Five knots, sir. Lookout's closing up now, sir."

Wilson slid down from his chair, crossed the Bridge and moved out through the screen door on to the port wing. As he did so a ragged cheer came up from the main deck below him. Realising that the First Lieutenant had arrived on the Bridge wing beside him, he turned with a questioning look.

"He's in the water, there, sir," said the First Lieutenant pointing ahead, then adding, "I've held back the seaboat, and stood-to the Duty Diver."

Wilson picked up a waterproof microphone, dragging the long coiled lead with it. Speaking into the microphone he said, "Officer of the Watch, Captain has the con."

As the bobbing light on the unfortunate logistics rating's life jacket moved slowly down towards the rescue party assembled in the waist, Wilson rattled out a series of engine and wheel orders to ease the ship gently to a stop alongside the man in the water.

The only reply he received over the conning intercom was "Coxswain on the wheel, sir."

There was a muffled splash as the black clad diver dropped the fifteen feet into the water and took two strokes to reach the man in his inflated lifejacket. This was a drill that had been practised repeatedly and within four minutes the whole thing was over, the 'survivor' was on his way to the Sick Bay and the upper deck crew were tidying away their gear as the ship picked up speed and began a gentle turn back towards her former course.

“Better make another pipe,” said the Captain to the Bridge in general. “Change the Datum arrival time to oh five hundred. I’m going down to the Sick Bay,” he said as he left without waiting for an answer.

*

On board the motor yacht *Sea Shadow*, Hamid was propped in the comfortable Bridge conning chair, dozing lightly. Khalid lounged by the wheel and engine console as the ship plugged on under auto-pilot at a steady fifteen knots. The crew members were still safely locked in the cabins and a two man armed guard had been placed outside the locked ‘owners stateroom’, where the Prince and his paramour were detained in reasonable comfort. The Prince had settled into a morose but quiet mood after calling down curses and divine intervention on the heads of Hamid and his crew. The woman spent most of her time curled in a foetal position, on the huge bed, sobbing.

Down in the Machinery Control Room, Melak was peering towards the bank of eight circular gauges indicating the contents level of the fuel tanks. Some gauges seemed to indicate a higher fuel state than others and above the two central gauges, two orange lights were flashing. He didn’t know why. As he stared, one of the gauge lights turned from flashing orange to flashing red, then to a steady, worrying, red light. Minutes later, the steady note from one of the big diesels began to falter. The engine, somewhere outside the Machinery Control Room, banged and coughed, died, picked up again, and then stopped.

Unknown to Melak, along the lower section of the control panel, a drop down flap covered a series of valves and circuit breakers with a network of engraved and painted lines running around and between them. This was the fuel management system, installed to enable the movement of fuel, and therefore weight, around the ship. It was possible to put the entire system into automatic transfer mode, supplying both engines equally from all tanks but it had always been the practice aboard *Sea Shadow* that the fuel transfer should be left under manual control.

The second orange flashing light turned to red flashing. Melak transferred his gaze and said a silent prayer. His prayer was not answered. The engine went through the same process of indicating fuel starvation and then stopped. The silence was almost tangible.

On the Bridge, Hamid awoke with a start. He hopped out of his chair, picked up the automatic from the shelf in front of him and turned towards the door to the Bridge ladder. Then he hesitated, turned back and fired off a rapid burst of Arabic towards Khalid. Dutifully, Khalid picked up the Uzi and trotted off down the ladder.

ELEVEN

"Captain to the con!" The tinny voice emerged from the speaker in the Captain's day cabin and John Reagan, Captain of the USS *Andrew James*, left his chair in one fluid movement without bothering to reply. Within fifteen seconds he was standing beside the two Officers of the Watch.

"She's stopped, sir. Seems to have lost power on both engines," said the First Officer of the Watch as Reagan arrived beside him. Reagan slid into his chair and took up his binoculars. The *Sea Shadow* was stopped, wallowing with the effect of the swell but lights were still on and there was no movement around the upper decks.

"Stop both engines, hold position alongside her," rapped out the Captain.

"Aye sir. Stop both engines," repeated the Second Officer of the Watch. The big warship slowed to a stop and then cautiously began to back up to a position about one mile on the beam of the *Sea Shadow*.

'What the hell do I do now?' thought Commander Reagan, but he kept the thought to himself. Instead he said from behind the binoculars, "See if you can raise *Carlisle* on Tactical and tell them what's happening."

"Aye sir," came the instant response.

*

Onboard the *Sea Shadow*, quite a lot of things were happening. Hamid had flown into an uncharacteristic rage and pushed Ali in the direction of the Engine Room with a shouted demand that he find out what was happening and then make the engines start working again. Ali was terrified. The changed motion of the now stationary ship had made his stomach churn and he felt very seasick. He didn't know what might face him in the Engine Room where a man had been killed and he didn't want to go back there. He didn't want to face the wrath of Hamid either. His journey from the Bridge was delayed by frequent stops while he waited for his stomach to settle, and during his passage along the upper deck, where he stopped to retch and vomit over the rail into the sea.

In his hideaway, Louis had been dozing. The change in the motion from smooth and steady movement through the sea to uncomfortable lurching from side to side caused him to wake in fear and uncertainty. He was petrified in case the ship should be sinking and he risked moving back to a position just behind the locked door into his pantry to try to find out what was happening. He could see nothing and hear only a series of unconnected noises, mostly of doors opening and shutting, with the normal 'ship noises' continuing in the background. He returned to his sanctuary and waited in silence and with only the light of his torch, since the second priority lighting circuits had shut down automatically following the loss of the engines.

After a while he decided to risk an attempt to use his mobile phone. He tried several numbers at random but failed to generate any response, but when he thought about his situation more rationally, he realised that any response to a mobile phone signal from within the steel hull of the ship, was unlikely. In this assertion he was almost right. Almost, but not quite.

The imprisoned crew, fearing abandonment in a sinking ship, had started to attack the locked doors of the cabins in which they were secured. Khalid, sent from the Bridge, arrived in time to see two of the doors being smashed off their hinges, but he waved his assault rifle about and fired a short burst down the passageway which caused the prisoners to retreat back into the cabins. Before they did so, Khalid caught sight of the white overalls of two of the engineers. He shouted, "You – Engineer man – you come here!" The immediate effect on the men was to encourage them to get as far back into the cabin as they could.

Another pirate arrived. While he stood covering the entrances to the cabins, Khalid went to the nearest cabin where he had spotted the white overalls. Using a contradictory mixture of bribes and threats uttered in fractured English he eventually extracted the two engineers.

A third Arab arrived from the Bridge and together with Khalid, the engineers were prodded and shoved in the direction of the Machinery Control Room. When they arrived at the entrance to the tiny room, sweaty and fearful, Khalid issued an unmistakable ultimatum.

"You make engine go or I kill," he said.

Sharkey Fisher turned to his companion and said, "I'll fix it Chief. They've just fucked up somewhere." Sharkey knew that the most likely reason for both engines stopping as well as at least one of the diesel generators would be fuel starvation. He elbowed his way past Melak and lifted the flap covering the fuel system layout and the problem became immediately apparent. Most of the tank connecting valves were shut off and the final engine supply tanks had in each case run dry.

Sharkey turned several of the switches controlling the tank valves and watched as the system indicated fuel flowing into the final engine supply tanks. Not quite knowing why, he connected enough tanks to carry the ship forward for a few days but not the remainder of the tanks. Sharkey went quickly through the start drill for each engine and stood back triumphantly as they grumbled into life. He didn't bother with the failed diesel generator.

Melak responded by throwing his arms around Sharkey and kissing him on the lips. Sharkey recoiled in shock and Khalid looked on, disgusted.

*

Before *Carlisle* appeared over the northern horizon, tactical communications were re-established between the two warships. *Carlisle* called first on the secure UHF net.

"Yankee Four Lima Mike, this is Golf Bravo Zulu Nine."

"Zulu Nine, this is Lima Mike. Welcome back. Standby sitrep, over."

"Zulu Nine standing by."

"Zulu Nine this is Lima Mike. I have you twenty-four miles north. Subject has stopped both engines approximately one hour ago. Some activity noted in Bridge and on upper deck but no gunfire or other violence. Subject now underway again but speed reduced to eight knots, heading two nine zero. I have no authorisation to interdict but am instructed to stand by. Over."

"Lima Mike, roger that. Zulu Nine is also instructed to watch and wait. Out."

What the *Andrew James* had not passed to *Carlisle* was that the highly sophisticated electronic interception equipment, which was part of the Aegis electronic detection and missile control system, had picked up several very brief attempts to contact various stations on a satellite phone. The signal had been weak but readable. None of the attempted contacts had been raised but that was probably because they were on the other side of the globe rather than inside a powerful warship half a mile away. The numbers called were being analysed but most important, the number of the calling phone together with its make, serial number, month and year of manufacture and the retailer who had sold it had all been identified. The purchaser, and registered owner had not yet been established but this was already being worked upon by the National Communication Analysis Team, a section of the CIA in Fort Langley, just outside Washington. The numbers called were interesting and instructive. These included the British Coastguard centre at Falmouth in Cornwall, an address in Spain, another in Ireland and two other cell phones, both with unregistered owners.

As both warships slotted into position on either beam of *Sea Shadow*, plans were developing in Wiltshire and Oxfordshire.

TWELVE

It was late evening before Jack was driven back to the Special Operations Group at Buckland House. The journey through light traffic took just under two hours and Jack spent most of that time on one or other of the two secure cell phones fitted into the back of the limousine. By the time the big car crunched along the last of the gravel drive leading up to the house, the outline of a plan was in place and the long table in Jack's office was laden with cardboard files of varying colour and thickness, set out in three groups identified by small 'tent card signs' – 'People' 'Ships' 'Equipment'.

A whisky tumbler half full of Loch Fyne blended Scotch and a small jug of chilled water completed the assemblage. Annette was still present despite the late hour and she followed Jack into the office, reading messages from a shorthand notebook as she walked behind her boss into the big office.

Jack began to wade through the files, starting with the pile labelled 'Ships'. The information here was fairly straightforward and described the frigate moored and forgotten in the upper reaches of Loch Eriboll as well as one alternative, an even older and smaller 'patrol vessel' privately built on speculation for a moderately despotic African government which had long ceased to exist and therefore had no further use for the ship. The small vessel had been sold on through several private companies and was now thought to be somewhere on the East African coast, awaiting further sale. An array of seven small tankers was presented, with a summary of the condition, location, state of preservation, service speed and range, and the likely availability of each.

The 'People' files contained information, much of which would surprise the subjects, on about a hundred men and women. Brief synopses of CVs were given for each with relevant qualifications (or those considered by Annette to be relevant) highlighted in each case. Current locations, availability, marital status and in some cases criminal records were also added.

Jack spent a long time with the 'Equipment' files. The first file, with no indication of where the information came from, gave a fairly comprehensive picture of the recent history and the materiel state of the frigate.

The old Leander had been built as a 'wide beam' batch three ship, slightly modified to meet the requirements of the Indian Navy and two other potential owners, both of whom had pulled out of the deal when they discovered that the British Government had actually expected to be paid for parting with the ship – albeit with a very modest sum.

The ship had never been operational and had been fitted with mountings for a variety of weaponry but not the actual weapons. Her boilers had been decommissioned and her big steam turbines had been ripped out, being replaced with four modified ex-minesweeper diesel engines and revised gearing arrangements capable of accepting large marinised gas turbines in the drive train to replace or complement the diesels. Most of the control mechanisms for this machinery had been located in a small Machinery Control Room not unlike those in most modern warships. The all important state of the hull, from the meagre information available, seemed reasonable although professional inspection was strongly recommended. The ship had spent very little time at sea and had been moored in predominantly benign fresh water, both of which Jack noted as being particularly helpful.

Another file listed a bizarre array of weaponry from rocket propelled grenades to army field guns which the author thought could be easily fitted to the frigate. Other files contained information on fuel, range, possible refuelling locations, communications kit and examples of how the appearance and the electronic signature of the vessel might be disguised. The most important file in this pile was a thin docket listing options for crewing the frigate, the patrol vessel and some of the tankers. It was estimated that a minimum of about twenty-five people could run the frigate but weapon operators and boarding parties could easily bring this number up to sixty. The patrol vessel needed a minimum crew of only eight and the small tankers could operate with between fifteen and twenty men.

By the time he had skimmed the personnel files and read the others in more detail it was well past midnight and when Jack finally left the room he took a selection of the personnel files with him to his bedroom. Annette had long since disappeared to some other part of the house but a list of immediate actions for the next morning was left waiting for her on the big polished mahogany table.

*

The unmarked turbo prop Jetstream, once the property of the Royal Navy Communications Squadron, bounced in light turbulence as it flew at ten thousand feet above the Cairngorm Mountains, heading for the airfield at RAF

Dounreay next to the huge nuclear power station complex. At Dounreay an RAF Puma helicopter was already waiting, rotors turning, to fly the party the thirty-nine miles along the northern coast of the British Isles, heading for the tiny settlement of Eriboll perched high above the loch and several miles inland from the sea. As the aircraft began the descent towards Dounreay they dropped below the ragged cloud base and the lonely mountains of the remote north of Scotland began to take shape below them.

Jack Lang folded the map he had been studying, unclipped his seatbelt and strode forward towards the cockpit. The noise inside the aircraft was not great and he was easily able to explain to the pilot that he wanted to divert slightly to the east to take a look at the loch. The small airliner banked to the left and continued the descent towards a glint of water that could already be seen emerging between two impressive looking Munros. The turbulence increased as they dropped still lower towards the mountain tops.

As the aircraft eased down in a wide descending turn to the right, the pilot could see clearly the long stretch of dark water, stretching away to the north which marked one of Scotland's most remote and isolated deep water lochs. Jack moved forward to peer over the pilot's shoulder while Maggie pressed her face to the window beside her seat and tried with limited success to peer forward and down. The other six passengers stayed put in their seats. Nobody saw anything except the grey ribbon of white flecked water dominated by heather clad mountains on either side, dotted with occasional stands of trees all leaning to the east, and a thin stretch of greener land connecting the base of the mountains with the loch side. As the coast came into view Jack returned to his seat and the aircraft banked steeply to starboard to begin the descent into Dounreay.

Less than fifteen minutes later the unmarked Jetstream was completing its landing run, turning off the upwind end of the main runway to come to a standstill on the perimeter track. As it did so, the Puma helicopter arrived alongside, touching down on the grass twenty yards from the aircraft. Within another three minutes, six of the eight passengers had crossed to the helicopter and strapped in. Annette and another man, the communications expert, were scooped up by an RAF Land Rover as the helicopter took off.

Both Jack and Maggie were handed headsets by the loadmaster, enabling them to talk easily to the two pilots over the roar and clatter of the helicopter. The Puma lifted off into a low hover and then, with a sharp nose down attitude, accelerated away towards Loch Eriboll.

The helicopter was swift and manoeuvrable. Following the contours of the valleys dividing the mountains it remained low and fast until, twenty minutes later it began to slow down and descend towards the surface of the water. In the deep gloaming under a lead grey sky, the loch and its immediate surroundings looked wild, forlorn and, at the same time, forbidding. The team inside remained silent as the aircraft slowed further to not much more than a walking pace, at about fifty feet above the surface of the loch. Sudden squalls of wind accompanied by flurries of short white crested waves rocked the helicopter as the loadmaster slid open the cabin door. The aircraft captain came on the intercom, “This is what you are looking for.”

The ship was moored fore and aft close in near the eastern bank. It was liberally covered with leaves, branches, guano and other detritus which had lodged on board over the years. The helicopter moved slowly down the side of the ship, around the stern and up the other side. Jack moved back from the door as his two photographers unstrapped and settled near the cabin doorway taking constant video and hundreds of still photographs. The helicopter circled the sad looking frigate twice before Jack said, "OK take us inshore and see if you can find a reasonably close landing place."

"Roger that," answered the disembodied voice in his ear as the Puma crabbed lazily across towards the shore line where a narrow road led to a small settlement without, so far, any sign of life or activity.

They landed with one wheel resting on a sloping grass patch and tumbled out one after the other while the pilot kept the other main wheel hanging in the air in order to keep the helicopter level. The loadmaster followed them out, still connected to the intercom and radio system by a long plastic covered lead, and in a hurried shouted, conversation it was agreed that the helicopter would return for them in exactly three hours.

As the helicopter climbed away the group started to follow the narrow road uphill to the tiny cluster of buildings. It started to rain with a fine penetrating drizzle. The first building was a single storey double fronted cottage with a straggly thatched roof. Notices in one of the windows suggested that the cottage did multiple duty as guest house, post office, village store and parish council office. The plan was that the team should be met by the local policeman, of whom there was no sign. The drizzle turned to raindrops as the small group squeezed into the even smaller space between the door and a wooden counter. A short, untidy woman appeared from behind an inner door and smiled enquiringly.

"Good morning," said Jack. "We have come from Dounreay and the local policeman was supposed to meet us here."

"Oh, that would be Constable MacGregor. But he has to come over the hills from Thurso. It can take a wee while." All this flowed mellifluously and steadily in a rich Highland accent.

"Oh," said Jack, looking at his watch.

"Can I help you at all?" said the small woman.

Maggie intervened. "We've come to look at the ship," she said as she began to drag a mobile phone from a pocket on the side of her workmanlike handbag.

"That gadget will do you no good here. We dinna have a signal." 'Gadget' was pronounced 'gajeet' and it took Maggie a few moments to take in the import of this news.

"Angus MacGregor is the Ship Keeper," continued the small woman.

Jack wondered if everyone was called MacGregor. "Where can we find him?" he asked.

"Why, he is in the parlour now, for I am Mrs MacGregor, and he is ma man." As if on cue the inner door eased open again and the frame was filled with the outline of a huge man wreathed in smoke and apparently clad entirely in coarse tartan, but not including a kilt.

"Am I wanted, mother?" He waited expectantly in the doorway puffing clouds of smoke from a curious pipe with an oversize bowl.

"This lady and her friends would like your help, Angus dear, I'm thinking."

Jack decided a direct approach was best. "We're from the Ministry of Defence," he said. "We need to get out to the ship and inspect it." He added emphasis by flourishing one of his several identity cards. This one labelled him as an official from Defence Sales.

Angus looked uncertain. "Will you be takin' the ship away?" he asked.

"Well, not today," replied Jack.

"I will get my boat," said Angus without further preamble. He turned and disappeared back into the inner room. The group glanced from one to the other.

At this point a crunch of tyres on gravel and a slight squeak of brakes announced the arrival of the constable.

Constable MacGregor stumped into the room with a dour scowl, matching the one which had just disappeared on the face of his namesake. "Ye need to visit the ship, I see," he said. "Angus will take you but I must go too." Jack decided not to argue.

The boat was a heavy sturdy open workboat about forty feet in length with a small cabin-cum-shelter in front of the steering position. A square galvanised steel tank was placed in the middle of the forward section. It smelt of fish and had two or three inches of dirty water slopping about in the bottom. Further aft the boat was fitted on both sides with small winches and most of the deck space was occupied by fishing nets, ropes and fenders. The inspection was to be carried out by a team of three – an engineer, a shipwright and one of the photographers. Jack was along to snoop about and gain a general impression but also to satisfy his curiosity.

As they approached the ship the reason for Angus's reserve became quickly apparent. The ship was festooned with nets, ropes and wires. Enclosures forming fish traps and small fish farms dangled just below the surface near the forecastle. Jack realised he had disturbed Angus's private fish, lobster and sea food farm. No doubt the whole loch was teeming with fish but the ad hoc arrangements dangling around the ship would ensure a continuing harvest from the sea without any of the usual risk, discomfort and hard work associated with fishing for a living. A sturdy rope ladder with wide wooden treads dangled from what had once been the flight deck and after a couple of circuits of the vessel Angus brought the boat expertly alongside the ladder. One by one they clambered aboard.

They moved around the main deck and then up over the superstructure and into the enclosed Bridge. The team had come well equipped with tools and powerful flashlights and these were soon in use as the heavy chromed steel retaining clips holding the upper deck screen doors closed against the elements were hammered back to allow the doors to be opened.

Inside, the ship was in remarkably good condition, having remained dry and largely undamaged except beneath the point where the main 4.5" gun turret had been removed. This section was a mixture of guano and bird nests but the mess looked superficial and would probably respond to a determined cleaning.

Jack confined himself to wandering through the accommodation areas, the galleys, the Operations Room and the Communications Office. The rest of his team donned head mounted flashlights and descended into the machinery and store spaces.

Two hours after arrival alongside, the group assembled on the flight deck and waved to the two MacGregors in the boat, which was drifting a hundred yards distant with three or four lines trailing over the stern. A puff of blue smoke signalled the opening of the throttle as the boat turned slowly towards the frigate’s quarterdeck while one of the occupants hauled in their fishing lines.

The overcast sky was darker and the rain heavier as the four explorers climbed gingerly down the swaying ladder into the boat which cast off and turned for shore as soon as the last man was aboard. No one spoke during the return journey.

As they alighted at the rough wooden jetty they could already hear the distant buzz of the approaching helicopter, just audible above the wind and rain. Jack thanked Mr and Mrs MacGregor for their help and set off towards the grass landing spot strolling jauntily along, swinging a walking stick, newly acquired from the MacGregors' little shop. The rest of the group trailed along behind with one man hanging back to place a couple of twenty pound notes into Angus's outstretched hand 'to pay for your time and fuel'.

THIRTEEN

The conference room built onto the back of Buckland House was crowded. Jack and Maggie sat in the middle of a long table opposite a projection screen hanging from a slot in the ceiling and currently displaying an enlarged photograph of the old Leander Class frigate. Another fifteen men and women were spread around the table so they all had a view of the screen. Perhaps twenty others were standing or seated around the edge of the room. The air smelled of fresh coffee and there was a low buzz of conversation.

Twenty-four hours had passed since the uneventful flight back from Scotland, and during this time every piece of information, photograph and impression had been analysed in as much detail as the time permitted. Several reports had been generated and these were about to be presented, discussed and either approved or torn to pieces.

Jack cleared his throat and, addressing the room, began. "We're here for what will now be known as Project Drake. I should like to remind all of you that this name is secret, as is the very existence of the project." No one spoke but heads nodded here and there. "In outline, we are going to try to take an old ship from here to the Indian Ocean, rescue some hostages and teach a group of pirates a lesson they won't forget." Jack paused to allow what he had just said to sink in. Several expressive profanities were uttered but most of the room stayed silent and waited. "First we will look at the means of transport available to us, then we will consider how they may be utilised," Jack continued. "Next we look at what we are going to do and what we will need in order to complete the task before finally, 'N' Section will take us through the timescale. Questions at the end of this meeting then decision before we leave this room on whether the scheme is a 'Go'. If it is I'll be briefing the Foreign Secretary tomorrow afternoon."

As Jack stopped speaking the tall engineer, now in the working uniform of a Royal Navy Lieutenant Commander, stepped towards the screen. With a billiard cue doubling as a pointer he began to point out the features of the warship. Half an hour later the picture changed to show a smaller, smarter and obviously younger ship with the typical streamlined shape of a Vosper construction. After this another man in civilian clothes stepped forward and took the assembly through a similar assessment of three small oil tankers.

They broke for afternoon tea, when the doors were thrown open to allow a cool breeze to run through the room, clearing the atmosphere and arousing tired brains. Several men and women drifted out into the garden and lit cigarettes. The various experts formed into their own tribal groups to comment and probe what they had heard so far. One or two, who had yet to speak, scribbled amendments on the notes they had prepared. After fifteen minutes they all trooped back into the conference room and the doors were closed once again.

As predicted by Jack's introduction, the briefing phase of the conference continued uninterrupted for another five hours. Just before 9 p.m. Jack called another pause while several trays of sandwiches, cheese and fruit were brought in. Once the doors had closed again behind the stewards, the conference continued with a series of presentations outlining several possible alternative plans, and ranging through lists of available and suitable weapons and equipment that might be needed.

Next, the leader of 'N' section, a short elderly bespectacled man who had once been the Royal Navy's star navigating officer laid out what he believed to be an achievable timescale for the operation from the moment of sailing from Britain to completion and withdrawal.

"I was told to do the approach within thirty days so I have suggested an overall passage speed of eighteen knots. We might get some help from the south going Canaries Current and the Equatorial Counter Current but we will have the Benguela against us and after rounding the Cape, both Aquinhas and the Mozambique against us to the East of Africa. There is therefore nothing to be gained except stealth by going around Mozambique." He had lost some of his audience but they took more notice as he continued, "Depending on the precise track followed, the total distance involved will be about ten thousand four hundred miles. It could be a little less but it would be reasonable to allow twenty-five days, plus another day to encompass up to four fuelling stops and we could be on station in twenty-six days."

Jack looked unhappy. "Can we not do it any quicker? The frigate is supposed to be able to maintain twenty-seven knots."

"No," said the navigation specialist, "the faster you go the more fuel you consume so you have to stop more frequently and you're back to square one. Plus, there would then be no allowance for bad weather and you will certainly get some." Jack wondered why 'we' had become 'you' then he sat in silence while the others waited.

The silence lasted for several minutes, disturbed only by the discreet click of knitting needles from the far end of the table to which Maggie had moved, apparently taking little interest in the continuing briefing, and now seemingly engrossed in her shapeless knitting. Eventually she stopped, peered pointedly towards the head of 'N' section and asked quietly, "Have you forgotten the patrol boat? I believe it is presently a lot closer to the scene of operations." Heads turned in her direction.

"It has been sold to Tanzania and is presently waiting, fuelled and stored, but without crew, unless you count a ship-keeper, at Dar es Salaam." She returned determinedly to her knitting.

FOURTEEN

In the Indian Ocean the overall situation hadn't changed very much, but there had been two significant developments. *Sea Shadow* was once again stationary, wallowing uncomfortably across a long swell and neither the pirates nor the accompanying warship crews knew why. One man did know. After the last fuel starved engine failure Sharkey Fisher had connected two further midship tanks but had left the fuel management valves shut for the remainder of the tanks. He had once again been hauled down to the Machinery Control Room but despite being punched and kicked he had maintained an effective charade, convincing his captors that his efforts had been properly applied but to no avail.

The other thing that had happened to cause some disturbance was that Louis's phone had rung. Louis had been sitting dozing in his comfortable chair when the phone, in which he had installed a ring tone consisting of a series of six depressed bleeps so it wouldn't disturb his customers, suddenly rang. In the stillness of his hideaway it sounded to Louis like Big Ben on amplifier. He prised himself out of his chair to reach for the phone when it stopped. Louis froze halfway between sitting and standing. His hands were shaking and lines of sweat were running down either side of his face. Slowly he exhaled, trying to ease the tension out of his body as he started to sit down once again. As he manoeuvred himself back into the chair his phone sounded again. Panic seized him once more as he lunged for the instrument. This time his hand had actually clutched the phone when it stopped. He put the dead instrument to his ear and said furtively, "Hello, who's there?" There was no voice or any noise even to indicate that the phone was live. Louis sat holding the phone and tried to think his way through the situation. He could not understand why and how his telephone had apparently managed to receive an incoming call. He sat and worried for several minutes turning again and again to the fact that the microwave signals could not penetrate the steel structure of the ship. Therefore, he considered, the attempts to contact him must have been made from within the ship's structure – which would mean that someone knew of his presence. In all likelihood, he deduced, that must mean the invading pirates were searching for him. In fact the ship was constructed of aluminium which did not have the same blocking effect. The other thing that he could not know was that the Aegis cruiser sailing only a few hundred yards away was able to channel a cell phone signal into an intense beam rather like a laser and increase its power so that it was in effect able to punch its way through almost any intervening structure without giving away its existence to any nearby monitoring equipment.

*

"Shall I try it again, sir?" said the Electronic Warfare Operator First Class.

"Give it two more minutes so he is holding the phone but has stopped panicking," replied the young 'Special Signals' Lieutenant who stood, peering over the operator's shoulder at the green screen in front of them.

"OK, call again. Stop immediately then call and respond when he answers."

"Aye sir." The EWO (1) started tapping buttons on the computer keyboard set into his desk. The calling signal sounded from a loudspeaker. He hit a button and it stopped. Counting silently but with moving lips to ten, he hit the button once more and waited. Nothing happened.

The Special Signals Lieutenant waited while the trilling tone continued from the speaker. Eventually, he made a chopping movement with his hand and the operator cancelled the call.

"We've spooked him," he said. "Wait an hour then we'll try again."

*

Hiding in his store, Louis was trembling and sweating. When the phone had rung once again he had recoiled from it crashing into a rack of bottles noisily in the process. Now he had convinced himself that discovery was imminent, to be swiftly followed by violent retribution. An hour passed, by which time he had just about reached the conclusion that to give himself up would be a better choice than waiting until he was dragged from his hideout.

The telephone trilled again. Louis reached slowly towards it. His hand hovered over it, hesitating.

*

"Time to give it another go, Sparks," announced the Special Signals officer as he pushed open the door of the Radio Room.

“Aye sir.” The Electronic Warfare Operator had not moved from his chair. He leaned forward and pressed an icon on the plasma screen in front of him. A light blinked on the desk mounted telephone handset and the shrill ringing tone emerged from the speakers. Abruptly, the ringing stopped. The phone had been answered in the captured ship.

“E-eh-’ello,” a quavery voice from the speaker flooded the small ‘Comms’ office, silencing the four occupants.

“Sir, this is the United States Ship *Andrew James* please give me your name and location.”

“Eh, Looeese.”

“Please repeat that sir. Also, what is your status and location?” The ECO pressed another icon on his screen, switching on a recorder.

“Eh, I am Loo-eese. I am Barman in *Sea Shadow*.” Louis’s clear grasp of English seemed to have deserted him as he struggled to make himself understood and to understand what was happening.

“What is your status, sir?”

“I no unnerstan’.”

The lieutenant stepped forward and plugged his boom microphone into an empty jack adjacent to the one being used by his operator.

In soothing tones he began, “Mr Louis, this is a United States Warship and we want to try to get you out of there but we need to know where you are, whether there are any armed men near you and some other things.”

“I gotta go, they weel ’ear me.” The signal went dead and an amber message flashed on the screen in front of the operator. ‘Signal terminated external’, it read.

“Give him a few minutes to cool down. He must be holed up somewhere where they can’t find him,” said the Lieutenant.

"How do we know he ain't been captured, sir?" asked the operator.

"If he had he wouldn't have the phone."

The Captain who had remained silent on the other side of the small metal walled room until now, looked worried. "Can we be absolutely sure we're talking to the right guy in the right ship and not some bum puttin' us on?"

"Sure as apple pie is American, sir."

"Tell me the story again," said the Captain.

"Sir, we were doing a standard electronic scan of the Subject Ship to see if we could detect any attempt by the hijackers to communicate with anyone outside the ship when we picked up a signal. Two, in fact. It happened twice. It takes the crypto panel here less than a second to analyse even complex signal detections; this one was a cert."

"How so?" interrupted the Captain.

"I think it was the closeness giving a strong signal strength sir. Also the structure in the topsides of that boat is light aluminium. What gave the man away was that his calls were to the British Coastguard Centre at Falmouth, England." They didn't answer because his signal strength was reduced by being in that tin can but we sure as hell could pick it up and read it clear as the Washington Post. There is one other thing, sir. To within a few feet we can tell where that guy is located in the ship."

"I see." The Captain stroked the stubble on his chin and looked thoughtful. "OK, wait for ten minutes then try again, but this time let me talk to him."

FIFTEEN

Silence dominated the room for three or four minutes, then, after Jack pushed back his chair, for another five minutes. All this time Jack sat motionless, staring at the far wall, his posture belying the racing turmoil of his thoughts.

Maggie laid down her never-to-be-finished knitting and leaned forward, waiting for Jack to respond.

At last he pushed himself to his feet, stood for a moment looking at the screen and said, almost absently, "OK we'll look at that in more detail later but now let's get on with the brief. Personnel next, I think."

A slim young woman stood up at the far end of the table and walked briskly towards the screen, stiletto heels clicking loudly in the otherwise silent room. The picture on the screen changed to show a list of roles needed within the ships and for the shore support.

"No problem here, sir," she began. Jack sat down again and Maggie remained leaning forward in her chair, elbows on the table, hands cupping her chin, knitting temporarily forgotten.

The girl picked up a pointer and turned towards the screen. "We believe we can run the frigate with a minimum deck and watch-keeping crew of four officers and about twelve crewmen."

"Ratings," murmured Jack. "They're called ratings, Alice."

"Yes sir," continued Alice, ignoring the interruption. "The engineering crew is a bit more difficult. If the ship is still steam powered we will need a lot of people, if not we can probably get away with six or eight and still have some hope of dealing with underway defects."

"Right, stop there," interrupted Jack again. Turning towards the tall naval engineer who had described the ships, he said, "OK. Engines, tell us the worst. What is her materiel and machinery state? The frigate, that is."

"I can tell you about both at the same time sir," responded the engineer as he stood, grasping his converted billiard cue pointer.

"Taking the frigate first," he began, "the news is generally good. Most of the muck and rubbish covering the vessel appears to be superficial and I think we could shift it in a day or so with not much more than a domestic pressure washer." He looked across at his boss and swiftly moved on as he sensed Jack's impatience.

"As far as the engine and power arrangements go, it could be our lucky day. The boiler room still houses two conventional steam boilers – both isolated – but the steam turbines in the engine room have been ripped out and replaced with what looks like a standard CODOG arrangement." Forestalling Jack's question, he continued quickly. "That's Combined Diesel and Gas. She has two big Deltic diesel engines for long endurance and slower running, supported by four Olympus Gas Turbines for rapid start and bursts of high speed. Of course until we get the ship out of the loch we won't know if any of this works but since she was an under-used trials ship I am hopeful that most of it will work with a little persuasion. Of course we don't know what the state of her underwater equipment is, propellers, rudders and so forth but again it won't take long to find out."

"Good," said Jack. He looked relieved.

The engineer ploughed straight on, clicking his remote control to flick the screen back to the picture of the smart patrol vessel. "This one is the prize, sir," he continued. As far as I can tell from the information we have been able to get, her owners are anxious to sell her and she is ready to go, fuelled and stored, now."

"Thanks." He gestured with his hand. "Alice, please continue."

Alice said, "In that case I suggest a maximum of eight officers and ratings in the engine department, so say twenty all together, to run the ship that is. If we need a boarding crew..."

"We will," interrupted Maggie from the far end of the table.

"…then that could increase the complement by another dozen, with perhaps another six or eight bodies if the weapon system you fit needs additional people. Say an absolute maximum of forty, including a couple of cooks."

"Right. What about the patrol boat?" said Jack. "Complement first, then engineering."

"That's pretty easy, sir," said Alice quickly. "The present owners are trying to sell the boat and they've put full details on the internet. Her normal operational complement is apparently four officers and twenty men. We could probably reduce that to fifteen ratings but the officer complement would have to stay the same. Again, if you carry special weapons you may have to carry additional personnel to man them." She turned to one side to make way for the engineer.

"This is a very easy one, boss," said the engineer. "The ship is fairly new and, according to the sales blurb, ready to go in all respects. Just add money."

"Tell us what we would get for our money, please," Maggie called down the table. "And how much money would that be?"

"She's a modified 'Brave' class fast patrol boat built twenty years ago by Vosper Thorneycroft," continued the engineer. "She's powered by three Bristol Proteus Gas Turbines with two small Rover Gas Turbines for domestic power. Not as fast as the original 'Brave' class but she can maintain forty-five knots in sea states up to force seven. After that she would have to back off a bit but could still keep up on the plane, judging the speed for the distance between waves."

"Get onto the key details, please," interrupted Jack.

"Right. Displacement one hundred tonnes, length a hundred and ten feet, beam twenty-one feet. Crew twenty-four. Can carry a mixed and interchangeable weapon load of guns and torpedoes." The engineer stood back, his pointer now held like a hiking staff, with the end resting on the carpeted floor.

"Range?" demanded Jack.

"Depends on the speed but cruising on the plane at thirty-five to forty knots she can achieve about eight hundred miles."

Jack looked disappointed and the engineer continued quickly, "However, she can also carry drop tanks, or ferry tanks, you might call them, which can give her up to another eight hundred miles, depending a bit on the sea state."

Both Jack and Maggie looked happier. "That's better," said Jack.

Maggie stood up. "Shall I summarise?" she asked, allowing her gaze to wander round the seated assembly before finishing on Jack.

Jack nodded.

"We have two ex-warships and we will probably need them both." Maggie spoke slowly and carefully, pausing to allow everyone to consider what she was saying and to interrupt if necessary. There were no interruptions.

"We need sixty sailors with various skills and we need an as yet undisclosed package of weapons, both for the ships and as small arms. It looks as though we have funding for the operation but how are we going to purchase the patrol vessel? That could be expensive."

"Not a problem," said Jack. "We sold it to the present owners in the first place. We trained the crew, and even gave them uniforms, I think. We should be able to sort something out through the Foreign Aid Budget, where no money actually changes hands."

Maggie smiled, said nothing more and returned to her seat.

"Thank you," said Jack. "We still need to know the materiel state of the frigate. How soon can we get her into a discreet dry dock?"

The question was addressed to no-one in particular but the engineer looked up and said, "She's on her way to Faslane now. That place is as tight as a drum. A rat couldn't get in and a whisper can't get out. There is a big floating dock used for the submarines and with luck she should be there waiting for it to complete flooding down by 0830 tomorrow. I've already had divers looking under her skirts but I should have a detailed report by early afternoon. Internally, as far as we can see, nothing essential is broken or missing but I will know more when we get her flashed up."

“OK,” said Jack. “Alice, start finding me the crews now. I want officer candidates summary on my desk by noon and…” he turned towards the engineer, “…I want to know for certain whether we can get the patrol boat and whether the frigate is fit to go to sea, by 1600 tomorrow. I will speak to the Foreign Secretary at five. That’s it for now. Wrap it up. Do your preps and assume that we will get the ‘go’ until I tell you otherwise. Thank you everybody.”

The big double doors were opened by two security guards and everyone began gathering papers and walking, some deep in conversation, to the door.

SIXTEEN

Remarkably, Louis had actually fallen into a doze by the time his telephone rang again. He awoke with a start, staring at the offending instrument. Then he grabbed it, intending to silence it but the phone was selected to 'any key' and so his touch on the keypad accepted the call.

"Good day sir, we mean you no harm," said Commander Reagan as quickly as he could, hoping to prevent Louis from cutting the connection. The line remained open.

Reagan continued, seeking to calm the man on the other end of the line by keeping him talking. "I am the Commanding Officer of an American warship which is stationed close by the ship you are located in." He paused for a moment then continued tentatively. "Can you hear me sir?"

"Yes." The voice sounded faint but no longer had the ring of panic.

"Is there anyone there with you? Are you alone?"

"Yes."

"Just to confirm that, you are alone, is that right?"

"Yes, I am alone."

"Can anyone hear you?"

There was another pause. "I don' know. I thing' no. Maybe."

"OK," continued the Captain. "We will both talk quietly. I want to help you but first I need to ask you some questions. You OK with that?"

"Yes." The voice was hesitant and barely perceptible.

Commander Reagan glanced down at a scrap of paper that the Lieutenant had placed on the desk in front of him. "Thank you, Louis. First, can you tell me where you are in the ship?"

"I yam inna my store. From the Grand Saloon. Behinda the bar."

"Do you know the location of the rest of your crew?"

"No."

"Have you seen any of the men who have boarded your ship?"

"No, not now, but before. Yes, then I seen them, but not all."

"Do you know how many of them there are?"

"No. Maybe, maybe ten, maybe twelve."

"Is your phone charged? Are you able to recharge it if it runs down?"

"Yes, I can do that."

The questions continued for another ten minutes. The Lieutenant made notes of the answers alongside a list of the questions printed on a sheet of paper. A small symbol on the screen in front of the operator indicated that a recorder was still running. Commander Reagan took the paper and left the Radio Room, heading for his cabin.

Thirty minutes later Reagan was talking to the Captain of *Carlisle* over the scrambled secure UHF radio frequency. He relayed the conversation with Louis, answering interrupting questions from Craig Wilson as he went along. The two captains agreed that they had little option other than to watch and await an opportunity to act. They each remained constrained by their respective governments to take no aggressive action but to maintain the status quo.

Electronic Warfare Specialist Petty Officer Kowalski, who had set up and was monitoring the secure communications channel summed up the situation rather well.

"What the fuck do they mean, maintain the status fucking quo," he muttered, addressing the steel wall in front of his desk as he clutched the single earphone to his left ear and glared at the dials on the electronic modules bolted to the steel topped table. "Same old routine, I s'pose," he continued. "Do fuck all and wait."

Within fifteen minutes of the end of the of the secure conference a messenger was offering each captain a small buff envelope with 'Top Secret Code Barnyard' stamped in red on the front and back. Each captain took the envelope, in *Carlisle*, to a discreet corner of the Operations Room and in the *Andrew James* to the imposing light oak desk in the Captain's Day Cabin.

The import of each signal was identical although the wording differed substantially. The flimsy signal sheet held by Craig Wilson in *Carlisle's* spacious Operations Room began with the eye catching line:

TOP SECRET CODE BARNYARD PERSONAL FROM CINCFLT PERSONAL FOR COMMAND.'

It continued: 'OPERATION DRAKE. OPDRAKE ONE. TASK GROUP 420.1 ESTABLISHED IMMEDIATE. USS ANDREW JAMES NOMINATED COMMANDER TASK ELEMENT 420.1.1. COMMAND OF TASK GROUP 420.1 WILL REMAIN CINCFLT. ADDITIONAL TASK ELEMENTS 420.1.2 AND 420.1.3 WILL BE ACTIVATED WITHIN 48

HOURS. OPCON OF BOTH T.E. 420.1.2 AND T.E. 420.1.3 WILL REMAIN WITH CINCFLT UNTIL FURTHER NOTICE.

It was followed on the same sheet of paper by

OPDRAKE TWO' the text of which read: 'OPDRAKE TWO. IT IS IMPERATIVE THAT SAUDI REGISTERED VESSEL SEA SHADOW IS NOT ALLOWED TO MOVE FROM PRESENT POSITION. PRINCIPAL RULES OF ENGAGEMENT REMAIN UNCHANGED. ARMED AGGRESSION IS NOT YET AUTHORISED AND LOSS OF LIFE MUST BE AVOIDED. REPORT PRESENT SITUATION (SITREP ONE) USING GRADE SEVEN REPEAT SEVEN ENCRYPTION. PRIORITY FOR ALL OPDRAKE SIGNAL TRAFFIC TO BE IMMEDIATE. BREAK BREAK. END.

Wilson sat and thought for four or five minutes. He reached a decision and pressed the intercom button on his desk. "Officer of the Watch," he said, "my compliments to the First Lieutenant and the Ops Officer and ask them both to come to my cabin please."

"Aye aye sir." The reply came instantly from the Bridge.

In less than two minutes there was a light tap on the door frame of the Captain's Cabin, the curtain was pushed aside and the First Lieutenant stuck his head into the space.

"Come in Number One," said Wilson. "Grab a chair. I've asked Ops to join us. There have been developments." The leading Steward peered expectantly from his pantry doorway.

"Pot of strong coffee for three please, Carter – and then pop off and get your own supper. We will need to be a bit discreet in here."

"Very good sir," responded the Leading Steward carefully, still behaving more as butler than Captain's Steward.

They waited while the coffee was brewed and by the time it was delivered to the small but sturdy circular coffee table, a relic that had sailed with Craig Wilson's father, the Operations Officer had joined them.

They remained seated around the cabin in somewhat stultified silence while the Leading Steward closed his pantry door and disappeared through the outer door in the direction of the Ship's Company Dining Hall. The First Lieutenant went to the door and checked that it was firmly shut. When he returned to his seat the Captain handed him the signal 'flimsy' without speaking. George Lee read the signal twice, looked up enquiringly towards the Captain, who nodded. George passed the paper to the Operations Officer.

The silence was broken only by the clink of china as the Operations Officer read the signal. He read it slowly and carefully and then placed it on the table between the three officers. "What exactly does it mean, sir?" he said, looking up towards the Captain.

"Well, the first thing CINCFLEET wants is for us to tell him what is going on here and now. You will notice that we have been placed under the tactical command of the *Andrew James* so before sending anything I intend to have another chat with him. While I am doing that I would like you two to come up with a foolproof way of guaranteeing that *Sea Shadow* cannot move, without involving a direct attack, boarding or any other obviously warlike activity." Wilson leaned back in his chair, stared at the ceiling then back at his two senior officers. "Any questions?" he said. "Other than, that is, what the bloody hell is going on?"

An hour later, as a thin layer of alto-cumulus began to cover the rising moon, the third OPDRAKE signal was received. Half an hour after that, a black and unlit rigid inflatable boat left the disengaged side of *Carlisle* and headed in a wide circle away from the group of ships before angling back in to the side of the *Andrew James*, keeping the American frigate between the boat and *Sea Shadow*. The RIB contained four British sailors clad in black diving suits and Commander Craig Wilson Royal Navy.

SEVENTEEN

Hamid was angry. He was very angry. He should have been taking his new prize into port, yet here he was still wallowing about, unable to move, over five hundred miles from his destination. He paced back and forth across the Bridge, fingering his revolver as he walked. The other three Arabs still on the Bridge stayed silent and tried to keep out of his way.

For once Hamid was uncertain. He had secured a rich prize but without outside assistance he could not move it. He could try to call one of the mother ships on VHF radio but that would only tell the world of his situation and whichever one of his rivals picked up his call would come down to steal his hard won wealth, for they were all thieves, were they not?

He thought of killing one of the hostages but the hostages were likely to be worth more money than the ship and, anyway, he had been convinced that the shaking sweating engineer had told the truth that the ship was out of fuel, for he had genuinely been in fear of losing his life. He considered waiting for nightfall and stealing away in his own boat, but then, one or other of the warships would detect him, and likely kill him and his men. He had no concerns for the health or continuity of life of the men he had brought with him but they were highly honed and useful tools that he had trained to achieve the means to make him rich.

He was stuck.

But by one hour before midnight Hamid, ever resourceful, had come up with a plan. He would trade some of his hostages with the British or the Americans for sufficient fuel to get him into port.

At precisely midnight, Hamid keyed the transmit button of the Bridge VHF Radio. "British ship, American ship, this is the Liberated *Shadow of the Sea* calling you." He waited. There was no immediate reply.

The radio message was received loud and clear on the Bridges and in the Operations Rooms of both warships but following instructions, no reply was given. In each ship the Officer of the Watch called down to the Captain.

*

In London it was three hours earlier than in the Indian Ocean and the Foreign Secretary was enjoying the grandeur of the Painted Hall in the former Royal Naval College at Greenwich while being served an elaborate dessert course – the opulent culmination of a four course banquet. This evening he was host at the annual dinner given by the Foreign and Commonwealth Office for all the ambassadors and high commissioners who were plenipotentiary to the Court of St James's. The chirruping chatter from the diminutive wife of the United States Ambassador who was seated on his right hand was flowing uninterrupted over his head as he contemplated the speech he was about to give.

The Foreign Secretary was still successfully locking out the buzz of conversation now surrounding him when he became aware of an urgent whisper into his left ear.

"Minister, there has been a development," hissed the young diplomatic aide. "They are seeking to make contact."

The Foreign Secretary did not need to ask who 'they' were. He had been lobbied brazenly and repeatedly on behalf of Prince Khalid and his unfortunate son, Prince Feisal, currently being held against his will by persons unknown.

Turning to his left he muttered out of the side of his mouth, as quietly as he could, "Do nothing and wait ten minutes. I'll come out then." The aide disappeared silently.

The stout red-jacketed toastmaster stepped forward and boomed, "Pray silence for the Right Honourable George Gray, Her Majesty's Secretary of State for Foreign Affairs."

The great man stepped back as a tinkle of almost applause started then stopped. The Foreign Secretary placed his cue cards discreetly on the gleaming white linen and stood up, noting with surprise that some magic had caused a small microphone and stand to appear on the table in front of him.

Twenty minutes later, the somewhat predictable speech having given way to a train of decanters containing port, Madeira, brandy and water which were following each other around each of the long tables filling the hall, the Foreign Secretary was sitting in the plain room adjacent to the hall that had been made available as an operations centre. He was listening carefully as his Permanent Under Secretary, Sir Gerald Carter, outlined the recent developments in the Indian Ocean.

"So they want to do a deal?" said the Foreign Secretary.

"I think they are stuck and trying to find a way of wriggling out."

"Who is this mole that the Americans have identified?"

"We don't know, Foreign Secretary. We and the Americans are working on it."

"Could it be some sort of ploy? A trick?"

"Yes, there's every chance that it is but if it is, it still seems that it has been forced on the pirates because they can't move the ship they have captured. They can't expect help or reinforcements because they have got two big warships riding one on each side."

"Yes, I see," said the Foreign Secretary. "Have you spoken with the State Department?" He waved towards the other chair in the room.

Sir Gerald sank into the wooden chair opposite to the Foreign Secretary. "Yes," he said slowly. "We are generally d'accord, and we have some agreement on how to react."

The Foreign Secretary wondered for a moment, and not for the first time, why these 'mandarins' took so long to get to the point. "OK," he said. "Tell me what is proposed."

Sir Gerald took a deep breath and leaned forward. "We now have more time because the *Sea Shadow* cannot, at least for the moment, move. The pirates, we think, believe they have run out of fuel, but having checked the ship's recent history including bunkering, we believe that cannot be the case. So it must be some other form of mechanical failure – or the pirates are being conned in some way. We now know there is at least one crew member who has not been captured and although we do not know the situation or location of the remaining crew members it is likely that they are alive and probably unharmed and it is also the case that there are only a few places where they can be held. As to the Prince and at least one girlfriend…" He made the word 'girlfriend' sound distasteful and unsavoury. "…They are obviously the high value hostages and threats to the safety, particularly of the Prince, could have serious international implications. I stress," he said, heavily, "that just the threat not necessarily the action, could provoke serious problems. Prince Khalid, for reasons we still do not quite understand, is looking to us, the British, to get his son back for him and to ensure the young man and his, ahem, friends, stay in one piece."

The Foreign Secretary seized the opportunity as Sir Gerald paused to draw breath. He plunged in, "OK Gerald," he said, "My view is this. We need to play for time. We need to know – one..." he began to count on his fingers, "...how many hostages are there? Two. How many pirates are there? Three. Where are they – hostages and pirates within the ship? Four. What is wrong with the ship? And, five. What kind of deal are they looking for?"

"With respect, Minister," interjected Sir Gerald. "We also need to sanitise the area to make sure the pirates don't have any friends about who might enable them to sneak away, and we also need to find out a lot more about the barman we have contacted."

The Foreign Secretary stood up, pushing his chair away from the plain table. "Right, I must go back, or they will think I'm stuck in the lavatory," he said. No one laughed. As he turned to go, he paused, turning back to Sir Gerald. "In summary, play for time, find out everything you can and keep me informed. Oh and I want to know how Jack Lang is getting on. I need to know as soon as he comes up with a credible plan to deal with the current problem, if he can put something together in time and in any case I want a contingency to respond to these people. I want to give them a bloody nose."

With that, he straightened his tie, tugged at his white waistcoat and strode back towards the painted hall.

EIGHTEEN

At Buckland House events were moving quickly. Twenty-four hours after the formative briefing for Operation Drake, Jack was once again facing Maggie over the polished walnut table in his study.

"Right," he began. "You will need to line up one or two of your 'specialists' to go to Dar es Salaam, ideally within the next three days. We have the authority to continue with the plan and we will need to get both the frigate and the patrol boat on station as quickly as possible. The operation, incidentally, is in two parts. Imagine a plague of wasps – your wasps, remember? We deal with the wasps that are giving immediate cause for concern and then we seek out and destroy the nest."

"Do you have clearance for that?" Maggie interrupted.

"I do," said Jack, pausing to look down at his scribbled notes on the table in front of him.

"I see."

"There is to be nothing attributable. Completely covert," continued Jack.

"That'll be a problem with the frigate, then?"

"I don't think so. We can sort that out. Remember this class of ships no longer exists."

"So where are you with the frigate?" continued Maggie. "Does it work? Will it work? Can you get it there?"

"Whoa. Slow down." Jack held up a hand. "Yes to all of that. I'll give you the details."

"Thanks." She stared across the table intently, her ever present knitting temporarily forgotten.

"Right," said Jack again. "The ship has been docked down. The hull and underwater fittings are sound, subject to a little pressure washing. Both diesels and the starboard gas turbines have been started and appear to be in remarkably good nick, probably because before the ship was laid up they had not been used that much. Number 2 port Olympus is a problem but, I'm told, should be resolvable. The team are looking around for a spare engine just in case."

Maggie raised her eyebrows. "Is that realistic?" she asked.

"Oh yes," said Jack. "These are the same engines that were used to power the Concorde and there are lots of almost unused spares hanging around. Also, they have been marinised and used in a variety of warships. We will lay hands on one but we are treading carefully because we don't want anyone to start asking questions." He paused again, marshalling his thoughts before continuing. "Her electronic systems are a bit shot but we can generate power and keep the lights on. Fresh water production remains a problem but capacity is pretty good. We have identified the weapons fit we want and I am about halfway towards sourcing a crew. With luck I will have that tucked away in another day, say two at the most. Given all of that, we could have her moving in seventy-two hours and the Nav. Team have suggested a Plan B. Go through the Med and the Canal."

Maggie looked unconvinced. "That's a hell of a risk," she said.

"Well," Jack paused for a long minute then leaned further over the table. "It's one we may have to take. Time, at the moment, is not on our side. Taking the ship around the Cape, at best, is likely to take twenty days. Going through the Canal will probably take twelve. The patrol boat can be on the scene within three days of getting a crew on board."

"I see," said Maggie. She continued to look sceptical.

"This is an old and obsolete ship," said Jack. "The Med and the Canal is the standard route for ships heading for the ship breakers on the northwest coast of India. She certainly looks the part and I don't propose to change that."

*

The Bag o' Nails pub in the West End of London had long been a haunt of lower ranking naval officers serving – many would say 'sentenced to' – the Ministry of Defence. At the same time that Jack was briefing Maggie, Charlie de Vere was enjoying the company of a very attractive and generous young woman. Charlie was nearing the end of his second gin and tonic while Anna, his companion and present benefactor, was halfway down her first. Anna was in fact a talent scout for the Special Operations Group and, in concert with several of her colleagues, she was busily head-hunting a crew for Operation Drake. Charlie was under the impression that she was from Johnson and Jameson, a small but exclusive firm of head-hunters who specialised in providing mariners to run the luxury yachts of the very rich.

Charlie was almost a retired Commander Royal Navy. He was, in fact just entering the final week of the four weeks of terminal leave provided by the Admiralty to those who have completed a term of service known as a 'Full Career'. He had spent the bulk of his early career flying helicopters from ship and shore, interspersed with a few 'fish-head' jobs, serving in a variety of mostly small ships as a seaman officer.

Having become too old for military flying and having been moved on from seagoing jobs by the pressure of younger officers struggling up the ladder behind him, he had been posted to a number of increasingly boring staff appointments and had spent the last six months cooling his heels in a non-job within the central staff of the Ministry of Defence. He was in the process of explaining to Anna just how much he was looking to start anew and how he had absolutely no ties, no wife, no children, no dogs, no cats – nothing except an old sailing boat and a small flat – to prevent him from seeking fame, adventure and fortune anywhere in the world. He had mentioned that he had passed all the exams and selections to command a frigate and had kept his civilian pilot's licence going although he was out of practice. Inside her generous Gucci handbag, Anna's small digital recorder was faithfully storing all these facts.

"So you haven't actually settled on a new career yet, then?" she said, smiling over the rim of her glass. "You must have had a pretty good security clearance?" Charlie thought it was a funny question but assumed that his wavy hair and finely chiselled features had captivated his companion. He was already starting to plot an evening of seduction when she came up with something which surprised and disturbed him – and certainly dented his partly formulated plan.

"I think I've got a job for you," she said, "but I need to make a quick phone call." Without waiting for an answer, Anna unwound herself from the banquette seat she was occupying, smiled her winning smile at Charlie and tripped lightly in the direction of the ladies' toilets. Glancing quickly towards Charlie's window seat and noting that he seemed to be staring through the glass, now spattered with the first heavy drops of rain from a lowering shower cloud, she slipped past the entrance to the toilets and continued towards the revolving door to the kitchen and the emergency exit beyond. As the one way emergency door slowly closed behind her she slipped a glove between the lock and the door frame, preventing the spring closer from doing its job.

She delved into her bag, switched off the recorder and pulled out a neat compact Motorola phone. She pressed the 'inbox' button and noted five messages, all left within the last two hours. She spent the next three minutes studying each message in turn, flicked quickly back through them once more and then pressed two buttons, summoning a pre-set number. The phone was answered monosyllabically on the second ring.

"Go," said Jack, from his study in Buckland House.

"I think we're there, Boss," said Anna. "I have first response from five of my team and we have, I think, almost enough to man both assets. I have a leader almost signed up but I must get back to him."

"Run a quick summary past me," said Jack.

Anna took a deep breath and paused. "If I bring in my current mark, we have a total of 80 candidates, including twelve officers and ten engineers. I am sure I can raise additional general hands and cooks if we need to. I should be able to get back to headquarters within three hours and the rest of the recruiters are already on their way."

"I want to reach decisions tonight. Can you brief me with names and main points by twenty-two hundred?" Jack waited listening to the hum of the open phone line.

The ten second delay seemed longer. "No," said Anna eventually.

"OK then, twenty-three hundred." Jack rang off. The phone went dead.

Anna shoved her phone back in her bag, switched on the recorder and extracted her glove from the door, pulling the door open at the same time. She peered around the door then quickly re-entered the bar room threading her way between the tables and walking briskly back towards Charlie at the table by the window.

Charlie half rose politely from his chair as Anna resumed her seat. He waited, punctuating the silence by lifting his glass and sipping the gin and tonic.

Anna waited until the glass had been replaced on the table. "I've got a job for you if you want it," she said.

"Tell me more," said Charlie.

Ignoring the interruption, Anna continued quickly, "It's a special job. Overseas. Won't take longer than sixty days. It pays one hundred thousand pounds, paid in any currency in any country, with a bonus depending on the degree of success achieved." She stopped and waited.

"I need to know more," said Charlie evenly.

"That's all you get right now. If I confirm the appointment and you sign up, you will be fully briefed before noon tomorrow. Give me a response now," she concluded somewhat harshly.

Charlie wondered where the charming and attractive easy-going woman had gone and how this hard nut had appeared so rapidly in her place. He lifted his glass again before noticing that it was empty.

"Well?" said Anna.

The silence stretched for a further thirty seconds. Charlie picked up his glass again, peered into it and put it back down on the small table. "Right," he said, "as far as it stands, and as far as I can see, which isn't far, I'll give it a go."

Anna's face twitched into a quick brief smile. Her hand emerged from her handbag with a small card, white except for a twelve digit number. "Phone that number at nine o'clock tomorrow morning." As she finished speaking she was already on her feet. Without waiting for an answer she turned and walked briskly towards the door. A few seconds later she was on the street outside walking rapidly away along the pavement, peering through the rain in the hope of flagging down a cab.

NINETEEN

In the spacious Captain's Cabin of the USS *Andrew James*, Commander John Reagan leaned across the coffee table and handed a thin piece of signal form to the Captain of HMS *Carlisle*. Commander Craig Wilson glanced at the form, read it through, then read it once again.

TOP SECRET. CODE BARNYARD. COMMAND EYES ONLY. OPERATION DRAKE. OPDRAKE THREE. RULES OF ENGAGEMENT LIFTED TO LEVEL ONE. ACTION IN FURTHERANCE OPDRAKE TWO NOW DELEGATED LOCAL COMMAND DECISION. BLUE CASUALTIES TO BE AVOIDED. RED CASUALTIES ACCEPTABLE. PROCEED AS NECESSARY TO ENSURE SUBJECT REMAINS STATIC. BEWARE FURTHER INSURGENT INTEREST. DO NOT ALLOW EXTERNAL CONTACT WITH SUBJECT. REPORT PROGRESS. AUTHENTICATE ZULU TANGO FOXTROT TWO SEVEN.

"The authentication suggests it's all been jacked up a level," drawled Reagan. "It seems that the British Chief of the Defence Staff is now giving it his personal blessing."

"Yes," said Wilson absently as he studied the signal once more. The desk mounted speaker crackled and the voice of the Officer of the Watch came through.

"We're ready to go Captain."

The Captain pulled the microphone across to him by its long curly lead. "Make it so, Mister," he said.

"Aye, sir."

The two senior officers stood and moved towards the door, passing through the curtain over the entrance, across the cabin flat and out through the screen door onto the main deck. Outside, the ship was completely darkened and as their eyes slowly became accustomed to the darkness, the shape of *Sea Shadow* blocked out the horizon only two cables away on the starboard bow of the cruiser. They stood and watched as black clad men moved about the deck.

A moment or two later, a battery of four powerful searchlights cut through the darkness and lit up the side of the motor yacht in an eye-searing reflective blaze. No more than a second later another battery of light beams hit the *Sea Shadow* from the other side. The ship seemed suddenly detached from the surface of the sea, suspended and transfixed within the brilliant cones of light.

On the disengaged side of the *Andrew James* the last of four black suited divers dropped into the long dark grey inflatable boat with an electric outboard motor which purred almost soundlessly. It moved slowly away from the cruiser's side, remaining in effect invisible by keeping just outside the brilliant cones of light still transfixing the *Sea Shadow*. The boat was towing a buoyed network of flexible stainless steel wire cables formed into an intricate 'cat's cradle' of metal. After covering two thirds of the distance between the American cruiser and the captured motor yacht three of the figures slipped soundlessly from the boat and instantly disappeared.

Working by touch they formed up on three sides of the partially buoyed steel net and, towing it just below the surface, swam towards the stern of the *Sea Shadow*, disappearing under the overhang of the ship's counter. Within six or seven minutes the steel net had been wound around both of the big bronze propellers, binding them immovably together. After another eight minutes three heads bobbed on the surface near the dark, almost invisible boat. The fourth man helped to heave his companions over the side and into the boat. The electric outboard hummed gently and the boat moved, slightly faster, back towards the far side of the *Andrew James*. Seconds later, all the searchlights switched off. The *Sea Shadow* was not now going to move under her own power without first entering a dry dock, and there were none bordering that part of the Indian Ocean.

TWENTY

The meeting at Buckland House didn't actually start until twenty minutes past eleven. Anna and three other members of the 'personnel' team were present together with five senior members of Jack's team. They were spread around the big sitting room in a variety of chairs. The meeting lasted until nearly three the following morning, by which time the eighty names originally considered had been whittled down to just fifty. A portable screen occupied one side of the room. Three lists of names were illuminated on the screen. The first list was headed by ex-Commander Charlie de Vere and was followed by the names of eight other officers, including four engineers. The second list set out the thirty-one men who were to crew the old frigate and the third list of ten were to man the fast patrol boat. Jack had one more name in mind but he kept that to himself.

In addition to Charlie, who would be in command, the frigate was to carry three more bridge watch keeping officers, two engineer officers and one warrant officer artificer, who would be the third engineer. Two of the bridge watch keeping officers were young short service officers, both of whom had previous experience of service in similar frigates, and the third was a Royal Marine who also held a bridge watch keeping certificate but who was expected to be more valuable as a weapons specialist. Both engineer officers were older and were Special Duties officers – they had each started their careers as ratings and had been subsequently selected for promotion to be commissioned officers.

Lieutenant Tom Clarke had left the navy eighteen months ago 'by mutual consent' – an expression he had begun to use to explain his somewhat precipitate departure after barely five years' service as a General List officer. The trouble was that he was easily able to adapt to everything he had been given to do, but a natural impatience with colleagues who were frequently unable to match his ability and a somewhat short fuse had left him isolated in a close-knit service. When he had started to criticise the decisions and actions of those senior to him and then to infuriate them further by pointing out after the event that he was right and they were wrong, his route towards the redundancies sweeping the Service was easily set out and he was one of the first to go – no less embittered than many of those who followed him. His general demeanour and outlook on life had not been improved by a failed marriage partly brought about by the abrupt termination of what he and his retired Rear Admiral father-in-law had identified as a promising career.

Tom had occupied the last eighteen months by spending his meagre gratuity on a number of improbable projects and then generally bumming around from one job to another. He had navigated a sixty foot ketch in a transatlantic sailing race, tried his luck as an irascible dinghy sailing instructor and more recently wasted his time as skipper of a shiny Arab owned gin palace which hardly ever ventured more than a mile from its berth in Monaco. Tall athletic and slim, Tom was attractive to women but a series of short, turbulent and unsatisfactory affairs had done nothing to improve his outlook on life or on the human race in general.

On the plus side, Tom Clarke was available with no strings, dependants or commitments to distract him from the task in hand. He was extremely physically fit and had proved his ability time and again as a natural ship-handler and an excellent navigator, one of the few who still retained the traditional skill of astro-navigation. He was fluent in French and Italian and was an expert shot both on the small arms range and in the rough with a shotgun. He had, in fact, represented the Navy at Bisley before he had even graduated from the Naval College at Dartmouth. His final attribute which secured his place as second in command of the team was his black belt in the martial art of Tai Kwon Do.

Jimmy McCoy was a different kettle of fish. Somewhat older than Tom, he had completed a twelve-year appointment on the Supplementary List of the Royal Navy, initially as a helicopter pilot before being selected for the Sea Harrier Force, where he had completed only one tour before a short sighted and ungrateful government had almost literally snatched his aircraft out from beneath him. Jimmy had left the Navy without recrimination and slipped easily into the commercial helicopter world. Two near disasters brought about by sloppy maintenance in one case and no maintenance at all in the second case had served to move him into the slightly more regulated world of flying to and from the oil and gas rigs dotted about the North Sea. In character he was quite the opposite of Tom. Gregarious, outgoing, happy-go-lucky and welcomed as a generous and amusing drinking partner he was most at home in the company of similar young men in an organised society. He never lacked for female company and he had at least three steady girlfriends in different parts of the country. He enjoyed their company and their different personalities so much that he couldn't reach a decision and so continued to vacillate between them. In any case, at the age of only thirty-five he believed he was still far too young to settle as a family man.

One thing that disturbed Jimmy and dented his wholesome outlook was the work he was doing in supplying the North Sea rigs. When he thought about it on the long boring runs out to the rigs through the inevitably foul weather, he listed three principle causes for his current dissatisfaction. First among these was Aberdeen and the Aberdonians. The place and the people were dour. The whole town was a series of dull grey slabs of wet granite. The airport was in dramatic contrast to the town but it did nothing to improve the scenery. Flat, barren and windswept with stands of pine trees providing some limited protection from the prevailing westerly gale, it consisted of a series of discordant multi-shaped and sized buildings apparently constructed from a giant's Lego kit.

The second reason for Jimmy's disquiet was the people. As a dyed in the wool Englishman from the south he had the constant impression that he was being tolerated by the locals who were offering the thinnest veneer of politeness while waiting the first opportunity to snarl and throw him out of their beloved, but to him, horrible country. Added to this was the fact that he seemed to have little in common with his work colleagues, who he thought of as uni-dimensional, unimaginative, ill-informed and with vision only as far as the end of their rotor blades. At first he had looked forward to a quiet beer at the end of the flying day, accompanied by the typical 'putting the world to rights' conversation he had enjoyed in the various Wardroom bars of the Navy during his formative adult years but now he rarely bothered to leave his 'Portacabin' accommodation because although the beer was good, drinking among the flight crews was frowned upon and even when stood down from flight duty on his days off, the companions to be found in the evenings were as boring as one could find anywhere. Their conversation seemed to be dominated by helicopters, oil rigs and competitive claims to have found the most dreadful weather.

The third reason which led to Jimmy's decision to move on was the generally awful climate and the type of flying. Like most commercial companies Jimmy's employers had no wish to waste a moment of expensive flight time, nor a pint of fuel. This manifested itself in a steady outpouring of often petty and sometimes irrelevant directions and restrictions imposed on exactly how the aircraft should be flown.

Jimmy was a free spirit, not a man who enjoyed being tied in this Gordian Knot of red tape, and when the company decided to take on a former Civil Aviation Authority examiner to run a series of airborne spot-checks on the regular company pilots, Jimmy decided he had had enough.

The new Airborne Standards Officer as the man styled himself had been discovered to have feet of clay. He had practically no experience in the unusual and frequently demanding task of flying to the rigs, having learned to fly in the Army Air Corps before leaving to join the CAA, first as an office bound administrator and then as a helicopter examiner. In this role he had spent relatively little time in the air and practically none at all with his hands on the controls.

When word of this background filtered through to the company pilots they almost immediately dubbed their irritating superior 'The Penguin'.

Before finally leaving the Aberdeen base Tom intercepted the 'Penguin' in the aircrew ready room, delaying his departure long enough to provide the 'Penguin' with an eloquent synopsis of how he was viewed by those he flew with, before marking the occasion by pouring half a cup of cold coffee over the Penguin's head. Jimmy had no intention of returning to a flying career in the North.

Both Tom and Jimmy had been located when they had responded to a small ad sent out in the routine email from the Officers' Association. The ad had offered short term exciting opportunities to former naval officers who were looking for adventure with good rewards.

Captain Brian Hall Royal Marines was already one of Jack's staff officers. He had been with the organization for nearly five years following a temporary secondment from the Royal Marines Special Boat Service. During that five years Brian had been sent on several operations but had spent much of the rest of his time becoming thoroughly familiar with those weapons and weapon systems with which he was not already expert.

As a 'sea-soldier' he had served in the jungle of Borneo, the mountains of the Yemen and in the generally miserable southern winter environment of the Falkland Islands. In this capacity he had collected a Military Cross, a Distinguished Service Cross and had been twice Mentioned in Despatches. He had also collected two wounds from small arms fire, one of which had put an end to a promising career as a marathon runner and left him with a slight limp.

Brian had a watch-keeping ticket and so he would complete the Bridge team but his main task – on which he was already, in fact, engaged, was to identify suitable weapons which could be easily fitted to the ship, to locate those weapons from untraceable sources and to prepare plans for their use onboard. When the team was finalised he would direct the necessary weapons training before departure and along the way.

Brian was twice divorced, neither time amicably, which meant that his opportunities to see his three teenage children were limited.

The three engineers came as a package, which Jack and Alice considered to be too convenient to reject.

For several years now, Dan Holloway, Mike Carter and ex-Warrant Officer Artificer John Banyard had been nursing elderly ships of all shapes, sizes and types from various parts of the world to their final resting place on the edge of the Arabian Sea to the north of Goa. Dan had completed his naval career as a Special Duties Lieutenant, having joined as a boy stoker and worked his way up to commissioned rank by taking apart, putting together, fixing, bodging and nursing almost every piece of mechanical equipment it was possible to find in a ship. He had survived the sinking of his ship in the Falklands, and was regarded as something of an unsung hero by the dozen men he had caused to survive with him. Although he could not resist turning his hand to any piece of engineering equipment, at heart he was a steam engineer and always would be, despite the fact that steam propulsion was now restricted to old railway engines and other museum pieces.

Mike had served together with Dan when they were both Petty Officers but their careers had parted when Dan had been promoted and gone off to be trained as an officer. Mike had eventually followed the same course but had left the Royal Navy as a Sub-Lieutenant. Mike was to electrical and electronic systems what Dan was to steam engines. Together they made a formidable team, each having picked up sufficient knowledge of the other's specialty to provide experienced and skilled help when the occasion demanded.

The third member of the engineering team, John Banyard, was the perfect foil for each of his two companions.

Originally a mechanical engineering specialist, he had been cross-trained some years previously as a Chief Electrical Artificer. In his mid-forties, John had been married until a Romanian lorry driver on his first long distance trip to England had fallen asleep at the wheel, crossed double white lines marking the centre of the road and, in no more than a moment, had wiped John's young wife from the face of the earth. The tragedy had been further compounded when the complexity and absurdity of English law had allowed the guilty man to walk free from the court and return to Romania. As he left the court the air of devastated remorse that had hovered over and around the man throughout the legal wrangling had been replaced by a self-satisfied smirk.

The fact of the availability of this tight-knit team arose simply because there had been a lull in the ship breaking business. Really big ships were being systematically dismantled in large graving docks and the smaller ones were only making the journey to the beaches of Northern India when it could be ascertained that the exercise would generate sufficient profit to make the operation worthwhile.

The remainder of the crew earmarked for the frigate consisted of sixteen seamen including four gunnery specialists, three Marine Engineering Mechanics, two electricians and two cooks. All twenty-one hands were to be led by ex-Chief Petty Officer 'Henry' King who had been recognised by the great and good as well as the lowly, as one of the most resourceful and knowledgeable seamen since Nelson's time. He had in fact been sculling around under-employed as one of Jack's fixers for some time. It was Jack himself who told him, "Henry, you're going to be a 'Buffer' again, so brush up those marlin spikes and get your splicing fingers in tune." Henry had immediately taken on the task of assisting in the selection of the men he was to lead.

Both dark skins and Arabic speakers were going to be needed and this was met by Samson Anatsui, originally from Ghana but more recently domiciled in Deptford, George Bedu, a big, grinning, amiable Nigerian, Mohktar Sulimi, who had served with distinction in the Sultan of Oman's Naval Force, Ali Serrana, a London based Egyptian and finally, Nobby Small, a tough and successful former amateur boxer with a polished coal black head and an accent that identified him as firmly coming from within range of Bow Bells.

The Gunners included Corporal Harry Smith Royal Marines who could easily pass for the young Clint Eastwood, and Corporal John Stevens formerly of the Royal Horse Artillery and the SAS who was as short as Harry Smith was tall and looked as if he was carved from the limestone of his native Portland. Henry King made three key selections who he believed would form the backbone of his seamanship branch. Hugh Campbell was a talented piper as well as a skilled seaman. Tom McCann, an Ulsterman, had left the Navy ostensibly as a Petty Officer but with an inflated pension in recognition of his undercover work in Northern Ireland during the 'troubles'. His partiality for Guinness had led to him moving up and down regularly between the various ranks in the Service, before settling into the dangerous work around the Falls Road. His long-time friend Will Taylor had been born on a farm and as a young man had harboured a desire to become a vet. Instead he had spent fifteen years in the small ships of the Royal Navy.

Apart from the skills required, the other qualifying factor for inclusion in the shortlist had been instant availability. As soon as the meeting ended, despite the late hour Anna and her team, now reduced to two assistants, began to put together that information necessary to start the project going.

A series of temporary files were started, growing steadily thicker as information and documents were added. Passport numbers, photographs and new driving licences were included as well as other paraphernalia necessary to support new false identities. Banker's drafts for advances of pay were made out as well as bundles of small denomination currency from several countries. Travel warrants and other documents vied with medical records and lists of necessary 'jabs'.

While this was going on, in another room, the final touches were being put to the team who were to crew the patrol boat.

This was a much simpler exercise, requiring the selection of a Captain and nine men which would be sufficient to turn the small fast craft into an effective fighting machine once more.

The selection of a Captain for the patrol boat was easy. Lt Cdr Harry Mullen had been one of Jack's men for over five years and prior to that he had spent a happy three years driving fast patrol boats, first in Hong Kong then in Gibraltar. His Executive Officer was a more recent member of Jack's team. Former Lieutenant Gerry Tan had been scooped up from a job as a watch keeping officer in a UK Border Agency cutter which he had thought, when he took it up, would provide the adventure that he craved but in fact it proved to be singularly boring. Gerry, whose family came originally from Hong Kong, had started out as a professional yachtsman, crewing ocean racing yachts for rich owners who sought ocean racing glory by proxy

The remainder of the crew were an unusual bunch. Mike Cowley, ex-Special Boat Squadron, had graduated from a career of patching up bits of kit broken – deliberately, he would often say – by his colleagues in the Special Boat Squadron, to a much more lucrative career by making himself available, at all hours and wherever he might be required, to maintain, salvage, rescue, recover and occasionally deliver back to their owners, a series of increasingly fancy gin palaces. It was great fun at first and there was no doubt that the money was exceptionally good, women were plentiful and readily available to Mike but despite this he became progressively bored with the high life and he had drifted, almost by accident, into Jack's team. Mike was a dab hand at anything mechanical and although he had no direct experience of gas turbines he was confident that he knew the principles, and that he could probably take them apart, and if he could take them apart he was certain he could put them back together again. However, to provide a little extra insurance he had suggested that Jimmy James, a former Fleet Air Arm Sea Harrier engineer might be useful to back him up. His suggestion had been readily agreed.

Of the remaining six crew members, three of them were women. All three were still in their twenties and each had amassed a tremendous amount of experience in ships and boats of various types. Karen Ford was an Olympic standard dinghy sailor. Raven haired, slim, tall and highly toned she was hooked on adventurous sports which was how she had found herself temporarily moving in the world of espionage. Recruited into MI6 while still representing her country as a solo dinghy sailor she had become involved in trying to smuggle some documents and small pieces of equipment out of St Petersburg and had been caught. Angrily she realised that she had been used as a high tech, high risk mule, probably, she reckoned, to divert suspicion away from someone else. Her sailing celebrity status had helped to get her out of Russia and she had found herself swept into Jack's headquarters, ostensibly for de-briefing. During an increasingly irritating few days of repetitive questioning she had encountered, quite by chance, the man who had honey-trapped her into doing his bidding. He was not top of her popularity list and when she saw him through the window of one of the other briefing rooms she waited on the outside of the door for ten minutes.

When he left his work at the desk and moved towards the door she waited until the door started to move and with beautiful timing threw her whole weight against the door. Taken completely off guard, Harry Carter, the MI6 man, was knocked back into the room. Following up her initial advantage Karen hurled herself after him and hanging onto his shirt front with one hand she had rabbit-punched him across the throat with the other. As he went down she kicked the side of his knee. The damage there was limited only because her formal court shoe wasn't heavy enough. Harry tried to roll to one side as a four door filing cabinet crashed down across his head and shoulders. Karen straightened her skirt, wiped her hands on Harry's unmoving shirt front and strolled off out of the room and down the corridor.

Harry spent nearly a week in intensive care and took nearly three months to recover fully. Unfortunately for Karen the whole episode was videoed by the security system. She did manage to talk her way out of a spell behind bars but at the cost of signing up with Jack.

Frankie Zambelas was black and sexy. She had at one time been a dancer in Fort Lauderdale, before moving through a couple of Bahamas nightclubs into a cruise line as a hostess and then, following a torrid affair with a senior ship's officer who had been since dismissed she had found herself ashore at Southampton.

Jane York was the serious member of the trio. She was a chameleon who could change successfully back and forth between different personas to meet the changing circumstances of the moment. A serious schoolmarm could disappear and then reappear as a vamp and then do the same trick, returning as a scruffy plain deck hand. Like the others she was tough and single minded.

The remaining three men in the team were also quite young. None of them were or had been married and only one, Paddy Stone who was recruited primarily as cook, was able to offer any relevant sea experience, but they were tough and adaptable. Both Billy Walker and Peter Archer were weapons experts and Peter, in addition, was an unarmed combat instructor. Altogether the crew was a mixed bag. 'Pirates to fight pirates' was the view of Harry Mullen.

Jack Lang had insisted, at Maggie's behest, that the patrol boat crew should be a mixed group of men and women. This would serve to reinforce the idea that the small group were a bunch of rich playboys and girls who would use the small fast boat for entirely pleasurable activities. In this way embarrassing questions might be avoided.

TWENTY-ONE

Hamid's repeated call was answered after ten minutes by the *Andrew James*.

"*Sea Shadow,* this is the United States Ship *Andrew James*. State your business."

"I need fuel for my ship. I am willing to trade," replied Hamid hesitantly.

"*Sea Shadow,* this is the *Andrew James*. We have reason to believe that you have boarded and seized the Motor Vessel *Sea Shadow* by the use of illegal force in contravention of the International Law of the Sea. You must release the prisoners you hold, lay down your weapons and come to the upper deck at the bows, unarmed with your hands in the air – over."

There was a protracted pause before the radio speaker crackled again and Hamid's harsh voice came through again.

"American ship, British ship," he said. "We have many hostages. We have women. We have Americans. We have British. I need fuel. You give me fuel, I give you two hostage. You no give me fuel, I kill two hostage. You unnerstan'?"

At a sign from John Reagan, the Comms Officer thumbed the transmit button once more.

"*Sea Shadow*, please understand that if you harm hostages, any hostages at all, then I am authorised to take action against you. I will sink your ship – over."

The verbal sparring continued for the next hour by which time Hamid had agreed to release two hostages of his choice in return for one thousand gallons of fuel. This would be insufficient to reach the Somali coast but Hamid did not know that. With the heavy steel wire rope wound round the propellers no amount of fuel was going to help Hamid. *Sea Shadow* was not going to move at all without a tug. But Hamid did not know that either.

Carlisle moved in close to the stationary motor yacht and lowered a small gauge fuel line, buoyed at intervals along its length, into the sea. A rigid inflatable boat appeared from around the stern of the destroyer, picked up the end of the line and towed it slowly across towards the motor yacht. As it reached the side of the *Sea Shadow,* two figures clad in white and wearing life jackets appeared on the side deck with an Arab gunman behind each one. A rope ladder with wooden steps was rolled over the side and another pirate scrambled down it, grabbing the end of the hose now trailing in the water. The boat's crew simply watched.

The hose proved too heavy and the Arab scrambled nimbly back up the ladder, appearing once more a few seconds later to go back down the ladder, this time clutching a light line. He stood with his feet on the lower rung of the ladder, waist deep in water, hanging onto the ladder with one hand while he wound the end of the rope around the hose end with the other hand. As he scrambled back up the ladder, other hands appeared and began to haul the fuelling hose up the ship's side. It was almost at the top when the rope unravelled from the end of the hose which fell with a plop back into the sea.

At the same time the two life-jacketed hostages hurled themselves forward, plunging over the rail to land with a huge single splash close alongside the boat. On deck, confusion, shouting and panic erupted, followed by a few rounds of automatic fire apparently aimed at nothing in particular.

Instantly two brilliant searchlights from the *Carlisle* flashed on and pinioned the figures on the deck of the *Sea Shadow* who were all holding up hands and weapons in a vain attempt to shield their eyes from the sudden glare. Alongside the *Sea Shadow*, the crew of the boat which had towed the fuel hose across were fishing the hostages out of the water. Within a few seconds the throttle was gunned and so far as the blinded pirates on the deck of *Sea Shadow* were concerned, the boat disappeared entirely.

On the Bridge of *Carlisle*, Ben Crossley, the Engineer Officer, looked across towards his Captain.

"Shall I bring the fuel hose back now, sir?" he asked.

"No, we said we'd give them some fuel so we shall, but it won't do them any good."

"They ain't gonna like it sir," said Ben.

"You mean when they find the props won't turn?" Craig Wilson turned towards his engineer with the ghost of a smile on his face. "Turn the fuel on as soon as they seem to have a connection, give them a few hundred gallons slowly – they can't measure it – and then disconnect."

"You mean get them to disconnect?" said Ben.

Craig half turned again. "Well, yes. But if they won't or can't just disconnect at this end. We need to get away from here as soon as we can – sooner if possible." He clattered down the ladder at the back of the Bridge, calling over his shoulder, "Keep the lights on them and move off as soon as we break the connection."

On the deck of *Sea Shadow*, a harassed and sweating handcuffed Second Engineer was scrabbling about trying to connect *Carlisle's* fuel hose to a large adapter which in turn was connected to one of the ship's fuel inlet points. It was proving difficult and diesel was beginning to spread across the immaculate teak planking. He wrapped a rag around the leaking connection which stemmed the spillage somewhat. For his trouble he was jabbed in the small of the back by the muzzle of a rifle and pushed away towards captivity.

The black rubber RIB was secured close alongside the port beam of *Carlisle* so that the bulk of the destroyer prevented anyone in *Sea Shadow* from seeing what was happening in the small boat. In fact the two trembling, soaking wet figures, still wearing their uninflated life jackets, were being manhandled up the ship's side before being whisked away to the Sick Bay and interrogation.

In the Sick Bay Leading Medical Attendant 'Doc' Holiday handed each of the men a pair of blue overalls and a scruffy pair of clean but well-worn gym shoes as he kicked the recently discarded pile of filthy and sodden clothes into one of the Sick Bay shower cubicles. He indicated to the two men, both of whom seemed to be mentally spent and defeated, that they should sit, side by side on one of the bunks. As they did so the door opened and the tall, heavy figure of Master at Arms Ronnie Vincent stepped into the room and stood, towering over the two exhausted, broken men.

Within fifteen minutes the Master at Arms was back in the Captain's Cabin reporting what he had found. Occasionally referring to a small leather backed notebook, he spoke quickly with few pauses while he brought the Captain up to date.

One of the men had been a steward in the *Sea Shadow,* while the other, younger, man had been a deck hand. They both came from Middle Eastern countries but the Master at Arms had not been able to identify their precise nationality.

They had been able to add little else but, with the rest of the crew, they had been locked away in a guest cabin without food but with a lavatory and access to fresh water. They thought that *Sea Shadow* had a crew of twenty-three or perhaps twenty-five men in addition to two passengers. Two of the engineers had been taken away and had not returned and after the initial round-up and incarceration they had seen or heard little from their captors until they were hauled out to handle the refuelling hose.

"Are they telling the truth?" said Craig.

"I don't see that they have any reason to lie, sir. They see us as their saviours, I think."

"Yes, I think you may be right," said Craig. "Anyway, get them cleaned up and fed and then lock them away somewhere under guard so they can't get up to mischief."

"Aye aye sir," said the Master at Arms as he pocketed his notebook, turned and left the cabin.

TWENTY-TWO

Less than forty-eight hours after the conclusion of Jack Lang's meeting, the Faslane dry dock had been flooded up and the frigate was once more afloat. More than that, both of her diesels and one of the gas turbines were running, though not under load.

The dock gates were opened and several small dockyard tugs nosed into the entrance to ease the frigate out of the dock and across the short stretch of water towards an empty concrete jetty. The whole exercise, taking place not long after midnight, was being done under the dim glow of the floating-dock lights and two or three floodlights mounted along the jetty. On the jetty itself, groups of men were appearing. Several cars, a mini-bus, a long articulated truck and half a dozen smaller nondescript vans littered the concrete surface.

Within forty minutes the ship was moored alongside the concrete jetty and the adjacent activity had expanded towards the ship then up the single gangway and onto the deck.

Jack Lang sat beside Maggie in the back of one of the unlit cars and smiled comfortably. "So far, so good," he said.

"Better than you had a right to hope for," said Maggie as a yellow painted mobile crane swung an unmistakable open sided crate carrying a gas turbine engine high over the frigate before lowering it down, out of sight on the far side of the superstructure.

Lights were popping on all over the ship as Jack turned back towards Maggie. "What about the patrol boat?" he said.

"All rolling ahead, in fact somewhat further ahead than this little foundling," she replied. Jack noticed, inconsequentially, that for once her knitting was missing.

Jack waited, silently. He knew there'd be more. When she didn't answer he raised an eyebrow – which was wasted in the darkness inside the car – and said, "Well?"

Maggie took a deep breath. "The crew left on two scheduled flights twelve hours ago," she said. "The ship is now owned by a small consortium of wealthy playboys who intend to disarm it and convert it to a fast cabin cruiser."

Jack raised his eyebrow again but said nothing, waiting for Maggie to continue.

"Our man came down from Mombasa and made the purchase. He confirmed that the ship is fully fuelled, stored – with non-lethal stores that is – and ready in all respects. She is due to leave harbour as soon as the delivery crew arrive at Dar es Salaam. That's just the Captain, engineer and two others. The remainder will be going on dude safaris in two separate groups. They will be picked up from the beach a few miles further south."

"What about weaponry?" asked Jack.

"No problem," replied Maggie as she began to root about in her large handbag. "That part of Africa is awash with weaponry of every description. If you have the money in hard currency, or better still, gold, you can get almost anything you want. Our weapons load should have left Beira within the last few hours and with a small modicum of luck it should be on board shortly after the boat leaves the African coast. By the way, the originally fitted Bofors forty millimetre is still attached, rather conveniently, I think, to the fore deck." She stopped, smiled and triumphantly produced from her bag, not the knitting that Jack expected but a small stainless steel drinking set comprising a flask with two cups. She poured two generous shots of Bowman fifteen-year-old single malt whisky and passed one to Jack. They continued to wait in silence inside the darkened car savouring the neat whisky and watching the feverish preparations taking place aboard the elderly frigate.

*

The engine room of the old Leander resembled a large white painted steel cavern now that the original steam turbines, diesel generators and evaporators had been removed. A small team of fitters, assisted by Dan Holloway and John Banyard, were labouring to fit a marinised gas turbine engine into its location and line it up to connect smoothly with the CODAG gearbox assembly. As they worked they were passed by a steady stream of men carrying boxes and bundles of various shape, colour and size into the engine room. The speed with which decisions were being made concerning the stores and spares likely to be needed for the voyage, as well as the lack of experience of the decision makers regarding this type of ship – which had last seen sea service before many of the organizers had left school – meant inevitably that preparing the ship for sea had been somewhat haphazard. Obscure dockyard and victualing stores all over the country had been prised open and had disgorged interesting looking lumps of machinery that in some cases could not be identified, and which had been subsequently thrown in the back of the collecting lorry. The collectors worked on the basis that there was plenty of room in the ship and the item might come in handy. Additionally the custodians of the various bits of kit were only too happy to accept a signed receipt in order to get rid of items for which they had no use but which they had been made to account for at each annual audit. Consequently the ancient frigate was filling up rather more quickly than had been at first envisaged.

The Proteus gas turbine was now in place and the drive shaft was fitting fairly neatly into the gearbox. Mounting bolts were all in place and were being torsioned now. Only the fuel lines remained to be connected. Dan had demanded that the ship's fuel tanks should be emptied and purged before being refilled with clean new diesel. The task had been resisted by the Faslane engineers at first but they had soon buckled under Dan's insistent and occasionally forthright profanities. Eventually the tanks had been cleaned, albeit cursorily and new filters installed and Dan was able to put aside his worry over the risk of contamination to his beloved new engine by dirty fuel. Nevertheless final fuel connections to the quadruple gas turbine system would not be allowed until Dan had sampled and tested every section and every fitting within the fuel system.

On the small flight deck and the presently empty helicopter hangar, boxes and crates were being delivered at a phenomenal rate. Only half the designated crew had arrived so far and even with the help of some of the shore people the work was piling up. Nobody had much idea of what the jumble of boxes contained, so nobody could yet decide where they should be stored except inside the hangar and the after senior ratings mess deck which occupied part of the deck immediately below.

Charlie de Vere, indistinguishable from his men in a blue overall, stood surrounded by confusion scratching his sweating head.

Over on the jetty, two long wheel base Land Rover Defenders had drawn up behind the shiny black limousine still occupied by Jack and Maggie. Charlie heaved a sigh and allowed himself a grin as men began tumbling out of each, clutching suitcases, holdalls and in one case an old-fashioned kitbag.

He made his way between the piles of crates and boxes to the head of the gangway where he waited. One by one the remainder of his crew came aboard, briefly introduced themselves with a handshake and then headed off down below to find somewhere to dump their kit.

As the last crew member disappeared forward, the main broadcast speakers all over the ship crackled into life and a voice boomed out, “Testing, testing, testing.”

“Great,” said Charlie to no-one in particular. “More and more bits and pieces working.” He arched and stretched his aching back, turned once more to try and produce order from the confusion spread around the deck in front of him. Within a few minutes he had been joined by Brian Hall, Tom Clarke and four or five of the other new arrivals. They worked steadily and order began to emerge from the confusion.

TWENTY-THREE

In *Sea Shadow*, Sharkey Fisher the Third Engineer was now in the Machinery Control Room. His hands were still handcuffed and Hamid and one of the other Arabs were squeezed into the remaining small space behind him. Sharkey was exhausted, dehydrated and hungry. He had lost his previous will to resist his captors and so he flipped all the fuel switches to flow, opened the by-pass restrictors, started the pumps and stood back. At a gesture from Hamid the other Arab seized the back of his grimy and sweaty shirt and dragged him back out into the corridor. Hamid carefully placed his automatic pistol on the desk surface, stared carefully at the layout of the panel and then firmly pressed a big green button marked 'No 1 Diesel Auto Start'.

At first nothing happened. Then as the auto start sequence worked its way through, there was a whine, followed by a bout of coughing like a giant smoker on his last cigarette, then the engine caught and ran smoothly up to one thousand revolutions, as indicated by the dial in front of Hamid.

Hamid paused for a moment, intoned a silent prayer and then went through the same procedure with the second engine. Nothing happened. Hamid waited, prayed again, more fervently, and pressed the button once more, this time holding it pressed for several seconds. A short pause occurred as before then the whine which seemed to go on for longer than the first time. The diesel coughed, the whine continued, it coughed again, and again, and again, then the whine stopped and the engine began to run. It rumbled and grumbled and did not seem to be able to hold the same steady revolutions as its twin but at least both were running. Already the emergency lights were going out and being replaced by the main lighting system as electrical power began to course through the ship, bringing it back to life.

The ventilation and air conditioning started up again and the foetid stink that had crept through the accommodation areas began to dissipate, or at least to ease slightly.

Much of the food in the ready use fridges was by now unfit to eat. As Hamid's men had progressively began to feel hungry so they had gone in search of food. They had hauled out the fresh produce they felt like eating, left the fridge doors open and food scattered over the surrounding deck. As for the hostages, all they had was the water from the washbasins in their cabin prisons, and even this had died away to a trickle when the fresh water system pumps failed.

Hamid called the Bridge on the now functioning Engine Room intercom and ordered Khalid to come down to the Machinery Control Room. As the two big diesels continued to rumble steadily behind the sound insulated bulkhead, he relaxed and allowed a shadow of a smile to appear around his beard. Truly, he thought to himself, Allah the Merciful is with me. I can do no wrong.

A noise caused him to turn, his expression changing as he did so to his usual one of truculent dissatisfaction. Khalid's wide frame filled the doorway. He looked expectantly towards his master, awaiting instructions.

"You know how to engage the engines to drive the ship?" Hamid spoke slowly in Arabic and Khalid nodded without speaking.

"I am going to steer the ship," said Hamid. "You will wait here and engage the engines to drive the ship when I call you on this." Hamid indicated the intercom speaker and handset. He moved towards the door, turned, waited for a moment then when Khalid said nothing he strode away quickly in the direction of the Bridge.

Khalid waited. Five or six minutes passed before the harsh voice of Hamid came over the intercom:

"Engage the engines – one at a time."

Khalid nodded assent then realised that he needed to speak. "Yes Hamid," he growled. He took the two chromium handled select levers and moved them quickly forward and they clicked as they stopped at the tally marked 'DRIVE'. There was a momentary pause then one after the other, the diesels faltered as the revolutions fell away then recovered. At the same time the hull shuddered and a metallic clattering and banging echoed throughout the ship. The ship continued to shudder and rattle for perhaps five seconds then one engine abruptly shut down. The running noise of the other was briefly submerged under a metallic scream as the main gearbox on that shaft stripped itself of all its gears. The engine picked up and continued to rumble gently. The intercom sprang into life.

"What have you done?" screamed the disembodied voice. Khalid shrugged, then again remembered the need to speak.

He said, "I engaged the engines to drive as you said." Hamid peremptorily ordered him to come to the Bridge. Khalid shrugged again, left the Control Room and made his way unhurriedly to the Bridge. When he arrived on the

Bridge he stood and waited patiently. Hamid was furious. Everyone on the Bridge was getting a loud tongue lashing. Eyes were downcast. All of the Somalis feared Hamid to one degree or another and nobody wanted to do anything to focus on themselves the towering rage that had become almost tangible.

"Bring me Captain! Bring me Engineer!" raged Hamid as he strode and whirled around the Bridge. Khalid took the opportunity to disappear back down the Bridge ladder. He was quickly followed by Melak who stumbled at the top of the ladder in his haste to get away from his leader.

*

The noise of the destruction of *Sea Shadow's* gearboxes and propellers had carried across to both *Carlisle* and *Andrew James*. Almost immediately the two warship captains were talking on the secure UHF channel.

"I guess they are not going anywhere any more, over," said Craig Wilson.

"How long do you think before they work out the exact amount of shit they are in, over?" responded John Reagan from the *Andrew James*.

"Any time now." Craig Wilson dropped the signalese endings of 'over' and 'out' and the conversation became more natural.

Reagan keyed his transmission button and held it down. He paused and then said, thoughtfully, "Well, she can't go anywhere, we aren't going anywhere. We are not authorised to take proactive action yet so the ball is in his court and we wait and watch."

"And if he starts killing?" Wilson came back quickly.

"How would we know?"

"We'll know because he'll either use them to try and squeeze something out of us, or alternatively, we'll hear the gunfire and see the splashes as the bodies hit the sea." Wilson waited for a response.

"He could try to cut and run – take as many hostages as he can cram in his boat." As he spoke John Reagan was staring across the short stretch of water dividing the two ships where *Sea Shadow* was now lit up like a cruise liner. He continued without waiting for a reply, "The blaze of lights suggest they must have at least one of the diesels still serviceable."

"Doesn't seem to matter – I think," responded Wilson somewhat uncertainly. Then, "We should get a response from Command now they know the latest development."

"Don't count on it. They know now that they have more time. They won't rush." Reagan seemed about to say something else but tailed off.

"Our lot certainly won't rush." Wilson stopped as he was interrupted by the Chief Yeoman who had appeared at his elbow clutching a clipboard with two sheets of signal form clipped to it.

*

In *Sea Shadow* Hamid had calmed down. He had retreated to one of the luxury guest cabins to think. In fact after thirty minutes or so his shortage of sleep coupled with the stress of his situation overcame him and he fell, still sitting upright on a plush sofa, into a sound sleep. None of his gang wanted to wake him and perhaps become the most immediate target if he relapsed once more into a towering rage when awoken.

Five hours later, in the early hours of the morning when he woke up, Hamid went in search of food and water. He prowled about in the passenger cabins, the saloon, the extensive ornate gilded dining room and it was here that he ran into Louis who had sneaked out from his hideaway to get rid of the faeces he had been forced to store.

Both of them stopped, shocked. Hamid recovered first and charged across the room, mentally cursing himself for leaving his pistol where he had slept. Louis recoiled in fear as the furious bearded Arab bore down on him, black eyes glittering. Louis carried two bags. He had a thin plastic bag in his right hand and a brown paper bag in his left hand. In desperation, as he staggered and tripped backwards, he threw first the plastic bag, then the paper one. Fear must have helped his aim and added strength to his arms. The plastic bag hit Hamid squarely in the face and burst apart on contact. About four pounds of semi-liquid shit covered Hamid's head. Instantly blinded, his headlong rush stalled, as he tried to claw the filth away from his eyes. The second bag – the brown paper one – was already disintegrating as it flew through the air. Most of the contents hit Hamid on his chest and beard and as the remainder fell to the deck Hamid stepped forward into it, slipped and fell.

Louis seized his chance. He had the advantage of better knowledge of the ship and as Hamid was levering himself up from the floor, using the edge of the big mahogany table for support, he ran through the doorway out into the corridor, turning aft towards a screen door leading to the side deck. Hamid was cursing loudly as he hauled himself to his feet and ran after the fugitive.

The first screen door was stuck so Louis ran on, scrambling up a stairway to the deck above. Hamid followed, gaining on the older, less fit man. At the same moment, Ali, who was on guard on the Bridge wing, saw the figures emerge onto the open helicopter deck. He levelled his Kalashnikov and loosed off a burst of three shots. All three missed Louis but the noise of the bullets hitting the deck and structure around him turned him momentarily from a human being to a fleeing mound of unthinking terror. He turned forty-five degrees to his left and threw himself bodily towards the ship's rail. It wasn't a clean dive and he hit the rail. He was briefly conscious of a searing pain around his ribs which was instantly extinguished as he hit the surface of the water and sank below it.

More shots came from various parts of the ship and bullets pockmarked the surface of the sea. Within seconds a battery of searchlights from the *Andrew James*, still only three hundred yards from the *Sea Shadow*, lit the scene in brilliant white light, pinning the *Sea Shadow* and the figures of pirates emerging onto the upper deck, against the backdrop of the night.

Of Louis there was initially no sign. To the pirates that didn't matter because the sudden glare of several million candle power directed into their eyes not only destroyed their night vision but disorientated them as well.

Louis had in fact surfaced but he was protected by the overhang of the stern of *Sea Shadow* and couldn't be seen from the deck.

"Look, sir," said Petty Officer First Class Hawkins. "There's a guy in the water." Commander Reagan, standing beside the Petty Officer on the Bridge Wing, trained his binoculars on the water beneath the counter of the motor yacht.

As the eyes of the pirates began to adjust to the brilliant white glare of the searchlights, two or three more appeared on the side deck clutching pistols or Kalashnikov rifles and began pooping off random shots over the side. Hamid was temporarily inactive because he was still scraping ordure from his face and clothing, while trying ineffectually to avoid the foul stink in which he seemed to be encapsulated.

Reagan flicked the switch on the loudspeaker by his side, picked up the microphone and his voice boomed out over the gap between the two vessels:

"Cease firing your weapons immediately – I mean now! – or I will open fire on you." Even those who were incapable of understanding the instruction could not fail to guess the meaning of the peremptory order. Hamid called his men away from the ship's side having reached his own conclusion that his unknown quarry must have drowned.

Four minutes later all the searchlights switched off simultaneously, causing the same problem to the eyesight of any observers in *Sea Shadow* as when the lights had been suddenly switched on. As the lights went out, on the far side of the *Andrew James* a matt black inflatable rubber boat hit the water and moved towards the stern of the cruiser. Seconds later it emerged from the shelter of the *Andrew James* and, using an electric outboard motor, headed silently towards the *Sea Shadow's* stern. As the boat re-emerged from under the overhanging counter of the motor yacht, all the searchlights came back on again, bathing the motor yacht in brilliant white light and playing havoc once more with the eyesight of those still on the deck of *Sea Shadow*.

Ten minutes later a shivering, shocked, blanket clad Louis was seated in a folding chair in the sickbay on board the *Andrew James*. The Captain and several of the ship's officers were gathered round him. Reagan sat immediately opposite Louis and spoke very gently. "We need your help, Louis. You can take it easy and we won't rush you but we need to know what you know so that we can help the rest of your crew. Do you understand?"

Louis nodded silently. He had been given a mild sedative and it was beginning to show. The ship's doctor was looking unhappy. He leaned close to the Captain's ear and said, "We need to keep this short, sir. He has been under stress for days and he has just suffered considerable trauma. He needs sleep."

Commander Reagan nodded curtly without turning away from the pathetic bundle in front of him. He waved a hand to his left where another officer was holding an internal deck plan of *Sea Shadow*. "Do you know where the crew hostages are, Louis?"

Louis leaned forward and for a moment Reagan thought he was going to be sick. He shook his head and then, as if an afterthought, he pointed a shaky hand towards the plans. "Has to be forward," he said, very quietly, "in the crew cabins." Then taking a long deep breath, he continued, "Not near me. I was hidden in the store behind my bar. They never came near that."

"He means the pirates," said a disembodied voice from behind the Captain. Reagan turned angrily and waved the man to silence, then looked back at Louis, whose eyelids were drooping and who was now being steadied to prevent him from falling out of the chair.

"One more question," said Reagan. There was no answer. Reagan reached out to hold Louis's shoulder and repeated, "One more question." Louis's head came up and his eyes gained a little more focus.

"How many pirates are there, Louis?" The question was louder and more abrupt than he had intended and Louis jerked back as if he had been struck. The doctor moved forward once more and was angrily waved back again. Everyone waited.

"How many pirates, Louis?" This time the question came softly and gently. Louis tried to respond.

After twenty or thirty seconds of silence his brow furrowed and he said, "I don't know exactly, more than five… more than seven… maybe ten. Boss man has a black beard and…" the frown of concentration was replaced briefly by a smile "and… and… and he's covered in shit." With that his eyes closed and he slumped forward in the chair.

"Thanks Doc," said Reagan over his shoulder as he headed back towards his cabin, followed by the Executive Officer and the Signals Officer.

When they arrived in the cabin the deck plans of the *Sea Shadow* were spread over the low coffee table in the centre of the room and Reagan looked at them thoughtfully.

"Well," he said slowly, "we know a little more but we couldn't say we know much more. Summarise for me, Exec."

"Well sir, ten pirates max ties in with what we've seen and eight or nine is more likely because of the size of the boat they came in. Keeping the hostages in the crew cabins forward would be sensible because they can be secured. They all have en-suite so there's no need to let them out to take a shit. The guy Louis told us how many crew there were and if he's right they'd need three cabins probably."

They continued poring over the plans and discussing the possibilities for another half an hour before putting together a signal reporting the developing situation.

TWENTY-FOUR

The old Leander class frigate was at sea once more. The clutter of stores and equipment had been sorted out into several broad groups but nothing had been properly stowed. Weapons and ammunition were below in the magazines, food, utensils, and other domestic stores were scattered in various locations leading off the main passageway along 'two' deck and a variety of other items filled the helicopter hangar while a quantity of paint and spray painting kit had been carried forward to the paint store in the forepeak of the ship. Wires, ropes, fenders, and other bits of rigging were still being sorted out. The tiny engine room team had achieved a near miracle by correctly identifying toolboxes, spares and other paraphernalia to the extent that they knew what they had got and where it was all located.

The trip down from Faslane had been surprisingly uneventful. All the old fuel in the ship had been removed, the tanks cleaned and refilled, and now both diesel units were running sweetly. A quick diversion, wearing the merchant fleet red ensign had been necessary into Carrick Roads, off Falmouth, in order to collect another bundle of stores deemed essential by somebody, but now the ship was out and running south. Everybody onboard seemed surprised at how such an elderly vessel, laid up for so long, had been able to respond to the sudden demands placed on her but some wondered how long that could last.

The truth, thought Charlie de Vere as he settled into the tall swivel chair on the Bridge, was probably easy to work out. Before the ship had been laid up very little demand had been in reality placed on her. Most of her early life had been spent in various dockyards while a steady flow of equipment was installed to be assessed at sea. This meant the heavy demands of service and weather normally placed on such a ship had been absent in her early days and when she had been finally parked in the remote Scottish loch it had been with a clear expectation that she was going to be sold. The Naval authorities wanted the ship to be able to attract a buyer as quickly as possible so time, money and effort was spent in making sure that she was serviceable in all respects and preserved as well as possible. Sadly for the Ministry of Defence, no foreign navy wanted to buy a one-off semi obsolescent ship so she stayed in her bleak Scottish home until called once more to duty.

The initial assessment that her hull and general systems were in good condition under layers of weed and dirt was an understatement. She was in fact, in very good condition, just a little bit old.

By the time they had worked their way across the Channel separation lanes Charlie, guided by what Dan Holloway was prepared to recommend, had nursed the ship up to eighteen knots and everything was still holding together. It was agreed that after rounding Ushant and keeping clear of another set of traffic separation lanes they would try to creep up to twenty knots or even a little more.

Refuelling was going to be a slight problem because they did not have sufficient manpower to do a proper underway replenishment. They were scheduled to meet an obsolete

Ranger class tanker between Cape Trafalgar and Gibraltar who would trail a fuel line so they could do an astern refuelling. This would be also necessary at the eastern end of the Mediterranean but no details had yet been offered for that rendezvous.

It would be necessary to maintain a discreet low profile and so several ruses with paint and canvas were to be employed to change the appearance of the ship from time to time, as well as continuing to fly the red ensign.

*

By the time they had passed Ushant and moved into the wide expanse of the Bay of Biscay the frigate was becoming organised for its task. One important point had been solved, which seemed to make everyone happier and less nervous. The ship had a name.

'Henry' King, the Chief Boatswain's mate, had announced that his last ship in the Navy had been a frigate of the same class, called *Andromeda.* He said that *Andromeda's* Mum according to mythological legend was *Cassiopeia.* Nobody else among the small crew was sufficiently knowledgeable to challenge this and so the ship became *Cassiopeia.* Very quickly this became *Cassie.*

Charlie de Vere spent most of his time on the Bridge during the first few days. As a naval aviator it had been quite some time since he had kept a watch on the Bridge of a warship and the layout of this old ship was entirely unfamiliar to him, as it was, he suspected, to the rest of his crew. In any case, much of the equipment surrounding him was commercial stuff that had been installed at the last minute and it was all a bit of a lash up.

If Charlie had made himself aware of what the rest of his polyglot crew were up to his outlook would have been considerably brighter.

Tom Clarke, assisted by Jimmy McCoy, had spent the thirty-six hours since leaving Falmouth very productively. The upper deck was now clear and although some boxes and packages still littered part of the ship's company dining hall and the larger adjacent messes, they had reached the stage where they knew what equipment they had, and in most instances what it was for. They were careful in identifying stowage spaces because they wanted to avoid the possibility of not knowing where to find important items when they needed them.

Food was easy to deal with. It was generally obvious when packages contained food and it was easy to decide where it should go. They had a good supply of frozen food and some fresh, as well as a lot of tinned stuff. Only about one third of the ship's cold room space was working and none of the main cool rooms but that had been addressed by shipping in several large one hundred and ten volt commercial freezer fridges and wedging them into position around the galley. The two cooks had identified what they needed and then modified it to match what they had. The galley stoves were both working and, given the circumstances, the whole crew were already feeding surprisingly well. There had been no complaints.

A boxed commercial Raytheon Radar Set was now up and running and a second set was almost ready as well. VHF, HF and UHF radios had been quickly unearthed and were now set up in the resurrected Operations Room, in addition to a sophisticated satellite phone which had been supplied and delivered by Maggie McGuigan. This compact and rugged little unit came with built-in encryption, burst transmission and a printer. It also ran from its own rechargeable battery. A number of UHF and VHF portable radios were spread around the ship to complete the communication arrangements.

Henry King with four of the seamen were busy with quantities of wire, rope, rigging kits, blocks, shackles, timber, canvas and a huge quantity of paint in different colours none of which matched the ship's original grey paint.

On the flight deck and in the hangar, Brian Hall and his two gunnery experts were carefully sorting through a bizarre selection of weaponry and ammunition while trying to understand what they had been given and how the extensive arsenal could best be used.

The ship had no main or secondary armament of her own and so someone had tried to redress the balance by supplying a range of weaponry, mostly small arms that could be used against unsophisticated foes. Two Mk 46 and two Stingray torpedoes gave the ex-Royal Marine his greatest headache. The ship had been fitted with one set of torpedo launching tubes on the port side forward of the hangar but nobody seemed to know much about launching torpedoes and the torpedo tubes looked as though they had provided homes for sea birds in the recent past. Brian could have tried to fit a torpedo into one of the tubes but he was deterred by the nagging thought of how he would explain away a sophisticated weapon like that being found in a ship that was supposed to be on its way to the scrapyard. He resolved the problem by sending one of the lads away to the paint shop and then painting along the side of each torpedo 'DUMMY – FOR DRILL PURPOSES ONLY'.

The rest of the weaponry was easier to understand and for the most part all that had to be done was sort it out, identify it and store it away down below as inaccessibly as possible.

By the time the last items had been cleared away Brian concluded that he had enough weaponry to start a small war and then had enough left over to make a substantial return at an arms fair.

From the brief discussions which had taken place when they had assembled before embarking at Faslane, Brian was aware that the likely tasks facing them would need primarily small arms and short range weapons of slightly greater hitting power.

They had thirty SA80a2 rifles with telescopic sights, a hundred and fifty magazines and twenty thousand rounds of 5.56 millimetre ammunition. Thirty bayonets and twenty grenade launchers made up the set.

Thirty Heckler and Koch SA80 Carbines and ten Bonelli M4 Combat Semi-Automatic Shotguns complete with about a thousand cartridges provided an alternative to the SA80 assault rifles. The haul of light armament was completed by several larger wooden crates which contained ten Minimi Light Machine Guns, six 7.62 millimetre General Purpose Machine Guns and One belt fed .50 calibre Heavy Machine Gun, all complete with ammunition.

The last items which Brian's team tackled were the heavy weapons. Several cases of Milan Shoulder Launched anti tank missiles, some boxes of hand grenades, two 81 millimetre mortars and one 120 millimetre mortar, were broken down into several crates, as well as a relic that resembled an old army field gun modified with some strange base plates.

Leaving his team to check – as best they could – the remaining large weapons, Brian hurried up to the Bridge to explain to his new Captain what they were carrying.

"What?" said Charlie when the list of weaponry was spelled out to him. "Are we supposed to be arming a battalion of pongoes?"

"Well," replied Brian, thoughtfully, "I guess we are supposed to be a ship on our way to the breakers yard so it would look a bit odd if we were bristling with nice smart Navy guns."

Charlie thought for a while. "OK," he said, "but there doesn't seem to be much in the way of heavy weapons if we need to defend ourselves at sea."

"Who is going to attack us?" responded Brian. "As I understand it our primary task will be to recover a rich Arab's yacht without anyone noticing and our only likely opposition will come from those chaps who don't want to lose their nice shiny boat. Anyway, so far as I know, there are no instances where pirates have captured any warships – and I can't see there being any…"

Charlie interrupted him, "But we're a ship. All those rifles and so on won't count for a row of beans if the enemy sits behind some steel bulkheads."

"We've got the mortars – and the Heavy Machine Gun." Brian waited for a reply.

Charlie looked belligerent. "What good are they – in a ship," he snapped back.

Brian was unmoved. "Well, if you know your naval history you will have heard of carronades," he said. "They are like an unsophisticated inaccurate mortar system and they worked quite well by all accounts."

"Yeah, but mortars, so my recollection of brown jobs tells me, need a steady flat base. This platform rolls around a bit," said Charlie.

Brian was unmoved. "OK," he said. "They won't be as accurate but we can fire when the deck is reasonably level –

we can measure that in fact, with a couple of spirit levels. And anyway, a few bombs raining down around the pirates will scare the shit out of them."

"We just want them to put their hands up and come quietly," said Charlie, drily. Brian gave up. "Suit yourself," he said, "I've got things to do. His stomach was calling him and he decided to join the others in the queue at the main galley.

Three hours later Brian was back on the Bridge clutching several pieces of paper. Charlie was still slouched in the chair and an empty plate was set on the shelf in front of him with the remains of sandwiches on it.

"I've worked out how we should set up the heavier weapons," said Brian carefully. Charlie swivelled his chair to face him. On the far side of the Bridge Jimmy McCoy was peering through binoculars. The Bridge was completely darkened with only the glowing red and amber instrument lights contrasting the blackness outside.

"We can set up the 120 millimetre mortar on the fore deck and the two 81 millimetre mortars on the flight deck." Brian ploughed on, "The GPMG should be set up as high as possible – probably the signal deck, and two LMGs mounted on the Bridge wings. The 'Milans' we can move around wherever we want and we can weld or bolt the mortar base plates to the deck and keep the rest out of sight."

Charlie was tired and didn't want to argue so he said, "OK give it to me."

As Brian opened his mouth to speak, Jimmy called from the other side of the Bridge. "Skipper there's a ship, wide on the port beam and he seems to be matching us for speed and is steadily closing."

Charlie jerked around, adrenalin rushing him to full alertness. "Can you make out what she looks like?" he called across the Bridge, and then back to Brian, "I hope you've got all your toys tucked away."

Brian had in any case moved to the back of the Bridge and was hidden behind a small curtained alcove, peering into the radar. "I have a contact at three and a half miles on radar but nothing in that position on AIS," he called, then followed up with, "No AIS, darkened and matching our speed suggests a warship – but I wonder whose?"

At that moment a bright white light stabbed out of the darkness from the port beam. Short, long, pause, short long, then again short long. "Bloody hell!" exploded Charlie, "have we got a signalman?"

"He's asking 'what ship?' I'll send him a long 'wait'," said Jimmy as he heaved open the port wing door. He threw the switch on the big signal projector and cursed when nothing happened.

Brian emerged from behind the curtain with a portable lamp in his hand. "Here," he said, "give him one long flash on this." Jimmy took the lamp and pointed it in the direction of the small corvette type ship which was now just becoming visible on the port beam. He pressed the trigger, counted one, two, and let go.

Brian was furiously whirling the handle of a sound powered phone to no effect when Charlie picked up the heavy rubber microphone for the main broadcast which had been hanging by its curly lead over the arm of his chair.

"Signalman to the bridge – now." His voice boomed out all over the ship, startling the others on the Bridge. They waited.

Less than a minute later, hasty noisy steps on the ladder heralded the tousled head of Tim Kay, sometime signals rating in Her Majesty's Navy.

Dropping back into a previous world he took the lamp from Jimmy and while aiming it out to port, said over his shoulder, "I'm rusty but I'll do my best, sir." Inconsequentially, Charlie was for a moment struck by the thought that this was the first time anyone on board had actually called him sir.

Pushing that aside he said, "Can you tell him 'British government owned ship *Cassie* heading zero nine zero, speed twenty. What ship are you?'" Tim started flashing the message, hesitantly at first, then faster and with more confidence. He waited a full minute until the light came stabbing out of the night once more.

Still staring into the blackness, Tim called out the answer he was reading: "French warship *Sourcouf,* bon voyage."

There was a collective and audible sigh of relief across the Bridge. Brian decided to tackle the weapons question in the morning.

TWENTY-FIVE

It was three hours later – nearly midnight – when the East African Airways scheduled flight from London rolled to a standstill in front of the arrivals terminal of the Julius Nyerere Airport at Dar es Salaam. The plane was not full but full enough to allow the four or five small groups of Europeans to pass through customs and immigration without calling any attention to themselves. The three couples and four men on their own gathered their meagre baggage, then waited at immigration while the usual irrelevant questions were posed by a bored immigration officer in a sweat stained uniform. Their British, Bahamian and American passports were given barely a glance before they wandered out into the cool African night to pick the least ramshackle looking taxis from the twenty or so waiting around in disarray, many with the driver fast asleep inside.

The trip from the airport wound through a variety of, old, new, traditional and modern suburbs heading for three different hotels in the centre of town. Curiously, each taxi meandered through the streets taking a different route to the others.

Harry Mullen who was to command the patrol boat checked in to the brilliant white Protea Courtyard Hotel with Karen Ford strolling along beside him. As they walked through the lush gardens, their luggage having already disappeared ahead of them, Karen looked wistfully around at the immaculate lawns and gently waving palms and said, “Perhaps we could stay for a week?” Harry said nothing. Not far away a taxi was stopping on Sokoine Drive outside the even more striking Kilimanjaro Hotel Kempinski. Two men piled out and, barely acknowledging each other, made their separate ways towards reception. Their separate identities were further supported by the vastly different grades of rooms booked for them. Gerry Tan had drawn the shorter straw and he was in a pleasant and well-furnished room in the main building – the older part of the hotel complex. Mike Cowley, the engineer, on the other hand, was to be cosseted in luxury in a suite near the top of one of the twin towers. Ten minutes later the third taxi arrived and deposited Paddy Stone the cook and ‘seaman’ Jane York who were ushered off to a spacious room with twin beds, armchairs and a long sofa underneath the window.

“You get the sofa,” said Jane.

A couple of miles away on the corner of Haile Selassie Street and Ali Hassan Mwinyi Road stood a much more modest, quieter and smaller establishment – the Protea Oyster Bay Hotel. This was where the remainder of the crew were staying. Peter Archer and Jimmy James arrived separately followed some time later by Billy Walker and Frankie Zambelas, whose journey had been interrupted while their driver paused to collect his wife, who rode the remainder of the journey in the front seat.

*

The life had gone out of the sea as the frigate, now known to everyone on board as ‘*Cassie*’, sailed steadily south keeping about one hundred miles to seaward of the Iberian

Peninsula in order to avoid the shipping routes emerging from the Mediterranean and the coastal traffic running up and down the Portuguese Coast. The ship's appearance had changed again as Henry King and his boys had continued to disguise the outline with canvas and paint. She had no guns or other visible weapons and had also lost her distinctive surveillance radar aerial. The hull and superstructure was now painted a dull matt black and canvas screens had been erected, also painted black, which to the casual observer made the hull look as if the ship was flush decked and not at all like the typical frigate shape of raised bow and dropped quarterdeck. Her black paint which looked uneven and scruffy, also had very effective radar absorbing qualities so any radar signals bouncing back from the unappealing black hulled ship would show up as a tiny contact more indicative of a small yacht, or perhaps they would not register at all.

As the previous night's middle watch – the 'graveyard watch' had handed over to the morning watch, a brief message had been received on the secure satellite phone providing nothing more than the prefix 'one' and a time and a position, followed by 'two' and a second time and position. These were the refuelling rendezvous arranged for the beginning and end of their passage through the Mediterranean.

As the sun nudged the eastern horizon Tom Clarke arrived on the Bridge and crossed to the starboard side where Charlie was slumped in the tall swivel chair, hunched down inside a thick sheepskin coat. Nobby Small was perched in the helmsman's seat opposite the set of handlebars which replaced the usual ship's wheel. Tom looked across and Nobby asked, "Coffee, boss?"

As Tom turned to answer, Charlie raised his head rubbed his eyes and said, "It would be great, Nobby, if you could convert that to a cup of thick steaming Kai made in the traditional way and keep it company with a big greasy bacon sandwich."

Nobby held up three fingers and looked questioningly across to Tom who nodded and said, "I'll watch the helm."

"OK." Nobby moved towards the ladder at the back of the Bridge. "She's in auto but watch it 'cos she drops out when you're not looking." With that he disappeared down the ladder.

Tom said, "Well, it's a beautiful fine morning Captain and if it stays like this I've got an idea that might be worth trying."

Charlie yawned and stretched, before slipping down from the chair. "OK. Shoot," he said.

Tom glanced across towards the helm and, turning back to Charlie, said, "The plan is to do a stern refuelling when we find the tanker because we may not have the kit to do an alongside replenishment, haven't got the muscle to pull over the jackstay or the hose and we haven't got the experience or knowledge to do it anyway. Am I right?"

"That's about it," said Charlie.

"Well, Henry reckons we do have the hands, we do have the muscle and we have the know-how to do the job alongside – and I'm bound to say I think I agree with him. But the main thing is if we can do an alongside replenishment we could save about three or four hours."

"He's a bloody good 'Buffer'," said Charlie. "There's no doubt about that." He pondered for a moment and then said, "Let's get him up here and talk it through."

At that moment two things happened. Nobby appeared back at the top of the Bridge ladder carefully carrying a makeshift tray laden with steaming mugs and a plate piled high with doorstep sized bacon sandwiches and the helm dropped out of automatic control, allowing the ship to start a slow turn to port. Nobby thrust the tray into Tom's hands and grabbed the handlebars, immediately easing the ship's head marker back towards one eight zero degrees. He pressed a button and the pair of flashing red lights showing the departure from the set course abruptly flicked out.

For the next few minutes the Bridge was silent except for slight creaking noises as the old ship responded to the needs of the sea. The three men munched the sandwiches and sipped tentatively at their steaming mugs of Kai – the thick sweet cocoa made from shavings from blocks of rich bitter chocolate, favoured as the invigorating drink of seamen who are routinely exposed to a harsh environment.

As the last of the sandwiches disappeared, Charlie said through a mouthful of bread and bacon, "Alright, let's talk it through." Grabbing the heavy rubber broadcast microphone he pressed 'transmit' and said, "Buffer to the Bridge." They waited.

Less than three minutes later the open face of the Chief Boatswain's Mate or 'Buffer' appeared at the top of the ladder. Ex-Chief Petty Officer 'Henry' King saluted smartly and said, "Morning sir."

"No need for the formality, Buffer. We're none of us in the Navy now," responded Charlie.

"If it's all the same to you sir, and since we're in a 'pussers' ship – even given that it's an old one, I think a bit o' the old ways wouldn't hurt. It'd make me feel a bit less lost anyway   sir." Henry tailed off into silence.

"OK. Have it your own way," responded Charlie, placing his empty mug on the front shelf.

Tom interrupted, preventing any further discussion on the niceties of shipboard discipline. "The Buffer reckons we have the kit and the manpower to do an alongside replenishment, and to quote him, it should be a doddle as well as taking half the time while keeping the ship going at twice the speed. Tell us how you'd do it, Henry."

At the back of the Bridge, Dan Holloway, still in his white engineer's overalls, had quietly joined the group, standing just behind the others.

Henry took a deep breath. "If this weather stays with us then I can't see much of a problem," he said. "The ship will be fairly steady and if we get everyone up here, less the Skipper and the Quartermaster, then we have twenty-nine blokes and that should be enough to haul in the Messenger and get the hose across."

"My boys will all be present at the fuelling point," said Dan Holloway.

Charlie turned away and stared out through the forward Bridge windows. It was true that they had on board the couplings, cordage, flags and other equipment necessary for an alongside refuelling but the equipment was ancient and untried. In the past he would have put thirty men to the task of heaving in the heavy fuelling hose and holding it in position until couplings were connected and the other lines were all in place. Although the ship could scrape together almost thirty men that would be using every man on board and if anything started to go wrong it would very likely escalate quickly and with possibly devastating consequences.

On the other hand, the planned astern refuelling, although a much longer process needing only enough men to grapnel the hose being trailed astern of the tanker and heave it inboard using the forecastle capstan, was much more certain. It would then be fairly straightforward to maintain station alongside the marker buoy being towed behind the tanker, but it would take ages because the tanker would necessarily be maintaining a speed of no more than about eight knots. Connecting up, although easier would take longer and the whole thing, in terms of distance, would leave them perhaps fifty miles further back than they would be if they tried the alongside method. But if that were to go wrong, he thought, we might have to turn round and go home. He continued to stare through the windscreen, not really seeing anything, for several minutes. The others waited in silence.

Gently and quietly, Henry interrupted the Skipper's thoughts. "If we put an extra block 'n tackle on the inhaul we could use less blokes," he said.

"Fewer blokes, Henry." Charlie regretted his pompous correction as soon as he said it and added quickly, "OK, we'll give it a try. Decision made. We go for an alongside refuel," he said to the group.

Henry looked pleased. Charlie turned to look out at the sea then continued, "Tom, can you get on the Satphone and see if you can get that message through to the tanker? I think they may well have been told just to set up for an astern run."

"Roger that," said Tom as he turned and left the Bridge. The others followed him away down the ladder, leaving Charlie climbing back into his chair and Nobby, now collecting empty mugs while casting suspicious glances back towards the helm which was back in automatic.

Down on the flight deck, Henry was already assembling his team, explaining in detail to each man exactly what was expected of him and patiently repeating his instructions until he was sure they had been hoisted in.

In the Main Communications Office, Tom had started to address the problem of contacting the tanker. The only Satphone numbers he had were the four numbers which had been made available in the written instructions they had been given before embarkation.

It had been made clear to the key people – the officers – Jack Lang had kept calling them, that the whole operation was to remain 'black' – completely deniable and therefore the only contacts that were to be allowed were between the two ships, Jack's base at Buckland House, and with Maggie McGuigan at Carrick House, and only there in the event of being unable to contact Buckland House. There was one more number which they had been told could only be used once and that was to contact the extraction force when that became necessary.

The two duplicate sets of Satphone communication equipment provided were curious lumpy metal boxes where communication was achieved by typing the message out on a rugged looking keyboard. This enabled a constant scrambling of any message. The message was stored in the unit and sent as a micro-burst transmission. Because of the scrambling system there was an extended delay before each transmission was answered, which made the whole process seem lengthy and cumbersome.

It took Tom over half an hour to get his message through and to confirm firstly that he was not asking permission to change the refuelling system but that he simply wished to announce the onboard decision. He asked the name of the tanker, which information was immediately refused to him with a directive that there should be no communication with the tanker other than directions concerning the fuel transfer when the rendezvous was made. His assertion that a great deal of time could be saved had convinced the operator at the other end of the line, and eventually Tom was able to make his way back to the Bridge to tell Charlie that the alongside refuelling could go ahead and to repeat the instructions he had been given about the tanker.

*

At an hour past midnight as the frigate passed through the sea which had once run red with the blood of the sailors of both sides in the Battle of Trafalgar, the Bridge radar picked up a firm contact fifteen miles ahead steaming slowly southwest. Charlie called for more power, and in the Machinery Control Room Mike Carter ran up each gas turbine in turn and engaged them to the drive system. The ship responded quickly to the demand for twenty-five knots and within only fifteen minutes the silhouette of a large ship could be made out in the thin moonlight.

In a further fifteen minutes the unlit shape had formed itself into the unmistakable outline of a small Ranger class former Fleet Replenishment Tanker. The sea was still remarkably calm and although his hands were damp with sweat, and the tension was like a bar across his shoulders, Charlie brought the *Cassie* up alongside the tanker in a textbook manoeuvre, slotting neatly into place and adjusting to the speed of the tanker as though he performed the operation every day. He eased the black frigate in as close as he dared and the big fuelling derrick leaned ponderously outward over the gap between the two ships. A gun line was fired from the tanker and the necessary ropes were hauled across. The Chief Boatswain's Mate's sweating heaving gang dug in their heels and laid back on the rope as the fuel hose came inboard. It took longer than it should have done to connect the hose to the deck inlet but as soon as it was complete Dan waved the signal and fuel began to flow. Two and a half hours later, everything was disconnected and the frigate sheered away in classic style. On the deck of the tanker two anonymous figures clad in blue overalls and white hardhats gave them a farewell wave.

Charlie made an adjustment to the course and increased speed as the ship pointed towards the Straits of Gibraltar, aiming to pass through before the night was ended. As they passed the familiar outline of the Rock, ablaze with lights, they received another message revising the next refuelling point at the far end of the Mediterranean.

TWENTY-SIX

In Dar es Salaam, Harry Mullen was sitting in the back of an air-conditioned Toyota Land Cruiser with Karen Ford, now in the guise of his Personal Assistant, seated beside him. In the front seat a man with a dark brown complexion and Arabic features was leaning over the seat back extolling the virtues of Tanzania in general and of their unwanted patrol boat in particular. They drove the short distance to the commercial docks then south along the dock line, threading their way carefully between the piles of containers and other detritus which inevitably clutter most docksides. The Tanzanian Government representative kept up a running commentary all the way.

Eventually they passed beyond the rows of bulk carriers and container ships waiting to complete loading and followed the road as it narrowed and curved inland around the edge of a new marina. As they drew to a stop Harry glanced towards a similar Toyota Land Cruiser, alongside which stood a small group. Gerry and Mike from the Kilimanjaro were already on board, wearing identical black blousons with the motif 'Hamble Ship Surveys' emblazoned across the back. Occasionally one or the other emerged onto the upper deck, one making notes on a clipboard and the other talking earnestly into a small hand-held recorder – which was not actually switched on. Jimmy James, Billy Walker and

Frankie Zambelas stood around looking like holidaymakers waiting for the tour guide, while of the other three there was no sign. Harry made a show of introducing himself and shaking hands with everybody on the dockside, making a statement to any unseen observer that they were all gathered together for the first time, for the purpose of collecting and ferrying the small warship to some unidentified third party.

When Gerry and Mike appeared, the handshaking charade continued afresh, then the government man who, curiously, went by the name of 'Maurice', insisted on leading Harry and his two 'surveyors' around the ship once more, proudly pointing out what he believed, erroneously, to be the salient features. Fatuous questions were asked by the tourists in order to show interest but in fact they knew the answers already. Finally, in the compact Wardroom a sheaf of papers was signed, one by one, by Harry while Mike went away to check fuel samples with a portable test kit. The group on the dockside had begun to wilt in the rising heat reflected off the concrete and had taken refuge inside one of the air-conditioned Land Cruisers.

At last, after two hours of inconsequential nonsense, Harry gave a little speech extolling the patience, skill, knowledge and understanding of their temporary chaperone 'Maurice' and shook him warmly by the hand while pressing a thick wad of twenty dollar bills discreetly into his sweating palm. All three men escorted their new friend to the gangway and waited while he boarded his Land Cruiser and was driven away, waving happily from inside the tinted glass window.

As soon as the Land Cruiser had disappeared the other three crew members emerged from the remaining vehicle, strolled over to the edge of the dock beside the boat, stood while they were given a loud summary of their duties by Harry, concluding with a stern lecture on the perils of going to sea in small boats and some general aspects of health and safety. Heads down and looking oppressed they slunk aboard. The driver of the second Land Cruiser slammed the back door shut, climbed aboard, turned the vehicle in a wide circle and drove off back along the docks.

Half an hour later all three main engines and one of the domestic gas turbines were running when a battered taxi pulled up alongside and disgorged the last three members of the crew. They opened the boot of the taxi and hauled out numerous bags of local groceries and dragged them on board. Ten minutes later, the lines were cast off and the small patrol boat moved slowly towards the harbour entrance leaving behind it a haze of hot air from the gas turbines.

The original plan of taking the boat away from Dar es Salaam with minimum crew and picking up the remainder from a beach further to the south had been abandoned as impractical. Firstly, the whole crew would be needed to operate the unfamiliar vessel and secondly, it had been discovered that no confidence could be placed in the willingness or ability of the safari guides to get them to the correct beach. Additionally, questions would be asked when the crewmen and women disappeared off the beach into a mystery boat. Bribes and a remote dockside would have to do instead.

During the tour round the boat, nobody had mentioned the object lashed securely under a tarpaulin in the centre of the fore deck. As they moved away from the harbour entrance Billy Walker and Peter Archer were gathered around the object loosening the yards of rope holding the canvas in place. Eventually Peter lifted one side and poked his head underneath. After thirty seconds or so he emerged, nodded to Billy and said, “Take a look.”

Peter held the side of the cover against the increasing wind as the boat gathered speed while Billy disappeared completely under the cover. He emerged more quickly than his companion, a wide grin spreading across his face.

"Bofors forty millimetre," he said. "And it looks to be fully automatic."

"A very shiny thing," said Peter, "and a lovely new toy."

Both men were former gunnery specialists and although neither had previously encountered this particular version of the famous Bofors gun they decided to take the weapon on as if it was their own. They didn't speak as they struggled to secure the tarpaulin around the gun once more. They were of one mind and words were unnecessary, and in any case the rising wind over the deck made it difficult to hear anything being said. Each man was happy at having discovered an unexpected new toy.

The patrol boat-cum-cabin cruiser, now thought of by its new crew as a 'gunboat', turned onto an easterly heading, gradually increased speed on the three gas turbines and climbed up onto the plane, slicing through the water at a relatively modest twenty-five knots. While most of the crew were getting used to the motion of the boat, Mike Cowley, now clad in white overalls with a big set of 'ear-defenders' clamped over an old naval beret and a set of safety goggles, was moving methodically through and around the cramped machinery spaces. He carried an adjustable spanner in his hand and in the leg pockets of his overalls, a pair of insulated pliers and a couple of screwdrivers, so his progress through the ship was heralded by a metallic clinking. He started with a grim expression and pursed lips but became more visibly relaxed as he checked each piece of equipment and found no liquid or gas leaks. Everything looked and smelled new and he was smiling as he completed his task and climbed up into the sunshine on the open Bridge.

By this time the low lying coastline had disappeared astern and the boat had altered course to the south.

"She's good," said Mike as he pulled off the beret and ear-defenders. "You can wind up the revs and see what she will do if you like."

Harry Mullen and Gerry Tan were both occupying the small Bridge and Harry ducked below the forward screen, nodded to Mike then shouted, "Ease her up to 40, Gerry."

"Aye aye skipper," responded Gerry as he grasped the three aircraft type throttle levers and pushed them together very steadily forward. The boat responded like a true thoroughbred. The bows angled up slightly as the speed increased but other than that and an evident increase in the power of the slipstream, nothing changed.

Underneath the Bridge the space had been utilised as Operations Room, Communication Centre and Weapon Control Room. Frankie Zambelas was working her way through several VHF radio frequencies in an attempt to contact the ship they were to rendezvous with and which hopefully would provide them with weapons.

*

The rendezvous they had been given was just off the southeast corner of a large island some ninety miles to the south of Dar es Salaam, near a lagoon-like inlet called Chloe Bay on the south-eastern tip of the island. The island was under-populated but it did have a small airfield with a paved runway about one thousand yards in length, near a place called Kilindoni, which appeared to be the only significant centre of population. The island presented the intriguing name of ‘Mafia Island’ and the airfield called itself ‘Mafia Airfield’.

The gunboat drove steadily south, settling down at just under forty knots in an almost flat sea while the sorting and storing activity continued below deck. Frankie patiently repeated her search of the air waves for their radio contact but apart from one indecipherable burst of static lasting ten seconds, without success.

Over the next three hours the gunboat continued steadily south until, with the sun hovering just above the western horizon they dropped down to ten knots and slid off the plane. They rumbled along deeper in the water, altering course occasionally to avoid distant contacts appearing on the radar and waiting for the sun to set.

As soon as the upper limb of the sun had dropped below the horizon and the short equatorial twilight had turned to night they increased speed again, sitting comfortably at eighteen knots and passing small islets, one after another like maritime signposts pointing the way towards the main island. They kept this up for about two hours, by which time the left side of the multi-coloured radar screen had begun to fill with the bulk of Mafia Island. Harry Mullen returned from a surprisingly good supper and took over the watch from Gerry. As soon as he was settled he eased the throttles back down again and the speed dropped to a crawl. In the Operations Room below, Frankie was once again trying to raise their contact but this time she was transmitting a three letter group T P B, with a break, then the numbers ‘Four’ and ‘Five’, before waiting for five minutes and then repeating the process.

It was nearly four the following morning before any acknowledgement was received. By this time the boat was just drifting with all lights extinguished and the engines just ticking over. Although the rest of the boat was quiet the Bridge was crowded with four lookouts and both Harry and Gerry. Harry was becoming increasingly nervous. They were completely unarmed and sitting in the lower part of what had become known as 'Pirate Alley'. If trouble discovered them they would need to use their speed in order to escape. He was also acutely aware that despite the assurances given before leaving England they could simply be walking, or rather floating, into an elaborate trap.

When the signal came in, a repeat of what they had transmitted followed by dot dash dot – the letter 'R', repeated three times, they had five tiny contacts within radar range. Two were fifteen miles to the west and behaving like typical fishing vessels, one more, on its own was ten miles to the southwest and moving north at ten knots – a course which would bring the ship to within two miles of the gunboat if they stayed still. Another very small contact had been sitting perfectly stationary eighteen miles to the east and only a few miles from the coast of Mafia Island. The fifth contact seemed to be steering an erratic course around the southern tip of a group of tiny atolls close to the main island.

"Repeat the recognition signal," said Harry into the speaking tube to the Operations Room. Immediately, they heard the dots and dashes going out on the Bridge speaker. A long dash signified the letter 'T', then dot dash dash dot, giving 'P' and finally a dash followed by three dots, the letter 'B'. Frankie was working the keys slowly and clearly, giving time for a novice operator to work out each letter before moving on to the next. Almost immediately, the three letter 'R's came bouncing back, rather faster than previously as if the operator somewhere out in the blackness was trying to demonstrate his familiarity with the code and the system.

"Did you get a bearing on that?" called Harry into the speaking tube.

Peter, who was peering intently at the screen of a radio direction finder that had travelled within his suitcase as medical equipment, chirped up, "Yes got it Skipper, clean as a whistle, and the bearing correlates with the radar contact just to the south and slightly east of us."

"We'll assume that's him," said Harry as he eased forward the throttles once more and, turning to the former lookout who was now helmsman, said, "Steer one six zero."

"One six zero," was repeated quietly as the boat picked up speed and turned slowly towards the apparent source of the signals some twelve miles to the south.

They travelled cautiously south, tension building up throughout the ship but showing mostly on the faces of the two 'officers' on the Bridge. Suddenly, the voice of Peter came up the speaking tube.

"Skipper," he said, "We should uncover the gun on the forecastle."

"We have no ammunition," said Harry.

"They don't know that, and if they're not friendly, waving it about towards them might bluff us enough time to get the hell out of it."

Harry thought for a moment. "OK uncover the gun," he said firmly.

Within seconds, two of the crew were scrambling down from the Bridge to the foredeck to clear the lashings and remove the cover from the gun. Harry looked uncertain then smiled quietly to himself. "Nothing ventured, nothing gained," he muttered half under his breath.

*

The first silver grey pre-dawn light was just beginning to change the sky above the eastern horizon when Gerry, staring through binoculars said, “Think I’ve got him.”

The boat was now moving slowly south and edging closer to the darkened looming mass of the island as several pairs of binoculars joined Gerry, who was still staring fixedly towards the target, which was fully darkened and hard to pick out against the thick line of trees and vegetation which swept right down to a narrow strip of beach.

“Give the light signal, Tango Papa,” said Harry without moving the binoculars from his eyes. Someone stepped up to the eight inch signal lamp mounted at the starboard side of the Bridge, flicked the master switch on and clattered out two letters in Morse Code. As the final dot of the letter ‘P’ dissolved into the night, a bright light shot a long beam out of the darkness ahead of them, went out and then shone out again, twice.

Harry opened the throttles once again and the bows of the boat angled upward as the three gas turbines thrust it forward. “Alert, everybody. Keep your heads down and watch out for any odd movements.” As they closed the distance their target began to take shape and formed itself into a steel hulled black and rust coloured fishing boat about fifty feet in length with two sets of masts and derricks, each of which supported a tangle of nets and ropes.

As they closed the boat the usual smell of burnt diesel which surrounded the gunboat was overtaken by a strong stink of old fish. Several of the gunboat’s crew clasped hands over mouth and nose as the smell increased to make it almost tangible.

Harry eased back the throttles and called across the diminishing gap between the boats, “Allah Ahkbar!” From someone unseen among the shabby figures lurking within the gloom of the fishing boat came an answering call, “Allah Ahkbar!” Nobody aboard the gunboat relaxed and Harry was conscious that Peter Archer, and Paddy Stone, the cook, were both standing on the deck below the Bridge and each of them had an impressive looking knife. The cook was holding a long black handled carving knife and Peter had what looked like a Malay parang hanging from his belt.

Harry could make out perhaps six men moving about the cluttered deck of the fishing boat. Most of them seemed to be African but at least two of them had distinctly Arabic features. One of these moved to the side of the fishing boat and looking up to the gunboat shouted, “You must be Harry.” His English was good but retained a slight trace of accent, although not strong enough to be identifiable.

“I am Anwar,” he said, and then, rather formally. “How do you do?”

Harry moved over to the side of the Bridge and called down, “I’m fine, thank you.”

“I bring greetings from my master,” called Anwar as the two vessels touched gently together.

“Do you bring anything else?” Harry called back, feeling some of the tension of the last few minutes begin to dissipate.

“Plenty,” came the reply. Harry caught a movement beyond Anwar and as he looked he could see crates and boxes small enough to be manageable, being brought up out of the hold and added to others piled on the fishing boat’s fore deck. As the pile grew bigger so the stink of rancid fish grew stronger.

Noticing the expressions of disgust which had appeared generally on the faces of the gunboat’s crew, Anwar looked up to the Bridge again and said, “Vile isn’t it – but then we do get used to it, and it tends to keep authority away from us;

they think their nice uniforms will never be the same again – and they're probably right."

Harry slipped out of sight on the Bridge and appeared a few moments later on the starboard side deck. "Do you know what you are giving us?" he asked.

"Nope," said Anwar. "It's better that way. If we don't know, we can't tell. I trust my boys all the way but they like a drink when we get in and when they've had a skin-full of mealy beer they'll tell anybody anything. Fortunately nobody ever believes them. They just think they are bragging to get more beer."

While Anwar was talking, the cargo was being passed quickly and efficiently across between the two boats and just as quickly disappearing into the interior of the gunboat. The whole operation was over in less than ten minutes but by that time a band of light had spread along the eastern horizon and the stars were beginning to dim and disappear.

"Skipper, I've got a contact heading this way fast from the direction of the mainland." Frankie had been left on radar watch and now, as she called on the upper deck broadcast her voice was etched with concern. "Twenty knots I think and it's about twenty-five miles away but heading exactly in this direction." As she spoke the tinny reproduction of the broadcast did not hide her concern.

"OK, everybody, we're off," called Harry as he started towards the screen door leading to the Bridge.

Behind him Anwar called out, "Hold on, I'm coming with you." He was already swinging across from the dilapidated fishing boat, carrying a dirty battered holdall in his right hand. As soon as he was aboard the patrol boat he shouted some instructions back towards the wheelhouse of the fishing boat in what sounded like Swahili.

An answering shout came from a black head thrust through the missing window in the fishing boat's wheelhouse. It sounded like, "Yeah, boss."

"Twenty miles, speed increasing, still approaching, contact in about twenty-five minutes. Gunnery range in about twelve minutes." Frankie's voice sounded more steady as she continued to report what she and Harry now regarded as a threat.

"Let go for'ard, let go aft, bear away." Gerry took over and started to ease the throttles forward as Harry reached the conning position in the centre of the Bridge. He was followed by Anwar, still clutching his holdall. Harry turned to face Anwar, bracing himself against the front screen and said, none too politely, "What the hell do you think *you* are doing here?"

"I'm your interpreter," responded Anwar evenly.

"The hell you are!" snarled Harry menacingly.

Anwar was unmoved. "You need an interpreter or you'll all end up dead," he said, staring challengingly back at Harry as the boat continued to gather speed and bounce on the bigger waves.

"Let's go below," said Harry as he unceremoniously shoved his way past Anwar and slid down the Bridge ladder, hands on the side rails and feet clear of the steps.

Anwar followed Harry down into the tiny Wardroom and, without speaking each man flopped down on the couches, facing one another across the table.

Harry glared towards the newcomer. "OK. Give," he said.

Anwar placed his holdall carefully on the seat beside him, rested his hands on the edge of the table and said, "Jack Lang sent me."

The effect on Harry was dramatic. He seemed to sink into himself and diminish like a punctured balloon. "Why didn't you say so?" he challenged.

"You didn't think to ask," came the reply. When Harry said nothing, Anwar continued, "I'm the back-up you might say. If you simply didn't show up for any reason, Jack would need to know why. My number one priority is to keep him informed and my number two priority is to translate any of the local languages for you and generally keep you out of trouble until things boil up."

Harry stuck a hand out "OK," he said, "Welcome aboard. What languages are you going to help us with?"

"Oh, Arabic mostly, and possibly a bit of Swahili," said Anwar. "I would also hope to be able to provide you with some local knowledge – where to get fuel for example."

"We will rendezvous with the other ship coming south from the Gulf of Aden."

Anwar smiled, and leaned forward in his chair, assuming the concerned expression of a schoolmaster about to put a struggling pupil on the right track. "But you will need fuel before that," he said, "and I believe you may need to refuel many times and perhaps you will not be able to return to the same source more than once?" This was posed as a question.

Harry sat in thought for a moment, clutching the side of the bench seat as the movements of the boat became more pronounced. "Increasing speed," he said absently, then, "You're right of course. We could need to refuel possibly three times before we can rendezvous; depends, I suppose, on what crops up."

"I understand that you will receive a signal granting authorisation for specific actions." Anwar spoke slowly, choosing his words with care and Harry wondered how much detail he had been briefed with. A lot, he thought as he framed his response.

"How much have you been told by Jack Lang?" he asked.

"I believe I know what your mission is – your secondary mission apart from rescuing certain important persons. I know that you will await instructions and guidance from time to time and I know a little about your consort ship and her mission – and I am here to help." Anwar smiled benignly. They continued to talk as the little ship forged on northward at a relatively sedate forty knots before reducing speed for half an hour to allow the cook to prepare some food.

TWENTY-SEVEN

In the Mediterranean things were not going quite so well. Shortly after completing the refuelling the weather had deteriorated and the old frigate had run into the Sirocco blowing a full gale out of North Africa. The newly installed Proteus gas turbine had refused to start and one of the seamen, George Bedu, had lost his footing while trying to tighten the gripes on the only boat the ship carried and had crashed to the deck. He had suffered concussion and sustained a nasty fracture in his left leg. He was in urgent need of medical attention but would have to wait until the next fuelling rendezvous which was set for a position in the Dodecanese in thirty-six hours.

Charlie de Vere reported the situation to Buckland House but received only a curt acknowledgement. For a further twenty-four hours the ship ploughed on, the weather eased, George's situation worsened and Charlie worried.

Down aft, Brian Hall was organising the vast amount of armament they had taken on board. He decided to pick out only what he believed he would need, train the operators in the use of what they were going to carry and, if time and energy permitted, do some generic cross training so as many of the crew as possible could become familiar with other weapons.

Brian decided to form three teams, a forward gunnery team, an after gunnery team and a third team who would form a boarding party when required but at other times support the other two teams. He had fourteen men including himself. Each mortar would need a team of three and two more would be needed for the General Purpose Machine Guns which he intended to mount on the Bridge wings. Assuming only two mortars in use, that would give him a maximum of six men as a boarding party. He thought that number would be adequate if they were all Marines but many of the men he had available were not and in most cases their capability was unknown.

In addition to the heavy weapons, everybody would be issued with a personal weapon. The Boarding Party would get Heckler and Koch carbines, with some carrying semi-automatic combat shotguns while the SA80 rifles with the telescopic sights would be deployed on the Bridge. Brian recognised that he had a mixed bunch and training was essential, but gunfire often carried far over water and so until they broke out into the Indian Ocean the weapon training would have to be carried out without firings. Furthermore, before entering the Suez Canal, every sign of weaponry would need to be removed and hidden away in the depths of the ship, far from the prying eyes of any inspectors.

As the vicious little Mediterranean storm abated another very brief message was received on the Satphone. The message consisted of a series of groups of five letters and numbers. Charlie took it away to his cabin, opened the safe and hauled out a thick 'one-time pad'. Laborious work with a pencil and the one-time pad produced a different set of figures which Charlie then fed into a portable machine, which eventually churned out on its green screen a time and position for the next refuelling session. This would entail sneaking in among the Greek islands, very late at night, tying up alongside the supplying tanker and then slinking away before first light.

*

Six days after leaving the English Channel, the frigate now known to her crew, but to no one else, as *Cassie,* slid gently through the mirror like surface of the Aegean Sea towards her rendezvous. The ship was completely blacked out and silent apart from the muted hum of the gas turbines, all of which were now co-operating.

The moon had not yet risen but the sky still seemed to be a brilliant dome of sparkling stars – set off by the bright white light reflected from the planet Venus, hovering low above the western horizon. Various islands, picked out by harbour lights, car headlights and occasional strains of frantic pop music, slipped past. Eventually, right on schedule, a dark, lengthy bulk ahead of the *Cassie* formed itself into an elongated ship-like shape. The ship showed no lights but appeared to be at anchor. There was no sign of human activity and to all intents and purposes it appeared derelict.

Cassie nosed slowly towards the silent ship and, with about a hundred yards to go one of the signalmen flashed the letter 'J' once in Morse. The dot and three longer dashes seemed to split the night but at first elicited no reply. Charlie stopped both engines and the ship continued to coast forward narrowing the gap between the two vessels. The nerves of everybody on the Bridge were strung taught and Charlie had just decided to back off when the answering signal flashed briefly across the gap between them. Dot – dash – dot, a miniscule pause and then the same again, followed by darkness even deeper than before.

There were no orders given in either ship. Men moved forward along the main deck of the frigate, some holding rattan fenders and others with heaving lines. The heaving lines snaked out fore and aft across the gap. One fell short in the water but the others were true and were picked up by unseen figures in the other ship. Heavier ropes were attached and passed across as the frigate nudged gently alongside the bigger ship, effectively disappearing into the shadow of the tanker.

Men appeared on the deck of the tanker at the same time as Dan Holloway and his team arrived. Within only five minutes a fuelling hose and a water hose had been passed across, with the two different liquid life-bloods flowing in each. Still no lights had been switched on in either ship and no-one had spoken in either ship.

When the fuelling had been running for twenty minutes or so, a plank was laid between the decks of the two ships and Tom Clarke danced the four or five steps across the gap to the tanker. He was grasped by the elbow and led, wordlessly, through a screen door into the Bridge structure.

"I need to see the Captain," said Tom and when that produced no response, he tried again. He attempted to repeat his request in French, then in broken Italian, which at least produced a twitch in the other man's face – but nothing else. At that moment a heavily Slavic accented voice came from the deck above as a pair of dull scuffed leather sea boots came into view on the ladder from the next deck.

"You want to speak me – I am Captain," said the man as he arrived in the lobby alongside the other two. "You should not be here – is not in the deal," he continued.

Tom found himself staring at a man of about his own age, heavily bearded with intense but curiously expressionless pale blue eyes boring into his own.

"We have an injured man," he began, "we need to land him – will you take him?"

The answer was a flat, uncompromising "No."

Tom couldn't accept that and he persisted, arguing that the injured man could not remain in a ship that was destined for a long voyage to the breakers yard but that all the tanker captain had to do was to sign on George Bedu as a crewman and land him at the first place with a decent hospital.

The tanker, it turned out was registered as a Greek ship but most of the crew, including the skipper, were Croatian. The ship seemed to be on some sort of long term contract to the Eastern Committee but – when it was not laid up quietly in the islands – was generally used for a variety of mostly clandestine tasks by Jack Lang.

After nearly an hour of fruitless argument, Tom returned to the *Cassie* to explain the situation to his Skipper. As soon as Charlie recognised the intransigence of the tanker Captain and had learned the man's nationality he decided that the emergency procedure should be used. This was to call the Duty Officer at Buckland House and using a series of innocuous phrases to outline the difficulty and the principal participants, leaving Jack's organisation to sort out the problem.

In this instance, the call lasted less than twenty seconds and described a difficulty in getting a return ticket to Malta for a nephew. Half an hour after the message had been passed, a hoarse call came from the fuelling point on the tanker's deck. The bearded skipper was standing by the fuel hose deck connection. Tom moved out onto the Bridge wing and peered over the edge.

"OK, I take him. He has good value for me so I make sure he OK." The tanker captain looked up towards the Bridge.

Fifteen minutes later, with the refuelling almost complete, George Bedu was strapped into a Neil Robertson stretcher and passed gently over the gap between the two ships. He was followed by a lightweight blue suitcase and a non-matching blue holdall, carrying his worldly goods. Fifteen minutes after that, still with no attempt at conversation from the men supplying the fuel and water to *Cassie,* the operation was complete. Lines were cast off, fenders kept, for the moment, in place and *Cassie* was allowed to drift gently clear of the still darkened tanker. As the gap widened, Charlie conned the ship's head slowly round to the southeast and they started the next leg towards the Suez Canal and the greatest risk to the operation.

TWENTY-EIGHT

FROM CARLISLE TO CINCFLEET. CODEWORD BARNYARD. OPDRAKE SITREP TWO.

SUBJECT VESSEL REMAINS DISABLED. THREE CREW MEMBERS RECOVERED ALIVE AND DEBRIEFED. NO SIGNIFICANT ADDITIONAL INTELLIGENCE EXCEPT PROBABILITY THAT AT LEAST ONE CREW MEMBER DECEASED DURING TAKEOVER. SOME SIGNAL TRAFFIC DETECTED FROM SUBJECT VESSEL. TRANSLATION NOT YET COMPLETE. BOTH GUARDIAN SHIPS WILL NEED TO WITHDRAW WITHIN NEXT SIXTY HOURS FOR REFUEL AND SOME RE-STORE. REQUEST INSTRUCTIONS. AUTHENTICATE TANGO TANGO NINE ECHO. MESSAGE ENDS.

Three copies of the signal from *Carlisle* were being studied in the secure communications room at Buckland House. Jack Lang and Maggie McGuigan each occupied one side of a square wooden table. The third side was occupied by an Asian man who was the Special Operations Group communications expert for the Indian Ocean area. The fourth side of the table was dominated by a large wall mounted television screen which displayed the troubled features of the Foreign Secretary.

"I'd like you to know, Jack," the Foreign Secretary spoke plaintively, "that I am getting constant pressure from the Middle East and I would be more pleased than you could ever possibly imagine if you can tell me where we have got to, what is going on in the Indian Ocean and what we can do about it."

"Well sir," replied Jack, staring earnestly and inappropriately at the larger than life image looking out of the screen, "the *Sea Shadow* is disabled and can't move anywhere without a tug, both *Carlisle* and *Andrew James* are still on station in close surveillance but each of them will need to refuel. Satellite imagery suggests there is quite a lot of surface activity within a radius of one hundred miles of the datum point – and of course three crew members have been recovered from the *Shadow* and the first of our own assets is operational and approaching the area of activity. Our second asset should bc entering the Suez Canal as we speak."

"OK. I've got all that but now please give it to me in English followed by a plan of what you intend to do." The voice boomed out from the screen.

Jack paused before replying, took a deep breath and began, "Right, the terrorists are still working out where they stand and may not yet have realised that they are not going to be able to move the ship without a tug. That means the ship is effectively of no further use to them but they still have the crew and at least one very high value hostage. The only way they are going to capitalise on that is by getting their captives away from the ship and they would probably try to do that under cover of darkness, and when one of our ships withdraws. They still have the boat they used for the attack but that is barely big enough for their own gang. That means, we deduce that they will at first attempt to bargain their way out with the lives of what they regard as the lesser value hostages. I mean, they will try to offer to leave a number of hostages on board on condition that we let them leave in another pirate vessel."

"How will you deal with that?" the Foreign Secretary interrupted.

Jack ploughed on. "Well the first thing we need to recognise is that any hostages left behind, with or without a deal, are likely to end up dead. So I think that our best bet is to try to be co-operative with the pirates. Remember that their focus outside their ship is on the two warships and they will have no idea that we are bringing other assets into the arena. As I said, our first asset is virtually there and we just need to stall them long enough to bring the second asset into play. I think we should gradually capitulate, or lead them to believe that we are, and allow them to leave the ship. The only way they will be able to do that is if they are able to bring another vessel close enough to transfer themselves and their hostages. All this of course depends on continuing good weather and so far it looks as if that is what we will get."

"How long to get the second vessel on station?" interrupted the Foreign Secretary.

At this point Sunil, the Special Operations Group communications man spoke for the first time. "We need to look at the problem through the eyes of the pirate group leader. Indications are that he has only eight men, nine or ten maximum – but in all probability only eight, otherwise their boat would have been dangerously overloaded. Most of the group will be from the same family or at least related but the leader is unlikely to be deflected by the possibility of taking casualties. If he has to call for help he can only do that on VHF radio, out to a practical range of perhaps twenty-five miles. The pirate situation in the area is fluid and continuously changing. When he calls for help he will not know who is going to receive his call and what they will do, particularly after they have turned up on the scene. There are many vessels, some legitimate, some not, milling about in the area." He paused.

"Well," said Maggie, looking up from the mess of needles and wool on the table in front of her, "he will concentrate entirely on his big prize – the Prince. He will probably try to hide the fact that he has landed a really big fish because the ransom value will outweigh all other considerations, and at the end of the day it is all about money – his money, and to hell with anybody else. This man is a pirate because he wants to convert himself into a western millionaire and he will kill anyone, destroy anything to fulfil that wish."

The room and the screen remained silent until Jack cleared his throat and glanced almost furtively from one to another of his companions. "I need assurance that you are alone, Foreign Secretary," he said.

"I am," came from the screen.

"And there is no chance of any recording or interception of this channel?" Jack waited for the reply.

"None."

Jack continued, slowly and quietly, "We will hold both warships on station for twenty-four hours. The first asset is a former fast patrol boat, coming up from Tanzania. She is arriving in the area of operations any time now but very short of fuel. She will rendezvous with the tanker who has already been instructed to refuel a small Korean warship. If the second asset, an old frigate already purchased by a scrapping company, gets through the canal without mishap – and I must admit that this is a critical point in the whole scheme – then she will take about five days to travel down the Red Sea and reach the area. She will also need fuel at that point but as soon as she has been refuelled she will be well placed to create havoc among the enemy."

"Meanwhile *Carlisle* will reluctantly agree to ferry the pirates and captives from the *Sea Shadow* to whichever mother ship turns up prepared to help out the pirates. This will be negotiated in exchange for as many hostages as possible. We think that the pirate boss will be amenable to this provided he gets to keep the star prize. Once the transfer is complete, we, or the Americans, will board the *Sea Shadow* and our other assets – remember still unknown to the enemy in general – will deal with the subsequent problem without constraint from the Rules of Engagement."

"How?" This from the Foreign Secretary.

There was another long pause before Maggie said, carefully and deliberately, "Foreign Secretary, it really would be better if you don't ask that question."

The ensuing silence continued for almost a minute, broken only by the steady ticking of an old-fashioned wooden framed clock.

At length the Foreign Secretary said, "I see. Or at least I think I see. You are going to prise all the people out of the captive ship, which you will then presumably attempt to recover, and then someone else is going to take on the pirates when they are more vulnerable and less prepared. Would that be about right?"

Maggie answered, "Yes, that would be about right."

"I'll tell the Prince to stand by for some better news." The picture faded abruptly from the screen.

TWENTY-NINE

The scruffy black hulled frigate joined the evening southbound convoy as number three in a group of eight disparate ships, none of which seemed in the first flush of youth. As they entered the western entry section of the canal at Port Said each ship was brought briefly alongside the stone pier while a canal pilot and two or three officials hopped on board. The pilot made his way up to the Bridge and the others began to wander around the ship. With the harbour side Gully Gully men still yelling about their wares the ship pulled out back into place in the column. A couple of hours later three more small ships emerged from the Eastern leg of the canal and joined at the head of the column.

Charlie de Vere stayed on the Bridge watching the pilot and attempting unsuccessfully to engage him in conversation. Most canal pilots were fluent in English but this one stayed silent for most of the time. His two companions were of a different nature and as they were accompanied around the ship by Tom Clarke, Henry King and a few others it soon became apparent that they were really just going through the motions of doing a few immigration checks while happily accepting, food, cigarettes and repeated cans of soft drinks.

It was early in the morning when the ships reached the Great Bitter Lake, where, without slowing down, a launch came alongside, deposited another pilot plus one minder and removed the previous team. This time the pilot talked endlessly as he monitored the progress of the ship, asking questions, comparing living standards, commenting on the end of ‘a fine ship’ and regularly eulogising on the hardships of canal pilots in the present times while hinting at the generosity of the men running his previous charges.

It was almost ten hours later that the old frigate pulled away from the dockside at Port Suez, watched by the pilot and his man, each with a pocket full of warm dollars and each holding a clear plastic bag containing a size ‘medium’ blue seaman’s jersey. As soon as the land had dropped away astern, Brian Hall and his two gunners, assisted by three or four other crewmen, were hauling out weapons and ammunition sufficient to turn *Cassie* back into a ship of war – of sorts.

The Satphone was used once more to declare, ‘Clear of the bottleneck’.

THIRTY

The Communications Officer waited patiently in the cabin doorway, his Leading Signalman beside him clutching his biro and signal pad, as Craig read the signal for the third time.

FROM CINCFLEET PERSONAL AND EXCLUSIVE FOR COMMAND. OPDRAKE FOUR. TOP SECRET CODEWORD BARNYARD. COMMAND EYES ONLY. COPY TO CHIEFNAVOPS WASHINGTON AND USS ANDREW JAMES. TASK GROUP 420.1 ACTIVATED. CINCFLEET TO REMAIN TASK GROUP CDR. EXECUTE REPEAT EXECUTE OPERATION DRAKE. ESTABLISH TASK ELEMENT T.E. 420.1.3 UNDER CINCFLEET CONTROL.

ANDREW JAMES IS TO WITHDRAW IMMEDIATELY TO RENDEZVOUS WITH RELIEF TANKER USS OKLAHOMA CITY NOW ESTABLISHING RACETRACK 200 NM NORTHWEST OF YOU.

CARLISLE TO REMAIN ON STATION, CLOSE TO HAILING DISTANCE WITH TARGET AND ATTEMPT NEGOTIATION TO RECOVER HOSTAGES AND AGREE TO TRANSFER BANDITS TO ANY VESSEL THEY NOMINATE. IF NEGOTIATION UNSUCCESSFUL, CARLISLE IS TO DEPART THE

DATUM AREA FORTHWITH. CARLISLE TO ATTEMPT RECOVERY OF AS MANY HOSTAGES AS POSSIBLE BY ANY NON AGGRESSIVE MEANS BUT TO DEPART AREA WITHIN 24 HOURS REGARDLESS OF LEVEL OF SUCCESS. IF REQUIRED, CARLISLE TO ASSIST IN TRANSFER AND EVACUATION OF HOSTAGES AND OR BANDITS. MAINTAIN EMISSION CONTROL POLICY SILENT UNTIL FURTHER NOTICE, EXCEPT TO REPORT RESULT OF NEGOTIATION.

RULES OF ENGAGEMENT REMAIN LEVEL ONE BUT NOW UNRESTRICTED.

AUTHENTICATE TANGO FOUR VICTOR DELTA.

Craig looked up. “Have you acknowledged?”

“Yes sir.”

“Who decoded this?” said Craig.

“I did sir – it was Deltext – Officers’ Eyes only.”

“OK, that will be all but just find the First Lieutenant for me please and ask him to come here, oh, and seal up the original un-decrypted text and secure it in your safe together with anything else referring to this signal. Got that, Sub?”

“Yes sir.” The young Sub-Lieutenant turned abruptly from the doorway and disappeared, followed by the Leading Signalman.

Craig closed his eyes for a moment, trying to muster and concentrate his thoughts. He rehearsed the signal in his mind trying to see if there was any nuance or hidden meaning he had missed. He thought, not for the first time that this could be a career breaker. He glanced again at the flimsy paper in his hand until a bulky shadow in the doorway and a discreet cough disturbed him. “Come in Number One,” he said. “Drag up a chair." Then nodding towards the pot on the low table he added, "Help yourself to coffee."

George Lee leaned across to pour a mug of steaming black coffee, noticed that there was no milk or sugar and plumped down in the maroon leather-covered swivel chair beside the desk. He looked expectantly across at his Captain through the steam rising from his mug. Craig Wilson continued to stare at the sheet of signal form in his hand and the silence stretched.

Eventually, still trying to decide how much or how little he was able to say in relation to his signalled instruction, Craig spoke, slowly and deliberately. "We have more orders," he said. He folded the paper carefully and put it in his pocket. The First Lieutenant did not miss the gesture and thought that whatever they had been told, it must be pretty ripe.

"At least we have been given something to ease the boredom," began Craig. George stayed silent and waited to hear more.

Craig decided that at least he must take George partly into his confidence. "The *James* has been told to go off and refuel," he began.

"They've already gone."

"Oh." Craig felt suddenly isolated, as though a new friend had become bored with him and had just wandered away.

"Yes, they just bimbled off without so much as a by your leave. Strange I thought, after we'd had so much fun together." George allowed a trace of irony in his voice as he finished speaking.

Craig ignored the interruption and pressed on. "We have a tricky little task to perform this evening. We just need to convince that gang of foul cutthroats over there to hand over their hostages and bugger off. Not a problem, I don't think."

"Can you explain that a bit further sir?" said George, sipping his now cooling bitter black coffee.

"Yes," said Craig. "Reading between the lines I reckon that the sudden absence of the bigger more bristly warship is supposed to send a signal to the bad bastards that we're all getting a little tired of the game and we have more important things to think about. We are invited to talk the buggers into handing over their hostages and standing by while they transfer themselves into a vessel that can actually move under its own power and shove off back home to Somalia."

George leaned forward, looking very sceptical. "And just how likely do we think that is?" he asked. He finished his coffee and placed the mug on the table before answering his own question. "About as likely as detecting a fart in a thunderstorm," he said.

"Well," said Craig, "maybe not. We should always try to put ourselves in the other guy's position and I've been trying to do just that. He must be getting just a little bit pissed off. Apart from being covered in shit, he's lost a couple of hostages – not important ones I grant you but the loss must be irritating all the same. He now knows that his propellers are wrecked, or at least he has a good idea that there is a serious problem, and he probably thinks that he has a fuel problem as well. His chances of motoring off happily towards his grubby cave or tent or wherever he lives have taken a dive towards zero. I would think he believes he is facing capture, death or at best, slinking away with one of his mates but without his rich cargo. We need to offer him a way out. How good do you think our interpreter is?"

"Do you think we should find out how good the bad guys' English is first, sir?"

"Perhaps you're right. This is what I want you to do."

*

Hamid was in a foul mood. He was way ahead of the discussion taking place in the Captain's Cabin on board *Carlisle.* His mood had not been improved by the failure of the air-conditioning and the pumps supplying fresh water. His dreams of ransoms and riches had collapsed into near despair as he realised that his predicament was incapable of resolution – although he thought of this in different terms. His men were already becoming restless and truculent because they too could sense that they were in a situation which was likely to end in disaster. Only Ahmed the climber and young Ali continued to show any faith and trust in their leader, but Hamid realised uncomfortably that their loyalty was matched only by their stupidity and fear of his wrath.

The light of the late afternoon bled away into a grey twilight as Hamid sat cross-legged in the centre of the comfortable sofa in what had once been the owner's suite. He could not avoid the fact that the ship was disabled and neither of the stupid engineers remaining among his hostages could do anything about that fact. He had sought to torture and beat them into submitting to his will and make the vessel come alive again but one was now almost dead and the other was physically and psychologically broken. He had forced them to start one engine but that had now failed again. The ship was a stinking filthy mess not helped by the incarceration of his remaining hostages and the unfortunate habits of his men in urinating and defecating whenever and wherever they felt like it.

At length, Hamid came to the conclusion he had spent hours trying to avoid. He was stuck in a ship that was incapable of movement and was furthermore being closely watched over by a foreign warship who would most certainly not allow him to escape. He did still have the hostages, or at least twenty-six of them. The barman had escaped, one engineer was dead and the other two were badly injured. He thought one might already be dead. Of the rest only about twelve or fourteen were fit to be moved, but that was irrelevant because he would not be able to fit more than two or three into his boat. If he could find the power to lower a ship's boat he could take perhaps five or six more – but there was no power and in any case, how could he escape and take any hostages with him while the infidels were watching? Even if he managed to escape the ship, perhaps during darkness, where would he go?

He would need to summon help but in doing so and trying to bring his mother ship to his aid, every deceitful cutthroat on the ocean would be alerted to his difficulty and would seek to relieve him of his captives.

As the night took command from the day, Hamid sat quietly in the darkness of the big cabin. He sat rocking slowly back and forth trying to summon inspiration, which would not come.

After two more hours, the big door to the corridor eased open and Ahmed entered the cabin carrying a mug of hot sweet tea. Angrily, Hamid waved him away, so Ahmed placed the mug carefully on a low table beside the sofa and silently withdrew. Hamid sat on alone. After perhaps ten minutes the sweet steamy smell of the tea slid in upon his thoughts and he moved across the sofa to reach for the mug, still sitting cross-legged. As he sipped the warm liquid his brain seemed to clear. The first thing that began to dawn on him was that it was likely that the ship's boats, or at least some of them, could probably be lowered without needing external power. He was aware of ships with lifeboats and tenders which could be lowered using their own weight so it was probable that this was also the case with *Sea Shadow*. He considered and rejected several possible plans before settling on one and then beginning to worry away at it, identifying the risks and trying to think of how to overcome them. His mood had begun to settle when the cabin door opened once more, none too gently this time. Ahmed stood framed in the doorway and even in the gloom of the unlit cabin Hamid could see, or sense, that his 'servant' was agitated, even before he spoke.

"Leader, leader, come quick, the Yankee ship is calling us! They want to talk to you!" Hamid didn't move or speak. His mind was racing. Inconsequentially he considered for a moment chastising Ahmed for confusing the British ship with an American then he thought, what does it matter? Ahmed is just a willing peasant whose skill is with his hands not his brain. As he eased himself carefully off the sofa his thought moved on fleetingly to the possibility of having to abandon Ahmed and perhaps others of his men. He had no doubt that his primary aim should be the preservation and wellbeing of himself, Hamid the leader.

Hamid strolled out of the cabin into the darkened corridor. He turned forward towards the command Bridge and stepped purposefully onto the stairway leading up to the Bridge deck. As he strode along, his composure was returning and his temper was receding. When he reached the Bridge he saw that all of his men were gathered there. His anger flared again as he demanded to know who was guarding the prisoners. Nobody spoke but two figures detached themselves in the gloom and disappeared down the other stairway. Hamid moved forward and peered through the clear view screen. Then he strode purposefully to each side of the Bridge, staring first at the unbroken starscape and finally at the brightly illuminated destroyer sitting stationary, less than one hundred metres away.

Hamid eased the retaining clips on the heavy screen door and opened it. As he stepped outside a metallic voice boomed across the expanse of water separating the two ships.

"I wish to speak to the Revolutionary Commander." The voice spoke in English very slowly and clearly. "If you are hearing me, show yourself by lighting a torch," it continued. Hamid wrenched the door open once more and demanded a torch. It was quickly thrust into his hand and he switched it on as he moved out to the edge of the Bridge wing.

"I am he," he called in halting, heavily accented English.

"What is your name?" The voice seemed to bounce across the water, becoming slightly distorted.

Hamid had no intention of giving his name. He replied with what he had heard others say. "I am the Commander."

"Well, Commander, I have a proposition for you."

Hamid kept the torch on but remained silent. If this unbeliever wants to offer me things, let him, he thought.

"If you are prepared to guarantee that the passengers and crew of *Sea Shadow* are safe and unharmed I will be able to allow you and your men to leave the ship in your own boat. Can you guarantee that?"

Hamid took a deep breath and roared back, "What is guarantee?"

There was a pause and a different voice responded, speaking in Arabic. "It means, my brother," said the voice, "that you pledge that you speak truly to the question and we should believe that all the people in your care are alive and want for little other than their freedom."

The switch to Arabic surprised Hamid and his thoughts transferred momentarily to what punishment would be appropriate to a man of his race who should align himself with the enemy. “You are not my brother!” he called back in Arabic.

But the answer came in English and this unnerved Hamid once more. “Your ship is broken and cannot move. Perhaps soon it will not be able to float. You will need to leave it. Do you wish to leave it?”

Hamid thought for a long minute before replying. “Yes,” he said. “I do want to leave this ship, with my men and my captives.”

“We will not allow that.”

“Then I will not leave this ship.”

“Then you will die!” Each word was punched out like a shot from a gun.

“I will not die!” roared Hamid, his body twitching compulsively forward with each syllable. He stood waiting for a reply but the Bridge wing of the other ship was suddenly empty and, very slowly, the destroyer began to move ahead, opening the gap between the two vessels. Hamid had been working himself up to meet the British ship’s demands with a scathing arrogant harangue and when the other ship simply drifted away he felt deeply deflated, as though his unseen inquisitor had just failed him.

*

As the *Carlisle* pulled away from the immediate position of the *Sea Shadow* Craig Wilson led George Lee down towards his cabin.

“We’ll give him a bit of time to think things over but I want a tight visual and electronic watch kept on that bugger throughout the night, then I think we’ll wake him up without a cup of tea just before dawn.” Craig flopped down into the one comfortable chair in his day cabin. "What's your take on that little exchange, George?" he continued.

"Well sir," the First Lieutenant paused, staring for a moment down at the arm of his chair. "We've opened the bowling and there can be no doubt at all that he knows he is stuck. Our problem is that we don't know how many hostages he has got – alive, I mean, nor do we know where they are and in what condition. My guess is that he will stall for time and some time in the next hour or so he will at last squeal to his mates. He must have some scruffs out there somewhere sitting in his mother ship because he sure as hell couldn't have paddled his little bum-boat all the way from the Somali coast. When he's had a good think he's going to try to extract himself and as many of his men as he can get away. But I think he will try and do a deal with us to only agree to leave, or perhaps not to harm the hostages, if he can take one or two with him as insurance."

"I reckon you're not far off the mark," said Craig. "Question is, how do we play it? We have a pretty free hand but the big deal is," – he started counting points off on the fingers of his outstretched hand – "One. We must recover the Prince. Two, we need to ensure the ship is clear. Three, we need to recover the remaining hostages, assuming that they are still alive. Four, we need to keep track of where matey chugs off to but we don't necessarily need to try to capture him or his mates when they arrive to help him out. I don't know for certain but I have the strongest feeling that someone else is going to do that."

THIRTY-ONE

Hamid spent another almost sleepless night. He went over and over his situation and it did not begin to look any better as the night moved on. He dozed for an hour around midnight and when he awoke he realised that his priority had changed. He was no longer on the verge of becoming a rich man but he still held many hostages and he must use these to extricate himself from the trap in which he now lay. He knew that the infidels were too squeamish to kill and this, he believed provided him with some advantage. He would not hesitate to kill men or women if it would advance his cause, and he believed it was now probable that he would have to demonstrate this determination to his immediate enemy. His priority now was to get away and preserve his freedom, nothing more. Although he would like to take his men with him they were, in fact, expendable, leaving before him one single goal – leave the ship and make his way to the nearest brother. To do this he would need to declare his difficulty to the many brothers who were patrolling the great ocean looking for opportunities just as he had been a few days before. If he was to escape he would need to entice a mother ship close to the *Sea Shadow* so that he had some chance of evading the Yankees and their lackey friends. He surmised that as soon as he was seen to depart in a boat the enemy would attack him but he could hold them at bay if he was able to take one or more hostages with him – or at least make his enemy believe that he had hostages with him.

At two o'clock he left the great state room and made his way through the darkened ship towards the Bridge. Melak was the only occupant and he was dozing in the tall swivel chair. Melak awoke with a start when Hamid pushed him roughly from behind.

"Give me the radio," said Hamid. Melak reached forward to the shelf under the windscreen, picked up the radio and wordlessly handed it to Hamid. Hamid switched it on and saw immediately that the battery capacity was very low. He glared at Melak and snarled an insult to his manhood. Melak reacted as if punched, thought for a moment of retaliating but then thought better of it. Hamid switched the radio off and slouched up into the now vacated Bridge chair. He knew that if he was able to rest the battery for a small period, even fifteen minutes would do, it would allow the battery to recover slightly and give a better chance of sending a recognisable transmission. He left the radio off and waited. Melak moved to the opposite side of the Bridge and sulked.

Twenty minutes later Hamid switched the radio back on and stared carefully at the little line of lights indicating the charging status. His expression settled into something which was not quite satisfaction as he noted that the radio battery did seem to have improved slightly.

He spoke quickly and quietly into the radio in Arabic, calling on any Somali brother who was near enough to come and rescue him. He repeated the call and then waited to receive any answer. After perhaps ten minutes two separate and distinctive voices came onto the channel. There was no direct answer to his call for help, just a demand for his position, his home location and the number of his men.

Although only two radio stations had answered, the calls made by Hamid had been picked up by at least thirty-four other radios, all within a radius of forty miles and each located in different vessels, themselves intent on pursuing plunder. The vessels receiving and understanding Hamid's call for help were mostly small boats operating as satellites and probes for six mother ships. Each of these ships had been previously taken by pirates and while attempting to appear and operate as what they had been originally, they were now the floating centres of pirate activity. They included two ocean going trawlers, a tug, two small coasters and a smart forty metre motor yacht, once the property of a wealthy Kuwaiti oil magnate.

Hamid had been concentrating his attention on his predicament and the depleted radio. As he switched the set off again and placed it carefully back on the shelf below the forward windscreen he looked outside and around the ship. There was no sign of the British warship. It had gone and its absence caused the ghost of a smile to curl at the corner of his lip.

Eleven miles away and just over the horizon from the *Sea Shadow*, HMS *Carlisle* was barely moving through the sea, slowly describing a large circle and in the Operations Room the command team were assembled in front of three multi-coloured radar screens with a fourth screen filled with green printed text. Hamid's radio call to his friends was faithfully printed out in Arabic and below it in blue lettering was a not quite accurate translation. Other messages on the screen indicated the position and movement – or rather lack of it – of *Sea Shadow* as well as several other lines, currently showing zero, which would otherwise list various electronic and infra-red transmissions from the immobilised ship. In the far corner of the Operations Room two men were leaning over the horizontal surface of a large plotting table onto which was projected an area radar picture, complete with bits of text and a few icons, of the ocean out to a radius of eighty miles. Red tracks showed several vessels moving erratically in the direction of *Sea Shadow.* Back aft on the flight deck the Lynx Wildcat helicopter was ranged ready for take-off with the crew strapped in and sweating behind the Perspex windscreen in the warm air.

THIRTY-TWO

"Let loose the dogs of war." Maggie looked up from her ubiquitous knitting and peered expectantly across at Jack. The meeting had been re-convened in the secure conference room at Buckland House. The big video monitor screen on the far wall was producing a soft green glow but there was as yet no image on it.

"Well we are now in a position to do just that," said Jack glancing down at a small pile of flimsy signal messages placed beside his open laptop. He shifted his gaze to the screen of the laptop which was showing a digitally adjusted image of the Western Indian Ocean. Small blue arrows showed the direction of friendly forces, similarly shaped red arrows showed known enemy forces and green showed the location of other vessels whose alignment was unknown. Near the top of the screen, some way to the south of the Gulf of Aden, a black arrow pointed south. Near the bottom of the screen a similar black arrow pointed north. Just below the centre of the screen a pulsing orange circle marked the location of *Sea Shadow.*

The picture was in fact a variation of the standard Automated Information System carried and operated by most commercial vessels, which sends a radio signal giving the location, course and speed, destination port and size of the vessel. Jack's version of this equipment was modified by a sensitive and discreet feed in from the Government Communications Centre at Cheltenham and an input from relevant military satellites. In addition to the standard information given to the world in general, by placing his cursor on the appropriate contact, Jack could learn a great deal more about a vessel. He could show the nationality, ownership, cargo, port of departure and names of the key crew members, but more interestingly he could also show on the screen a list of all the electronic emissions given out by the ship. Radar and other similar emissions were simply listed with frequency, power, bandwidth and so forth, but the really interesting information was the transcription of radio calls made by each ship. In most cases these were printed in the language used but with about three clicks on his keyboard Jack could produce an instant translation. In fact he could also get a real time translation as a call was being made and in several cases small pinpoints of light were flashing up alongside the target's icon to show that a radio call was being made. His equipment was pretty smart. A complicated-looking grey intercom sat on the table beside the laptop with two buttons glowing orange and one green. The orange buttons indicated lines of communication on standby to the office of the Foreign Secretary and the green light indicated an open line, instantly available, to Jack's Communication Centre in the basement of a building set in a stand of trees on the other side of the lawn behind Buckland House.

Jack leaned forward and pressed the green button. He spoke quietly but clearly. "Give both units the signal to go. The show is on."

*

In the Indian Ocean, on the Bridge of the old frigate now known as *Cassie*, the Captain and his officers were grouped close together examining a small piece of signal form with a single paragraph of instruction written on it. It had emerged only five minutes beforehand from the secure teleprinter connected to the Satphone.

Charlie allowed his gaze to move around the three men facing him then folded the paper and stuffed it in the top pocket of his shirt.

"Aren't we supposed to destroy that?" said Tom Clarke.

"It's our 'Get out of Jail Card'; we keep it," said Charlie.

"Yeah," added Jimmy McCoy, thoughtfully. "Yeah," he repeated.

Charlie broke the spell. "OK. Anything we see that has bearded men on it and isn't painted grey is ours for the taking. Gentlemen, I think we've just become twenty-first century buccaneers."

"So that signal in your pocket is a 'Letter of Marque', I think," mused Jimmy. The others nodded and turned away to prepare for battle, as the former Captain of Marines, Brian Hall, put it.

Within an hour the frigate was completely blacked out, with the hotch-potch of weapons mounted in various locations around the ship. Half of the crew had gone to the dining hall to eat, leaving the remainder to man the essential elements of the frigate, in particular the newly established weapon stations. The ship was now doing twenty knots, ploughing through a glassy calm sea under clear and almost dark skies towards the position indicated in the signal, just one hundred and fifty miles further to the south.

Four hundred miles beyond that position, the Captain and officers in the gunboat had just completed a similar discussion and another piece of signal paper was resting in the top pocket of Harry Mullen. It was in fact the second signal they had received. The first had instructed the boat to be taken further inshore towards the coast of Kenya where a darkened tanker had awaited them eight miles from a deserted coast lined with thick secondary jungle and mangroves, which would almost certainly provide an impenetrable barrier to the narrow strip of sandy beach. The rendezvous position had been chosen well and the two ships were able to sit undisturbed only thirty yards apart while fuel was quickly transferred from the tanker. The gunboat approached at slow speed from seaward, keeping the tanker between the boat and the beach so that any casual observer on shore would see just one more tanker loitering for a couple of hours, probably waiting to go into Mombasa, further to the north.

The refuelling of the gunboat was complete within just over an hour but before the two ships parted company, five large cylindrical heavy duty rubber fuel tanks were floated across from the tanker, and hoisted laboriously onto the deck of the patrol boat. Each tank was half filled with fuel to make it possible to handle, and then manoeuvred into position on the deck of the smaller vessel. Another smaller diameter hose was then floated across and each tank was topped up with diesel. With two tanks lashed down on each side deck and another on the stern, the gunboat had completely changed its silhouette but at the cost of becoming a little more unstable at slow speed.

"The really important thing," said Harry as they moved away to seaward of the tanker, "is that we've just trebled our endurance."

An offshore breeze had begun to kick up small waves as the boat was brought up onto the plane, gradually increasing to a cruising speed of forty knots and setting course to the northeast.

As in the frigate far to the north, preparations for battle began almost immediately. Weapons were brought out of the various stowages and issued. The boat slowed down to allow the cover, still not without difficulty, to be removed from the Bofors gun on the fore deck and, magically, ammunition was also located for it.

*

Back in the Buckland House Communications Centre, two switches were flicked from off to on and in both the frigate and the patrol boat, transponders began to transmit an identification in EHF (Extreme High Frequency). The transponder signals were transmitted using a frequency well above the bandwidth of any normal military or commercial receiving equipment. They were also encrypted and transmitted using burst transmissions moving constantly up and down the limited frequency spectrum. Four thousand six hundred kilometres above the Northern Indian Ocean, the tiny signals were collected by an American geo-stationary military satellite and immediately re-transmitted to another geo-stationary satellite above the North Atlantic and then, almost immediately back to earth. In this way the location of the transponder was hidden and in the unlikely event of the signal being detected it would appear as nothing more than random interference – unless it arrived at one of the compatible but highly secret receivers.

Jack Lang had such a receiver, as did HMS *Carlisle.*

The satellite above the Indian Ocean had a secondary purpose. It was also a photographic satellite and, on command, it could take high definition video or still photographs of the area beneath it, and providing there was no heavy cloud cover, the pictures could be beamed to a receiving station below. In this case the receiving station was the *Andrew James* which could then transmit the data to other suitably equipped locations – such as the *Carlisle.*

THIRTY-THREE

Hamid had been sitting silently on his own in the big guest cabin for the last three hours. He was sure that the British or the American warship would soon reappear, probably at dawn so they could observe the *Sea Shadow* more easily. He thought he had another two or possibly three hours in which to act. He had worked out a plan which was very far short of his original intention but one that might just keep him alive and free, although possibly not all of his men. He planned to put one of *Sea Shadow's* boats in the water and together with his own boat he would make his escape taking as many hostages as he could in each boat. He had told no one of his intention but he planned to leave the ship two hours before dawn, when even if the warships returned they would be less likely to spot two small boats and the plastic and wooden hulls of the boats would not show up on radar.

Hamid reckoned that if he headed due north he would be bound to run in to at least one of the 'Free Somali' vessels that must by now be heading in his direction. He had a moment of uncertainty when he wondered whether his radio call would be heeded but he comforted himself with the thought that despite the diminishing power indicated in his radio his words did seem to have been transmitted. In any case, he thought, if he headed north there were so many ships milling about in the area that he would be bound to encounter one of them. He intended to take most of the money from the Captain's safe, leaving just heavy coinage and currency notes that were unlikely to be readily exchangeable. He had in fact spent some time secreting high denomination dollars and pounds about his person, making his appearance slightly more bulky about his torso.

His men would be divided between the boats, he would take the two most important hostages himself and try to make room for others – the ship's Captain and officers in the other boat. He wondered for some time whether he should set fire to the *Sea Shadow* before he left it but came to the reluctant conclusion that to do so would merely attract attention from the lurking warships and their helicopters. He was completely unaware of the fact that he was now under surveillance from a satellite, indeed he was a little hazy about what satellites were, or could do.

Shortly after reaching his decision, Hamid arrived on the Bridge and curtly issued a series of instructions to the dozy men who were lounging around doing little except occasionally peering through the windows.

Sea Shadow carried four boats. Two of them were high speed twin engine motor boats designed to provide luxurious and swift passage to and from *Sea Shadow* on occasions when it was deemed necessary for the ship to remain at anchor outside a port. These gleaming boats seemed to have every electronic gadget and accessory imaginable but they were not intended for open ocean work and, Hamid guessed, they were likely to have limited endurance.

The other two were much more workmanlike utility vessels which were also supposed to double as lifeboats. They were each powered by two diesel engines and had none of the luxury of the other boats. Several rows of seats, each equipped with safety straps, ran across the boats and, together with more seats along the side, each boat was able to accommodate all of the crew and passengers that *Sea Shadow* would be likely to carry – although in conditions of marked austerity. In between the transverse rows of seats were large spaces also equipped with restraining straps to enable bulky stores to be carried. The whole boat was covered over with a fibreglass curved roof with raised steering and observation platforms poking above each end. These two boats were as ugly and practical as the others were smart and impractical. Their final and overriding advantage was that they could be lowered and launched under their own weight and without the assistance of any external power.

Hamid decided to use one of the *Sea Shadow's* utility tenders to tow his own boat, into which he would place some of his men and some of the ship's crew. He decided to travel in the much bigger tender with the remainder of his men, the key hostages and as much loot as he could get aboard in the time remaining. In this way, any warship that tried to intervene would see that he had captives under guard by men with guns but they would not be able to see what was inside the bigger boat – or so he thought.

Once the men were prodded into action it didn't take long to get the big utility tender loaded and launched. Weapons and ammunition were split between the tender and Hamid's open cutter with the bulk of the armoury in the tender. The Prince and the girl were pulled roughly from their locked cabin, stripped and then forced into jeans and blue working shirts, so that thcy wcrc indistinguishablc from thc other occupants of the boats. The *Sea Shadow's* Captain and remaining officers as well as another five crewmen, selected at random were ordered from the stinking locked cabins that had been their prisons, and roughly pushed and shoved to the upper deck. There were fourteen prisoners in all, many of them in a bad way, starving, filthy and suffering from the effects of their incarceration in the oven-like, airless cabins. Their feet were hobbled with lengths of rope and their hands were loosely tied in front of them. Hamid's open boat was brought around to the ladder near the stern of the ship and one by one, five more captives were pushed to the ladder to climb awkwardly down to the boat. All of this was being done in darkness and the third man attempting to climb down the ladder missed his footing and fell several feet, landing with a cry of pain on the side of the boat before rolling into the sea. Khalid, who was standing in the stern of the boat waving a Kalashnikov about, spun round and as the unfortunate crewman rolled onto his back, gazing open mouthed and wide eyed while desperately trying to tread water, Khalid, barely raising the automatic above his hip, shot him. A burst of four or five rounds tore into the man's chest and brief fountains of blood sprayed momentarily into the air, the boat and the sea. No one said anything as the body began to drift away and the red stain marking the sea surface and the end of a life, disappeared.

Further along the deck the remaining nine hostages were being loaded into the utility tender whose supporting davits had been turned out and which now hung from the davits at deck level. Weapons, ammunition, bags of money, valuables robbed from the hostages, containers of water and ten litre cans of diesel fuel as well as some food and other assorted packages had been tossed into the boat. Melak and Abdullah, each looking like a walking armoury, joined Khalid in the open boat while Hamid and three others took their positions inside the tender. Two men remained on deck operating the lowering mechanism and tending the 'falls'. As soon as the boat hit the water they followed one another down a thick rope and joined the others in the boat. The engines fired up at the first push of the starter button and the handle of the disengaging gear was jerked open allowing the boat to drop with a startling crash the few inches to the water. After banging along the *Sea Shadow's* side for a few feet the big tender veered away from the ship and turned in a wide circle to come up alongside the other boat. A rope was passed between the two and they grumbled away ahead of the once stately yacht, turned around the bows of the still drifting vessel and set a course to the north.

Onboard, seven men and three women remained locked in the big crew cabin. They were all dehydrated, injured and starving. Before the end of that day, four of them would be dead.

THIRTY-FOUR

The old frigate *Cassie* had now reduced speed to fifteen knots and she was approaching the nearest of several unidentified targets. Her bizarre array of weapons were spread around the ship, loaded and manned. On the Bridge, powerful binoculars and night vision glasses were being used to try to locate the quarry being stalked by the frigate. Charlie de Vere was confident that he would be able to see the other ship before his own was spotted. The entire ship was now painted in matt black radar absorbing paint. Her slower speed was not producing any significant bow wave or wake so Charlie believed he would remain invisible and silent to the other ship until, from their point of view, it would be too late. The target on the discreet radar screen in the Operations Room had been confirmed by the transmission of a single letter from Buckland House, as enemy, and Charlie was free to attack it.

The intercom from the Bridge buzzed briefly. "Got it visual," said Tom. "It's a trawler and it's not fishing."

"That's the one," responded Charlie, and then, using the Armament Broadcast, he said, "All positions, target confirmed ahead at seven miles, red twenty. Clear to engage but stand by for my order." With that he left the Operations Room and ran up the ladder to the Bridge, two steps at a time.

The target was, or at one time had been, an ocean going trawler. Registered in Mauritius, and owned by a French company, the *Aquarius* had been captured by a Somali pirate gang nearly two years previously. She was now a 'mother ship' acting as support and headquarters for four or five small boats which would be despatched out to a radius of sixty miles, probing for further potential victims. Before her capture, she had fished very successfully and lucratively for blue fin tuna but now her fishing gear was long gone and she had been converted into a form of armed surface raider manned by gangsters. As with most such captive ships, the *Aquarius* was so filthy that she could often be located by smell before she could be seen. Her original crew of Skipper and fourteen men had been removed and were still held captive in another vessel anchored in the Bay of Lefar, the pirate's main operating base. Now, the main fish deck amidships was occupied by two boats and an array of loaded weapons casually distributed in convenient locations, while another boat was being towed astern. The ship was packed with up to forty men, many of whom spent most of their time in the boats, casting far and wide for new victims. At the point where she had been identified from the Bridge of *Cassie* there were twenty-eight men on board, two of whom were in the Engine Room and three, including the pirate skipper, were on the Bridge. The remaining twenty-three were scattered about the ship, on deck and below, sleeping.

Cassie altered course slightly to starboard as the distance between the two ships closed to four miles, then three. Charlie, whose eyes were still adjusting to the darkness inside and outside the Bridge, despite the red lighting system in the Operations Room, climbed into the tall Bridge chair. "You keep the con, Tom," he said, "until I can see properly." Tom who was peering through night vision goggles which gave him a clear view ahead into the night, in various shades of green, raised a hand in reply.

Back aft, Brian Hall was in his element. His mortar crew of three men were standing by the big 120 millimetre mortar which was now fixed firmly on its base plate, with a 'ready use' pile of twelve mortar bombs stacked within easy reach. Brian was standing on the port side of the deck peering through binoculars around the side of the hangar structure. He had set up the mortar for an opening range of three hundred yards and he was trying to estimate the point at which he could order the first bomb to be fired. Up on the forecastle, ex-Corporal Harry Smith was directing a similar team who waited expectantly around the 81 millimetre mortar. They would open fire at a slightly closer range.

So far, the target ship had done nothing to indicate that anyone was aware of the presence of the black frigate bearing down on them.

With eight hundred yards still to go a man was seen to burst out of the trawler's Bridge door onto the port Bridge wing. He waved his arm, and was seen to open his mouth. The trawler started to heel to port as the wheel was put hard over to starboard. Simultaneously *Cassie* surged towards the trawler. Thirty seconds later Brian gave the order to fire. A mortar bomb was dropped into the mouth of the 120 millimetre tube and almost instantly the bomb whooshed into the air in a high curving trajectory to drop into the sea about twenty-five yards ahead and slightly to port of the trawler. Ten seconds or so later the 81 millimetre was fired from the forecastle, looping high through the air in a perfect parabola to land on the foredeck of the trawler with a blinding flash. Two bodies were thrown cartwheeling through the air. One landed sickeningly on the deck which was now on fire and the other disappeared into the sea.

The .50 calibre heavy machine gun mounted above *Cassie's* Bridge opened up, creating a line of tracer into the wheelhouse structure of the trawler. The man on the Bridge wing who was still trying to give the alarm to the pirates scattered about the deck was cut in half as the heavy bullets tore through him and his twitching torso toppled sideways, spurting blood as it fell. The roof mounted machine gunner brought the tracer line deftly to the left and the machine gun began to chew the Bridge and wheelhouse to pieces. Several 120 millimetre rounds had been fired from *Cassie's* Flight Deck and finally one landed square on the trawlers after deck, causing the biggest explosion so far. A second blaze started on the deck and below. Other automatic weapons had opened up from the black frigate and lines of bullets were chopping through structure and men. Splinters of wood and chunks of structure flew into the air in all directions. The fire on the after part of the vessel had taken a serious hold as the ship slowed to a listing stop and wallowed, dead in the water. A misplaced 81 millimetre mortar round landed on the boat being towed, into which four or five of the pirates had dived, seeking refuge. There was a big flash and the boat simply disappeared. Charlie had his night vision by now but the scene of devastation before him was lighting the sea around both ships. The trawler, now only two hundred yards on the frigate's beam, was well alight both fore and aft. The after fire, probably fuelled by a ruptured diesel line was sending flames over fifty feet high. It was now a blazing wreck and rapidly settling lower in the water. Every part of the upper deck that was not ablaze was littered with blood-soaked shattered bodies, mostly dead but some still moving. Four or five men, apparently unharmed, stood still in front of the ravaged superstructure, hands held high in the air.

"What do we do about them, boss?" said Tom, turning to look at Charlie as the trawler started to list further to starboard. As he said it another, lighter, automatic opened up from somewhere above and behind them. Two of the men were blown dramatically backwards to lie twitching on the deck.

"Let them swim for it." Charlie stared fixedly ahead as he spoke. He picked up the Armament Broadcast and spoke into it: "All weapons, cease firing. All weapons cease firing."

The silence was like a cocoon, blotting out everything else. Men began to emerge through the upper deck screen doors to stand silently and watch the still floating inferno. The trawler was by now over at an angle of ninety degrees and the splintered remains of the bows were below the sea surface. As they watched the ship seemed to shudder before rolling right over and extinguishing all the deck fires with a steamy smoky elongated hiss. Charlie eased down from the Bridge chair and slid down the ladder, heading for the Operations Room. At the top of the ladder he paused and called over his shoulder, "Stay here and circle until she has completely gone, Tom." He didn't wait for a reply. His mind was already focusing on the next target.

By the time he reached the Operations Room, Jimmy McCoy had already identified what was thought to be the next target. This process was fairly straightforward because they had been told that, other than a few positively identified ships, everything within their area of operations should be regarded as potentially hostile. Jimmy was concentrating on a contact about sixty miles to the southeast of their present position. He also had a real time grainy photograph on the desk, courtesy of Jack Lang's electronic wizardry and an American satellite. It showed a pretty powerful looking tug.

*

Six hundred miles to the south of *Cassie's* attack on the trawler, Harry Mullen's former patrol boat was planing at forty-five knots through a slightly rising sea, heading just east of north and moving purposefully towards the position of the derelict *Sea Shadow.* The sky was overcast and with no moon or starlight the boat was forging through the darkness, relying heavily on the radar set. Karen Ford was peering into the radar display, occasionally speaking quietly into a microphone, passing ranges and bearings of possible contacts up to the Bridge crew. As each report was received, Harry or Frankie Zambelas would peer through their binoculars in the direction indicated and if nothing was immediately seen the course would be altered sufficiently to pass a mile or so clear. The height of the radar aerial mounted on the low mast meant that the maximum range of detection was only about twenty miles – fifteen if the targets were small. At forty knots the patrol boat would reach most of the contacts within half an hour and would become visible to the target in less than fifteen minutes, so Karen was locked into her task and the stress was demonstrated by the sweat streaming down her face.

It was as Karen paused to wipe the sweat from her eyes that she missed a single pinpoint of light that appeared briefly on the screen, disappeared and then reappeared in the same place. By the time her disturbed concentration was re-focused the pinpoint was steady on the screen, almost right ahead and at a distance of less than three miles. By the time the message was passed to the Bridge, and binoculars were trained on the bearing the contact was only two miles away. Neither Harry nor Frankie could see anything at first until Frankie shouted, "There it is – turn to port!"

The small outboard powered boat was only about twenty-five feet in length. It was a nondescript greyish colour and carried about seven or eight men. It was very low in the water which was why nobody had spotted it until it was within a hundred yards. In six seconds the patrol boat roared past the boat, passing less than fifty yards distant and causing the boat to rock violently in its wake. As the patrol boat surged past a wild burst of gunfire came from the small boat. At least two weapons seemed to be firing but the bullets flew wide and above the speeding gunboat which was passing quickly out of range. Nevertheless everybody on the Bridge had automatically reacted by ducking down below the screens.

"Try and keep the glasses on them," shouted Harry as he knocked the steering out of autopilot control and eased the powerful vessel around to port in a wide turn, increasing to maximum speed as he did so. As the boat settled out of the turn they began planing out of sequence with the swell and started an uncomfortable slamming.

Harry had judged the turn to attempt to cross their previous track at a right angle. "Can you still see them?" he called over the slipstream wind.

There was a pause before Frankie, still peering ahead through her binoculars, called, "I have them, skipper. Come left ten degrees and they will be right ahead."

Harry followed the instruction and looked up, while gripping the wheel firmly and saw the open boat almost immediately. In fact what he saw was a series of pinpoints of light caused by the gunfire now aimed at his ship. The noise of the firing was drowned by the combined noise of the wind and the roar of his three engines. He stared grimly ahead as bullets began to ping off the front of the Bridge screen, and made a tiny adjustment of course, bringing the bows of the gunboat about two degrees to starboard. Seconds later the firing stopped as the open boat seemed to rush beam-on towards the gunboat.

The flared bow of the gunboat loomed momentarily above the pirates' vessel. At the last moment two men were seen to leap overboard then, at over fifty knots, the hundred ton warship smashed down and through the wooden boat which disintegrated. Harry had a fleeting view of a shiny new-looking outboard motor sliding into the sea, taking with it a large chunk of the wooden stern. Frankie saw a body turning end over end through the air like an Olympic diver, before it fell out of sight into the sea. When they took the patrol boat around once again to pass through the collision point there was nothing remaining of the other boat or its occupants except for a patch of very small pieces of wreckage. Harry risked illuminating the wreckage with the big searchlight and loitered slowly while the beam of light played over and around the wreckage. After two or three minutes a single leg emerged on the surface, then the torso of a man, clearly very dead, bobbed up. As the Bridge crew stared silently at the carnage pinioned by the powerful light against the blackness of the sea surface they saw movement beneath the water and then the leg disappeared. Eyes were still riveted to the spot when with an upwelling surge the torso also disappeared. As it went down it was rolled over and a bearded face stared upward with wide accusing eyes. Harry eased the throttles forward and brought the boat back around onto her original course. They settled down at a comfortable forty knots, nicely adjusted to the length of the swell and drove steadily on towards their ultimate target.

*

In Buckland House, both Jack and Maggie, now accompanied by two men and a woman staring at other laptop type screens, were aware that action had taken place. The result of the brief battle between the trawler and *Cassie,* which to them was just 'the frigate' was determined by the fact that their screens showed that *Cassie* still existed whilst the other contact did not. They were both puzzled by the sudden manoeuvring of the patrol boat because throughout that action and despite their sophisticated surveillance system neither of the 'spooks' had been aware of the existence of the small pirate boat.

Maggie had long since discarded her knitting as well as her trademark casual disinterest. She was now controlling the communications and gleaning incoming information as well as fending off questions from the office of the Foreign Secretary. She was collecting and interpreting raw and analysed satellite intelligence as well as drafting and sending questions by burst transmission to *Carlisle* and to the *Andrew James*.

She stood and walked around the table to where Jack was rapidly manipulating buttons under one of the two screens facing him. Maggie waited for a pause in Jack's activity before leaning forward and, speaking softly, said, "OK, I have an update if you want it."

Jack looked up and spun his swivel chair to face her. He looked tense and tired. "Shoot," he said.

Maggie consulted a shorthand notebook and said, "This seems to be the picture. I stress *seems to be* because there are gaps."

Jack nodded, tilted back his chair and looked up expectantly.

"At least six major units are controlled by pirates, being operated as mother ships and cruising in the general area.

That has been correlated against vessels reported captured but not quarantined at Lefar. Working from the likely number of attack boats that would be supported by the mother ships there could be as many as thirty of them out looking for victims. The mother ships are now, of course, reduced to five because the frigate has attacked one of the bigger ones – a long range trawler. It has disappeared from the surface and satellite plot and is presumed sunk with all hands."

"How do you know it's with all hands?" interrupted Jack.

"Because if there had been survivors we would have been told."

Jack nodded. "Right," he said.

Maggie glanced back at her notebook and continued in a balanced, matter of fact tone, "Of course, with the sinking of the mother ship we can reasonably assume that several attack boats will be out of the action as well. If they were with the trawler at the time they have been destroyed and if they were out prowling then they have no home to go to – unless, that is, they find a victim," she added thoughtfully.

"I know less about the other possible action in the south but I have asked for a report on EHF. I think it is likely that the patrol boat came across one or more attack boats, and since our boat is once more heading for the centre of operations I presume whatever was encountered was sunk." She stopped as one of the assistants handed a sheet of paper to her. "Yes," she paused, glancing again at the signal, "I was right. They stumbled across one attack boat which fired at them before it was sunk, again with no survivors."

"Two down," said Jack.

"More than that. Remember the attack boats controlled by the trawler. That will be at least three more out of the picture."

Jack started to turn back to his screens when Maggie caught his arm.

"Hold on," she said. "There has been a development around the *Sea Shadow*. *Carlisle* reports that boats have left the *Sea Shadow* with about twenty people and are moving away to the north. The report is confirmed by radar, satellite, infra-red and electronic emission detection. *Carlisle* believes that the pirates who took the *Sea Shadow* have been forced to abandon the ship and are running for the security of a mother ship. The numbers estimated to be in the boats, one of which seems to be a ship's lifeboat, suggest that they have taken about a dozen hostages with them and will use these as a bargaining chip to get themselves safe passage to a mother ship. The distances obviate any attempt to reach any shoreline. We must also assume that they will have taken with them the star hostage. *Carlisle* is asking for approval to close the area and investigate. What do you think?"

Jack sat still, staring at Maggie, deep in thought. At length he bounced the question back. "What do *you* think?" he said.

Maggie was primed and ready for the question. "It can't do any harm provided they go in carefully and as silently as possible – to the ship that is. They, or the *Andrew James* must also keep close tabs on the pirates' boats though. We can't afford to lose touch with them now that they have taken hostages and are more vulnerable." Jack nodded and Maggie walked back to her position at the table.

THIRTY-FIVE

Commander Craig Wilson peered across the rim of his coffee mug and waited for his First Lieutenant to respond. George Lee glanced down once more at the short signal resting on the low circular table between them. "It doesn't tell us much does it, sir?"

"It tells us, I suspect, all they know." Wilson sipped his coffee and continued, "In any case we haven't much choice. We have to go back to the *Sea Shadow,* see if they've left any of their dodgy friends on board, check out any hostages left alive, get the props sorted out and cart her off to her owner so the bloody politicians can reap some glory."

"Well I think we should send the Lynx down to have a shufty round before we risk any of our blokes," said George Lee. The strain of the last week was etched in his face and he was beginning to look tired.

"I agree that caution is better than haste," Wilson said carefully. He paused before continuing. "We're running back down towards the drifting datum and I want to arrive before last light. If we arrive at about six, that will give us an hour for an initial search. We've got four hours so I intend to launch the Lynx two hours from now. I want you to get your head down for a couple of hours, George. You look like you've been eaten by a horse and shat out of the other end. I want Young John Temple to lead the Boarding Party and

Andy Stephens can rig the gear for towing. If there is enough light I propose to put the diving team in the water to see if they can untangle the 'cat's cradle' we left on their propellers. Now, off you go and don't re-appear for at least two hours." With that, Craig Wilson turned in his chair and picked up the intercom microphone to the Bridge. The meeting was closed.

George Lee didn't protest at the direction to get some sleep. He levered himself out of his chair, brushed through the curtain hanging in the doorway of the Captain's Cabin, crossed the 'cabin flat' to his own cabin in four long paces, fell onto his bunk and was asleep in less than thirty seconds. As his head hit the pillow the main broadcast clicked on and the Quartermaster's voice announced, "Lieutenant Temple and Lieutenant Stephens are requested to go to the Captain's Cabin. Flight Commander is requested to go to the Ops Room."

Half an hour later, as the Lynx was being ranged, a full flight briefing was taking place in the Operations Room. Paul Bycroft the Operations Officer, was giving the briefing while Commander Craig Wilson was sitting listening. As well as Joe Hardisty the Flight Commander, Keith Walker, the Lynx Pilot was listening intently while noting key points with a 'chinagraph' pencil on the knee-pad of his flying overalls. The Flight Deck Officer was also present but wearing his 'other hat' as Met Officer. A synoptic chart of the weather situation was pinned to a board and propped above the Operations Officer's desk, with cloud levels, wind speed and direction, temperature, sea state and a few other bits of paraphernalia hastily scribbled along the bottom of the chart. A young-looking girl with a leading seaman's badge and, incongruously, two 'good conduct' chevrons on her left arm was carefully transcribing the information scribbled below the chart onto the display board above the Helicopter Controller's console. The two Helicopter Controllers, an older-looking female Sub-Lieutenant and a fresh faced Petty Officer who, to the casual observer, looked as though he should still be at school, sat on swivel chairs turned away from their radar screens, each making notes as the briefing progressed.

"OK is everybody clear?" said Paul Bycroft, staring intently towards the two aviators. "You get airborne at fifteen hundred, climb to two thousand feet so you are reasonably safe from shoulder launched missile attack, then go to the target and initially orbit at no closer than one mile. Report what you see using 'Scramble One – UHF'. Then wait for clearance to proceed further. Make sure you have both cameras primed and ready and be prepared to return here for a role conversion to 'rapid roping' in case we want to put a boarding party in. Any questions?"

There were no questions and the two aviators hefted their big 'briefcases' and headed for the door. "Stay safe," said the Captain as they passed out into the passageway.

*

The small, grey painted helicopter climbed away, turning steadily to port as the *Carlisle's* Main Broadcast announced: "Relax from Flying Stations, Flight Deck Crew remain closed up."

In the Lynx, both men were completing their 'Post Launch Checks'. Joe Hardisty brought the radar up to 'standby' and switched on his electronic Emissions Detector. This would pick up any electronic signal being transmitted from any equipment within forty miles of the aircraft, analyse it and quickly state whether the signal was being emitted by equipment that would pose a threat to the aircraft. There was evidently nothing significant as all the little threat lights at the bottom of the screen remained green. Joe gave a 'thumbs up' to his pilot, who was in the process of engaging the radio altimeter and auto pilot, before switching the radar to 'sector scan' and pressing the green 'Transmit' button. They settled down to wait while the Lynx approached the last known position of *Sea Shadow* at a steady speed of one hundred and forty knots.

"Got it, I think." Joe peered carefully at the circular screen in front of him where a green dot had emerged at the top of the screen. "Come left ten degrees."

Keith said nothing but just concentrated on flying the aircraft accurately. The westering sun was low now and it was shining through the thin cloud overcast. Keith pulled down his smoked Perspex visor so it was impossible to see his face. He nudged Joe and pointed towards the right hand window. "Look," he said. "Boats, about three miles away." Joe looked across the cockpit in the direction still being indicated. Far below and away to the west were two small blobs moving northward through what looked, from this height, to be an almost calm sea. The boats themselves would not, in fact, have attracted attention. It was the wake they were creating and the reflections of the sun from it that had given them away. Joe checked the position and made a note in the pad strapped to his knee. He reached for the radio on the centre console and turned a small switch which would scramble his next transmission. "Xray Yankee," he called, "two small contacts close together, course north, speed estimated five to ten, mark, two miles west of me, over."

A cultured female voice answered with the single word, "Roger."

Fifteen minutes later Keith had set the helicopter in a wide turn to port, following a circle with the stationary *Sea Shadow* at its centre. There was no movement of any kind on or around the ship. Joe reported this and asked permission to go closer and lower. After a few moments this was approved and so Keith took the little aircraft down to a thousand feet, continuing the turn and at the same time edging in closer. There was no reaction from the ship and Joe began to form the view that it was abandoned. Once again he reported what he had seen but kept his opinion to himself. As they continued to circle around the ship which still showed no sign of life, Joe began taking a series of photographs with a high definition digital camera. On the second circuit he repeated the process with a small digital video camera. As he was completing the video record the radio came to life again. "Charlie, immediate," said the girl with the nice voice. They had been summoned to return to the destroyer without delay. Ignoring the 'immediate' for another half a circuit, Joe switched on and aimed the powerful infra-red detector. It remained silent and the miniature screen remained blank.

Keith pushed the nose down, increasing to maximum speed as they turned back towards the north. In just over twenty minutes the Lynx was secured by its 'Harpoon' restraint system to the metal grid in the centre of the flight deck. Keith remained in the cockpit while Joe had dashed off with his notepad in the direction of the Operations Room. The ground crew were taking the opportunity to refuel the aircraft, but they broke off as the Flight Deck Officer pointed one of his batons at the helicopter and twirled the other one around, signalling Keith, who was still strapped in the cockpit, to start the engine.

Joe reappeared followed by the Flight Aircrewman, Andy Stephens the Boarding Officer, and his eight-man boarding party. The helicopter was going to be crowded and heavy. Joe stood by the cabin door as ‘Shiner’ Wright the aircrewman checked that all the weapons had safety catches set to ‘on’ as their owners entered the cabin. It was a tight squeeze to get them all in but Joe left Shiner to organise the ‘passengers’ and walked around the aircraft, taking the opportunity to do another quick external check before climbing up into his seat on the left side of the cockpit.

In only three minutes the Lynx was airborne again, this time moving in a slightly more staid fashion as they settled the aircraft to approach the *Sea Shadow.*

Before approaching the ship, Keith made another circuit, low and fast this time. There was still no sign of activity from the ship and since the after deck provided plenty of space with no obstructions Keith decided to dispense with the fast roping technique and instead took the helicopter down to a low hover so the boarding party could jump the few feet from the aircraft cabin.

As soon as they were all clear of the aircraft, Keith hauled in power and climbed away to orbit the ship once more.

The Boarding Party split immediately into three groups and began to follow a well-practised routine. Andy led two men, weapons cocked and ready for action, towards the Bridge. Another three men made their way cautiously down towards the machinery spaces while the third group moved equally cautiously into the accommodation area, kicking open and searching every compartment they came to.

Each man was wearing a head-set connected to a miniature two-way radio so although within the ship, they could all communicate clearly and easily.

The first to report was Andy. "Bridge clear," caused each man to relax slightly. If they were facing trouble it would most likely have come from the Bridge.

Each of the machinery spaces was reported clear but the Machinery Control Room was caked with crusted dried blood. The main accommodation spaces, guest cabins, bars, dining rooms and galley on the main through deck were also quickly searched with no result. Then, when Andy was beginning to frame a report to *Carlisle* to say that the ship was deserted, a voice announced into his ear, "Crew cabins forward – locked doors."

Andy left a man on the Bridge and set off for the crew quarters. He had to go down through four decks so by the time he arrived both the machinery section and the accommodation searchers were assembled outside three adjacent cabin doors – all locked.

The doors were made of light steel in wooden frames but looked fairly substantial. Two men appeared with large fire axes taken from a damage control locker. "Go to it," said Andy. "I want to be in there in one minute."

In fact it took two minutes to smash down the first door and when the men started into the room they recoiled at the sight and smell that met them.

They found eight men and two women in the first two cabins. The third cabin had been occupied at one time but was now empty. Only five of the men and one woman were still alive. Dehydration, starvation, the stink of defecation and hordes of black flies had killed four of the captives. The remaining six were also in a very bad way. Andy's men moved them as gently as they could from their hellish dungeons. They kept them inside the ship because they had all been left in darkness for days and even the gloom inside the rest of the crippled ship was painful for them.

Andy moved away from the scene of carnage out to the upper deck and ignoring signal protocol he called the *Carlisle*: “We need medics with saline as soon as possible. We have four dead and six survivors who are all in a serious condition.” He thought for a moment before adding, “And we need engineers to get some domestic power in this thing.” As he completed his radio call he happened to glance over the side. Floating face down and nestling against the white painted steel side of the ship was a man’s bloated body. The body was dressed in a pair of engineer’s overalls. The body seemed to be full of black holes and had no shoes. Something had chewed away most of one foot. Andy vomited.

THIRTY-SIX

The USS *Andrew James* was at Action Stations. The powerful Aegis cruiser had been instructed by signal from the Task Group Commander to return to the area of operations, locate the boat convoy discovered by the Lynx from *Carlisle,* to shadow it and try to determine how many hostages were in the boats, where they were and who they were. A second signal had been received as the ship was powering southwest through the long swell at full speed. This instructed the *Andrew James* to prepare to assist *Carlisle* in providing medical and humanitarian support. The signal also announced that the *Sea Shadow* had been recovered and that *Carlisle* had evacuated survivors and was attempting to prepare the ship for movement to the north, probably under tow.

While the *Andrew James* was charging down towards the location of the *Sea Shadow*, Harry Mullen's gunboat had already passed well to the east of the datum point occupied by the *Sea Shadow* and was moving further to the north trying to keep themselves up-sun of any action in the hope that the glare from the rising sun would make it more difficult for them to be spotted by any of the boats they were hunting. The gunboat had already despatched a pair of skiffs lurking in wait for passing victims in the first light of dawn. The fuel from two of the additional tanks had been used and the empty rubber cylinders had already been jettisoned. The three remaining fuel tanks served to change the silhouette of the high speed hunter and possibly confuse the occupants of the pirate boats they were hunting. Harry Mullen had been able to surprise the pirates by approaching at reduced speed until the skiffs were within range of the Bofors gun. As the two boats manoeuvred to place themselves on each side of the misshapen gunboat Harry waited, allowing them to creep up to a position broad on each beam. As the Bofors was trained round to starboard its cover was wrenched off and at the same time the heavy machine gun mounted on the port side engaged the nearest boat. The Bofors opened fire a few seconds later and the first shell hit the water in a flat trajectory ten yards in front of the skiff. It ricocheted off the sea surface and sailed ineffectually over the heads of the men in the skiff, a couple of whom opened fire at their aggressor. The second shell sailed high above the target and the third hit the small boat amidships. The fourth shell plunged accurately but ineffectually into the floating mess of wreckage and broken bodies. On the port side the machine gun had done its job rather more quickly and the small vessel was still intact but full of holes and men who were evidently dead, and it was sinking. As the gunboat increased speed to move away the only remaining trace of the pirate boats was the bows of one pointing vertically upward and being dragged lower by the weight of its outboard engine and a slightly discoloured mess of flotsam where the other had been.

It was two hours later that the gunboat came across Hamid's two boats still journeying slowly north. At about the same time they received a burst transmission on the Satphone warning them of friendly forces in the area, describing Hamid's convoy and requiring extreme caution because hostages were known to be aboard the boats.

A quick conference took place in the tiny Operations Room below the Bridge while the boat was slowed to keep pace with the targets three miles to the east.

"The problem is we can't recognise who are the hostages and who are the bad guys," said Harry Mullen.

"There is a way to reduce the problem, I think," said Gerry Tan carefully.

"Go on," said Harry.

"Well, it's highly unlikely that the guy steering the boat is a hostage. In fact, if we can get close enough to take a careful look we can probably easily identify who is who."

"Only in the open boat," Jane York joined in the conversation from her position in front of the radar screen.

"I said we might reduce the problem, not solve it," Gerry replied. "In fact if we can deal with the open boat we can halve the task."

"If you can get that close I could call them in Arabic and see who responds." Anwar's deep and sonorous voice emerged from the Wardroom. He stepped out, wiping traces of his meal from his mouth with the back of his hand. Nobody answered but they all turned to look at him. Eventually Jane York spoke from the gloomy corner where the radar was placed. "Suppose we could separate the two boats, would that help?"

"Who are our best shots?" asked Harry. The others thought for a moment. They waited, looking from one to the other.

Anwar broke the silence. "There are sniper rifles among the weapons," he said, looking at Harry.

"Peter Archer, then Billy Walker, then, probably me," Jimmy James spoke slowly.

They continued for five minutes, by which time they had developed a plan. Harry identified key targets as the man steering the second boat, any head that might appear through the steering hatch and the stern hatch in the first boat and finally the point of tow.

The gunboat accelerated and turned in a wide circle to the left before speeding away in the opposite direction. By the time the remains of the small boats had disappeared astern Jane had placed a moving marker set for the course and speed of the targets and the gunboat idled along in a trailing position, while everybody took the opportunity to eat. "If we wait long enough they might assume we have gone away," said Harry.

It was nearly an hour later when Harry brought the gunboat cautiously up to twenty knots and Jane started to count down the distance to the marker she had placed on the screen. When the distance to the marker had reduced to four miles Gerry spotted their targets through binoculars. "Got them," he said quietly.

"Remember that the steersman in the second boat will be looking ahead and his friends will be watching the hostage," said Harry.

"Or hostages," interrupted Jane.

Harry ignored her and continued, "In the first boat only two of them can really be looking out and they will have more hostages to watch as well." As he spoke the attack team were positioning themselves. Gerry Tan took the wheel and placed himself well over on the left hand side of the Bridge. Peter was crouched in the centre of the Bridge and Billy Walker went down on one knee balancing his rifle on the side screen. Jimmy was down on the after deck lying prone with his rifle supported on a wardroom cushion. Harry equipped himself with an ordinary SA80 Assault Rifle.

As soon as Gerry had spotted the targets the speed was eased to ten knots so the boat came off the plane and the small white bow wave disappeared. Jane continued to count down the distance as they crept up behind their targets. Remarkably, neither the heads protruding from the hatches in the first boat nor the helmsman in the second boat looked back. At four hundred yards distance another man suddenly stood up in the second boat and shouted something, pointing an agitated arm towards the gunboat.

Gerry shoved the three throttles all the way, through the detent and hard forward. The stern dug in, the bow angled up and the patrol boat leapt ahead. They roared up behind the towed boat and within three minutes they were passing close alongside. By that time Peter had loosed off three careful shots at the helmsman in the second boat. The first shot missed, the second hit Khalid between the shoulder blades, catapulting him forward and spinning him round and the third shot hit him in the left shoulder punching him to his right and toppling him over the side of the boat, leaving him spread-eagled and face down in its wake.

In the front of the open boat a second man was standing, bracing one leg against the side of the boat and spraying inaccurate bursts from a rifle. As they came abreast, Billy's rifle fired and three bullets in perfect grouping kicked Melak's dying body into the air and over the far side of the boat to land with an impressive splash. Billy shifted aim and continued firing short bursts at the tow rope attachment as the bigger boat shot past.

Peter was still pointing his weapon forward as they came up with the enclosed tender. The man steering from the forward hatch had already dropped out of sight but a head and shoulders appeared in the after hatch with a weapon. He was killed with a single bullet to the head, only to be replaced immediately with a second head which ducked out of sight as the fusillade continued.

Gerry threw the gunboat into a hard turn away from the pirate boats causing the ship to heel into the turn and deflecting Jimmy's aim from his position on the after deck, but not before he got off three aimed shots through the fibreglass side of the tender adjacent to the steering hatch. The violent lurch of the tender to starboard suggested that the helmsman had been hit.

As the gunboat roared away from the damaged pirate convoy other heads peeped out of the tender's hatches and fired off a lot of un-aimed shots at the departing gunboat. It was one of these shots that hit and killed Jimmy James instantly as he was climbing to his feet on the after deck.

*

The gunboat roared away from the battle zone while several crew members tended to Jimmy. There was nothing they could do and his body was wrapped up as best they could and a sombre crew buried him with a small ceremony at sunset that evening. Another empty fuel cylinder was dropped over the side at the same spot.

Although it had been short the adrenaline flow and the loss of their shipmate caused a wave of despondent tiredness through the crew and Harry decided to hold off from further action for a few hours to allow everyone to get as much rest as possible. By midnight the distress and sadness had been replaced throughout the boat by a cold anger and they went hunting for more victims.

THIRTY-SEVEN

Hamid was beside himself. Shortly after the gunboat disappeared, the bows of his skiff where the tow rope was attached broke away. The stem of the boat where the tow was attached had been shattered by the gunfire from the small warship. Anxious to keep moving out of the area he paused only long enough for Abdullah, the sole survivor of the skiff's crew, to scramble onto the tender. What Abdullah saw when he arrived inside the tender made his heart sink. There seemed to be blood everywhere. One man lay dead on the floor of the boat and two others had been wounded but each still held onto their weapons. Only Hamid and Ahmed remained unhurt. In his frustration and rage, Hamid decided that he would kill the hostages, but in the act of cocking his rifle he realised that they still offered possibly the only pass out of his situation. He sat and brooded in silence for ten minutes or so and tried to console himself with the thought that the three hostages left in the open boat would die of thirst and sunstroke before the day ended. In this he was wrong.

*

One hundred and twenty miles to the north of the battle with Hamid, the old frigate *Cassie* was preparing to go hunting. In the briefing he had received from Jack Lang on the dockside at Faslane, Charlie had been told that this was a 'one-off' operation. There would be no second chances and although his primary purpose was to assist in the recovery of the *Sea Shadow* and her crew he was expected to strike a major blow against the pirate system. He was not told how but Jack had suggested that the curious array of weapons he had been given should be used to damage or destroy every element of piracy that could be located and identified. Maggie, who had also been present, had pointed out carefully that the Naval ships in the area were all governed by the rule of law, both national and international and so their actions were strictly limited by the Rules of Engagement imposed on them. These could be loosened or tightened but nevertheless always tended to give the enemy the initial advantage. This, she emphasised firmly and slowly, did not apply to Charlie's temporary command nor to his gunboat consort. "They do not exist," she had said, "so how can they be governed by rules – any rules?" She did not add that Charlie's little force was expendable but he didn't take long to work out that if they didn't exist while doing the job assigned to them, they could hardly suddenly appear after the event. It was a point that continued to bother him as his darkened ship prowled through the night in the Northern Indian Ocean.

That night was to be an exceptionally busy one for Charlie and his crew, and the events that would take place before dawn were to form the germ of a plan for the major strike that his masters expected.

*

As *Cassie* cruised slowly to the south, waiting for complete darkness, Charlie asked for Dan Holloway to come up to the Bridge. When Dan arrived he pre-empted Charlie's first question. "We have plenty of fuel, boss," he said. "We could probably get to Australia if we keep the revs down."

"We may have to," said Charlie.

Dan looked concerned. "I didn't mean it literally," he said, scratching the back of his head.

"Don't look so worried. We may be able to top up without bothering our masters at home." Charlie peered through his binoculars as he spoke.

"Where from?" Dan continued to look worried and slightly puzzled.

"We could try using the same sources as the people we are looking for."

Dan decided not to pursue the point so he simply nodded towards Charlie's back and said, "I'd better get back down below."

In the Operations Room, Nobby Small was peering intently at the radar screen in front of him. At the same time he was switching the range control and fiddling with the 'gain' and 'clutter' buttons at the base of the screen. Every few minutes he would jot something on a pad of paper to his right. After half an hour he paused, leaned back in his chair, massaged the ache in his lower back and picked up the intercom handset. "Bridge," he said. "Ops sitrep."

There was a pause then, "Bridge."

Nobby glanced down at his pad and started to list what he had found. "Four significant targets altogether," he said. "Target one is eighteen miles due south, heading slowly west, speed erratic but averaging about six knots. Target two is fifteen miles south east, stationary, and only painting intermittently. Target three is right on extreme range to the south, popped up about ten minutes ago and is heading north at ten knots. Target four is about eight miles south of target two, heading north slowly and looks like it will be joining up with target two. As well as those four I have a dozen or more very small and intermittent targets. They are difficult to keep tabs on and they seem to jump around a bit but I'm sure that there are small boats or similar things in those positions."

"Thank you." There was a protracted pause while the information was digested on the Bridge. Nobby waited patiently until the speaker crackled into life once more.

"Ops, Bridge, we will investigate targets one and three. Can you give me a course and speed to intercept 'one' please? Keep the speed below fifteen."

"Roger," said Nobby. He pressed a button and fiddled with a 'four-way' switch, pressed another button and read off the small figures on the screen that had now appeared alongside the circle surrounding target one. He pressed the switch on the intercom handset. "Bridge, Ops," he said. "Course to intercept target one is two zero five. Time to intercept at fifteen knots is one hour thirty-one minutes.

This time the answer was immediate. "Ops, Bridge. Thank you. Watch that one please and report any change in course or speed." Even before the call had ended Nobby felt the slight change in the ship's motion as *Cassie* increased speed to fifteen knots.

Seconds later a different speaker burst into life. "D'ye hear there, the ship will go to action stations in one hour. Make sure you have been able to eat before then." *Cassie* altered course a few degrees to starboard and headed purposely towards her unsuspecting target. Those men who could, snatched a quick meal in the dining hall but others, despite the broadcast instruction were already assembling and checking weapons.

Forty minutes later everyone was closed up at their allocated 'Action Station' and the curious old frigate was completely blacked out and advancing towards a ship some six miles ahead. "Anybody make out what it is?" called Charlie as he stood on the starboard Bridge wing peering intently through a pair of binoculars.

"Looks like another trawler," a disembodied voice answered from somewhere beyond the open Bridge door.

"Slow ahead both, come to port onto one eight zero," said Charlie. Immediately the ship's head began to move around twenty degrees to the left. "It's a bloody big trawler," said Charlie, still peering through his binoculars at the quarry they were stalking.

Tom Clarke slipped silently through the door and took up a position alongside Charlie. He aimed his binoculars at the darkened ship and twiddled with the focus ring. "I think it's a whaler," he said at length.

There was a pause while both men, now steadying themselves with elbows leaning on the mahogany rail, continued to study the ship, now only a couple of miles ahead and to the right of them. "I think you're right," said Charlie without moving the binoculars from his face. "The big question is, is she our whaler or their whaler?"

No one answered but Nobby's metallic voice announced over the Bridge intercom, "Range four thousand yards, course still west, speed now eight knots. No transmissions. Contact still unidentified."

"We'll try her out," said Charlie as he lowered the glasses and stepped back into the Bridge. "Half ahead both engines – give me revolutions for twelve knots, come round onto her starboard beam." This last was addressed to Jimmy McCoy who deftly conned the frigate through ninety degrees until she was following a parallel course to the whaler. As they began to overhaul her, the darkened ship stoically maintained her course and speed.

They were just coming abeam of the whaler when Tom stepped back into the Bridge, closing the door to the Bridge wing behind him. This action probably saved his life. Without warning a dozen rocket propelled grenades were fired towards *Cassie* from various locations in the whaler. Simultaneously *Cassie* came under attack from both light automatic fire and heavy machine gun fire. Bullets thudded into the port Bridge wing where both men had been standing and a rocket propelled grenade hit the screening on the port side. A Bridge window on the same side was shattered, spraying shards of glass among the seven men inside the Bridge. With great good fortune there were no serious injuries but there was a lot of blood flowing freely from cuts inflicted by flying glass.

Not everyone was so fortunate. Down aft on the flight deck Will Taylor and ex-corporal John Stevens had been standing by a mortar when they were both hit by wildly spraying light machine gun bullets. John, a tough man with a background in the Royal Horse Artillery and the SAS, was hit by eight or nine bullets and killed instantly. Will, a great bull of a man who had worked as a farm labourer since leaving the Navy fifteen years before, was hit in the left arm and left thigh, a wound that narrowly missed his femoral artery, but he remained conscious and stayed at his post.

"Hard a starboard, full ahead both engines." Charlie shouted above the ringing in his ears and the helmsman who had held on desperately to the small 'wheel', threw the helm over and shoved the electronic engine room repeater forward to the full ahead position. Two red lights came on and the engine room telephone buzzed. No one answered it.

Back on the flight deck, as Will stood in a pool of his own blood, he felt the ship heel hard to port as he saw the 'trawler' begin to pass behind *Cassie*. By instinct, or perhaps just wishing to let go of the mortar bomb in his hand, Will dropped it into the mouth of the firing tube. There was a click, a seemingly long delay of only one second and a whoosh as the mortar bomb was hurled into the air in a high trajectory. Will sank slowly to the deck beside the weapon. He was still looking aft towards his target and he saw the bomb land square in the centre of the other ship's after deck. There was an explosion followed immediately by a smoky fire and accompanied by a cessation of firing throughout the ship.

As *Cassie* charged away from the whaler, first-aiders moved around the ship patching up the wounded. The body of John Stevens was collected, carried carefully down to the Sick Bay and placed in a bunk behind drawn curtains. The same team collected Will, attempted with some success to staunch the flow of blood and carried him down to a different part of the same Sick Bay.

Charlie sat in his cabin while cuts on both arms were bandaged. Brian Hall stood in the doorway. "That one's a right bloody floating porcupine," Charlie said ruefully. Then, "We were over-confident."

"We can fix him without getting too close I think," Brian said slowly.

"Explain."

"Torpedoes."

"Will they work?" Charlie waved Brian towards a chair.

"We won't know till we try, but we should try because that bastard outguns us at close quarters – and you can bet he is now very alert."

*

Charlie took *Cassie* out to a position six miles north of the whaler which was still travelling west but now at very slow speed. They drifted along in that position while Brian and John Banyard struggled to understand the vagaries and complexities of the ship launched torpedo system. No form of instruction manual had been supplied with the four torpedoes so John had to dig deep into his memory to dredge up what he could about electric torpedoes and to supplement that knowledge with initiative and experimentation. All the torpedoes were powered by banks of batteries and it seemed that the launch process should activate the weapon, arm it and start the powerful electric motor. The torpedoes were designed primarily as anti-submarine weapons but it seemed possible to set them to run shallow so they could be used against a surface target.

The morning was well advanced before the ad hoc torpedo launch team was ready to try the first weapon. Streaked with sweat, John stood upright and eased his aching back. "Right," he said, "we need to load the first one into the tube and we should be able to launch it either from the torpedo console in the Ops Room or locally from here."

John stood back as Brian and several other men struggled to align and raise the torpedo on its trolley and then, using a block and tackle as well as brute force to push it into the tube. It took three attempts to get the first weapon in, by which time they were getting slightly better at the task. Eventually, after a few more struggles and false hopes they all stood back admiring the row of little coloured lights on the launch control panel.

After John had explained that the Mark 46 was a less complicated weapon they had opted to try this first. As far as he could recall the torpedo would run for up to about six thousand yards before its inbuilt sonar would go active and search for a target to home in on. The tube mounting was wound out to point over the side and one of the team was sent up to the Bridge to invite the Captain to take the ship into the recognised firing position. They stood back and waited.

On the Bridge Jimmy McCoy, who had the 'watch' manoeuvred the old frigate towards the whaler which was still limping along on a westerly heading.

The thin layer of cloud had cleared and the sun was beating down on the men assembled by the torpedo launcher when Charlie strolled out onto the Bridge wing and waved his arm in a signal to launch. Brian sighted along the tube and noted that it was pointing towards the pirate whaler about two miles distant on the beam. John pressed the launch trigger. There was a delay, then when they were all convinced that nothing was going to happen, the torpedo shot out of the tube and disappeared below the surface with an impressive splash. Brian, John and the others peered towards their target, straining to see if they could detect any tell-tale track in the water. The sea surface between the two ships remained undisturbed.

John had just said, "It should be there by now," when there was a frustrated cry from behind them.

"Christ! Look at that!" Five men peered silently at the red nose of the Mark 46 torpedo bobbing in the sea about eight yards from their own ship.

They tried the second Mark 46 torpedo, which they fired about an hour later but with almost the same result, only this time the weapon appeared to have travelled about fifty yards before it felt the need to come up for air. Despondently, Brian trudged up the deck and climbed the ladders to the Bridge.

In response to Charlie's unstated question Brian said, "I think we've crapped out as far as torpedoes are concerned.

We can try the missiles we have but we'll need to get a bloody sight closer and will probably take more RPG hits."

"We need to take that ship out," said Charlie. "I propose to stay here and eliminate any boats they are controlling then have another go tonight." Brian nodded and turned to make his way back down to the deck. As he started onto the Bridge ladder he saw John gesticulating from the torpedo mounting. He seemed excited about something.

Brian stepped back into the Bridge. "I think John wants to give it another go, skipper," he said.

Charlie was beginning to lose interest in the plan. "Can't do any harm to try, I suppose," he said without enthusiasm.

When Brian arrived back at the mounting there was a new air of anticipation among the men. "Look at this," said John. "We've got a different arrangement of lights on the control panel and it sounds as though something is buzzing inside."

"OK let's launch it," said Brian, not really expecting much difference from the previous attempts.

Brian pulled the launch trigger. This time there was almost no delay before the Stingray shot out of the tube, describing a graceful arc through the air before plunging into the sea. "The propellers were turning!" John stared at the expanding ripple where the Stingray had entered the almost completely calm sea. Once more they stood and waited patiently, straining to see any sign of the torpedo running. There was no sign and most of the men standing around the torpedo launcher had begun to search the sea surface closer to the ship looking for yet another 'non-runner' when there came a rumbling thunder-like noise from the direction of the whaler. The five men stared in fascinated, awe-struck silence as, apparently in slow motion, the whaler was lifted bodily clear of the surface under a mantle of flame, and then, as it flopped back down the ship broke completely in two. The stern part of the ship did not re-appear but the bow section thrust out of the water, hanging in suspension and pointing forlornly skyward.

The silence gripping the small group of men became oppressive as they watched the drama play itself out. The whaler's bow section stayed pointing upward while pieces of loose equipment and bodies tumbled down into the sea and then, very slowly the wreckage slid backward below the sea surface. leaving nothing but an oily scum dotted with bits and pieces of wreckage.

Cassie was already turning towards the whaler's last position and in fifteen minutes she was cruising through the rapidly dispersing remains, mostly consisting of small pieces of floating junk and some shredded clothing. As he peered over the side, Brian saw first one, and then a second glistening grey back surmounted by a fin, break the surface. The black frigate cruised several times through the area of the wreckage looking for survivors. There were no survivors.

Cassie turned onto an easterly course and increased speed to intercept 'target three'.

*

Three hours later *Cassie* was loitering slowly along still heading east and waiting for the last crimson streaks of sunset to fade from the darkening sky. Most of the damage from the skirmish with the whaler had been tidied up or covered with temporary repairs. Will Taylor had been sedated and was now relatively comfortable. The mortal remains of former corporal John Stevens had been cast into the ocean in a brief but dignified ceremony with funereal sentences improvised from uncertain memories. Everybody had eaten an evening meal and Charlie had assembled his key people for a tactical conference.

Charlie looked around the eight men assembled in various states of relaxation around the Captain's Cabin. "This one might be a little different," he said, surveying the expectant faces. He paused, "The reason is that I would quite like to capture a ship." Several men sat upright in their chairs. "If we can get hold of a mother ship not only will we be able to wreak havoc among unsuspecting attack boats but we might be able to confuse the enemy a bit more." He looked across at his two Arab crewmen, seated close together on the banquette that ran along one bulkhead. "That is where I hope you two will come in," he said.

Tom Clarke interrupted, "If the last one is anything to go by, skipper, trying to capture a ship could be a bit bloody."

"We will need to use stealth and subterfuge," continued Charlie. He turned towards Mohktar and Ali Serrana. "Do you think you could pass for Somalis?" he said.

"Do you mean look like Somalis or speak like Somalis?" Mohktar responded.

"Both, but speech might be more important."

The two Arabs looked at each other uncertainly. Mohktar cleared his throat. "Thing is, I'm Iranian. I can speak Arabic but it would be my accent that would give me away. That and the smell when we get closer."

Charlie looked puzzled.

"I mean they stink and I don't," retorted Mohktar.

Charlie allowed his gaze to shift to Ali who shifted in his seat and said, "You want me to sound and look like a sewer rat, I'll do my best but I will be spotted. Maybe it's best we don't get near them, just call them, eh boss?"

Charlie thought about this and was about to reply when he was interrupted by a call on the Bridge intercom.

"Ops has got a firm radar contact fourteen miles ahead as well as three or four intermittent contacts a bit closer to us. He thinks the returns might be bouncing off outboard engines but the contacts are definitely there although being intermittent makes the picture confused."

"Does the main contact fit the one we were looking for?" asked Charlie.

The answer was hesitant. "Well, Nobby says it's in about the right place, give or take ten miles or so. It's following a different course and he can't be sure that it's the same one – but he is pretty sure that it is one of them."

"What's its course?"

"A bit erratic but generally about one one zero."

"Thanks," said Charlie. "Keep tracking it and see if you can identify exactly how many boats there are. Let me know if any of them start to move towards us."

"Aye skipper."

Charlie looked around his cabin and smiled. "I think I have a plan," he said. "We are going to be a tethered goat. Henry, how long to rig canvas screens to change our profile?"

"It depends, boss. How good a job do you want?"

"I want to be able to fool someone in an open boat in the dark that we are a small tramping bulk carrier." Charlie stared at Henry, waiting for an answer.

"We've got some paint so I can rig up a name and port of registry that might do. We've got plenty of canvas." He thought for a moment and said, "Give me an hour, maybe an hour and a half and we can come up with something that might work."

Charlie nodded. "OK. Start now. Let me know when you think she will be presentable."

Henry got up and moved to the door. As he stepped over the threshold he turned and said, almost to himself, "I don't know that she'll ever be presentable, but I can make her interesting – like a Union Street whore, if you know what I mean."

Charlie smiled but everyone else ignored Henry King's parting shot.

"Right, a good metaphor that. What I want to do is to parade up and down looking worthwhile to any 'Jack the Lad' that is floating about waiting for a prize. If the ship we are trailing is a mother ship, and I think it is, and if he has got his boats out looking for trade, and I think he has, then we let the boats have a go at us. We give them a surprise, and with the help of Mohktar and Ali we should be able to give the mother ship a surprise."

They continued talking, going over 'what-ifs' and other variations to the plan, allocating jobs and positions. After an hour they dispersed to set the operation in motion, with a final reminder from Charlie. "Remember," he said, "they generally operate their boats in pairs, sometimes in threes, so we don't rush into action at the first sign – and we keep the noise down as much as possible. Finally, if at all possible I want to keep their boats."

Half an hour later Henry knocked on the cabin door. Charlie was dozing, stretched out on the banquette. "She's as ready as she will ever be, boss," said Henry from the doorway, "and I think, with the right lights she'll pass muster."

Charlie got up, stretched, and followed Henry out onto the upper deck. What he saw surprised and impressed him. He strolled around the deck followed by Henry, then, one foot on the Bridge ladder he turned and said, "Yes, she will pass muster, I think; well done Henry." By the time he reached the Bridge *Cassie* was showing the steaming and navigation lights of a medium sized trading vessel, and with canvas and paint she had been completely transformed from any indication of being a warlike ship.

"Steer for a position five miles astern of the target," said Charlie. "Set revolutions for ten knots and put a slight weave in the course." They settled down to wait.

It was just after midnight when the first boat was spotted. It was a fairly big rigid inflatable and was trailing *Cassie* about a mile astern. Shortly afterwards a second rigid inflatable was spotted gradually overtaking the ship on her starboard side, this time a little closer than the first one. A third smaller boat was following some way behind the other two.

Tom was using night vision goggles. "Eight men in the one astern," he said, "but I can see no more than six in the other boat." They watched and waited as the two boats crept cautiously closer, and the mother ship opened up the gap between her and *Cassie* to eight miles.

The speed was eased to eight knots and 'reception' teams were placed at likely points of attack all around the ship. The boat which was pursuing them crept gradually closer until from about two hundred yards right astern it made a sudden rapid dash towards the port side of the flight deck. The adjustable nets that surrounded the flight deck were raised in the vertical position and disguised with sheets of black canvas around the outside.

A three pronged grapnel came sailing up over the side and lodged on the top of the net rail. Seconds later a second one followed it. A scuffling noise preceded the arrival of the first pirate who reached the top of the rail and vaulted over. As he landed he was shot once with a silenced pistol at close range and he flopped down, twitching onto the non-skid surface of the deck. His companion appeared at the top of the second grapnel rope and met the same fate. Unfortunately this one toppled backwards, arms spread wide, and dropped with a noisy splash into the sea. A third man appeared at the top of the first rope and was grabbed by Harry Smith rising up from a crouched position behind the cover of the canvas. A fire hose held by two seamen, Tim Kay and John Baker was aimed over the side in front of the boat and pointed at the occupants. The helmsman in the stern sheets was hit by the powerful water jet and blasted straight over the side of the boat and as the four other occupants shielded their eyes they were swiftly and expertly shot dead.

Tim Kay swarmed up and over the rail, down the after rope and into the boat. Within minutes he had tipped the four dead men over the side to join their companions floating away in the wake of the ship, and finally neatly secured one of the grapnel ropes so that the boat, a big modern rigid inflatable with a fifty horsepower Honda outboard, was now being towed by the frigate. On the starboard side in two places, similar actions had taken place. However the last boat to attempt a boarding had become alerted and attempted to haul off after the first two pirates had arrived on deck. Following Charlie's instruction that under no circumstances were any of the pirates to be allowed to escape, the boat was riddled with small arms fire. And left as a tattered mess of rubber barely afloat and being dragged down by the weight of the outboard on the stern.

So far, the plan was working. They had captured two boats intact and, a bonus, they had recovered a working UHF radio, which was taken as quickly as possible to the Bridge.

Charlie held the radio in his hand and waited. Both Mohktar and Ali stood by his side waiting and watching the radio. For five minutes nothing happened and then with a background of hissing, the radio produced a burst of staccato

Arabic. Mohktar took the radio from Charlie and spoke briefly into it which produced a protracted response followed by another shorter answer, this time from Ali.

Charlie looked quizzically towards his two men as he took the radio back. "What did you say?" he asked.

Mohktar answered. "They have heard gunfire and wanted to know what happened," he said. "I told them that we – they – have taken a few casualties, not serious but we are in charge of the ship. Ali told them we have lost a boat. They were not happy but they told him to follow them into their harbour."

"Thank you," said Charlie, somewhat formally. "Now for phase two. Man the two boats please and proceed." Two teams each of five men, headed respectively by Mohktar and Ali, set off from the Bridge down the main deck and over the side into the big rubber boats.

One by one the boats cast off and moved forward towards the port side of the ship ahead. As *Cassie* increased speed to overhaul the pirate mother ship, Tom, still peering ahead through night goggles suddenly exclaimed, "It's a tug!" He lowered the goggles from his eyes and waited to adjust to the ordinary light level while Charlie edged the frigate closer to the tug until, as the two rigid inflatables arrived one behind the other alongside the low towing deck of the tug, *Cassie* turned a few degrees to port and thudded neatly alongside the starboard side of the tug. Men poured into the tug from both sides and as three or four heads appeared from the superstructure they were efficiently shot down. Within less than two minutes both ships were firmly secured together and the battle was over, leaving small groups of the boarding parties methodically searching through the ship for survivors. Three men were produced, a cook and two from the engine room. They were trussed up and hauled bodily up into the frigate.

THIRTY-EIGHT

The *Andrew James* was steaming south at high speed. Men and women were battling on the forecastle against the thirty knot wind created by the American cruiser's speed. They were still stowing the last of the hoses and couplings that had been used to complete yet another refuelling exercise.

John Reagan glanced up at the United States Navy ensign streaming aft from the starboard signal halyard alongside the stubby mainmast. He held the Bridge Main Broadcast microphone in his hand and paused to gather his thoughts before making his announcement to his crew.

"Now hear this," he began, using the traditional opening words for any broadcast instruction. "This is the Captain. We are heading south to join up with the British destroyer *Carlisle*. I have been informed that the Somali Illegals have left the hostage ship *Sea Shadow*. *Carlisle* is attempting to clear up the *Sea Shadow*, check for booby traps and ensure the ship is sufficiently seaworthy to be towed back to a friendly port. There are reports of six survivors from the hostages but they are all very sick indeed. *Carlisle* has no doctor on board so as soon as we are close enough our Medical Team Alpha will be transferred by helicopter to the British ship. Any of the survivors designated fit enough to travel will be transferred to this ship for ongoing treatment.

There are plenty of enemy vessels in the area and we know that even very small boats can deliver lethal force. Therefore at sunset there will be no external lights – that includes smokers. Upper deck patrols will be maintained and action lookouts will remain closed up. The message is – stay alert guys. That is all." He replaced the microphone back in its stand and climbed slowly back into his chair.

With barely half an hour to go to 'last light' there was a shout from the lookout stationed on the port Bridge wing. "Officer of the watch – port lookout sir, I have a single object at red thirty, range estimated at four miles sir, possibly an empty boat sir."

The report was quickly relayed to the Captain who was now down in his cabin, eating a sandwich. The Aegis cruiser turned thirty degrees to port and began a speed reduction to ten knots. As the distance closed, several pairs of binoculars were focused on what seemed to be a damaged and abandoned skiff, about twenty-five feet in length. As they eased closer the boat became the target for several automatic weapons, aimed from high on the flag deck and lower down on the main deck. John Reagan took in the tension ranged above and below him as he brought his ship closer to the skiff. He reached for the broadcast microphone again and said tersely, "Captain speaking. All weapons tight. No firing until cleared by me." As he placed the microphone on the top of the compass repeater the *Andrew James* had reached a position where he could actually see down into the boat. There were three men lying in the bottom of the boat and as he was assuming that they were dead he saw a movement.

He called over his shoulder to the Officer of the Watch, "Get a seaboat away with a medic onboard and get those men over here – be quick."

The reaction was indeed quick. In less than ninety seconds a black rigid inflatable was cutting through the small waves at speed and heading for the skiff. Restraint stretchers were propped in the boat, with red-cross marked medical bags. Two men knelt inside the rubber tube at the bows aiming small automatic weapons at the skiff. When the rubber boat bumped alongside the skiff, men scrambled over the side and tenderly began to move the three bodies and strap them in the stretchers. After a further four minutes the boat was back alongside the cruiser and the stretchers were being hoisted out. Another small boat raced across and took the skiff in tow.

The three men were taken carefully and gently down to the Sick Bay and Hamid's one time skiff was hoisted on board covered in heavy duty polythene and retained for later detailed forensic examination.

The *Andrew James* got under way once more and before midnight she had re-joined *Carlisle* and *Sea Shadow*. Some eighteen hours later the search teams in *Sea Shadow* had satisfied themselves that there were no hidden booby traps in the ship and other groups of men and women had carried out a rudimentary clean-up to make it generally habitable for a towing crew to man it. The cat's cradle of wire hawsers had been expertly cut away from the propellers but the combined damage to gearing and propellers determined that the ship would need to be taken home under tow.

Eventually, with George Lee heading a small towing crew, *Carlisle* set up the tow and started to work up to the modest speed of six knots while *Andrew James*, in the words of her Captain, rode shotgun on the towing group to ensure that there would be no interference. As the three ships started to move north an urgent conference was taking place in the Captain's Cabin aboard HMS *Carlisle*. The big problem the two Captains were addressing was their failure to locate and apprehend the pirates who had taken *Sea Shadow* and even more important, where was the Prince?

One of the hostage survivors rescued by the *Andrew James*, although seriously ill, had confirmed that he and the other two had been taken hostage on board *Sea Shadow*. He had been locked away for most of the time that the pirates had been in control and although he was unaware of what had happened to the Prince he confirmed that the boat towing the one in which he had been held captive was one of the tenders belonging to *Sea Shadow*.

A 'flash' precedence signal had been sent off from *Carlisle* to the Task Group Commander at Northwood Fleet Headquarters in England which in turn had been rapidly relayed to Buckland House.

There were two copies of the signal and they were being studied independently and intently – as though intent study might change the contents – by Jack Lang and Maggie McGuigan in the conference room of Buckland House.

"Shit," said Jack with feeling.

"They've done quite well," said Maggie. "They've recovered the ship and accounted for most of the crew. Our two renegade bulls in the china shop are also creating mayhem among the opposition as well." She tried to sound upbeat, but not very successfully.

"But they haven't got the big prize," said Jack, "and I think that is deeply disappointing."

"Yes I suppose it is." Maggie was capitulating to Jack's mood.

*

The reason for the failure of the anti-piracy forces to find Hamid and his remaining pirates was that he had found a mother ship – not his own mother ship, but one with whom he was hopeful of coming to an understanding.

It had been shortly after the attack from the small warship that Hamid had spotted another skiff. It was very low in the water and contained only four men and in fact Naseem, the crew leader, had spotted Hamid's boat well before Hamid had spotted him.

Hamid reflected that, once more, his luck had held. When Abdullah had scrambled into his boat Hamid had only four fit men including himself. He also had eleven hostages, too many to take with him if he transferred to the skiff, but he learned that the skiff had a consort boat a few miles away and the two boats were hunting together. After nearly an hour of fruitless bargaining the second boat, a rigid inflatable, was already approaching. While the bargaining was going on one of the wounded men lying on the floor of the tender finally succumbed to his wounds. Minutes after he died his body was tumbled out through the side hatch without ceremony and almost without interrupting the debate with the skiff, still cruising alongside as they argued.

Hamid's negotiating position was not strong and was becoming weaker as time moved on, and which brought a rendezvous with the mother ship closer.

Eventually it was agreed that Ahmed and Abdullah would go with the wounded man and four of the hostages who would all be squeezed into the skiff. Hamid, Ali and Quasada would take the seven remaining hostages in the big Rigid Inflatable. The sea was rising slightly so the two boats, each packed to capacity could only travel at reduced speed when they disappeared in a direction which the helmsmen hoped would take them to their mother ship.

The yellow painted tender was left empty but for one dead man heading under reduced power in a completely different direction, ready to become a decoy.

By nightfall Hamid and his men were safely aboard a small green painted coaster, previously employed as an inter-island trader in the Maldives Archipelago. All of Hamid's hostages were down in one of the empty cargo holds, chained and padlocked to strong points set into the bulkhead. The coaster was heading for the Bay of Lefar where the man in command intended to remove the hostages from Hamid's care and then to ransom them himself.

*

Hamid was not a stupid man. It was true that he had no formal education but he did have the education of the street. He knew how to look into a man's eye and see what often lay behind gestures and smiles of welcome. Above all he was a hard man and an unforgiving man. He was able to rationalise his activity as a pirate because that was the way his god had sent him. His priorities were simple. First came himself, then his family, then his clan and finally the men who served him. He had no notion of patriotism or loyalty to a country because he didn't understand what a country was, nor what benefit a country might bring to a man. Throughout his thirty-five years he had lived in a society where the strong prevailed and the weak died. Strength, he believed, came through possession, knowledge and ruthless application of weapons, as well as firm and unbending control of those who served him. However he was also acutely aware that men would only continue to serve him if he continued to be successful, and without his men he was nothing.

As soon as Hamid and his diminishing band of warriors had been taken aboard the mother ship he had sat and taken food with Yusuf who now owned the ship and its attendant boats. Expressions of welcome and friendship had been floated about but the eyes on the other side of the metal table told a different story. And Hamid was not fooled.

No attempt had been made to relieve Hamid or any of his men of their weapons for to do so would have produced a violent response and everyone knew that the outcome would be bloody, and unpredictable. Hamid had acquiesced to the suggestion that Yusuf should take his ship quickly back to the Bay of Lefar and that, on arrival, the hostages should be landed and sold to a 'negotiator', the payment to be shared equally between the two men.

That first night onboard, Hamid and his men had settled down to sleep in a mess hall in the base of the ship's superstructure. One man was always to remain awake as a guard and as the others began to sleep Hamid remained awake, considering his position and what actions he might take. Including himself he had five men, one of whom was wounded, but still able to fight. Yusuf had at least sixteen men at his disposal but his 'cruise' had not been successful and he might be encouraged to send his boats out hunting once more, in which case Hamid might have a chance to turn the tables. Also, Yusuf was unaware of the special value of one of Hamid's hostages. Hamid thought that it would be better to keep Yusuf in ignorance for as long as possible.

THIRTY-NINE

While the *Andrew James* was patrolling in a wide circle around the centre of operations where *Carlisle* was preparing to tow *Sea Shadow*, crews from both warships were still working in difficult conditions to recover as many services as possible in *Sea Shadow* and to clean and fumigate the ship so that George Lee and his towing crew would be able to work in a reasonable environment. In the Ship's Hospital aboard the *Andrew James*, the three hostage survivors were being treated for malnutrition, and severe sunburn as well as several other injuries. Although still seriously ill they were all showing signs of recovery.

Sixty miles to the southwest, Harry Mullen's gunboat was powering steadily north through a rising sea. The men and women on board were hunting for enemy boats on whom to wreak their revenge.

Fifty miles to the north of the patrol boat, Yusuf's coaster was moving purposely towards the Somali coast but Yusuf had picked up two possible contacts on his radar set and was even now planning one more sortie by his attack boats. In this he was guided by the knowledge that on return to the Bay he would be required to pay his backers and the only means he presently had to that end were the few miserable hostages brought to him by Hamid.

Well to the north of Yusuf's coaster, Charlie de Vere was transferring men and weapons to his newly acquired tug. His intention was to take both ships into Lefar Bay and cause mayhem.

Unfortunately for Yusuf, he slowed his ship and launched two of his three attack boats at almost precisely the same time as his coaster began to show on the radar of the former patrol vessel approaching at high speed from the south.

Yusuf's big rigid inflatable boat powered away to the south, leaving the slower skiff trailing in its wake. Their targets were a further ten miles or so to the south and were travelling slowly north. Yusuf and his lieutenants believed these were probably private sailing yachts travelling in company for mutual support.

*

Onboard the yacht *Sundowner,* the owner, Jerry Howard, a retired United States Navy Captain was on watch and, being well aware of the risks inherent in this sea area, he was keeping a keen lookout. By his side he had a small portable UHF radio which he used from time to time to keep in touch with his friend's yacht, *Red Rover,* half a mile on his starboard beam. A thick leather belt was strapped uncomfortably to his waist. The belt supported a holster containing a Colt 38 automatic pistol and several ammunition pouches. In the locker beneath his seat and within easy reach was a Remington repeater shotgun.

Jerry picked up the radio with the intention of making a routine check with *Red Rover,* when something far ahead caught his eye. He peered into the evening gloom but could not see anything. He put down the radio and picked up his binoculars, again examining the horizon ahead. Almost immediately he saw what had attracted his attention. It was a small but distinct white bow wave being produced by a small fast vessel coming straight towards his boat.

Jerry grabbed the radio and spoke tersely into it. "Trouble ahead John," he said. "Get ready." The only reply from the other yacht was an audible click.

Jerry stood and deliberately scanned the horizon all around the boat. To his horror he saw another white bow wave approaching from the south. Without hesitation he reached into the emergency bag hanging from the cabin bulkhead and brought out a small yellow box with an aerial attached. He thumbed the protective guard clear and pressed the red button. Immediately an orange light began flashing on the unit.

At the same time another orange light began flashing above a screen in the Combat Information Centre of the *Andrew James* and a similar light began working in the Operations Room of the *Carlisle.*

A hurried consultation took place between the captains of the two warships and thirty seconds later the *Andrew James* peeled away from the towing operation and settled on a heading to take the ship 'down the bearing' of the 'Pirate Alert Signal', simultaneously winding up to thirty knots.

Jerry watched the shape behind the white bow wave gradually form into a big black rigid inflatable boat but to his surprise, it didn't head straight towards him. Instead it slowed down and began to circle the two yachts at a range of about three hundred yards. Jerry could not know that the pirates were waiting for their second boat to catch up. Instead, he assumed that the bigger boat approaching fast from the south was another pirate vessel and he hauled his shotgun out of the locker.

The man leading the crew in the rigid inflatable had also spotted the boat coming from the south and assumed that he had competition in his attempt to capture the yachts. He began to circle closer to the two yachts and Jerry knew his worst fears were confirmed because he could clearly see armed men in the boat.

The gunboat roared up from the south and while the pirates were watching what they still believed was one of their own, Harry Mullen opened fire with the Bofors. The first two shells straddled the big RIB, the third shell passed through it without exploding and the fourth and fifth shells blew the boat into a thousand shards of rubber and plastic. The six men simply disappeared.

*

The gunboat roared on past the yachts and through the expanding pool of wreckage, focusing now on a second small contact which, through the night vision goggles, had formed itself into a wooden skiff with at least four armed men aboard. Too late the skiff attempted to turn away and out of the path of the bigger vessel charging towards them. At fifty-one knots the bows of the gunboat towered over the skiff before running right over the top of it. The small boat broke in two. With precise timing hand grenades were dropped into the two halves of the wreck. The gunboat slowed slightly and continued north, blending into the horizon within a few minutes.

"Holy shit!" said Jerry Howard.

*

Fifteen miles ahead of the gunboat, Yusuf's coaster was wallowing beam-on to the short cross sea. His boats had not returned nor had he heard anything on the radio. He waited with three of his men, lounging and squatting in various parts of the Bridge. He had one man in the engine room and another lurking below keeping an eye on Hamid and his gang.

Hamid was also aware of the time that the boats had been away and was calculating when to make his move. He intended to attack Yusuf and capture the ship but, in the base of the superstructure he was a long way from the Bridge, several floors above him. Yusuf's man was watching them from across the mess hall when Hamid saw a packet of Egyptian cigarettes on the table. Although he didn't smoke he pulled a cigarette out of the pack and ostentatiously started looking for a means of lighting it. Looking pointedly towards Abdullah he walked easily across to Yusuf's man indicating that he was looking for a light. The man shoved a hand in his pocket and pulled out a box of matches which he tossed onto the mess table. Hamid picked up the matches, selected one and lit his cigarette. As he drew in the smoke he started coughing, bending forward as he tossed back the matchbox. Instinctively the man brought up both hands to catch the matchbox. As he did so, Abdullah uncoiled from his position leaning against the bulkhead and with a continuous flowing movement, he threw his knife. It hit Yusuf's man in the throat and he went down, gurgling as he clutched at the handle of the knife. Hamid took one long step, pulled out the knife and, without compunction, slit the man's throat.

Hamid and his three fit men moved towards the staircase leading to the Bridge. They had just started upward when there was a series of explosions from above them. A searing wave of heat and smoke rolled down the stairway amid further explosions. Hamid changed direction and ran from the stairway to a screen door leading to the upper deck. He opened the door and shut it again quickly. In the brief moment of looking out he had seen several missiles coming towards the coaster, and he realised a separate gun was also firing at them. The superstructure above him was a pillar of flames.

Hamid's enhanced sense of survival cut in. He ran back into the mess hall and out through a door on the opposite side. A second RIB was sitting on the main deck just in front of the superstructure and between the four men they managed to drag it to the ship's side and tip it over. As it hit the water, one after another they leapt into the darkness.

Abdullah was first aboard and he stuck out a hand to pull Hamid in. The other two dragged themselves over the side while Hamid was fiddling with the outboard, which surprisingly was still in its place secured to the boat's transom. Having left the ship by the disengaged side they stayed where they were, keeping the bulk of the burning coaster between them and the attacker. Another man emerged from a hatchway, ran to the side and jumped overboard landing with an ungainly splash alongside the RIB. At a nod from Hamid he was hauled in. They waited for five minutes or so when the noise of battle died away. As they tentatively crept the boat out around the bows of the stricken coaster they saw, with some relief that the attacker had gone. Hamid set a course by the stars which he hoped would lead him home. He had lost his hostages but he still had a huge amount of money strapped around his body.

FORTY

It took several hours for the *Andrew James* to locate the two yachts and when the cruiser arrived at the scene a boat was sent across to get the story of what had happened from Jerry Howard. Jerry was coming down from his adrenaline fuelled 'high' and his description of the events which had so recently occurred was somewhat disjointed. The story that was relayed to the Captain boiled down to a couple of boatloads of armed men suddenly appearing in a threatening manner and then, when disaster was imminent, an avenging angel, in the guise of some sort of gunboat, had roared out of the night, instantly destroying both of the threatening boats and all their occupants, before charging off into the night once more.

When the boat had returned and the Boarding Officer was able to report the gist of what he had learned, Reagan held a quick conference in his cabin. In fact he simply posed a series of questions and answered most of them himself. As the Aegis cruiser drew away from the two yachts, now looking small and lonely in the night, Reagan sat in his chair and briefed the Officer of the Watch on his intentions. "The gunboat or whatever it was is supposed to have left the scene heading north and going fast. We don't know what that ship is or where it came from but we will move north for fifty miles to see if we can find anything. Keep a sharp radar watch and report any contact as soon as it is seen. After fifty miles it is my intention to turn back to the east and re-join *Carlisle* in the escort role. Have you got that? Any questions?"

The Officer of the Watch had no questions. "Aye sir," he said. "As well as the radar I'll double the lookouts."

"Good," said Reagan as he slid off his chair and made his way down towards his cabin.

Just two hours later the intercom in the Captain's Cabin buzzed urgently.

"Captain."

"Officer of the Watch sir. We have sighted a glow on the horizon and we have a stationary radar contact in approximately that position. I think it could be a ship on fire, sir."

"How far away is the contact?" Reagan climbed out of his comfortable leather chair, shaking off the sleep that had just been interrupted.

"Six miles sir," said the Officer of the Watch.

"Go to flank speed. I'm coming up."

When Reagan arrived on the Bridge he saw that his Executive Officer was already present. He climbed into his chair and said quietly, "Stand the helicopter to, X.O."

"Already done sir," came the reply.

"Come down to fifteen knots as we approach and then go around the contact in a wide circle. I want to stay beyond effective small arms range," said Reagan.

"Aye sir."

They were now approaching a small coaster which appeared to be well on fire but with the fire largely confined to the superstructure, parts of which seemed to be melting in the localized heat. The *Andrew James* was taken all the way around the burning vessel and several pairs of eyes peered at the ship as the big warship cruised around. No-one could see any sign of life.

"OK let's see if we can range up close enough alongside to see if we can do anything about that fire," said Reagan.

As the *Andrew James* was brought in towards the burning coaster, close enough to feel the heat from the flames, six hoses aimed powerful jets into the burning section. Reagan noticed that the fire was not only confined to the superstructure of the coaster but it did not appear to have spread down the structure all the way to the main deck. The combined effect of the six hoses pouring seawater under full fire-main pressure into the heart of the fire began to douse the flames. Within fifteen minutes of the *Andrew James's* arrival alongside the burning ship the flames had been replaced by smoke.

"Right, let's board her," said Reagan. "Use the 'Seahawk'."

Five minutes later the Navy Seahawk helicopter was waiting on the flight deck with rotors spinning as the Executive Officer led a boarding party of ten men and women into the aircraft.

Reagan watched as the helicopter lifted easily into the air, pointed the nose down and moved in a steady turn through three hundred and sixty degrees to hover adjacent to the main deck of the coaster. Having checked carefully for obstructions the pilot moved the helicopter sideways until it was hovering over the deck, then reduced its height until the wheels were no more than a foot above the coaster's deck. Led by the Exec the boarding party hopped, one by one, out of the aircraft onto the deck. Each individual presented a strange bulky shape because they were all wearing bullet proof vests as well as automatic life-jackets. As he moved away from the helicopter the Exec leaned down and placed both hands on the deck. He ran to the side and did the same again. Then standing where he could be seen clearly from the cruiser he raised both arms to the horizontal. He was signalling that the deck was not unduly hot and so the fire did not appear to have spread from the after superstructure tower.

The party split into two teams. The second team included the medics and they waited near the door into the base of the superstructure while the others cautiously passed through the door. Inside there were stairways leading up and down. Smoke was pouring down from the upper stairway, so led by the Exec they moved down the other stairway. At the bottom of the stairs they were faced with a big steel door, clipped firmly shut. Hammers and boots knocked off the clips and the door was pushed open. Before anyone stepped through the doorway noises were heard – like a cross between a human voice and an animal in pain. Flashlights were poked through the open doorway and they identified the area as a big unlit open space, undoubtedly one of the ship's holds.

Smoke had also entered the hold from somewhere, making the atmosphere inside hazy and causing some difficulty with breathing. Men and women stepped through the door and peered into the gloom being randomly pierced by the beams of the flashlights.

"Holy fuckin' shit!" said the Exec as he took in the scene before him. Ten men and possibly one woman were manacled and chained to ringbolts along the side of the compartment.

The Exec recovered from the initial shock, turned and shouted, "Harman, Reilly, get up on deck, get the 'chopper' back and have them fetch bolt croppers – big ones!"

"Aye sir." A man and a woman ran from the room and sprinted up the stairs. When they arrived on deck the instruction was relayed to the deck team who passed it back to the *Andrew James* by UHF radio. A quick word to the deck group and they were followed back down below by two medics.

*

When the four men and women from the deck party arrived back in the hold, the scene before them seemed actually worse than previously. Six of the hostages chained to the bulkhead were unconscious. The others were dehydrated and barely conscious. The two medics hefted their medical bags in through the door and began to dribble water between parched lips where the patients were able to respond. Others tried gently to move the bodies into more comfortable positions.

It seemed to take ages but was certainly no longer than ten minutes before the helicopter was back hovering above the deck and bolt croppers, portable cutting gear as well as several stretchers were being handed down and then rushed down to the ship's hold.

It took nearly two hours to free all of the hostages and carry them up to the deck of the coaster. The helicopter could only accommodate three stretchers at a time together with a medical attendant and so it was another hour before they were all transferred to the *Andrew James*. As the last of the stretchers was being carried below the man strapped onto it opened his eyes and said in a barely audible voice, in English, "I am Prince Feisal." Then he closed his eyes again.

The news that one of the hostages was the Prince was not conveyed immediately to the Command, because the man who heard it, he said, had more important things to do. Nevertheless before the *Andrew James* steamed away from the derelict, Commander John Reagan had gone down to the

Ship's Hospital and confirmed from photographs that had been supplied, that the man, who was now heavily sedated, did indeed closely resemble Prince Feisal.

'Flash' precedence signals were sent off to *Carlisle* and to the Task Group Commander. The information was then relayed by secure telephone to the Operations Room at Buckland House. It took a few minutes to write the report carefully on a signal pad which was then taken in to Jack and Maggie who were in the middle of a meal break.

Jack looked at the paper, thought for a moment and then said, "We've done it, Maggie," and then, more cautiously, "At least I think we've done it."

Maggie just smiled. "Well done Jack," she said, "but I think we should wait for DNA proof before we break out the champagne."

"We had better call off the wolves," said Jack.

"After the champagne and the DNA," said Maggie.

FORTY-ONE

Because the activities of what Jack had begun to call his 'wolves' could not be officially recognised, neither the Captains of *Cassie* nor the gunboat were made aware of the development and the likely consequence that the operation would soon be called off.

In fact Charlie, on the Bridge of *Cassie* had just finished briefing his key people on a plan which was so audacious that it would be remembered in the 'Spook' world for years to come.

At the same time, the gunboat was actively hunting for more victims not far to the south, and having used all of the deck carried tanks, Harry Mullen was beginning to worry about fuel. Neither ship knew the location of the other.

Charlie had explained that he was going to try an old fashioned 'cutting out' operation. His intention was to make his way into the Bay of Lefar where the pirates seemed to have a base and where about eight captured ships were anchored close to the shore. Within the contents of his captured tug Charlie's crew had discovered two sets of metal cutting gear, numerous shackles, hawsers and towing gear.

Among the anchored ships was a big gas carrier, distinguished by the gas containing spheres which dominated the outline of the ship.

*

Charlie's intention was to sneak in and steal the gas carrier, then take it out to sea, clear it of any enemy and use it to create a diversion while releasing as many of the other anchored ships as possible.

Tom Clarke now headed a crew of twelve men in the tug, including both Arabic speakers. Weapons had also been transferred to the tug but many more had been found abandoned onboard.

As they approached the low coastline a heavy overcast had drifted off the land and obscured moon and stars. The two ships, completely blacked out, with the tug leading, crept slowly into the bay. As the radar picture became clearer nine ships were located anchored between one and two miles offshore. The gas carrier was easily identified by its unusual silhouette. It must have been one of the more recently captured vessels because it was anchored a little further out than the others.

With almost no noise the tug backed in under the overhanging bows of the huge ungainly ship. A big shackle was fitted across the links of the anchor cable which seemed to have no strain on it. A towing hawser was connected to the shackle before cutting equipment was produced which effortlessly sliced through the anchor cable below the newly fitted shackle. The severed end dropped into the sea as the tug eased forward to take the strain on the towing hawser. In less than an hour all three ships had cleared the bay and nobody seemed to have noticed.

*

The next part of the exercise was more problematic. With the tug still towing the bigger ship out to sea, *Cassie* eased alongside the gas carrier and to the accompaniment of squeaking rattan fenders, men crossed from one ship to the other. It took some time to search the ship and it was nearing dawn before the boarders were able to determine that there were no hostages in the ship. They had however located, disarmed and captured three young men who suddenly seemed very anxious to please.

The gas carrier was a modern vessel and equipped with an autopilot. On the stern of the ship, set at the top of a steeply angled launch ramp was a pod type life raft which could be launched by tripping a lever from inside the craft, whereupon the small orange painted pod would shoot down the launch ramp and into the sea.

Jimmy McCoy and the engineers Mike Carter and John Banyard comprised the 'scuttling crew'. Jimmy went up to the Bridge and the other two disappeared below to start the powerful diesel engines. The ship was eight miles offshore when she started to move ponderously forward. Jimmy brought the bows slowly around until they pointed directly towards the shallow sandy beach and the scattered settlement beyond. As she began to move John opened the last of the valves on the gas containing spheres and the liquefied gas under huge pressure began to pour out and fill the hull of the ship through doors and deck hatches, as many as possible having been opened.

Gas carriers are built to be fast ships. With six miles still to go and the big diesels at full throttle this one was already touching twenty-four knots, and was settled on a course aimed straight for the centre of the shallow sloping beach and disaster. Jimmy stayed on the Bridge long enough to ensure that the ship was going to pass clear of all the other vessels and have an unrestricted run to the beach. When he was sure of this he left the Bridge, meeting Mike on the Main Deck and John as they reached the lifeboat pod. All three were conscious that they were surrounded by the stink of gas as they walked carefully along the main deck. The hatch opened easily and they climbed into the pod. There were straps round the edge of the pod so they each strapped in. Jimmy reached up and pulled the handle. Nothing happened. "There must be a door relay," said John as he unstrapped and moved forward. They opened the entry hatch again, slammed it as hard as they could and pulled the launch handle. There was a click but nothing else. Jimmy started to unstrap with a view to jumping over the side when there was another click and without warning the capsule shot down the ramp and plunged into the sea astern of the ship. Jimmy moved forward to open the hatch but John grabbed his arm. "Leave it," he said, "we're safer in here if she blows." They waited as the sweat ran down their faces.

Cassie was stationed well outside the bay and several people were crowded into the Bridge watching the speeding gas tanker through binoculars. Dawn was just breaking over the eastern horizon.

Charlie stood at the front of the Bridge, sweaty hands gripping binoculars trained on the stern of the gas tanker. He relaxed a little and breathed again as he saw the small orange escape pod come hurtling down its launch ramp to crash into the sea.

*

"She should hit the beach any time now, boss," said Henry King as he stared at the gas carrier. His words were prophetic. The big ship began to rear up as it was propelled by the enormous momentum through the shallows and up the almost flat beach. The ship was completely clear of the water before the first explosion came. The watchers saw a huge flame cover the deck of the tanker almost in slow motion. A few seconds later the sound reached them. First there was a heavy rumble rather like a prolonged thunder clap, then came several sharp reports followed finally by three enormous explosions which actually hurt the ears of the watchers on the Bridge wings. All sound was now blotted out by a rushing roaring noise as a tower of flame shot skywards to be followed by sheets of fire emanating apparently from the sides of the ship. The gas tanker was now at the top of the beach and still moving, albeit more slowly. It looked like the irrepressible advance of Armageddon as the remains of the ship continued to move through the sand, accompanied by more explosions which were jetting large sections of burning debris in every direction.

Within moments fires seemed to be burning all along the beachfront. Massive columns of dark blue smoke were obscuring most of the shore area while flattened buildings could be glimpsed through occasional gaps in the firestorm. There was a second shattering roar with more flaming jets, this time shooting in all directions. The ship came to a stop among the first buildings before the third explosion came. The ship was still burning furiously when it literally blew apart with flaming debris flying high into the sky like a macabre firework display. The flaming pieces fell among the other buildings of the settlement. Everything beyond the waterline was one huge raging, popping, hissing, crackling inferno.

With the cutting gear shared between the two ships, *Cassie* and her tug consort began to move in towards the billowing wall of oily smoke. As they each entered the smoke visibility became very difficult. *Cassie* was better placed because she could feel her way by heading for the big radar contacts that surrounded them. The tug blundered about largely by following timed runs until something loomed out of the smoke. There was at first no attempt at interference and by midday the two ships had broken the anchor cables and dragged eight unmanned ships out of the bay and cast them adrift.

*

It was as *Cassie* was casting off the last ship, another, smaller, tanker, that men appeared on the upper deck of the tanker and started firing down onto *Cassie's* deck. Two light machine guns promptly returned fire from the Bridge roof and the men disappeared from sight.

As *Cassie* cleared the area, heading south, Charlie decided it was time to report progress and he drafted a signal to be transmitted to the secure Satphone at Buckland House. He reported that the base at the Bay of Lefar had been destroyed following an accident with a captured liquefied gas carrier and that there were likely to be few survivors. He added a second paragraph stating that eight hijacked ships had been towed out of the bay and were now adrift and probably unmanned to seaward of the bay. He ended the message by repeating the precise position of the drifting ships.

Further to the south things were not going quite so well. The gunboat had continued through the night looking for more victims. Four more small boats had been located and destroyed and then, as the sun climbed higher in the sky they came across a white painted luxury motor yacht. The yacht seemed to be drifting and there was no sign of any crew on board.

*

Harry felt it would be worth a look because there might have been innocent people in need of help on board the motor yacht. Several members of his crew suggested caution but with the heady success of the night's hunting, Harry had allowed his guard to drop. Cautiously they eased in towards the motor yacht. Harry had just decided to go alongside the vessel and board it when a shower of rocket propelled grenades hurtled out from the motor yacht. Several missed completely but one hit the open Bridge, killing Harry and devastating the Bridge. Two more penetrated the Hull near the water line but only one of these exploded, blowing a huge hole in the starboard bow. Gerry Tan had been standing beside Harry when the RPG landed but curiously, apart from instant deafness he was completely unharmed.

Most of the rest of the crew were shocked by the suddenness of the attack and reacted slowly as men began to pour out of the motor yacht and leap across to the gunboat. The air was suddenly full of gunfire, smoke and fire.

Karen Ford had been thrown off her feet by the original blast from an RPG in the forward mess deck. She lay stunned for a few moments but as she recovered her senses she couldn't see because of the thick smoke swirling around. She felt hands clutching at her breasts and more hands tugging at the waistband of her jeans. Her tee shirt was in tatters and the rest was being ripped off. Am I going to be raped in a sinking ship, she thought. Then answered her own thought, shouting aloud, "Hell, no! Not in a million years!" She realised that a bearded face was inches away from hers and responded by jack-knifing her body and smashing her forehead into the nose in front of her. There was a strangely feminine scream and one pair of hands slipped away only to be replaced by another. She brought her right hand around to the back of her belt, clasping the handle of her knife. Rolling onto her left side caused the hands pulling at her waist to loosen, giving her the opportunity to slash upward with the knife. Unaware of who or where she had struck she was sprayed with warm blood. She put her feet flat on the floor and scooted backward along the deck, followed by the man scrabbling after her. She seized her second opportunity, bringing her knees hard up towards her chest then kicking out violently with both feet hard into the man's crotch. He went down gasping.

Further aft, the tide of battle was turning but the gunboat was definitely sinking. Mike Cowley's head popped out of one of the engine room hatches followed by a hand holding a Smith and Wesson automatic pistol. No-one was looking in his direction so he calmly squeezed off five shots, each one finding a target. A shadow loomed over the hatch and he ducked down simultaneously firing up into the shadow. It fell with a thump across the hatch so Mike withdrew and squeezed around the front of the gas turbines aiming for the hatch on the port side. When he looked out there was no-one there so he climbed through onto the upper deck. The ship was heavily down by the bows and blood mingled with twitching bodies covered the decks. A burst of automatic weapon fire came from the Bridge which looked like a disaster that no one could have survived.

Suddenly it was all over. Harry Mullen and Jane York lay dead, one an unrecognisable mess in the Bridge, the other on the starboard deck. Paddy Stone, the cook, was doubled over in a pool of blood but as Mike looked around he could see no living pirates. There had been nine of them to start with. One was drowning in the water rising in the forward mess, with Karen's knife sticking out of his throat, another was concussed behind him; three bodies were lying in the water and two on the upper deck. One more was hanging out of the flybridge of the motor yacht also looking fairly dead.

Gerry Tan leaped across the small gap to the motor yacht and Mike ran up the side deck to join him. They kicked open the door to the saloon and ventured carefully in. A cabin door was swinging open at the far side of the saloon. Without hesitation, Gerry fired off a short burst through the door. The door was shattered and swung forward at the same time as a young bearded Arab toppled forward into the passageway.

The gunboat was sinking rapidly and Gerry cajoled the six uninjured crew members to move as many weapons and as much kit as they could into the motor yacht. They were all shocked and dazed so the work went slowly but with Anwar who seemed to have more energy than any of the others, they had managed to transfer most of the remaining weapons and ammunition, as well as a good quantity of food and some water. The engineers shifted tools as well as the secure Satphone and several portable radios.

It took thirty-five minutes in all, by which time the bow of the gunboat was below the sea surface and progress below the main deck had to be through water at least waist deep. Gerry shouted, "She's going," as the last two loads were bundled across to the motor yacht. They all stood silently on the deck of the motor yacht as the gunboat paused with deck awash before slipping quietly below the surface, taking its skipper with it as well as a brave woman.

FORTY-TWO

The news that Prince Feisal had been recovered alive was treated with expressions of great joy and delight in Buckland House. The Foreign Secretary had been informed but Jack had tempered his enthusiasm by explaining that there had been casualties and it was also apparent that a series of explosions had occurred in a coastal village at the Bay of Lefar. Information was sketchy but the disaster seemed to have been caused when a gas carrier, loaded with liquid petroleum gas had run aground and caught fire. The vessel apparently had been taken hostage by Somali pirates recently.

Later reports based on satellite information suggested that at least six large ships were drifting, unmanned in the Indian Ocean. An urgent demand was sent via the Task Group Commander to turn round the *Andrew James* and send the ship back to deal with the situation. The Captain of *Andrew James* was not impressed since he had only just re-joined *Carlisle* and her tow.

In Buckland House the back slapping had subsided but Jack and Maggie were enjoying a bottle of chilled Moet et Chandon between them as they discussed what should happen next. It was at that point that news of the loss of the patrol vessel came in.

Jack stared silently as the lines of bubbles sparkled up to the top of his glass. "We've lost good men," he said at length.

"And a good woman." Maggie was looking pensive and the room remained in silence, punctuated only by the steady tick of a walnut cased clock on the sideboard.

"I will write to their families," said Jack.

"We knew there would be casualties and to be honest, they could have been much worse. I think we need to concentrate on the extraction of the ones we have left." Maggie peered intensely at Jack, willing him to shake off the mood of despond which seemed to have overwhelmed him.

Jack looked up and took a long deep breath. "The original plan was to ferry the crews into Mafia Island using the patrol boat and then scuttle the frigate in deep water. We could have flown a C130 into the airstrip on the island and the whole operation would have been wound up in twenty-four hours. Now we need to think again."

Maggie waited until he had finished, leaned forward across the table and said quietly, "Kerguelen."

"What?"

"Kerguelen Island."

"Where's that? And so what?" said Jack.

"It's the way we can wrap it all up neatly and get our boys and girls home in one piece," responded Maggie.

Jack waited, then said, "Tell me more."

"Kerguelen is an almost uninhabited island deep in the Southern Hemisphere. It is owned by the French and they have up to five hundred research scientists located there. But the island is the size of Wales and extremely inhospitable. The scientists are all located in the western peninsular and the rest of the island is mountainous, wild, with a filthy climate and hundreds of deep unexplored inlets."

"How do you know all this?" said Jack.

"I read. It used to be called Desolation Island which about sums it up. If we don't like Kerguelen there's another much smaller one – Heard Island, completely uninhabited and about four hundred miles to the north. It has the same filthy climate though."

Jack stroked his chin and looked pensive. "Neither place would encourage visitors," he said at length.

They sat, thinking, for a few moments. Jack climbed stiffly out of his chair and began to pace the room, his hands occasionally moving to illustrate his unspoken thoughts. Maggie sat and watched. She had seen this pensive mood many times before and knew that it was best not to interrupt. However, as Jack was starting his second turn about the room, the door opened and a woman entered clasping a handful of signal sheets. Without speaking, she divided the papers into two identical groups and placed them on the table before leaving as quickly and silently as she had arrived. Jack opened his mouth to speak, thought better of it and reached for the small pile of paper in front of him. Maggie was already speed reading her papers, skimming swiftly through each one before placing them carefully side by side across the polished surface of the table in front of her. She looked up, waiting for Jack to finish reading.

At length he put his papers back in a small pile and looked up. "Well, it looks like mopping up and closing up time," he said.

Maggie nodded. "What about Kerguelen?" she persisted. Jack didn't answer her directly. He kept looking towards the signals, still trying to marshal his thoughts.

"What about Kerguelen?"

A shadow of irritation crossed Jack's face. He waited then said, "It sounds as if it might be a possible exit course but can they get there? How long will it take them? If they do get there, how do we extract them?"

"Do you have an alternative?" said Maggie.

"Yes, of course. Stick to the original plan. Scuttle the ships in deep water and bring the crew home in another vessel. Maybe as shipwrecked mariners."

"Kerguelen is better." Maggie held up a hand to forestall interruption and continued, "It's a two-thousand mile run heading almost due south and it's through what will be almost empty ocean. I believe the frigate has the fuel. I don't know about the tug they captured but if they can take it with them that is their ticket out and home." Still holding up Jack's response with her hand, she continued, "Before you ask, I don't include the gunboat crew. They are down to seven with one wounded. They should take the vessel they have captured and head for Mafia Island. Anwar would be grateful to take it off their hands and they can answer any questions by claiming to be a delivery crew who were attacked by a gang of pirates that they managed to beat off. It's close to what actually happened and will account nicely for the injuries and bullet holes. Anwar should be able to deflect any close interest and the airstrip is long enough to get an unmarked aircraft in and out without fuss. What do you think?"

Jack sat, continuing to think about what Maggie had said but finding his thoughts confused by wondering about how it was that this remarkable woman seemed to have the ability to think herself – and himself, he silently corrected – out of any seemingly intractable problem. "I buy the plan for the gunboat crew," he said, "that seems on the face of it pretty straightforward and safe. What aircraft could we use?"

"We could use the trucker," said Maggie.

"Do you think he is reliable?" Jack looked troubled. "If he isn't we could be responsible for the incarceration or death of a lot of people."

"We are already responsible for the death of a lot of people," retorted Maggie. "And we can make him an offer he can't refuse."

"You know what I mean," said Jack, tetchily, "our people!"

Maggie waved her hands in submission. "Alright, that was being a smart-arse," she said, "but just listen to me. It will work. I'm sure of it!"

"Tell it to me then," said Jack, not wishing to admit that he had no better plan to offer.

Maggie took a deep breath and reached across to the coffee pot as she considered how to begin. "As of now," she said, "the frigate is somewhere parallel to the southern point of Kenya with hopefully a good load of fuel. The gunboat crew are further south by now and within easy striking distance of the Comoros Islands. We don't know the fuel state or seaworthiness of the boat they have requisitioned but we should ask them if they can get it to Mafia Island. If they can't, plan B would be to pick them up in the frigate which will have to pass them going south, and sink the boat in deep water. They would all then carry on south to Kerguelen. It's about a two-thousand mile run down to Kerguelen and I'm hoping that they have sufficient fuel to cover that..."

"We'll ask them anyway," interrupted Jack.

Maggie continued as if he had not spoken. "If they don't have enough fuel we would need to risk a refuelling with a tanker, probably out of Mauritius. We would need to do it at night and keep it quiet but I've been doing my sums and I have good reason to believe it shouldn't be necessary."

"What about the tug?"

"The tug," continued Maggie "is a different, and easier, problem. The tug is a straightforward commercial vessel which has spent an unforeseen period in different ownership.

If she needs fuel, I think we arrange for her to simply go and get it, from Reunion, or Mauritius, or anywhere else en route for that matter. It is important though, that she has enough fuel to get to Kerguelen and back again as far as the Comoros. We could even bring her all the way home and if her proper owner pops up we announce that she has been found abandoned on the high seas."

"It would be useful to own an ocean-going tug," mused Jack.

"As I was saying," continued Maggie, "once the fuel situation is clarified we take the two ships south in company, hide or scuttle the frigate at Kerguelen and bring the crew back in the tug."

"To Mafia Island?"

"To the airstrip at Kilindoni," said Maggie. "The Hercules is a very versatile and rugged aircraft and I see no reason at all why the trucker shouldn't be able to get his old C130 into Kilindoni and out without any problem at all."

"OK, I'm convinced," said Jack, smiling for the first time that day. "Let's get the boys and girls working on the details, before I speak to our lord and master the Right Honourable Secretary of State for Foreign Affairs."

Maggie nodded as Jack paused in the act of picking up the telephone and asked, "What about all those ships that de Vere cast adrift?"

"They are being attended to by the United States Navy," said Maggie triumphantly. Jack held the phone and pressed a single digit. He spoke rapidly into the handset and as he placed it back on its cradle he turned once more towards Maggie.

"You haven't mentioned the tiny difficulty of how the frigate is going to get into Kerguelen Island without being spotted by the French?"

Maggie looked patient. “Kerguelen,” she said, “is about ninety miles long by about sixty miles wide. It has permanently filthy weather, and the western side consists of a range of high snow-capped mountains. The whole coastline is covered with hundreds of deep water, fjord-like inlets. The French contingent of research scientists is cosseted in the peninsula at the southeast corner of the island, that being about the only habitable area in the whole place. If the two ships approach from the northwest they will almost certainly remain in the radar shadow of the mountains. Although the French have a satellite ground station they are looking for other things in other places. Nobody in their right mind would actually want to go to Kerguelen.”

“Have you been there?” said Jack.

“Yes.”

“I’m impressed.” He thought it best not to enquire further.

Maggie continued, “If everything conspires against them then I suggest they set the tug to towing the frigate and go back to the story of going to the breaker’s yard.”

“And got lost, I presume?” said Jack.

“Something like that, yes,” said Maggie, “anyway if they go in at lunch time the locals will all be busy with the claret and beouf bourguignon and will never spot them.”

“I hope you are right,” said Jack as he left the room heading for the Operations Room.

FORTY-THREE

Charlie de Vere held the Satphone print-out in his hand and peered across the table towards his 'officers'. "Looks like it's all over bar the shouting," he said.

Brian scratched his chin, looking both puzzled and concerned. "Where the bloody hell is Kerguelen?" he said.

The others looked towards Charlie but Tom chipped in, "Used to be called Desolation Island. That, by all accounts is a pretty fair description of it. Makes the Falklands seem like Shangri-La and it's something like South Georgia only more remote."

"That might be a little over-pessimistic. Apparently only half of it is like South Georgia – the rest has got a bit of vegetation and fewer mountains. The main thing is it is over two thousand miles to the south and probably through bloody awful seas." Charlie looked across the cabin towards the Engineer. "Have we got the fuel?" he said.

"We have enough fuel to get there," said Dan Holloway, "but bugger all after that, and it would be nice to have a little bit of comfort zone, boss."

"How much has the tug got?"

"Not enough," said Dan.

"OK, we need fuel." Charlie paused. "We'll just have to ask home base to fix up some arrangement in Mauritius or somewhere. How much do we need?" He looked expectantly at Dan.

"As much as we can get."

"Typical bloody plumbers' answer, that is! Tell me what we need in numbers of tons, please."

Dan looked uncomfortable. "Eighty to a hundred tons minimum, however three hundred tons would top us up nicely. But the tug should top up with every drop it can get because that, presumably, is our bus ride home."

"Right," said Charlie, "I'll get on the UHF and tell Tom the score. I'll also see if he can give me an estimate of his fuel," he paused, "and I suppose I should warn him that he's going to be a bit crowded on the way home."

"You've forgotten that we have another problem." Brian Hall looked worried as he continued, "We've got six prisoners."

"I haven't forgotten them," said Charlie rather brusquely, while privately cursing himself because he had done just that.

Dan broke the ensuing silence by clearing his throat noisily. "If the boot was on the other foot," he said, "they would just chuck 'em over the side and bugger off."

"But it isn't," snapped Charlie. The silence continued.

"I suppose we can't just shoot the bastards because we're supposed to be civilised," Dan muttered grudgingly.

Charlie glanced across at Dan. "The problem we have is that we can't hand them over to any authority," he said slowly as though feeling his way through his argument, "because we don't exist. Therefore we either release them somewhere or we kill them."

"In cold blood?" This came from Brian. The others looked shocked and stayed silent.

"We've killed a helluva lot in hot blood," said Dan.

Charlie was still deep in thought. Eventually he looked up and said, "Get Mohktar up here." Brian picked up the sound-powered telephone above the desk and relayed the request to the Bridge. They sat and waited.

In a couple of minutes there was a polite tap on the door. Dan opened it and ushered Mohktar into the room.

"Take a seat," said Charlie. Mohktar perched uncomfortably on the end of the banquette. "I want to talk to you about the men we took off the gas carrier. You have questioned them, I know," said Charlie, addressing Mohktar. Mohktar nodded.

"Do they speak or understand English?"

"Very few words," said Mohktar.

"Can they read English?"

"No."

"Are you sure?"

"Sure," said Mohktar, emphatically.

"How can you be sure?" Charlie leaned towards Mohktar.

"They are young and simple men. They are so much fodder for the warlords. They know guns and how to kill but they know little else. They are ignorant, even in the language of their birth. They speak but they understand nothing of what may be written." Mohktar spoke confidently and with feeling.

"OK, thanks Mohktar. Treat them well and tell them we are going to release them providing they do not give trouble." He nodded to Mohktar, signalling the end of the interview. Mohktar stood and left the room.

Charlie waited until the door closed. "Right, here's what we do," he said. "We transfer them to the tug which will have to go for fuel and I would guess that this will be somewhere in the vicinity of Mauritius. When they have finished fuelling they put the six prisoners in one of the inflatables – without the outboard – and cast them adrift close enough to give them a chance of paddling ashore." He raised a hand to stifle evident protest before continuing. "The clever bit is that we give each of them a sealed envelope and tell them that in it is a document giving them safe passage back to Somalia. We tell them they should present this to the authorities when they get ashore. What we actually put in the envelopes will be a full account of who they are, how and where they were found and what we believe they have done. This will be set out in English but in a form that looks like an official certificate. The fact that all the accusations will have to be anonymous will weaken any case against them but we can put sufficient factual information in to make it very difficult for them to talk their way out." As he finished, he looked up and around the group with an air of triumph, waiting for questions or challenges. There were none.

"Well we better get on with it," said Brian. "I'll brief Mohktar on what to tell them."

"OK, but do it carefully," said Charlie. The group broke up.

An hour later *Cassie* was heading southeast through a rising sea at fifteen knots – Dan's estimate of her most economical speed with four hundred miles to run to Mauritius. The tug was lumbering along about two miles astern and steadily dropping further behind as she pitched and rolled, struggling to keep up. Tom had established that the tug had plenty of fuel but he was far from certain of its rate of consumption. The fuel gauges seemed to be giving changing readings as the vessel was thrown around but Tom seemed confident that they would make it to Mauritius but wouldn't commit himself further. Charlie pondered the situation for some time before sending a carefully constructed signal by Satphone. It took a further hour before the machine chirped and chittered out a reply. 'Continue towards Mauritius,' it read, followed by 'underway replenishment both vessels. Rendezvous position follows.'

Charlie called Dan up to the Bridge, showed him the terse instruction and asked his opinion on whether it was possible to obey the order.

"Depends what they send to refuel us," said Dan. "We can manage an underway refuelling if the weather calms down a bit but the tug is going to have a problem. I really would like to know her rate of consumption and fuel capacity…" he lapsed into silence.

Outside, the tropical twilight fell away quickly into night and the wave train began to come from a different direction so that they were no longer pounding straight into it. "I'll ask for advice," said Charlie.

"They won't like another call," said Dan.

"Well they can fucking well lump it. We've done the job and done it well," said Charlie, showing his frustration. He slid off the tall chair and, followed by Dan, rattled down the ladder to the Operations Room.

Dan's estimate of the reaction from Buckland House proved correct. The signalled response concluded with the terse instruction to 'keep traffic to a minimum'. However they had the information they were seeking. On full tanks it was suggested the tug had a range of over five thousand miles and the estimated rate of consumption suggested that the vessel would have plenty of fuel to reach Mauritius.

Charlie slowed down the ship and called Tim Kay up to the Bridge. When the signalman arrived Charlie gave him a clipboard with a lengthy message pinned to it. "Can you send that by light?" he asked.

Tim scanned the paper and nodded. "Can do, boss," he said, "but I'll have to send it slowly so the reply will take some time."

With *Cassie's* reduced speed, the tug had caught up and only a mile of sea separated the two ships as Tim started to send the signal. He did it carefully and slowly, dividing the lengthy instruction into several sections. Forty minutes later he switched off the ten inch lamp and turned to Charlie. "Shall I wait for a reply, skipper?" he asked.

"Yeah, I think so," said Charlie, now back in the tall chair.

Only twenty minutes later a bright light flashed from the wheelhouse of the tug which was now wallowing along close on the port beam. The short waves had all but disappeared but the long lazy ocean swell remained.

The reply from the tug was brief. 'Roger. Awaiting transfer.' The two ships were eased closer together and brought to a stop. One of the captured RIBs was lowered over the side from the frigate, eight men climbed down into it and, with several machine guns tracking its progress from the deck of *Cassie* the boat motored quickly across to the low towing deck of the tug, where six of the men climbed out of the boat, this time covered by guns from the deck of the tug. The whole operation took no more than fifteen minutes before the boat was hauled back aboard *Cassie* and both ships started to make way again.

*

Onboard the motor yacht Gerry Tan had received a similarly short signal from Buckland House which seemed to be as vague as it was short. Gerry had been told to head for Mafia Island, destroy his weapons and stores, then dispose of the vessel and wait at Kilindoni. He decided to hedge his bets and keep some of his weaponry available for the present. There was an open discussion among the remaining crew as to what 'dispose of the vessel' meant, with a general feeling that there should be no haste in obeying the instruction.

Mike Cowley summed up the view of the crew. "We won the bugger in a hard fight and we should hang onto it until we're certain we're not going to get our feet wet."

At this point Anwar stepped in with an attractive solution. "I will take the ship," he said, and I will hide it away until I have changed the ship into a different ship," then he added, "after I have landed the shipwrecked victims of a pirate attack, of course."

This seemed to satisfy everyone and the tension flowed quickly away, only to come surging back, following the roar of powerful engines from somewhere astern of the motor yacht. There was a quick scramble for positions and weapons as three small boats, two RIBS and an outboard powered skiff, in a broad line abreast came into view, rapidly overhauling the big white vessel.

Men could be seen standing and sitting in each of the boats as one swung to starboard of the motor yacht and the other two rushed in close on the port side. Gerry held the wheel and crouched down behind the flimsy structure, trying to avoid becoming an obvious target. The two boats on the port side were surging past the ship only twenty feet away when the man standing in the leading boat loosed off a prolonged burst of fire from an automatic weapon. Small spurts of water close to the motor yacht's, bows marked the entry point of the bullets.

Gerry whirled the wheel hard to the left and shoved the twin throttles forward. The bigger vessel began turning quickly to port and heeling as it responded to the increased engine power. It took only seconds to close the gap between the two vessels and although the driver of the RIB spun his wheel hard left he was not quite quick enough to prevent the bows of yacht and boat banging together. The rubber tube of the RIB caused it to bounce back off the side of the bigger ship. The sudden reversal of direction caused the gunman in the bows to tumble forward, falling over the front of the RIB and disappearing between the two vessels.

Several things then happened at once. The other RIB on the starboard side of the motor yacht suddenly found himself astern of his quarry and unsighted from all possible targets.

On the port side, while the RIB was still pressed against the hull of the motor yacht, three grenades sailed over the side of the yacht. One landed in the sea and began to sink, followed by a muffled ineffectual explosion, the second exploded in the air just behind the RIB and the third landed in the boat, exploding as it landed. The shards of steel from the exploding grenades shredded the rubber of the buoyancy tubes and the men inside the boat. The RIB seemed to disappear to be replaced by a sheet of cracked and splintered fibreglass.

Of the men with their weapons there was no sign. Gunfire erupted from the skiff, only to be silenced seconds later by a rocket propelled grenade which hit the bows of the vessel, followed by a second RPG which hit the water alongside and blew the skiff into two parts. By this time also, the third boat was dead in the water, having come under a hail of automatic fire at close range from three weapons. From start to finish the whole incident lasted no longer than two minutes.

As Gerry spun the wheel back to starboard to resume course a silence brooded over the vessel and the smell of cordite hung heavily about the ship. Karen was the first to recover from the adrenaline rush and she began calling the names of the remaining crew. Remarkably, nobody had been hit and the only demonstrable reaction came from Anwar who became vociferously annoyed at the damage, slight though it was, to his newly acquired motor yacht.

This was the last encounter of the gunboat crew with the 'enemy' and thirty-six hours later, in the early hours of a dark and moonless morning the motor yacht slipped quietly through the entrance of the big lagoon on Mafia Island and stopped thirty yards from a deserted shoreline. Two men and two women eased quietly down into a rubber dinghy and paddled towards the grove of gently waving palms that backed a small sandy beach between clumps of mangrove. The two women and one man climbed out of the dinghy and walked up to the edge of the palms where they waited while the second man paddled the dinghy back towards the motor yacht now standing outlined against the far shoreline. The two remaining men climbed down into the dinghy and were paddled ashore. As soon as they were ashore the dinghy was deflated and shoved deep under one of the mangrove bushes. Gerry said, "It will probably be found, but hopefully not until we're long gone."

The small column of six, the remainder of Jack Lang's patrol boat crew, then set off following a bearing on a hand compass towards the west. An hour later they were all sitting on the grass near the end of the Kilindoni airport runway. They had not long to wait. Within another ninety minutes a black speck appeared in the lightening sky away to the west. It steadily formed itself into the shape of an aircraft and then into the familiar shape of a C130 Hercules.

The big aircraft, grey painted and without markings, roared down the runway in a cloud of dust to the southern end of the tarmac strip, before beginning to turn and face the way it had come. As it lined up facing north the stern ramp was lowered and the six men and women ran from their places on the grass.

As they climbed the ramp into the rear of the aircraft, it was already accelerating into the take-off run. A few minutes later they were climbing away over the sea heading northwest.

"First stop Diego Garcia," said the Loadmaster as he handed out flasks of hot coffee and packs of sandwiches.

FORTY-FOUR

The remaining swell had already died away by the time the small convoy approached Mauritius. The wind had continued to veer and drop until it was little more than a gentle breeze. As they moved into the lee of the island the sky cleared apart from a few cumulus clouds marking the position of the isolated land fifteen miles away to the northeast and the breeze continued to drop until the sea was glassy calm, there being no movement to mark the remainder of the weather system they had passed through. The unbroken warmth of the afternoon sunshine began to revive spirits.

By late afternoon there was still no sign of the vessel they were to rendezvous with and Charlie was contemplating another call on the Satphone despite the recent terse instruction. With only an hour to go to sunset Charlie picked up the portable VHF set and called Tom in the tug.

"I want you to detach and go into Mauritius to refuel," he said.

"What do I use for money?" replied Tom.

Charlie thumbed the transmit button briefly. "Wait," he said. The requirement for payment for anything had not yet arisen and Charlie had to think hard to recall the instructions he had been given in the back seat of Jack's car on the jetty at Faslane. A whole lifetime seemed to have passed since he had taken command of the old frigate and the weeks of worry and action seemed to have formed a mental barrier. He thumbed the transmit button once more. "I need to work that out Tom," he said. "Just stay listening." With that he slid off the stool and made his way down to his cabin, where he dimly remembered a package he had been given at the end of his briefing. Ordinarily, such instructions to a captain embarking on a voyage would have been placed immediately in the captain's safe. *Cassie* however, had no safe at all so Charlie had stowed the package in a safe place. His current problem was that he could not remember the location of that 'safe place'. It took him nearly half an hour before he found the package and started opening it. The first thing he pulled out was a small leather folder, inside which was a black and gold credit card issued by a Swiss bank that he had never heard of. As he took in the printed instructions on the reverse of the card he was interrupted by the Bridge intercom. "We have a contact twenty miles ahead," said the disembodied voice. "It seems to be moving slowly towards us." Charlie returned the card to its folder and put the folder carefully back in the manila package before climbing back up to the Bridge.

The sun was very low on the western horizon and the Bridge was illuminated by the warm twilight as Charlie reached the top of the Bridge ladder. Jimmy, who had the watch, glanced at him and pointed ahead. "There," he said, "about twelve miles fine on the starboard bow. I've closed the lads up to modified 'Action Stations'."

"Hopefully it will be refuelling stations we'll need," said Charlie, peering through binoculars. Then he picked up the VHF portable and thumbed the 'transmit' button. "Tom," he said. "Disregard our last conversation. We might have a tanker up ahead. Stay with us but just be prepared in case there are any hostiles, over."

The reply was short and swift: "Roger that. Out." The tug began to move up from its position astern of the frigate, opening out onto the larger ship's port beam. Charlie picked up the binoculars again and focused on what was now plainly a small tanker, now only five or six miles ahead and turning slowly to match the course of the frigate and tug.

Within twenty minutes the frigate was cruising slowly on the starboard beam of the small elderly and chunky looking tanker. Every part of the old ship seemed to be streaked with rust and a thin dribble of smoke emerged from the squat funnel above the superstructure in the after part of the ship. No flag was being flown and no name or port of registry was discernible anywhere on the vessel. Charlie could see half a dozen men of indistinguishable nationality struggling to drag sections of dark grey armoured hose along the deck towards the stern. As each section arrived it was deftly locked onto the end of the previous section and as the fuelling hose grew it was being streamed over the stern, trailing along the sea surface behind the old 'rust-bucket' and kept in place by buoys attached at intervals along the length of the hose.

Jimmy said, "Bugger me, it's another old Ranger class – or maybe it's just the ghost of one."

"She's certainly very ancient," said Charlie as he continued to watch the other ship's preparations through the gathering dusk. "If she is an old 'Ranger' that would make her about fifty years old, but all we need her to do is to last about another hour or so – and hope that she can pump fuel." He lowered the binoculars with a worried frown.

Somebody called, "Ready on the fore deck," from the Bridge wing.

Charlie lowered the binoculars, stepped smartly out onto the wing and said, "I have the con. Slow ahead both engines. Port ten, steer for that float marker."

With both ships moving slowly through the calm sea it took only ten minutes to grapple the end of the floating fuel hose, haul it in and connect it up to the frigate's inlet valve. Unfortunately things slowed down a lot after that and it was pitch dark with only the glimmer of a moon beginning to show above the horizon by the time the frigate was able to ease the fuel hose back into the water and move aside to allow the tug to line up.

Again, the hose was brought in quite quickly but this time no fuel at all came through. Doggedly, Tom hung on and remained in position astern of the geriatric tanker and after about twenty-five minutes, to everyone's relief, fuel began to trickle through. It was another two hours and the quarter moon was now high enough to ease the blackness of the night before the tug was able to break the connection and drop the hose back in the sea.

Both ships turned together slowly away from the tanker, which continued on its easterly course. Charlie reflected that during the entire ponderous refuelling operation no communication of any kind had passed between the old tanker and the two privateers. As the tanker blended into the eastern horizon Charlie turned *Cassie* to the south at ten knots, while the tug sped off in the opposite direction, towards the island of Mauritius. When they had reached a position only two miles from the southern shore of the land which was now filling their northern horizon, the tug stopped. A small engineless RIB was shoved over the side of the towing deck and six frightened men were ushered down the deck and into the boat. As the men clumsily experimented with a pair of oars, the tug's propellers started turning and the helm was set to the south. Within ten minutes the RIB had merged into the night.

Five hours later, in the first grey light of the pre-dawn, Tom Clarke, who had remained in the wheelhouse throughout the night, was nudged out of an exhausted sleep to be told that their frigate consort was visible eight miles ahead.

When they had re-joined, the two ships increased speed together and adjusted their course slightly to the east of south and began the long run towards their remote destination at the bottom of the world.

Charlie reckoned that it would take about six days to reach their destination. Although he would have liked to make the final approach at night he recognised that this would introduce a significantly increased risk, so his compromise was to try to run the last fifty miles at dawn. He realised that he would be faced with a further problem in that the Antarctic autumn was moving towards winter and the hours of daylight were being steadily reduced.

Within three days the warm seas and skies of the mid-latitudes had been replaced by the short violent storms of the Southern Ocean, with a seemingly constant wind beating out of the west. They were entering the Roaring Forties. When they had left Scotland their destination had been the Indian Ocean and no provision had been made for the biting cold and slashing spray that was their lot throughout each day. Men scratched around for additional clothes to try to keep out the bone chilling cold, which grew worse as hour followed hour through the night and the ships trudged and lurched further to the south. Sea sickness began to take hold as the violent movement of the ships, particularly the tug continued without any easing, save when the two vessels were turned to put the raging seas on their quarters so that some attempt could be made to cook hot food in the galleys. Whenever possible, Charlie tried to keep *Cassie* upwind and up-sea of the tug to provide the smaller vessel with some relief from the big seas. Sometimes this worked but more often it provided little respite for the tug which continued to slam, pitch and roll alarmingly.

By the fourth day, with at least eight hundred miles still to run, the wind picked up even more and huge, mountainous white capped waves reared up to stop the ships in their tracks. Both ships were beginning to suffer structural damage and Charlie decided to heave-to until the worst of the storm passed by. In fact it simply grew even more violent at first and small groups began to gather on the Bridge of the frigate, staring silently into the afternoon gloom as giant waves, sometimes a hundred feet high reared up and towered over the frigate, occasionally to crash down on the warship, effectively causing it to disappear completely below the surface of the boiling, foaming maelstrom. At one point, someone could be heard muttering a prayer in the darkness at the back of the Bridge.

In the tug the violence of the movement was even worse but the smaller vessel was actually coping with the vile turbulent weather better than the frigate. The tug was being tossed about on the slopes of the giant waves as if it was merely a piece of driftwood. Although the dizzying upward heaves of the whole ship and the stomach churning plunges down the face of the mighty waves was very difficult for the human anatomy to take, there was no alternative and most of the men simply found some niche where they could stolidly wait out the rage of the storm. As the weather continued to deteriorate there were repeated occasions when cliff-faced sea mountains actually broke and crashed down right on top of the tough little vessel, which still managed to emerge, shedding water like a wet dog, to thrust once more into the black hellish night.

After twenty-four hours of this beating the storm began to ease and the two ships were able to make way again, tentatively at first, and then with a few hours of unaccountable lull in the tempest, they were even able to increase speed and turn to try to recover the ground they had lost, having been swept far to the east of the track to their destination.

An albatross appeared and ancient fears began to rise deep in the psyche of those who were able to stand and watch it. The great bird appeared out of nowhere to cruise effortlessly, first alongside the tug, then moving forward across the half mile gap between the two ships, it took up station alongside the frigate. Throughout the day the great bird stayed, wings outstretched, occasionally swooping down towards the still turbulent waves but always returning to the same position, a little to the left of the ship and ten feet or so above the level of the Bridge. By nightfall the bird had become a talisman for safety in the eyes of many of the crew as one after another they came up to the Bridge to stand and stare silently out towards it.

As dawn broke late in the following morning, the bird was still there and a perceptible swell of relief washed through the whole crew of the frigate. Then, in the early afternoon the snow came and the bird was gone. The wind rose but not to the level of the previous storm, but the temperature began to drop and ice started to form on the decks and superstructure of both ships. This really worried both Charlie and Tom in the tug. They were both aware that ice forming as it was could be a ship-killer. There were many documented instances of ships with accumulated ice on their upper surfaces simply disappearing, leaving not a trace of man or machine.

Charlie studied the GPS satellite navigation receiver for perhaps the twentieth time. The ship's progress was traced by a dotted line and the readout of the distance to the waypoint that marked their destination suggested that they had a day and a half to run, but only if they could maintain the present rate of progress. Outside the steady snow had been replaced by a series of flurries and the temperature had steadied, and then even begun to rise a little so that it was now fluctuating around freezing. Charlie stared through the gloom trying to decide whether the ice covering most of the deck was still forming. Should he risk sending people out onto the deck to try to chip it away with the consequent increased risk to them or should he carry on for the thirty-six hours that he judged necessary to reach Kerguelen?

A voice beside him interrupted his thoughts. "There is one good thing about all this shitty weather," said Nobby Small. "If it keeps up everybody on the bloody island will be hunkered down in front of a fire and won't want to get up to look out of the bleedin' window."

"Yeah," said Charlie," I hope you're right."

"Yeah, boss." Nobby wandered off towards the ladder leading down from the back of the Bridge and disappeared. Strangely, Charlie felt his mood lift as the stocky black seaman with his permanently cheerful air left the Bridge. He squared his shoulders, took a flashlight and pointed it down at the parts of the main deck that he could see. It looked as if the layer of slick ice had not grown any more and although the decks were treacherous the stability of his ship was not likely to be reduced. He put the flashlight back on its shelf and stood, feet braced wide apart, standing across the centreline of the ship, feeling for any change in the motion of the deck which might forewarn of a reduction in stability.

Three quarters of a mile behind the frigate, Tom was trying to make the same assessment, but in his case without the cheering intervention of Nobby Small.

Another day passed, by which time several of the crew members of the frigate were reduced to a state where they were no longer able to make any useful contribution. Nevertheless both ships wallowed and lumbered on through the westerly near gale and it was just after midnight when the radar picked up the returns from the mountain peaks at the northwest of the island. They had about fifty miles to run in and Charlie decided to reduce speed to allow them to close the coast in the early daylight.

Next morning, as the grey dawn crept up on them, the cloud lifted sufficiently for brief glimpses of the northern coast of the island to be seen – and the albatross returned. The effect was like a tonic suddenly being administered to each man.

The wind had risen at first but it was blowing from just south of west so the two ships found themselves in the relatively calmer waters in the lee of the great mountain range to the west.

While the frigate stood a mile or two offshore, Tom took the tug in to probe the various inlets along the northern coast. From seaward they gave the appearance of fiords similar in size and appearance to those along the western seaboard of Norway but most of them contained a hidden danger which might have spelt disaster to any ships venturing in. The problem was the massive fields of kelp which had grown untrammelled for thousands of years and would now act as a living barrier able to obstruct, then grip, then destroy any ship venturing into the clutches of the giant seaweed.

By mid-afternoon when fifteen likely fiords had been investigated, their luck began to change. The tug cautiously entered yet another inlet and Tom quickly reported that there was no kelp. Then he dashed the raised hopes on the Bridge of the frigate by announcing that the sea bed was shoaling rapidly and he was able to see below the surface, huge rocks scattered about haphazardly.

It was almost dark before their luck finally changed. Tom nosed his way cautiously in through a narrow entrance which immediately opened out into a wide passage without a sign of kelp anywhere. Also he noted several smaller leads out from the main fiord all with steep sided rock walls. It was too dark to investigate further so he brought the tug back out and the two ships cruised slowly offshore in the surprisingly calm waters, still to leeward of the western mountain range.

It was mid-morning once more before the thin grey light began to penetrate the layers of dark cloud. After a hurried conference on the radio it had been decided that the frigate should now attempt to enter the fiord, followed by the tug. Charlie took *Cassie* carefully in through the narrow entrance and then waited half an hour for the light to improve. He found himself in a wide calm sea loch bounded on all sides by tall mountains, several of which were snow-capped and all of which had near vertical sides descending to the sea surface. In various places picturesque waterfalls tumbled several thousand feet, carving vertical gullies out of the living rock before crashing with distant roaring into the sea. In most cases the upper lengths of these falls were lined with walls of ice. From the Bridge of the stationary ship Charlie could see at least a dozen fissure-like entrances cut into the surrounding walls of the loch. At least three of these looked promising so he moved out onto the Bridge wing, shivered as the crisp air struck him and began to con the frigate carefully towards one of the openings.

By mid-afternoon all three of the likely entrances had been investigated. All of them had sufficient depth to allow the frigate in and two of them were several hundred feet deep, enough to scuttle the ship if necessary thought Charlie, although the idea depressed him and he didn't dwell on it. In both instances if he took his ship far enough into the inlet, the vertical side of the fiord gave way to a more gentle slope and vegetation grew all the way down to the water's edge. Within the vegetation grew large clumps of rough cabbages. Charlie had done his homework and took pleasure in explaining that these Kerguelen Cabbages had been much prized by the whaling fleets of a hundred years ago, the crews of whom had used them to supplement their diet and ward off the seaman's curse of scurvy.

With all the fenders they could muster hung out along the starboard side Charlie eased his ship gently in towards the rock wall. *Cassie* was only about twenty feet off when Charlie suddenly pointed at the rock surface. "Bloody hell!" he shouted. "Would you look at that!" Several pairs of eyes peered in the direction pointed by his outstretched arm. At first nothing could be seen then, several voices at once began to exclaim.

What Charlie had seen was a row of rusty iron stakes which had been hammered into clefts in the rock. And below two or three of the iron spikes were signs where something had been chiselled into the rock. It was evident that at one time the marks had formed words but the words were now indistinguishable.

In a gesture unfamiliar to his companions, Charlie threw his hands in the air. "We've found a bloody whaling station!" he shouted. Then he repeated it in case anyone had not heard the first time.

They had indeed discovered an old whaling station, hidden within this complex of fiords for over a hundred and fifty years. The old whalers of the southern oceans had been intensely competitive and in many cases whaling ships had sought out hidden bases to which they could return for rest and to carry out repairs. Often they had built and stocked refuge huts at their secret bases to be used as a last refuge in case of disaster. Up through the cabbages and scrub trees on the far side Charlie and his people did find the remains of such a hut. It was by now barely recognisable as a hut but there were various accoutrements and bits of clothing scattered about inside the square the hut had once occupied. On the sloping ground behind it were six small cairns made of piles of stones, set out in a rough semi-circle. The assorted group of ill-clad sailors stood silently contemplating the graves, two of which were marked by wooden crosses on the ground behind them, which had once presumably stood upright at the head of the grave.

After the tug had been brought in it was decided that they should leave the frigate afloat and camouflage it using the abundant foliage lining the hillside as well as rock and shale covered canvas to disguise the outline of the ship. At the same time preparations were made to accommodate *Cassie's* twenty-nine survivors in the tug as well as transferring fuel from the frigate to top up the tug's tanks and installing a careful selection of weapons, equipment and food. Water was likely to run short on the return trip so as many containers as possible were filled with clear spring water from one of the nearby falls and stowed deep in the bilges of the tug.

It took a further two days to complete the transfer of equipment and then carry out a thorough search of the frigate to ensure that nothing incriminating should be left behind.

The heavy weapons were cut away or unbolted and tipped over the side, to be followed by every other embarrassing item that was able to sink out of sight. Lighter things were bagged and weighted and any small items which could not be trusted to remain forever hidden in this way were tucked into various corners of the tug. While this was going on, the weather eased to a relatively benign state. The wind dropped to a steady twenty knots and the skies cleared. A party was sent out to climb the fiord slopes as far as they could in order to check that the spot they had selected for *Cassie's* last mooring was truly isolated. On return they reported that not only was there no evidence of human habitation or visitation as far as the eye and good binoculars could see, but in fact, after climbing only a thousand feet the twisting structure of the fiord hid *Cassie* completely. Charlie fretted at the waste of what seemed to be an unusually benign 'weather window', but by the time the tug was ready to leave on the third morning the weather god still seemed to be smiling on them.

The last act on the evening before departure was to drag huge skeins of kelp from further along the fiord and drape them over the decks and superstructure of the frigate, the effect of which was to blend the outline of the ship so thoroughly into the vegetation covered hillside that it would be necessary to come within a few yards to discover it.

In the first grey light of mid-morning the tug backed away from the side of the old frigate and turned ponderously to point towards the junction with the main fiord half a mile distant. The wind had dropped away almost entirely within the fiord network and the sky was obscured with an overcast of high-level stratus cloud which the experienced seamen onboard took to be a good sign.

Men were posted on the forecastle to warn of any beds of floating kelp as the tug moved slowly down the fiord. It took over an hour to enter the main sea loch but after that, with advancing daylight they were able to increase speed so that by mid-afternoon when the light was once more failing they passed out of the fiord entrance and set course to the northeast. Almost immediately the weather began to deteriorate. The overcast cloud layer started to descend and darken, while the wind backed once more to the west, increasing as it did so. With the rising wind striking the tug almost beam on the small vessel began to roll uncomfortably until Tom, who remained as skipper, turned more to the northwest, putting the sea on the port bow and easing the turbulent motion.

It was at this point that the men lounging around the wheelhouse heard a triumphant shout from the helmsman. Henry King was on the wheel and he had been poking around the binnacle and shelving in front of him with one hand while maintaining a reasonable course with the other. "Samson!" he shouted, "in fact she's called Samson II. She's got a name!" Nobody seemed to react directly to this discovery but thereafter it was noticeable that the vessel became *Samson* rather than just 'the tug'. This simple discovery seemed to give life to the vessel which had now become lifeboat to thirty-one men and it seemed to give heart to the weary crew.

Samson plugged on into the steadily rising sea while the men who were not engaged in operating the ship tried to wedge themselves into various corners and spaces where they struggled against the lurching, churning motion of the tug. The weather continued to deteriorate until it settled into a bone chilling force nine gale screaming out of the west, occasionally dumping thick flurries of wet snow on the decks. The curse of sea sickness began to overcome one man after another and misery was prominent. The one easement that Tom remained thankful for was that the temperature remained constant at a few degrees above freezing. They covered two hundred and fifty miles in the first day, two hundred in the second day and barely one hundred on the third. However by midday on that day the wind began to ease slightly, there were breaks in the ragged cloud cover and the temperature rose a few degrees turning the snow flurries into stinging blasts of icy rain. Even this tiny respite served to ease the mood of gloom which had pervaded the ship. This was the point at which the starboard engine started playing up.

The engine began to run rough and then to overheat. Tom and Charlie agreed that it must be shut down while Dan Holloway and John Banyard tried to discover the cause of the problem. The tug struggled along on the labouring port engine barely able to make two knots while the wind, still nearly a force eight gale, drove them inexorably to the east.

One after the other Dan and John had to crawl out of the engine room to vomit and then retch dryly into a bucket. It didn't take very long to discover the source of the problems but resolving them took the rest of the day. The cooling water inlet for the starboard engine was jammed with a mixture of kelp strands and other detritus all of which had served to reduce the flow of cooling water to a tenth of what it should have been. All the filters were blocked but these could be cleared fairly easily by dismantling them. The real problem concerned the connecting pipes which were also blocked. The best method of clearing these would have been to do it from the outside of the hull but the turbulent conditions made any attempt to do this impossible. After several hours of probing and poking as well as eventually having to deal with an inrush of seawater before the sea-cock could be closed, the blockage was cleared. That dealt with the overheating problem but not the reason for the engine failing. The violent motion of the tug during the approach to Kerguelen and since their departure from the island had stirred up the sludge and rust that had formed in the bottom of the fuel tanks causing progressive blockage of every fuel filter in the system. It was a long and dirty job to clean the filters and some of the elements were so damaged that they needed replacement. Two replacement filter elements were found and after more than ten hours the starboard engine was started once more. It ran sweetly but Dan immediately dented the slight air of euphoria by declaring that the port engine was probably suffering from the same problems and should be shut down before it failed of its own accord.

He was right. As the starboard engine took the load the port engine was already running rough and the big diesel was labouring to keep going.

As soon as it was shut down and cooled the weary team set to work once more. They quickly established that there was no serious blockage in the sea water cooling system but Dan dismantled the filters and cleaned them anyway. The fuel filters presented a much more serious challenge. Again they were becoming seriously blocked but there were no more replacement elements so after various experiments home-made versions were cobbled together from canvas and hessian. After several hours of debilitating work in truly horrible conditions the engineers emerged, the engine was restarted, ran sweetly and the tug started to make headway once more. By midnight *Samson* had worked up to twelve knots in a much reduced sea but which was still over-ridden by a long and heavy westerly swell. The epidemic of sea sickness had eased but largely because the men had nothing to throw up and were in many cases too exhausted to do so.

In the thin morning light, Tom could see that the rage had gone from the waves, there were breaks in the cloud and the temperature was rising. Tom had brought the course around to northwest which made the motion easier as well as helping them to return to the track they needed to make good.

It was at this point that the Satphone squawked into life and chittered out a brief message.

FORTY-FIVE

Jack Lang sipped contemplatively at glass of vintage Moet et Chandon and waited for the empty communications screen to be filled with the familiar image of the Secretary of State for Foreign Affairs. He was on his own in his study at Buckland House, Maggie having been called away to discuss another potential problem which had not yet become Jack's concern, but, he thought cynically, soon would be.

The screen shivered and the familiar head and shoulders appeared. The Foreign Secretary smiled. "Well done Jack," he said, and there was relief as well as gratitude in his voice.

"Thank you sir," said Jack rather formally.

The Foreign Secretary cruised on smoothly, "The prince is well pleased, the Prime Minister has been congratulated, my phone has stopped ringing and we have been paid – handsomely!" He ended on a triumphal note.

"What is the state of play with the Somalis?" said Jack.

"Well there's a lot of fury and name calling flying about but a UN relief team has been flown in to the site of the explosion and they seem to be rounding up a surprisingly large number of survivors but that place as a base will be out of action for a long time. The Americans have sent a lot of ships in to support *Andrew James* and as of this morning they had no less than eighteen ships under tow or under control. A lot of hostage crews have been released and we have in excess of sixty prisoners although God knows what we will do with them."

"We are winding up the operation now sir," said Jack. "I believe that the frigate reached Kerguelen but we can't confirm that by satellite yet. I have sent an instruction to the tug but again I don't have any further information. Given the timescale they should be on their way back from the island but the weather in the Antarctic region is appalling and our search capability is limited because we want to keep it discreet."

"What about the gunboat crew?" said the Foreign Secretary.

"No problem there, sir," said Jack. "They took some casualties but…"

"I'm sorry to hear that," interrupted the Foreign Secretary. "How many survivors?"

"Five uninjured and one wounded," said Jack. "They are all now in Cyprus, being kitted out for return to the UK."

"I see." Then after a moment's thought the Foreign Secretary continued, "You have a lot of men on that tug and I expect the going will be tough. I'm going to release *Carlisle* to your operational control. You might want her to probe to the south to see if she can locate the tug."

"Assuming she's still afloat," said Jack, quietly.

The Foreign Secretary didn't answer directly. "Keep me informed," he said, as the image faded from the screen.

Jack sipped his champagne and continued to stare at the blank screen. He sat thinking like this for half an hour or more until he was disturbed by a discreet knock on the door. One of the operations officers was there. "We have a response from the tug," said the man. "Communications are difficult but they seem to be making slow progress to the north and are looking for instructions. We also have *Carlisle* available at our disposal."

*

The starboard engine had run sweetly for two days but it was now struggling and coughing. The weather had continued to ease though the wind, now from the southwest, maintained a steady twenty-five knots. Food was running low and what there was of it was unappetizing. Thankfully the water they had embarked at the island supplemented by the small amount produced onboard remained plentiful. Dan Holloway was exhausted and it was John Banyard that led Mike Carter back down into the bilge of the engine room once more to clean the filters as best they could. The tug struggled on for another eight hours at eight knots which was better than during the first emergency, but Charlie was now becoming seriously concerned for some of the men who had been the worst sea sickness sufferers.

The GPS showed that they were now over twelve hundred miles to the north of Kerguelen and this was borne out by the general improvement in the weather, although the roaring forties wind still tried to clutch at them. Charlie was mentally calculating how far he might have to go to reach various ports and at the same time wondering why there had been no instructions received since leaving Kerguelen.

"Look at that, boss," said one of the seamen in the wheelhouse. He was pointing towards the HF radio set on the shelf by the navigation station. A pair of red lights were winking urgently on and off. Charlie walked unsteadily across to the set and switched it from 'standby' to 'receive'.

He thumbed the transmit button. "Station calling, this is tug *Samson*, over."

There was a pause then the set burst into life. "This is Tango Tango Lima Four, Rescue ship *Carlisle*, give your position, course and speed, over." Charlie didn't hesitate; he read off the latitude and longitude from the GPS lying on the chart table and added their course and speed.

The response was quite quick. "Tug *Samson* we are three hundred miles to the north of you. Maintain your course and speed. Maintain listening watch on this frequency. We expect to reach you in approximately twelve hours provided you are able to maintain your course and speed. Report your condition and any casualties." Charlie responded to the instruction, his voice thick with emotion. It was over.

Carlisle arrived on schedule just after midnight. The tug wallowed in the lee of the big warship as several boats ferried men across to the tug, returning with most of the exhausted crewmen. Charlie, Tom, Henry King, Dan Holloway and John Banyard elected to stay with the ship that had brought them this far. *Carlisle* took the tug Samson under tow while a fresh team of engineers tackled the blocked fuel systems once more and together they headed north.

*

Maggie was back at Buckland House, passing the time of day, she said.

"So you've got yourself a nice little tug boat to add to your fleet. I'm surprised the owners didn't want it back," her eyes glistened over the rim of her teacup.

"It's salvage," said Jack. "*Samson* is a bit battered and I, or my men, recovered the ship so the owners must pay me a substantial sum in salvage. The Penang and Malacca Steam Navigation and Towing Company have, following discussion with their insurers, very sensibly decided to award the vessel to me in lieu of a very large payment for the salvage of the said vessel. She has now joined my other modest little group."

"It seems strange to be referring to something called *Samson* as 'she'," pondered Maggie.

"Quite. But that is the tradition of the sea."

"So it is all over?"

"We lost some good men," said Jack.

"And a woman."

"Yes, but I have taken onto my team some tough and resourceful seamen."

"And a couple of tough and resourceful women," countered Maggie.

"Yes, you are right."

"The bill in blood was quite high, I think," said Maggie.

"There was no other way," said Jack.

The End